He wasn't what she had expected.

Her knight would be gentle, kind and chivalrous. This man looked big, tough and slightly dangerous. But the strange feeling of recognition persisted. Isabel felt the soldier's hand gently cradle her face. His thumb tilted her chin up.

'The rose is for you, little maid,' he said, his voice husky. 'And this is for me.'

He bent and brushed her mouth fleetingly with his, before lingering for a heart-shakingly tender kiss.

Dear Reader

We welcome back Janet Edmonds with her Regency, A NABOB'S DAUGHTER, where India and Viscount Bardolph form an uneasy alliance. Julia Byrne is back with MY ENEMY, MY LOVE, a sizzling action-packed plot set in the Anarchy. Our American authors are Lindsay McKenna, well known to Silhouette readers, and Lucy Elliot, who offer an Apache heroine, and the Civil War respectively. We hope these four stories will enthral you—enjoy!

The Editor

Julia Byrne lives in Australia with her husband, daughter and two overgrown cats. She started her working career as a secretary, taught ballroom dancing after several successful years as a competitor, and presently works part-time in the history department of a Melbourne university. She enjoys reading, tapestry, and playing Mah Jong.

Recent titles by the same author:

GENTLE CONQUEROR

MY ENEMY,
MY LOVE

Julia Byrne

MILLS & BOON LIMITED
ETON HOUSE, 18–24 PARADISE ROAD
RICHMOND, SURREY, TW9 1SR

First published in Great Britain 1993
by Mills & Boon Limited

© Julia Byrne 1993

Australian copyright 1993
Philippine copyright 1993
This edition 1993

ISBN 0 263 78239 5

Set in 10 on 11 pt Linotron Times
04-9311-87718

Typeset in Great Britain by Centracet, Cambridge
Made and printed in Great Britain

PROLOGUE

Tracy Castle, Herefordshire
March 1136

'EDMUND, I swear if you tear your clothes again, climbing that wall, I won't sit up half the night to mend them before Dameta sees the damage you are wreaking.'

The grubby face of a young boy, not more than ten summers in age, peered down at the speaker through the tangled mass of overgrown shrubbery atop a high stone wall.

'I'm scaling the ramparts of a castle in Anjou,' he protested somewhat breathlessly. 'And you're the Empress. Prepare to be taken prisoner, lady.'

'A fine ambition,' scolded his victim, unmoved by the fate about to befall her. 'What has the Empress Matilda ever done to you, pray tell?'

''Tis not on my own behalf,' claimed the would-be hero. 'I am for King Stephen.' He scrambled over the wall and fell with more haste than skill into the enclosed, sun-warmed garden below. Jumping to his feet, Edmund swung a makeshift wooden sword in a reckless arc. 'Yield, thou troublesome female,' he commanded in a youthful treble. 'You are my prisoner.'

The young lady thus addressed jumped back a prudent pace or two. 'By our Lady, Edmund, you nearly had my head off!' she exclaimed indignantly. 'Go and take a few more lessons from Osbert.'

Edmund heaved a disappointed sigh and let his sword arm fall. 'Sisters are no fun,' he complained. 'You'd better take care, Isabel. You're becoming as prim-faced as Alice and Constance.'

Isabel elevated her small nose with all the hauteur of a young lady who had attained the lofty age of thirteen, and had therefore ceased climbing walls and brandishing wooden swords herself.

'I'm sure if King Stephen ever did have the Empress in his power he would not wave a sword in her face,' she declared severely. 'He would be more gallant. And, moreover, we still don't know if our father will shift his allegiance to the King.'

Edmund dismissed this remark with another perilous sweep of his sword. 'Of course he will. A man such as Sir Guy fitzAlan would not be acting as the King's messenger if Stephen was not confident of Father's support. We de Tracys will never back a woman.'

Isabel decided to ignore this annoying example of male arrogance. 'What is Sir Guy like?' she queried curiously, not having been present in the hall when their visitor had arrived.

Her brother heaved another long-suffering sigh. 'You're *worse* than Alice and Constance,' he declared. 'They, at least, confined themselves to giggling like village idiots when they watched him from the tower. Girls! No wonder we don't want one on the throne. Take heed!' he shouted, reverting to his character of besieging knight. 'Stay here in Anjou and leave England to the rule of a man.'

Before Isabel could retort in kind, Edmund scrambled nimbly back over the wall with the assistance of its thick covering of climbing roses, putting a long slash in his white linen shirt in the process.

'You horrid little toad,' his sister yelled after him in exasperation, foreseeing a long night of sewing ahead of her. 'I hope you turn into an eel and Tom puts you in a broth.'

'I can't be a toad and an eel,' floated back the voice of her brother. 'And if that's the best revenge you can think of, we definitely don't want a woman on the throne.'

Inside the ancestral home of the de Tracy family, a more serious discussion of the same subject was under way.

'As a man of the Church, I must object,' stated a portly cleric in the bombastic tones of a man accustomed to a respectful, if not enthusiastic, audience. He folded complacent white hands over his considerable girth and frowned at his two listeners. They remained unimpressed by either the measured words or the frown.

'Let me remind you, Brother, that your own superiors have recognised the Count of Mortain as King. Stephen is crowned and consecrated, by William de Corbeil, no less.'

The man who spoke was enough like the priest in face and build to indicate their relationship, but, instead of the severe black habit and tonsured head which proclaimed the cleric to be of the Benedictine order, he was dressed in all the splendour of a prosperous baron. His knee-length red woollen tunic was lavishly trimmed with fur, and the chain of solid metal links about his neck gleamed with the sheen of precious gold.

He was the only one who matched the colourfully embroidered wall-hangings and solid oak furniture of the private solar. The youngest of the trio was severely, even ominously garbed in chainmail over serviceable brown woollen leggings and tunic. A sword hung at his side and a plain iron helmet lay close to his hand on a nearby table. The afternoon sunlight, shining through the western window embrasure, highlighted the number of dents in the cone-shaped headgear, testifying to its effective and frequent use.

'We had heard 'twas so, of course,' muttered the

priest in answer to his brother's statement. But, despite
the unwilling admission, he looked across the room at
the soldier rather in the manner of one who hoped he
had heard incorrectly.

The younger man nodded polite confirmation. 'Aye,
Brother Prior, the Archbishop of Canterbury blessed
the King this last December, just before Christmastide,
and had the support of the Bishop of Winchester and
Roger, Bishop of Salisbury, the justiciar. Stephen also
held the treasury,' he tacked on drily, a slightly amused
gleam in his eyes.

The Prior didn't notice the amusement. He sank
down on to a convenient chair and shook his head
dolefully. 'Of course Stephen had Henry of
Winchester's approval,' he grumbled. 'The man is the
King's brother, and we all know of his ambition. Don't
tell *me* Henry didn't plan Stephen's dash for the throne
down to the last detail, because I'll never believe it. The
Bishop is more statesman than priest.'

'But a good one,' murmured the soldier, unable, this
time, to hide a smile as the priest shook his head again.

Baron de Tracy grinned openly and grabbed a drinking-horn, splashing some wine into it from the jug on
the table. 'Here, William, you look as though you need
a drink. 'Tis not so bad that Stephen is King. Would you
rather have a woman on the throne of England?'

'Matilda is the late King's daughter, Hugh, and we all
took that oath to recognise her as the future queen after
her brother went down with the White Ship,' protested
the Prior. But he accepted the proffered wine and took
a long draught, letting a thoughtful silence fall. After
all, he reminded himself, he was Prior William now and
had his eye set on further promotion. One must tread
cautiously, however, when kings, or, in this case, a king
and a former empress, squabbled over the crown.

'An oath sworn nine years ago and under considerable duress may become invalid in certain circum-stances,' stated Hugh firmly. 'What say you, fitzAlan? You know more than we who live in this backwater on the Marches. There is rumour abroad that King Henry disinherited Matilda on his death-bed. And who can blame him? The woman was at war with her father at the time.'

The young soldier looked carefully from one man to the other. His host he could count on, he thought. Like so many others, Baron de Tracy knew which way the wind blew and where gain was to be had. A churchman's conscience over a sacred oath was the stumbling-block here. But he would not lie. There were too many stories flying from one end of the country to the other that Stephen's rapid seizure of the throne, before the late King was even decently interred, was based on lies and deceit.

'There was a knight who swore that King Henry disinherited Matilda,' he admitted. 'But to say truth, sirs, 'tis doubted by many. What is more certain is that the Bishop of Salisbury claims the oath sworn years ago was conditional upon the King's not marrying his daugh-ter to anyone outside England. Since Matilda is now the wife of Geoffrey of Anjou, your oaths are no longer binding.'

'Well said,' nodded Hugh de Tracy. 'Besides, in times such as these, men must be practical. Stephen has shown himself capable thus far.' He turned to his brother. 'Could a woman have beaten back the Scots, forcing King David to come to terms before he plundered the entire north?'

'Matters of warfare are not fathomed by such as I,' countered the Prior, taking refuge behind his priestly garb. 'Although one assumes David only crossed the border because his niece had been cheated of her crown and gave him no peace until he avenged her, haranguing him with letter after letter. Besides,' he added, descending from these dramatic heights, 'Matilda's husband would have led the army.'

Hugh made an impatient sound. 'We don't want Anjou here, interfering in England's affairs. Keeping him from snapping at the heels of Normandy is bad enough.'

Although worry still clouded his face, Prior William nodded immediate acceptance of this statement. Man of the Church he might be, but no Norman worthy of the name wanted any truck with Geoffrey of Anjou. Apart from the fact that Anjou was the hereditary enemy of the Normans, the man was a cold-blooded brute who hadn't hesitated to let his army of barbarians ravage the Norman countryside even while his father-in-law was still alive. If Henry, King of England and Duke of Normandy, *had* disinherited his daughter, as Stephen claimed, one could understand why.

'And remember,' Hugh continued forcefully, 'Stephen is as much a grandchild of the Conqueror as Matilda.'

'On the female side,' the Prior felt impelled to point out. Another thought occurred to him. 'But what of Matilda's son? Young Henry was the joy of the King's last years and——'

'A child!' scoffed his brother. 'A babe scarce two years old. Don't tell me you can see *him* on the throne. Even Robert of Gloucester would be preferable.'

'That was suggested,' murmured young fitzAlan, moving restlessly in his chair. He was growing impatient with the argument, deeming it useless. The Prior would eventually have to obey his superiors, no matter what his private thoughts on the matter, and he couldn't see de Tracy going against the majority of England's nobility.

Stephen's quick action in marching to head off David

of Scotland had impressed most of the barons and the King looked forward to a well-attended Easter court, which would confer upon his kingship the final confirmation of acknowledgement by his nobles. It was Guy fitzAlan's task to deliver Stephen's invitation to de Tracy and to persuade him to accept the inevitable — if such persuasion was necessary. He hadn't counted on the opposition of Hugh de Tracy's priestly brother, who should have been safely at home in his monastery, where he couldn't cause any trouble.

The subject of this exasperated thought sent him a look of enquiry, bringing him back to the present debate.

'While King Henry lay in state in Normandy, several barons went to the Earl of Gloucester to ask if he would be willing to take the throne,' Guy elaborated. 'He is the late King's son when all is said. But he refused on the grounds of his illegitimacy.'

'Not because of the oath he swore to Matilda?' queried Hugh interestedly. 'I remember how he and Stephen quarrelled over who should be the first to pledge alliance to her. The jealousy between them was the talk of the Court at the time. Stephen won, as I recall.'

'Aye, again on the grounds that a legitimate nephew of King Henry came before an illegitimate son. But, though Gloucester refused the crown, he did attend a meeting of the barons in Normandy to discuss an alternative to himself. After all, Robert mistrusts the Count of Anjou as much as anyone.'

'I believe Stephen's elder brother, Theobald, was put forward,' said Hugh briskly. 'Until they were told that Stephen himself had already been crowned. You see, William, that Matilda has precious little support in Normandy *or* in England. Where is the problem here?'

'The problem, Hugh, is that England will be torn

apart by strife and ill deeds. Matilda has the reputation of being a shrew — do you think she will stay tamely in Anjou? You only have to cast your eye on Normandy. 'Tis already in a state of uproar, ready for that ambitious husband of hers to pluck it like an over-ripe plum, rotting and falling from the tree, and —'

'God's holy fingernails,' burst out Hugh, impatiently interrupting his brother's flowery passages. 'That is precisely my point. Mark my words, before the month is out we shall have Earl Robert crossing the Channel to make his peace with Stephen along with the rest of us. As for his sister, the woman is tied to Anjou, producing infants, and we have a competent man already on the throne, and one,' he added shrewdly, 'who has promised to confirm all the liberties of the Church.'

The Prior had opened his mouth to state that, in his opinion, Robert of Gloucester was unlikely to throw casually aside his loyalty to his half-sister, no matter what councils he might have attended, but this statement made him close his lips on the words. Seeing that the priest was carefully considering the Church's position in the situation, fitzAlan stood up abruptly, ready to put an end to the debate. His host quickly crossed the solar and laid a conciliatory hand on the younger man's arm.

'Leave the rest to me, Guy,' he said softly. 'William can be as stubborn as the devil when he chooses, and the sight of a soldier will only make him dig in his heels further. Let him take a favourable tale back to his abbot when he leaves us tomorrow. Meanwhile, stretch your legs outside before supper. I warrant you've seen nothing but the road between your horse's ears for days.'

FitzAlan laughed and agreed. A brisk walk around the bailey to work up an appetite sounded good, and a glance at the Prior, who was still shaking his head gloomily over his drinking-horn, convinced him that there was no more to be gained by pushing the issue. Let Hugh de Tracy handle his brother, and the tricky question of broken oaths. He wanted to study the fortifications more closely in any case. It never hurt to know in advance what well-provisioned castles could be put at the King's disposal at short notice.

An hour later Guy refreshed himself with a jug of water drawn from the well and wondered how his host would take a few suggestions. Like most strongholds which dated from the Conqueror's day, the original Saxon palisade enclosing the large compound had been replaced by a stone wall, with a barbican protecting the gate, but the place was assailable. There was no moat, and though the hall was constructed of stone the other buildings within the bailey were of wood and thatch and therefore vulnerable to fire.

His eyes wandered further. In a grassy corner a large eel pond lay smooth and serene beneath the branches of a chestnut tree and, near by, several pigs rooted contentedly in the muddy shallows. A girl emerged from the dairy with a pan of milk and was instantly surrounded by the stable cats, mewing pleadingly as though they had not caught a single mouse for days. It was a peaceful scene. The girl bent to stroke one of the cats, murmuring to it, and from somewhere behind the hall came the cooing of doves.

Aye, peaceful, thought Guy. The harmless noises of the countryside surrounded him. But he knew how quickly peace could be overcome by strife and warfare, how quickly the cooing of doves could be silenced beneath the clash of arms. Prior William had been right about one thing. Anarchy *was* rife in Normandy. As soon as King Henry had breathed his last the barons had turned on each other like ravening wolves, attacking their neighbours and ripe for every type of lawlessness.

A strong man was needed there, as well as in England, and those loyal to the King needed strong fortresses.

Guy turned to consider the stone hall. It was flanked by two towers and its entrance was reached only by a narrow stairway, but by no stretch of the imagination could it be called a fortress.

And Guy was uneasily aware of another fact. No one could say for sure if Robert of Gloucester would support Stephen, or if he would remain in Normandy to throw the considerable weight of his position, wealth and experience behind his half-sister. And if he landed in England with Matilda, estates such as Hugh de Tracy's were at risk, placed as they were in Herefordshire and Gloucestershire, where the majority of castles were held by men who owed fealty to the Earl rather than the King.

However, it was no use pondering on unanswerable questions. The King was steadily gaining more support. One could only hope that the Earl of Gloucester would realise the futility of remaining isolated in Normandy when Matilda's cousin was already annointed and crowned, an act that even the Pope acknowledged as irrevocable, despite his disapproval of Stephen's methods.

As Guy sat contemplating this conclusion, a fair-haired child came racing around the corner of the north tower. A short wooden sword was clutched in one grimy hand and the boy's shirt had been well and truly ripped. He scampered up the outer staircase and disappeared into the hall.

Guy grinned suddenly. The imp was either fleeing from female reproaches or about to fall into that trap. He wondered where the boy had come from. There was little behind the main building apart from the usual outdoor privies and midden heaps, and the little devil wasn't *that* dirty.

Still idly curious, Guy got to his feet and strolled across the bailey and past the hall. He really should go in search of his squire and order some hot water so he could wash away his own grime before sitting down to table. He'd been on the roads for days and they still retained their winter mire, despite the advent of finer spring weather. But instead he wandered past the neatly laid-out kitchen garden, strangely reluctant to give up this rare moment of peaceful solitude in the sun.

Then, from somewhere beyond the imposing stone wall, came a sweet voice singing a haunting ballad. Guy paused, spellbound. The poignant melody made him think of soft feminine sighs, warm arms and whispered words of love in the dark of night.

By the Saints, he must have been without a woman for too long, he thought wryly. And he'd probably have to resign himself to that situation until he returned to Winchester. His host had mentioned three daughters, but they were definitely not the sort of girls one could tumble into bed and then forget.

On the other hand, maybe that soft, slightly husky voice belonged to a nicely rounded wench willing to indulge in a little loveplay as well as sing about it. And as this notion made his mouth curve upward in amusement at his optimism, he found what he was searching for.

A small wooden door, set into the stone wall, and half hidden beneath the hanging tendrils of a climbing rose. If it had been later in the season, and the roses in full bloom, he might have missed the portal altogether, but there was just the one unopened bud on the bare branches, of a delicate peach shade with hints of rose which made him think of a girl's skin. A country girl, he decided, with the bloom of health and youth.

On impulse, Guy reached up and plucked the bud, avoiding the surrounding thorns. Still grinning faintly at

such unaccustomed fancies, he grasped the iron handle
and carefully pushed the gate open.

Isabel loved her great-grandmother's garden, although
she had never known that lady, who had expired bearing
her lord a son, the present Baron's father. Thus, when
the stone ramparts had been constructed years ago,
there had been no mistress of Tracy Castle, and the
pleasance had been abandoned and left outside the
boundaries of the bailey. Its crumbling wooden fence
and the wealth of overgrown shrubs was considered
useful only in shielding the postern gate from any but
the most discerning eye.

Every few months Hugh de Tracy would mutter about
seeing to the building of a proper barbican over the
postern. However, under King Henry's harsh but effective rule, England had remained peaceful, so nothing
had ever come of her father's plans and Isabel was free
to indulge her girlhood dreams in the quiet haven, shut
off from the bustle and constant noise of castle life.

When Edmund had left her she had wandered as far
as the orchard, and had just pushed aside the crooked
wicker gate to re-enter the garden when she heard the
latch of the heavier postern rattle. Isabel paused, the
refrain she had been absently singing fading away as the
soldier stepped into the pleasance at the same moment.

Across the warm, sun-filled expanse of wilderness
their eyes met with an impact that held them both
motionless. In the sudden silence Isabel thought she
could almost hear the life of the garden, preparing for
its spring blossoming. Every other sound that she had
hitherto been conscious of—the distant bleat of sheep
in the field, the wind in the trees, the mewling cry of a
hawk far above her—disappeared, vanished from her
awareness.

Then her hand clenched involuntarily on the gate and

she jumped, a startled murmur on her lips, glancing down at her finger where a splinter had pierced the skin.

'Don't be frightened,' Guy said at once, his own hand still grasping the postern gate. He had never seen such a beautiful girl in all his life. So unexpected was her appearance that, for a moment, until she'd moved and cried out, he'd wondered if she was real. No sturdy country wench this, but a slender, fairy-like creature who seemed part of her wild, otherwordly surroundings. He was hardly aware of moving, but when he pushed the postern closed behind him she stepped back into the gateway, eyeing him with very human caution.

'Don't be frightened,' he repeated softly, not daring to move again in case she fled. Or vanished. In the shadowy corner where she stood, she seemed almost insubstantial. 'Who are you?' he murmured, only half expecting her to answer. Perhaps he really *had* dreamed her up after months of travelling.

'Isabel de Tracy,' she whispered, and, releasing the gate, took a tentative step forward into the sunlight, the skirts of her close-fitting blue kersey gown swaying gently about her ankles.

Guy caught his breath all over again, so captivated by the sweet face upturned to him that he missed the strangely puzzled wonderment in her wide-eyed gaze, his own eyes tracing features drawn with exquisite delicacy, though her gently flushed cheeks still retained the rounded curves of youth. Her long, sable-dark hair was confined in two braids, each as thick as his wrist, but several shorter tendrils had escaped and curled enticingly over her brow and temples, almost mingling with the sooty lashes feathering luminous grey eyes that would probably show her every emotion. And her soft, full-lipped mouth was made for kissing.

She was tiny, he saw. He could have spanned her waist between his hands and, had they been standing

closer, the top of her head would not have reached his
shoulder. Guy had always liked tall women, preferably
those built on rather buxom lines, but right now he
couldn't for the life of him remember why. In fact he
would have had trouble recalling his own name. He
remembered hers, however.

'Isabel,' he murmured, making the name sound like a
poem. Then, as his eyes fell to the way she was cradling
one hand in the other, he added, frowning, 'You're
hurt.'

Isabel glanced down at her injured finger. ''Tis only a
splinter. . .' she began, but her voice died away as the
soldier moved swiftly towards her.

She stifled a desire to turn and flee, wondering what
was wrong with her. She was in no danger. She was not
afraid of the soldier, who was probably one of Sir Guy
fitzAlan's men and therefore no threat to her.

This thought reminded her that he hadn't volunteered
his own name, but somehow it didn't seem to matter.
She knew him. He was a complete stranger, and yet she
knew him. The shocked sense of recognition made her
breathless; her heart fluttered in her breast like the
trembling of a captured bird.

It wasn't supposed to happen like this, Isabel told
herself, trying to regain control of her disordered
senses. She wasn't supposed to have this kind of tremulous reaction to a soldier encountered so casually.
Especially one who looked glaringly out of place in the
still serenity of her garden. He wasn't right.

He wasn't what she had expected.

She had dreamed, as very young girls did, of a
handsome knight who would one day arrive at her
father's castle, fall in love with her, win her heart by
some brave deed, and carry her away across his saddle-
bow. But he had ridden up on a valiant steed with all the
trappings of chivalrous knighthood. He hadn't just

appeared from nowhere. And, though Isabel hadn't really pictured a face, she had known that he would be gently bred, slender, a little taller than herself, perhaps, and handsomely clad in the raiment suited to his station.

Not so tall and powerfully built that she felt as though she might break if he so much as touched her. Not dressed in travel-stained wool and dusty chainmail with his sword hilt gleaming harshly in the sunshine. And definitely not with several days' growth of beard on an aggressively masculine jaw, or with so much. . .so much compelling *strength* in his face, in his ice-blue eyes.

Her knight would be gentle, kind and chivalrous. This man looked big, tough and slightly dangerous.

But the strange feeling of recognition persisted.

"'Tis really nought,' she whispered nervously as he reached her and held out his hand. Then she stared, amazed, at the fragile rosebud lying across his palm. It was flawless, completely unbruised for being held in that strong, long-fingered hand.

'See, I won't harm you,' he said, smiling down at her bemused face.

Isabel looked up at him quickly, startled anew as she realised he was much younger than she'd first supposed. Somewhere in his early twenties, she decided, fascinated by his unexpectedly boyish smile. But the smile was the only thing he had in common with her fantasy knight. Close to, he was even more intimidating. He must have stood at least two inches over six feet, and his obvious physical strength caused an unfamiliar quivering to start up deep inside her.

'Give me your hand.'

It was a command, but his deep voice was so soft that Isabel hesitantly held out her wounded finger. Her hand hovered above the rose, not quite touching it.

'I think you will not be able to remove the splinter, sir,' she said, struggling to recover her usual practical common sense. It took an amazing amount of effort. 'But Dameta will easily do so. She is my maid and her fingers are much smaller than yours and then she'll want to put a salve on it and. . .'

Under the soldier's intent gaze Isabel subsided abruptly into silence as she realised how she was babbling. She was behaving like a fool. And to think she had always poured scorn on her older sisters when they had put on such fluttering airs in front of a man. For the first time Isabel wondered if those airs had been caused by the same stupid helplessness which seemed to be gripping her.

When she made no move to take the rosebud, Guy tucked it into one of the mail links on his hauberk and captured her hand before she could withdraw it again. The flash of heat that surged through him as their fingers touched took him completely by surprise. Desire, immediate and powerful, tightened his entire body. It took every ounce of self-control he possessed not to crush her fingers with his and pull her into his arms.

Had she felt it also? Her little hand trembled in his much larger one, but Guy was too stunned to notice that she didn't pull away, although he continued to hold her as though she were as fragile as glass. Never, *never* had he felt such a violent reaction to a woman.

Isabel raised questioning eyes to his face. 'See, 'tis but a scratch,' she murmured, in a voice so shy and uncertain that something else shuddered deep inside him.

He wrenched his gaze away from hers and glanced down. The jagged sliver of wood piercing her finger caused a peculiar chill to sweep over him. He found himself rocketing from desire to protectiveness in the space of seconds, and felt suddenly impatient with such irrationally see-sawing feelings. God's teeth, he must be more tired than he knew. After the wounds he'd seen in his time, how could one little splinter have such an effect? How could *she* have such an effect?

'You're right,' he said brusquely. 'I won't be able to grip it.'

Her face clouded over in confusion at his curt tone, and another set of emotions rioted through him.

I'm not ready for this, he thought almost desperately, not even knowing what 'this' meant. He couldn't even begin to untangle the sensations buffeting both mind and body. The only thing he recognised with any surety was intense desire, so intense that the vague awareness at the back of his mind of something wrong was stifled.

Holding her captive with his eyes, he raised her hand quickly to his mouth.

Isabel gasped, her eyes widening in shock as warm lips enclosed her finger. She felt his teeth against her skin for a split-second, then the splinter was gone.

And, with it, the image of her bland, faceless knight. If she dreamed of him again it would be this man's face she would see. Isabel looked up at him and knew every feature was indelibly impressed on her mind. His fair, almost silvery-blond hair, the broad, high cheekbones, the strong aquiline nose, the firm line of his mouth. And his eyes — piercing, vividly blue, and glittering with a light that she was yet too young to understand, but which called to something very feminine within her.

'The splinter is gone now,' Isabel managed, finally breaking the spell of his gaze. She gave a tentative tug at her hand. He didn't release her. 'My finger is not even bleeding,' she pointed out uncertainly.

'No, it isn't,' he agreed, not even glancing at the small wound. His other hand retrieved the rose. Very carefully he placed the flower in her hair, just above one silky dark plait.

Isabel had meant to ask for her hand back, but now her breath seemed to have been stolen as well. A strange anticipation held her completely immobile. Unable to meet his eyes, she stared at the garden, wondering vaguely why it looked the same when she felt so very different.

She felt the soldier's hand gently cradle her face. His thumb tilted her chin up.

'The rose is for you, little maid,' he said, his voice husky, deeper than it had been before. 'And this is for me.'

He bent and brushed her mouth fleetingly with his, before lingering for a heart-shakingly tender kiss.

It was the kiss that finally brought Guy to his senses. Her mouth felt warm and soft — and totally unawakened. Hell, what am I doing? he groaned silently. She's only a babe.

The swift understanding cleared his mind for a moment. He drew back immediately, only to stifle another low sound of longing at the wondering expression in her eyes.

She was too young, and, even if she was not, she was his host's daughter. Not for him. He had to leave the garden. Before he forgot where he was and why he was there. Before he did something he'd regret for the rest of his life. Before the quick rush of protectiveness was swamped by the passionate need growing more insistent the longer he stayed.

She's barely more than a child, he told himself again. But sweet. So innocent and sweet. How long ago was it that I looked on the world with such innocent eyes?

'Is-a-bel.'

Several seconds passed before Isabel realised her name had come from beyond the wall and not from the man whose fingers still gently caressed her cheek. The intrusion of the world brought her back to reality with a thud.

Blushing hotly, she sprang out of reach and hurriedly

backed away. 'I must go,' she whispered, avoiding the soldier's eyes, watching his hands fall to his sides instead. Merciful saints, she had let a complete stranger hold her, kiss her. . .

Had not her sister Alice cautioned her of the dangers in being alone with a man, now that she had reached marriageable age? Had Alice not warned of men who took advantage if a maid was compliant? But she had forgotten all the warnings. She had stayed willingly in the secluded garden with the soldier, had not voiced a single protest at his boldness. She went hot all over at the thought, too upset to understand that she had only escaped his hold because he had let her.

Without so much as a glance back to see his reaction to such an abrupt departure, Isabel scurried to the postern, yanked it open, and fled. She wondered wildly if a scratched finger would excuse her from supping in the hall so she wouldn't have to face the soldier again.

CHAPTER ONE

Empress Matilda's Headquarters, Gloucester Castle
October 1141

THE flames of the rushlights burning in the gallery overlooking the great hall flickered gently, as though reaching out warm fingers to caress the girl passing beneath them. Their lambent glow danced over her sable-dark hair, touched her face briefly, then slid reluctantly away as she moved into the shadows between each one.

The last was more fortunate. At the end of the gallery the girl halted, gazing down into the hall through one of the archways cut into the wall. The flames seemed to burn brighter in her presence, illuminating her finely etched profile and the hand resting on the stone wall beside her. It was a small hand, with slender, tapering fingers. The hand of a lady, unmarked, but for a tiny, crescent-shaped scar on the middle finger. In the light of the flaring sconce the girl could see the scar quite clearly. As clearly as she recalled that spring day so long ago when she had received the small wound.

She hadn't needed to offer such a weak plea as a scratched finger after all, Isabel remembered. Dameta had taken one look at her heated countenance when she'd emerged from the pleasance, and had ordered her to bed, muttering about fevers and the carelessness of wandering about in gardens without a mantle. And she had climbed between the sheets without a murmur, another circumstance which had convinced her nurse that she was about to succumb to a chill.

The memory hurt.

Determinedly Isabel tried to shut off the thoughts of Dameta, of home and family. For some reason it wasn't so easy tonight. She lingered still beneath the rushlight, the mark on her finger drawing her eyes irresistibly. It was odd how the scar had remained all these years. It had been such a little hurt. And yet today she had glanced again and again at her hand, and found herself remembering.

Remembering how she had stood on the tower battlements the next morning, watching her knight ride away. She had known who he was by then, had known that he was returning to the King with assurances of her father's support.

He had looked different. With a safe distance between them the impression of strength and toughness was not so overwhelming and, now that he was washed and shaved, with the morning sun turning his fair hair to gleaming gold, she had seen that he was handsome. His clothes had been brushed also, and the harness on his magnificent black destrier had been cleaned. Isabel remembered how the horse had tossed his head and sidled playfully, like a huge, overgrown puppy, when Guy had tried to mount him. She remembered his laughter, and her father's voice shouting farewell.

He had ridden away without a backward look.

'You are reluctant to go down to the hall, *demoiselle*? Allow me to escort you.'

Roused abruptly from her memories, Isabel looked around to see one of the young knights from the castle garrison. He liked her, she knew, although he never seemed to gather the courage to do anything about it. Just as well, she thought thankfully. She would never marry a man such as Sir Richard Fiennes. But at least he respected her. She was glad not to have to hurt his feelings by spurning any deliberate advances.

'My thanks, sir,' Isabel murmured, turning to walk
with him. The noise of conversation from the hall below
bounced off the walls around them. It seemed louder,
more raucous than usual, and she sighed at the prospect
of another evening spent listening to the same arguments and bitter reproaches.

The boy keeping pace beside her must have heard the
sigh; he glanced at her, his expression concerned. 'I
regret I must leave you at the door, Lady Isabel. I'm on
duty tonight. But you need have no fear. You are under
the Sheriff's protection here.'

A faint smile crossed her face, but she remained silent
until they had descended the stairway and stood at the
entrance to the great hall. It stretched before them,
appearing huge, despite the crowd gathered for the
evening meal.

Off to one side, several men, still wearing their mail
hauberks, were warming themselves before the fire.
Drinking-horns were passed around, and a burst of
laughter greeted the end of a tale being recounted by
one of the soldiers. On the opposite side of the room
another fire burned brightly behind the high table, and a
page was carefully setting the finger bowl in its place.
Though the benches at the lower trestles were filling up
quickly, Isabel saw that none of the nobles had as yet
put in an appearance.

Fiennes glanced doubtfully into the room. 'Would
you rather wait for the other ladies?' he ventured,
obviously torn between his duty and the thought of her
sitting alone in such rowdy company for several
minutes.

'No one will accost me,' she assured him, and smiled
with gentle irony. 'After all, as you just reminded me, I
am under the Sheriff's protection.'

The irony was lost on Fiennes. Like all men, he saw
only the smile and not the sadness that lay behind it. She

didn't mind. It was safer that way. He bowed reluctantly, and took himself off to his post.

Isabel forgot him instantly. She glanced down at her hand, wondering yet again why the memory of that day should be so insistent tonight, then her lovely face became expressionless as she wrapped herself in the familiar cloak of indifference. A remote, cool air enveloped her that caused more than one man to think twice about approaching her as she walked slowly down the length of the hall.

Entering a room full of rough soldiers, unescorted, and sitting alone at the high table, exposed to their speculative eyes and lewd jokes, held no fears for her.

It was raining again when he reached Gloucester. The hollow clatter of his mount's hooves on the castle drawbridge mingled with the heavy splash of water rapidly filling the ditch. Further along the embankment a few miserable beggars huddled close to the stone ramparts, seeking the meagre shelter afforded by a jutting tower.

Ordinary sights and sounds on a night like this, mused Guy. There was no logical reason why they should add to the vague tension he'd been conscious of all day. His mission was going well, and he had even managed to save some precious time by arriving before the curfew was rung and the drawbridge raised for the night. Instead of having to seek shelter at an alehouse, he would be able to deliver his messages immediately and leave in the morning.

He spared a glance at the ragged specimens of humanity crouched against the wall and wondered how many of them had once been prosperous farmers or innkeepers or tradesmen. How many had been beggared while the war between the royal cousins had swept across their fields or through their towns, while the

barons who should have protected them looked only to
their own gain, shifting loyalties so often that the
ordinary common man found himself constantly
besieged and attacked by both sides?

Of course there were those who remained staunch,
Guy reminded himself, as he reached into his tunic for a
few coins. Men who had stayed loyal to Stephen
throughout his misfortunes, and, on the other side, men
who followed the Empress Matilda unreservedly.

This fact was abruptly brought home to him by the
commanding voice ringing through the gloom of the
overcast evening.

'Hold there!'

A young soldier appeared beneath the arched gateway, flanked by two men-at-arms, wielding pikes. 'Let
me see both hands—slowly,' he instructed, his voice
strained.

Guy's mouth kicked up at one corner in a wryly
amused smile. Despite the fact that the war had ground
to a halt while the commanders-in-chief of both armies
languished in their respective prisons, the young sprig
confronting him obviously took his guard duty seriously.

'I'm fitzAlan of Ashby Chase,' he announced quietly,
withdrawing the hand concealed in his cloak. The other
retained its firm grip on the reins. He wasn't going to
risk having his horse spooked into the ditch by a nervous
sentry. 'I carry letters from the Queen to the Countess
of Anjou.'

He noted the awed curiosity on the younger man's
face on hearing his name, but the boy came back with a
swift answer. 'You mean the Empress, sir. I'll see that
she gets the letters, if you'll be good enough to wait in
the guard-room.'

Guy muttered darkly and dismounted. 'I mean the
Countess of Anjou, boy,' he snapped with barely

concealed impatience. 'Where's your commanding officer?'

As he had expected, the sentry came to attention automatically at the suddenly terse voice.

'I'll take you to him, Lord fitzAlan,' he responded stiffly. 'You'll understand our caution, I trust.'

'Very commendable,' Guy growled. 'But since it's obvious that I don't have a bloody army at my back you can take me directly to the Countess, or the Sheriff of Gloucester, if he's here.'

'Aye, sir.' More rigid than ever, the boy turned to lead the way.

Guy followed, taking the time to throw the coins in his hand to the beggars. They scrambled to retrieve them, croaking out blessings and thanks.

At least he'd made someone happy, he thought drily, regretting that he'd snarled at the lad in front of him. The boy was only obeying orders. But the odd tension which had been nagging at him seemed to be increasing.

He looked up at the formidable stone keep of Gloucester Castle towering three storeys above him and wondered if there was danger within, although his task was straightforward enough. Behind him, along the road leading down to the town, he could see lights start to glow as home fires were kindled against the cold night. No danger there, either. And yet, as the sentry yelled for a stable boy to take Guy's horse before they mounted the outer stairway of the forebuilding, he felt every muscle in his body tighten.

Shrugging off rational assurances, Guy let the warning sensations roll over him. More than five years of rebellions and civil war had honed his instincts to a fine edge, and he knew better than to ignore them. No matter what awaited him tonight, he was braced and ready.

* * *

'Isabel, look!'

'What is it, Adele?' Isabel didn't trouble to glance up from her stitching. Repairing her already threadbare clothes was not her idea of an entertaining evening, but she had learned that if she appeared busy no one bothered her.

Sometimes she even managed to shut her ears to the arguments going on around her. They were always on the subject of war anyway. She was sick of battle plans, plots and schemes that never succeeded, and the angry railing against failure. Why couldn't the Empress Matilda see that she was beaten?

It had been a different story earlier this year after the Battle of Lincoln had seen Stephen's army defeated and the King himself taken prisoner. King Henry's daughter had been triumphantly proclaimed Lady of England until she could be crowned queen. Even the powerful Bishop of Winchester had turned his back on his brother and had acknowledged Matilda.

But the tide had turned. Unable or unwilling to curb her arrogance while her star was in the ascendency, the Empress had alienated nearly all those who had abandoned the King. Her overweening imperiousness had finally driven the Bishop to send a message to the Queen, begging for her forgiveness and her help. Furious, Matilda had besieged the Bishop in his own castle, but the surprising determination of Stephen's gentle wife had prevailed.

Only too glad to regain the support of her brother-in-law, the Queen had gathered her army and surrounded Winchester. The besieger had become the besieged, and Matilda had only escaped because of the gallant rear-guard action of her half-brother, Robert, Earl of Gloucester, as they fought their way out of their castle before they were starved out. Robert had been taken prisoner in his turn and, for the time being, hostilities had ceased while both sides licked their wounds and took stock of the situation.

But had the Empress been grateful that her brother's sacrifice had meant her freedom? No, thought Isabel. Matilda was still ranting and raving against the absent Earl for getting himself captured. She was beginning to hear that strident, angry voice in her sleep.

Adele's softer tones were a welcome change.

'Oh, Isabel, do look. He's so handsome.'

Isabel finally turned to regard the girl sitting next to her. Adele was in a similar position to herself—caught up in the middle of a war, alone, and without the protection of close family. But she was also distant kin to the Sheriff of Gloucester, and thus treated with more consideration than Isabel.

'Who have you fallen in love with this week, Adele?' she asked, smiling indulgently.

'No one,' protested Adele indignantly, then blushed. 'I mean, I haven't changed my mind about Philip, you provoking creature. I'm talking about the man who just came in.' She cast a glance down the table from beneath her lashes, and added, 'I see our lady is quite interested, also.'

Isabel's eyes followed the direction of Adele's to rest on the woman seated midway along the high table. She was flanked by two men. Men whose stern faces and seasoned appearance proclaimed their experience in war and hardship. And yet the woman's personality overshadowed them both.

Matilda, Countess of Anjou and Princess of England, occupied her great, carved chair as though she sat upon the throne she stubbornly insisted was hers. She was a tall woman, dark of hair and eyes, still considered strikingly attractive, although she was nearing forty. But there was a hard veneer to her, a cold ruthlessness, which repelled many who came into contact with her.

'One doesn't think of the Empress as being interested in men,' observed Adele in a gossipy whisper. 'She is usually so impervious to any softer womanly emotions, and we all know her opinion of her husband. Philip tells me they fight like cats every time they come within sight of each other, and Count Geoffrey is so occupied with annexing Normandy that he refuses to help her cause here.'

'Matilda argues with everyone,' Isabel pointed out.

'I think she has other plans for this man,' murmured Adele. 'Perhaps he has come to offer his support. Why else would anyone come here?'

Why else, indeed? wondered Isabel. *She* certainly wasn't in this forbidding place by choice.

Her curiosity mildly aroused by Adele's close interest in the stranger, Isabel glanced across the table, her gaze sliding past the sentry announcing the visitor.

Big, was her first impression. The man stripping off his helmet as he strode down the room was tall and broad-shouldered, and moved with the leashed power of the hunter. A hunting wolf, she thought, shivering suddenly. That lithe, muscular grace told of awesome physical strength under perfect control. Intrigued almost against her will, Isabel shifted her eyes to his face — and, in the space of a heartbeat, five and a half years vanished from her life.

It was her soldier!

Guy fitzAlan.

Not a longed-for dream, but the man himself.

For a breathless instant, made dizzy by the fierce uprush of joy sweeping through her, Isabel could not think beyond the fact that he had come. He was *here*. Almost within reach. She was conscious of nothing else. She heard nothing else, saw nothing but his face, felt nothing apart from the out-of-control pounding of her heart. The entire world shrank to the mere fifteen feet separating her from the man she had thought never to see again.

'Isabel? Are you all right? You've gone as white as snow.'

Isabel stared blindly at Adele's concerned face. 'A. . .a sudden toothache,' she improvised wildly, hardly knowing what she was saying. Reality swung back with another dizzying rush that made her head swim. Without understanding why, she knew she had to distract Adele's attention away from her. 'It must have been those honeyed cakes,' she added hurriedly, and gestured to the Empress. 'Hush, Matilda is speaking.'

Adele turned away, apparently satisfied, and Isabel shrank back on the bench, half hidden by Adele's body as the other girl leaned forward to hear what was going on. Struggling desperately to regain control of her senses, Isabel forced herself to listen also, to silence the clamouring questions in her head.

Matilda was contemplating the man before her, tapping the letters in her hand against the table. 'So, my cousin is becoming anxious to have her husband back, my lord.'

The tone of voice was gently musing, but Guy wasn't fooled for a minute. This wasn't his first encounter with Stephen's rival and he knew the woman seated on the other side of the high table was a formidable opponent, probably more dangerous than the King, and possessing in full measure the strong will and harsh determination that had characterised her father and grandfather.

It was her misfortune, Guy reflected briefly, that Matilda hadn't also inherited the Conqueror's skill at diplomacy. If she had, she might now be wearing the crown of England instead of being holed up in Gloucester Castle, her supporters scattered and dwindling, and what little popularity she had once possessed destroyed by her own hand.

Guy stared into hostile eyes, his own gaze ice-cold. 'No more anxious than you are for the return of the Earl of Gloucester, madam,' he countered.

He felt a sudden sharp impulse to look to his left, but controlled it, his eyes never leaving the Empress. Her face took on a mask-like stillness at the lack of title with which he addressed her. She'd better get used to it, Guy thought inflexibly. Matilda was the Countess of Anjou. Damned if he was going to call her Empress when her first husband, the Holy Roman Emperor, had been dead for years. And she was no longer Lady of England.

'I seem to recall that you don't believe in wasting time on gallantry, Lord fitzAlan,' Matilda bit out, her eyes narrowing to hazel slits. 'You have not changed, I see.'

'Gallantry is wasted, madam, when 'tis repaid with threats and ill treatment. But I am not here to bandy words with you,' Guy continued, ruthlessly forestalling another angry retort. 'The Queen *is* anxious for the negotiations between our two parties to be concluded satisfactorily. It is the natural anxiety of any wife who is concerned for her husband's well-being. Since more formal arrangements seem to be delayed, she has ventured to address you herself, one woman to another.'

Even if it's useless, Guy added to himself. He caught the eye of the man seated on Matilda's left and nodded curt acknowledgement. 'My lord.'

Miles, Sheriff of Gloucester and Constable of Gloucester Castle, nodded back. 'Lord fitzAlan. 'Tis some time since we met.'

Guy didn't bother with any further conversation. He and Miles had last faced each other across a battlefield strewn with the dead and dying. Miles had managed to vanish before Guy could get to him. Apparently his escape from the rout of Winchester hadn't been so easy. Guy had heard that Miles had finally reached

Gloucester on foot and practically dead from exhaustion, his weapons and armour long since abandoned so he could travel faster. He had not been alone in fleeing thus ignominiously. The field had been littered with riderless steeds and discarded equipment. As a result, Earl Robert had not been the only valuable prisoner taken, a fact that obviously rankled with Matilda.

'Such arrangements as are proposed take time to consider, Lord fitzAlan,' she pointed out. 'My brother is but an earl, and yet you expect us to give up a king in exchange. I believe the release of all your prisoners for my cousin's freedom would better suffice.'

Guy raised a mocking eyebrow. 'In that case, are you freely acknowledging that Stephen should remain King, madam?' he asked smoothly.

Matilda's eyes flashed. 'Never!' she cried angrily. 'That false perjurer and defiler of oaths stole the crown from me. He has no right to it!'

'Then, madam, the exchange of one commander for another is fair, is it not? The other prisoners will be released on payment of ransom, as is the custom.'

Isabel couldn't help it. No one spoke to the Empress like that and got away with it. She leaned forward to see Matilda's reaction to Guy's brutal logic just as he turned his head slightly in her direction, as though he sensed her watching him.

Their eyes collided with a force that deafened and blinded Isabel to everything else. She vaguely heard Matilda's angry voice, but it came to her from a great distance. She glimpsed the Sheriff's movement, but through a blurred mist. The only thing Isabel saw with any clarity was the startled recognition in fitzAlan's ice-blue eyes. Transfixed by the sudden intensity of his gaze before he turned back to the Empress, she was totally unprepared for what happened next.

'I see you are still human enough to be attracted by a

pretty face, my lord,' Matilda purred with patently false sweetness.

FitzAlan narrowed his eyes at her. 'I once knew the girl's father,' he said abruptly. 'How does she come to be here?'

Matilda's smile was mocking. 'Why, Tracy Castle is held for me, of course.' She cast a glance at Isabel's still face. 'This dear child's loyalty is my greatest pleasure, and *so* useful. Men will often behave. . .rashly, shall we say?. . .when the reward is thus sweetly packaged. You see, I give you fair warning.'

It was Adele's indignant gasp that wrenched Isabel out of her frozen state. Her eyes flashed swiftly to fitzAlan, only to recoil at the look of blazing fury and contempt he turned on her. She shook her head slightly, making a move as if to rise, but Adele grabbed her arm.

'No,' she whispered in Isabel's ear. 'Let it go. You know Matilda is always looking for a reason to punish you.'

Sick and shaking, Isabel obeyed, slumping back on the bench and gazing helplessly at fitzAlan. When he at last looked away from her, she felt as though she had been seared to the soul by the scathing dismissal in his eyes.

Oh, how could she explain? How could she tell him why Matilda had made such a spiteful remark? She would never be allowed to see such an important visitor, let alone speak with him. Oh, God, what was she to do? The prospect of Guy leaving, thinking the worst of her, was unbearable. The idea that she might be able to leave with him didn't even occur to her.

'Isabel? You really *are* in pain. And no wonder, after that. Poor girl, you must retire.'

Barely hearing Adele through the strange roaring in her ears, Isabel gazed blankly at her friend.

'Go up to our room,' instructed Adele firmly. 'I'll

send a serf with some vinegar, oil and sulphur to rub on your tooth.'

This practical suggestion got through the haze. 'I. . .I can't,' Isabel stammered, not wanting to leave the hall while Guy was there. Then she realised that he had gone, and she hadn't even seen him leave. Had shock held her deaf and blind for so long? She glanced distractedly around the room. He was nowhere in sight.

'Where. . .?'

'Oh, don't worry about our visitor. Uncle Miles suggested that Lord fitzAlan retire for the night while he and the Empress read through the Queen's letters. I wager they've put him in the meanest, coldest room, without even a brazier, after the way he spoke to Matilda. I thought she would have a fit on the spot. And she obviously didn't like the way he looked at you.'

'Me? Adele, what. . .?' Frantically Isabel gathered her wits, trying to suppress the sudden queasiness in the pit of her stomach.

'Well, she might have been angry with him,' Adele chattered on, 'but he's not the sort of man one can ignore, is he? Matilda would love to have him on her side, and not only because of his reputation.'

'Reputation?' She felt sicker than ever. 'You mean with women?'

'Heavens, no! I don't know anything about *that*. But I remember Philip telling me of a man he admired a great deal, and 'twas Guy fitzAlan of Ashby Chase. It must be the same man. Apparently he fought with incredible bravery at Lincoln, only retreating when the King was captured. And he is one of the few who have never changed sides. Of course, that doesn't mean he won't take a woman if he fancies her, especially after what Matilda said, but. . .'

Adele saw Isabel's pale face turn even whiter and broke off, patting her hand consolingly. 'Don't fret,' she advised kindly. 'I'm sure Lord fitzAlan will be kept much too busy to accost you. Although I have to admit, if he had stared so at *me*. . .' Adele shivered dramatically. 'Holy Mother, those eyes!' She seemed to realise that this comment was not exactly reassuring and hastened to make amends. 'But keep to your room if you fear him, Isabel. And, see, Matilda is retiring also. Now that she's vented her spite for the evening, she won't even notice you're missing, but if anyone asks I'll tell them you're suffering from toothache.'

'Aye,' gasped Isabel, remembering her hastily manufactured excuse and rising. 'My thanks, Adele.'

Hurrying from the hall, she stifled her guilt at deceiving her innocent friend, knowing that Adele had entirely misunderstood her fright. But the need for solitude to pull herself together was too imperative. She would confess her deception to the castle priest later, Isabel promised her conscience, and then wondered if, in fact, the chapel might provide the privacy she craved. It would be empty at this hour. Then she saw that, in her haste to leave the hall, she had fled to the nearest exit, which opened on to a passage running along the side of the great-room. It was seldom frequented since only the Empress's suite of rooms lay here in the south-west tower.

Isabel hesitated, considering her choices. She could reach the chapel from here, but it was situated in the forebuilding, beyond the staircase turret at the other end of the corridor, and, though a rushlight burned in its sconce above the steps leading to Matilda's rooms, the rest of the passage lay in heavy darkness.

She hated the dark.

But the alternative of returning to the hall, and traversing its crowded sixty-foot length to gain the opposite staircase leading to the upper storey, where

she shared a tiny chamber with Adele and two of
Matilda's ladies, was just as unappealing.

It would have to be the chapel, Isabel decided,
scolding herself for her cowardly hesitation. The only
danger in the dark passage was the risk of a collision
with the odd piece of furniture, and surely she was not
afraid of a table? Placing one hand on the cold stone
wall for guidance, she plunged forward.

Blackness closed around her instantly. But there
would be lights in the chapel, Isabel assured herself,
peering ahead for a sign of them and flinching from the
feel of the rough stone beneath her palm. The chill from
the bare wall seemed to penetrate to her bones. Surely
it was odd that no light at all shone in the corridor? It
was Matilda's private route to the chapel, after all.

That's if the woman ever prays, Isabel reflected,
holding on to the random thought to steady her shaky
nerves. Matilda was more likely to rant at her Maker
than supplicate, even when she hadn't been put into a
rage. She found herself wondering how long Matilda
would rant against Guy, and another stray thought
flashed through her mind.

Everyone had called him *Lord* fitzAlan. Some time,
then, during the intervening years, he had been granted
a barony. A reward for unswerving loyalty, no doubt.
Despair washed through Isabel again as she remembered the cutting disdain in fitzAlan's eyes, too distressed at the moment to be angered by his instant
acceptance of Matilda's explanation. So many families
had changed sides, and she was not imprisoned, nor
even a slave. He had seen her sitting at the high table
among the other ladies of noble birth who served the
Empress.

Oh, God, she prayed silently, show me a way to let
him know how wrong he is. I but saw him the once, and
yet cannot bear for him to despise me so.

'He despises me! Did you see the scorn in his eyes? I'll not endure it! Do you hear me, Miles?'

It took a moment for Isabel to realise that the low, passionate words, so like those inside her head, had been spoken aloud. She stopped immediately, her heart thumping in sudden fright as she saw that the chapel was occupied. At the same time her groping fingers felt emptiness and she knew where she was.

Ahead, a narrow sliver of light showed where the chapel door had not been properly closed. The shadowy form of a woman crossed it before the Empress moved out of Isabel's line of vision. To her right, as her eyes adjusted to the faint lifting of the darkness, she could just make out the first steps of the spiral tower staircase. Then, before she could decide whether to retreat and wait for the Empress to leave, a man murmured softly. Isabel couldn't hear the words clearly, but she knew the voice. And she knew who it was they were discussing.

Matilda was with the Sheriff, and there was only one reason why they would be here, seeking privacy like herself: to plot against Guy.

Holding the skirts of her worn grey woollen gown close about her legs, Isabel glided into the darkness of the stair turret, hugging the wall. She no longer felt the cold, or worried about the unlit passage. Every sense strained to hear the low-voiced conversation in the adjacent chapel. For the first time she was grateful for Matilda's notorious temper, which made it impossible for the Empress to keep her voice down.

'How dare he speak to me like that? "The natural anxiety of any wife for her husband's well-being." Did you hear him, Miles? And look at this letter. That puling creature has the gall to remind me that Stephen is a consecrated king and should not be treated as a felon. What else should that perjurer expect, but to be chained in a dungeon? Do you tell me that my brother is not treated in a like manner?'

'You forget, my lady, that the Queen has treated Robert with the utmost honour.'

'Honour? *Honour*? They offered him the highest position in the land, second only to that traitor, if he would forsake me! Is that honour?'

'I meant the way he is housed. My lady, try to calm yourself and consider carefully. Do you think it wise to continue to hold Stephen bound and chained in that dungeon at Bristol? The reports of his health are not good.'

'Then let the man sicken and die.' The words dropped into the darkness like shards of ice.

Isabel, listening in the tower, shivered at the implacable hatred in Matilda's voice. She saw a shadow move across the wall opposite her as the other woman paced violently.

'If that happens while he is in our custody,' continued Miles, 'you can give up any hope of getting your brother back; and we need him.'

'Don't tell me my business, Miles,' stormed the Empress. 'God, why did Robert have to be captured? Why am I served by incompetents who can only advise surrender?'

''Tis not surrender, my lady. 'Tis true that releasing Stephen will put him back on the throne, but our army can do nothing without my Lord of Gloucester at its head. Holding Stephen is no longer an advantage.'

The shadow suddenly stopped moving. 'That may be,' said Matilda, and her voice was now soft and deadly. 'But we can hold him for a while yet. Time enough, perhaps, to break his health so that he does not long survive his freedom.'

'And how do you intend to convey a delaying answer to the Queen, my lady?'

'Very simply,' replied Matilda silkily. 'Even that whey-faced simpleton who calls herself Queen will understand a message pinned to fitzAlan's dead body. Where did you put the arrogant lout?'

'In one of the chambers off the gallery, but you can't. . .'

Isabel did not wait for more. Reluctant to brave the corridor again in case the conspirators emerged and caught her, she turned sharply and fled up the tower stairs, just one thought uppermost in her mind.

She had to warn Guy. He must leave at once. Matilda must have run mad to suggest such a thing. To murder a man while he was under her roof. . .

Shivering with fear and the need for haste, Isabel stumbled up the narrow stone staircase, slipping once and bruising her knee when she fell. She hardly noticed. At last she reached the floor above the hall and began to cross to the diagonally opposite tower, grateful that there were lights here to guide her way. A room off the gallery, the Sheriff had said. But which one? There were one or two built into each thick wall of the rectangular keep. How could she find fitzAlan without anyone becoming suspicious? Apart from disturbing the wrong occupants, the gallery was open to the hall below it in several places and she might be seen.

But then, if she waited until everyone slept, she might be too late.

The idea of Guy being killed while he lay sleeping quickened Isabel's steps. She hurtled down the north-west turret staircase with a reckless disregard for life and limb, and emerged at the point where she had entered the hall earlier that night — was it only hours ago? She felt as though she had been running forever. Her legs quivered and her chest heaved as she struggled to control her breathing. The north and west galleries stretched before her; every door was shut. Below her, the hum of voices was reassuringly loud. She should have brought a wine jug from the hall, she chided herself as her breathing steadied. It would have given her an excuse to be searching for a particular room, but she had been so frightened. . .

And she must not hesitate now. The memory of the fear induced by Matilda's vindictive rage spurred Isabel towards the nearest door. She would just glance quickly into each room and hope she didn't encounter anyone who knew her.

It was not only fear that drove her forward. Guy's safety was the only conscious thought in her mind, but deeper, in a dark, secret place in her heart, Isabel knew she was also impelled by the urgent need to see him again. To speak to him. Perhaps, by her action, to convince him that she had not turned traitor to the King. The barely acknowledged hope caused her heart to beat faster as she reached for the first round iron latch.

Then every drop of blood drained from her face as a man's hand reached past her. Strong fingers clamped brutally around her wrist, staying her action, and she was swung roughly about to meet the hard, questioning glare of one of Matilda's Angevin guards.

CHAPTER TWO

'UNGRATEFUL wench! Thankless creature! For years have I housed and fed you, and this is how you repay me! Traitorous slut!'

The vicious epithets struck Isabel's ears like blows. She stared stoically at the tapestry wall-hanging in front of her. It was the only concession to comfort in the Empress's room. The bed, table and stools were of plain, sturdy oak, rushes covered the floor, and the fire had not been lit. Matilda lived as hardily as her men.

'I have sworn no oath to you, my lady,' retorted Isabel, refusing to cower. 'Nor did my father.'

'You dare to answer me so?' shrilled Matilda. 'Fool! Ignorant wench! You will soon learn the penalty for your disgraceful conduct.'

'I have committed no disgrace,' insisted Isabel. ''Twas you, my lady, who would have been dishonoured by killing a guest.' She didn't have to wonder where such reckless courage was coming from. The worst had already happened to her. She had been intercepted outside Guy's room and would be severely punished, perhaps even killed.

The Empress was right, she thought wretchedly. She *had* been a fool not to anticipate that a guard would be keeping a hidden watch on fitzAlan's door. Her despair at this belated realisation had rendered her only half aware of being dragged down the gallery stairs and across a hall humming with surprised murmurs. She had vaguely noticed Adele's startled, anxious face, before she was shoved roughly across the threshold of Matilda's chamber to be confronted by the Empress, the Sheriff

44

and the one man who thought Matilda could do no wrong — Brien fitzCount, Lord of Wallingford, who, except for her half-brother, was the Empress's most devoted follower and, some said, her lover.

But he was also a man of fixed principles in matters of warfare. When Matilda had demanded an explanation, Isabel had given it to her, omitting nothing. She might not have succeeded in warning Guy, but she didn't think Brien fitzCount would stand by and allow the Queen's equerry to be murdered while he was on official business.

Matilda's harsh laughter cut through this hopeful belief.

'Are you telling me you were concerned for my soul?' she mocked. 'Look to your own, girl. Skulking about in private passages, listening at doors, betraying your rightful queen.' She paused in her furious pacing and thrust her face close to Isabel's. 'I should despatch you to hell this minute, where your soul will be justly rewarded.'

Determined not to show fear, Isabel stood her ground before the rage in Matilda's eyes, staring back at the other woman defiantly. With a strangled sound of frustrated fury, Matilda drew her arm back.

'My lady, wait!'

'Don't try to stop me from punishing this ingrate, Brien. I'll make sure the drab never interferes in my plans again.'

'You will do as you see fit, my Lady of England, but am I right in thinking this girl has a brother?'

Matilda's arm stayed. She turned slowly towards Brien. A look passed between them that Isabel, braced for the blow and hardly daring to breathe, couldn't decipher.

'Don't we hold him at Tracy Castle?' fitzCount

continued with careful emphasis. 'The girl would not like any harm to come to him, I warrant.'

There was a long, heavy silence. Isabel felt her defiant bravado disintegrate like shattered glass. She watched, numbly, as Matilda lowered her arm and stepped away.

Miles of Gloucester, who had remained quietly in the background since Isabel had entered the room, now moved forward. He carefully closed the door to the antechamber where some of Matilda's ladies sat, trying to ignore the scene going on in their hearing. 'What do you have in mind, Brien?'

'The girl was going to warn fitzAlan of the danger to his life, presumably so he could escape.' FitzCount's voice held no inflexion of either censure or approval of Matilda's plan. 'Perhaps we should allow her to go ahead with her virtuous deed. Under certain conditions, of course.'

Another look passed between the three. 'Why?' asked Matilda at last.

She seemed to have completely forgotten her rage, or perhaps it had been channelled into a more dangerous, calculating form, thought Isabel in dread. Terror caused her heart to jolt sickeningly, and her hands became damp. She had not cared about risking her own life, but Edmund. . . Her mind shut off the thought. She must not show fear. She must listen and wait.

'The last man I sent to Winchester has had more success in gaining entrance to the castle than the others,' explained fitzCount. 'But he can't get close enough to anyone of importance. He needs a contact—someone who can listen and not be noticed, someone whose presence is unremarked. A lady-in-waiting to the Queen herself would be the perfect answer.'

'You're saying I should let the wench escape with fitzAlan?' Matilda swung around and stared narrowly at Isabel.

Isabel stared back, trying not to let her flimsy hope show in her eyes as Matilda's appraising look swept down to her feet and back again.

'The creature has possibilities,' the Empress pronounced consideringly. 'Aye, 'tis more than time that she made herself useful. How will your fellow know her, though, Brien?'

'I'll send Rainald a message,' responded fitzCount. 'Telling him to expect word from this — what's your name, girl?'

'She's Isabel de Tracy,' Matilda answered for her, still thoughtful. 'A rebellious family, but their blood is good enough. My tender-hearted cousin will not refuse to take such a nobly born orphan into her household.' The Empress nodded once and became suddenly brisk. 'You are spared, girl, to carry out your self-appointed task and one of greater importance. My Lord of Wallingford's man will tell you what information to listen for, but know this: one false step and your brother's life will be forfeit. One word from Rainald that you are not proving useful to us and young de Tracy dies. Do you understand me?'

Isabel nodded carefully. She would agree to anything to save Edmund. There was only one doubt in her mind. 'What. . .?' Her voice came out as a hoarse whisper and she had to clear her throat. Matilda's satisfied expression at the betraying sound roused Isabel's pride. 'What if my lord fitzAlan refuses to take me with him?' she managed to say quite steadily.

'Because of what I said earlier?' Matilda laughed scornfully. 'Look in a mirror, girl, and you'll see what that insolent cur saw in the hall tonight. Of course, he'll be suspicious, but he's a man just the same.' She looked over her shoulder at the other two, smiling archly. 'Don't you agree, gentlemen?'

Brien fitzCount didn't even glance at Isabel. He sent

Matilda an answering smile that immediately caused Isabel to suspect that the gossip concerning the pair was true.

The Sheriff, however, remained grim-faced. 'FitzAlan may be a man,' he argued, 'but he's a man on a mission—not likely to saddle himself with female company on a hard ride. The girl's still a maid, isn't she? Do you think she'll be persuasive enough?'

'With her brother's continued good health at stake?' derided Matilda. 'She will do whatever she has to, won't you, Isabel? After all, what is your maidenhead compared to his life?'

Isabel didn't reply. There was no answer anyway. Her growing indignation at the way they were discussing her as though she were so much merchandise was abruptly swamped by misery at the thought of giving herself to the man she had dreamed of for years in such a cold-blooded manner. She had survived much. This might finally destroy her.

Through a haze of despair she noticed that the Sheriff was still frowning at her.

'Can't you look a bit less like a nun?' he demanded with masculine vagueness. 'Loosen your hair. . .and what about that poor excuse for a gown?'

'We don't want to overdo it,' objected Matilda, gesturing to Isabel to unfasten the braid hanging down her back.

Feeling like a puppet, Isabel obeyed.

'The dress can stay,' continued Matilda. 'If seduction doesn't work, she can play on fitzAlan's sympathy, if he has any.' Her lips curved suddenly in an unpleasant smile. 'And just to help arouse it. . .'

The vicious, open-handed blow landed on Isabel's cheek before she had any warning of the Empress's intention. It was hard enough to make her stagger and fall to her knees. Her eyes filled with tears of pain and shock, but Isabel refused to let them fall. She would not give the other woman that satisfaction.

Pushing herself upright again, she met Matilda's triumphant expression with impassive calm. 'How do I contact Rainald, madam?'

It was very late. In the hall a few sleepy serfs cleared away the debris left from the evening meal. Others, their duties finished, were settling down for the night on their pallets in front of the fires. The castle dogs crept closer to the flames also, snapping lazily as they squabbled for their accustomed places near the warmth.

Despite the almost empty room, Isabel had been taken back to the gallery by a circuitous route through little-known passages deep inside the castle walls. It was a trip she would rather have forgotten — the cold was biting and the whispering patter of rodent feet made her heart jump every few minutes — but she knew she would have to face it again when she and Guy escaped from the keep. Matilda had told her that their escape had to look genuine if fitzAlan was to believe her story.

At the moment, however, as she stood outside the door she had intended trying before, one trembling hand hesitating over the latch, Isabel could only think as far ahead as the next few minutes. She did not have any idea, she realised abruptly, of what she was going to say to fitzAlan. The breathless warning she would have uttered earlier would at least have had the ring of sincerity, but now she was only too conscious of having to play a part. And the fact that she wanted nothing more than to entrust herself to fitzAlan's protection made her nervousness all the more acute.

What if he didn't believe her? Worse, even if he accepted her warning, what if he refused to take her with him, thinking what he did of her?

The impatient gesture of the guard who had escorted

her caught Isabel's eye. No doubt he wanted his task over with, so he could return to his companions and his ale-cup in the soldiers' quarters. The man was ignorant of the Empress's scheme, but when Isabel glanced back at his face she saw only too clearly his opinion of her visit to their guest's room. And by morning the entire barracks would share his belief.

Suddenly Isabel knew she *had* to succeed. If she did not, and survived the failure, her life here would be unendurable.

Unable to bear the lustful, knowing mockery in the guard's eyes any longer, she closed her hand over the latch, pushed the door open, and slipped into the room. The door shut again on pitch-blackness. Isabel stood pressed back against the wooden panels, trying to listen for the sound of breathing over the drumming of her heart.

It seemed an age before she thought she heard movement over to her left. Her feet felt like leaden weights, but she eventually managed to take a step, and then another, one hand held out in front of her to feel for the bed. She only hoped there *was* a bed, and that she wouldn't fall over a low pallet. Why hadn't the man left a sconce burning? Was there an economy drive on rushlights tonight?

Then, just as this nonsensical question darted through her mind, something huge and heavy slammed into her back with all the force of a boulder slung from a catapult. She was flung violently forward, to land face down in a heap of blankets, the crushing weight of her assailant forcing all the air out of her body.

It was a woman, Guy realised in surprise.

When the door had opened to admit her, the waiting tension still gnawing at him had finally transformed itself into swift action, and he'd been too busy quitting the bed and judging the right moment to attack to identify the intruder. But there was no mistaking the soft fragility of the body beneath his, or the fragrant silkiness of the long tresses brushing across his throat as she tried to turn her head.

At her desperate movement, Guy promptly shoved his unexpected visitor's face into the bedding with a large, relentless hand before she could let loose a scream.

'Make one sound when I release you and I'll break your neck,' he growled in her ear.

Isabel barely heard him. Almost fainting from lack of air, she could only answer in choked gasps. Apparently it was enough, because the heavy pressure on the back of her head eased and she could turn her face to the side, dragging air back into her lungs.

It took a couple of deep breaths before she recovered enough to grasp what was happening. The oppressive weight above her had lifted slightly, and she was being searched. Systematically and with devastating intimacy.

Her faint scream of shock was abruptly stifled by a hand clamped over her mouth. She tried to struggle, flinching away from that intrusive touch. It was useless. Sobbing with rage and fear at her utter helplessness compared to the superior weight and strength of the man above her, Isabel could only submit. When fitzAlan had satisfied himself that she didn't carry a weapon, she felt as though no part of her body remained untouched.

'Don't move a muscle,' he ordered.

Too dazed by the rapid succession of shocks to disobey, Isabel stayed prone on the bed. She heard a flint strike and, a moment later, light flickered, dimly illuminating a small area around her head.

'Now, then, let's have a look at you,' came fitzAlan's voice, and she found herself flipped over on to her back to encounter a pair of hard blue eyes.

In the ensuing silence she could have heard a flea move in the rushes on the floor.

Then, with a rough jerk, fitzAlan pulled her to her feet. 'Just what the hell are you doing in here?' he snarled, towering over her.

'I. . .' Isabel's voice was scarcely a whisper. She had to stop and try again. Before she could utter a word, however, he suddenly slid his hand down to hers and raised it to the candlelight. His eyes scanned her bare fingers and returned to her face, their icy glitter freezing her to the floor.

'You're still unwed?' The words were flung at her like an accusation of felony.

Thrown mentally off balance by such an unexpected, seemingly irrelevant question, Isabel could only nod, her attempt at speech failing completely.

FitzAlan uttered an impatient curse and pushed her down on to the bed again. She went easily, her trembling legs no longer capable of supporting her, watching in silence as he strode over to the table next to the window embrasure and stood with his back to her, leaning both fists on the oak surface. Isabel saw the powerful muscles of his shoulders flex beneath his tunic as he controlled whatever emotion was driving him.

Dear lord, she had to speak, she told herself, staring down at her hands gripped tight in her lap. But she was being battered by so many conflicting emotions that her brain felt numb. She had never experienced such roiling confusion before in her entire life. A strange mixture of dread and tremulous joy at seeing fitzAlan again battled for supremacy with outrage at his rough treatment of her. What had happened to the icy indifference with which she had surveyed the world for the past few years?

'Well, you've certainly come a long way from the child who ran from me in that garden.'

The contemptuous tone of the words brought Isabel's head up. FitzAlan had turned and was now half sitting, half leaning against the table. He was still fully dressed, she noted distantly. For a moment they stared at each other — and, though the anger and hostility in the room were almost visible, the memory of that long-ago day hung in the air between them.

He looked bigger, thought Isabel. Stronger. More powerful. It was not only physical strength. She saw now that his tough appearance, which had so overwhelmed her five and a half years ago, had then been tempered by his youth. But if there was any softness, any tenderness in his nature now, it was buried too deeply to be easily discernible. Though still handsome, he looked hard, ruthless, and twice as dangerous as Isabel remembered.

What, Guy wondered, furious with himself, had possessed him to bring up that day? It was too dark in the small room to see by her expression if Isabel remembered also, but he knew she did. He could *feel* the memory they shared. Damn it, he hadn't meant to betray that he'd never been able to forget that afternoon, and the sweet innocence that had touched something very deep within him. Because she was certainly far from innocent now. Her presence in his room at this hour confirmed her role in Matilda's household only too plainly.

Well, if Isabel had any ideas of playing on that one unguarded remark she could think again, he vowed grimly. She might still be the most beautiful woman he had ever seen, but it wasn't going to affect him. Guy pushed the image of innocent vulnerability out of his mind and forced himself to look at Isabel objectively.

She was taller, of course. No longer a child. And although her slenderness gave her an air of fragility, Guy had felt the gentle curves of her body when he'd

searched for a concealed weapon. She was all woman —
soft, warm and enticing. He ruthlessly banished that
memory as well, concentrating on the rest.

Her hair was loose, falling in thick waves to her waist,
a dark frame for her exquisite face, with its delicate
bone-structure, softly curving mouth and expressive
clear grey eyes. No, not expressive any more, Guy
acknowledged, as the candle flared briefly in a gust of
air from the open window. She stared back at him now
with an indifference that almost rivalled his own. For
some reason that angered him. He said the first thing
that came into his mind that would eradicate any
suspicion she was harbouring that he might soften
towards her.

'If Matilda sent you here after warning me of your
"usefulness", she must be losing her mind.'

Isabel ignored the scornful statement. The long
silence had given her time to pull herself together.
Dragging about her every shred of the detachment she
had learned over the years, she forced herself to
concentrate on the immediate future. If she had to lie to
get herself and Guy out of this place, she would lie. If
she had to beg, she would beg.

'I am not here for Matilda. I came to warn you,' she
said, and her voice held determination.

'Another warning,' Guy observed sceptically. He
might as well have said, Don't bother with the rest.

'Aye. Your life is in danger.'

He gave a short laugh that sounded genuinely
amused. 'That's nothing new,' he informed her, and
added sarcastically, ''Tis one of the hazards of warfare.'

'But you are here on honourable business, not to
fight,' persisted Isabel, beginning to lose some of her
composure in the face of his blatant disbelief. 'Matilda
planned to kill you and send a message back to the
Queen pinned to your body.'

His eyes narrowed. 'Planned?' he questioned, in a voice of such ominous quiet that Isabel's heart leapt into her throat. Holy Mother, she had blurted out the wrong thing already.

'I. . .I mean she *plans* to ——'

She was abruptly cut off. FitzAlan strode forward and captured her face in one powerful hand. His long fingers held her in a grip that Isabel knew she could not escape without hurting herself — and probably not even then.

'You don't lie very well, little schemer. Try again. The truth this time. What was your task? Seduction and murder? Or just plain seduction to serve the Countess's ends?'

This was so uncomfortably close to the truth — at least as Matilda had ordered it — that Isabel flushed guiltily. Though her face was in shadow, she knew fitzAlan could feel the betraying heat beneath his fingers. This time his laugh was unpleasant.

''Tis true,' she cried as vehemently as possible with her jaw clamped in his hand. 'Her plan to kill you, I mean,' she stammered. 'Not. . .not. . .'

' "Seduction" was the word I used,' he mocked her hesitation. Releasing Isabel's face, he stepped away from her, his hard eyes raking her up and down with casual appraisal. He grinned insolently. 'Don't let me stop you from trying, though. I might enjoy sampling what I was touching a few minutes ago.'

And suddenly, unexpectedly, out of the whirlwind of Isabel's emotions, anger gained the upper hand. Furious, reckless anger.

How dared he speak to her so insultingly?

She remembered her fear for this man's life, the way she had fled through the castle to warn him, her useless defiance of Matilda's wrath and the threat hanging over her head if she refused to co-operate with the Empress.

She also remembered five and a half years of girlish dreams and fading hopes.

So much for that gallant, knightly rescuer, she berated herself with sudden savagery. You may put *him* out of your mind. He doesn't exist in this man, if he ever did. Matilda was right for once. He *is* a lout. A sneering, arrogant, unchivalrous *lout*.

'You fool!' she cried, leaping to her feet and gesturing frenziedly with both hands. 'I came to help you escape from here. I am *not* lying! You *will* be killed! And I wouldn't care now. I wouldn't——'

This time the words were stopped by his mouth. She was seized and held in a crushing embrace before she could do more than tense at the look on his face. Anger emanated from fitzAlan in waves, the force of it completely overwhelming her, even as the physical impact of that ruthless kiss stunned her into frozen immobility. Then, before she could struggle, before she could even unravel her wildly mixed reactions, Guy broke the kiss and, with one smooth movement, picked her up and tossed her on to the bed.

Isabel bounced once against the plump straw mattress, then made a frantic bid for freedom. She got as far as the other side of the wide bed before being dragged back and pinned beneath fitzAlan's forceful weight for the second time that night.

'I wouldn't like you to think your visit was wasted, pretty traitor,' he grated tauntingly, and lowered his mouth to hers.

Struggling would be useless. Her soft feminine frame was no match for fitzAlan's solid muscularity. Heart pounding, Isabel waited until his mouth had almost reached its goal, then jerked her head to the side.

She half expected Guy to wrench her face back up to his and braced herself to resist, but to her astonishment he laughed softly. There was no harshness or mockery in the sound now. Rather, his low laugh held a note that sent unexpected shivers down her spine. Quite involuntarily Isabel began to tremble. Then she stiffened, a startled gasp escaping her lips when his mouth began to string a row of tiny moist kisses down the side of her throat.

'Is this what it takes to silence you?' he murmured, the movement of his lips sending waves of heat along her neck.

The heat didn't stop there, but spread lower, stealing her breath and jolting her heart into an even wilder rhythm. The rest of her body seemed to have melted into a useless tangle of arms and legs. The iron grip Guy had used to subdue her had relaxed into a hold that now cradled rather than constrained, and yet she couldn't lift so much as a finger to defend herself, could barely summon the will to press her face harder against the bed in a futile attempt to escape that warm, spine-tingling touch.

'That's better, little one,' he whispered against the junction of her neck and shoulder. 'I've kissed you before, remember. Do you remember, sweet deceiver? You were only a child then, but now you're a woman, and this time I'm going to take what you came here to give me.'

Sweet deceiver?

The murmured words finally pierced the haze of unfamiliar pleasure induced by those hot, insistent kisses. What was she doing? Isabel wondered in bewilderment. Exactly what the Empress ordered, a cold little voice in her head replied. But she couldn't. She *couldn't*. The man despised her, hated her. And she ——

With a muffled cry of rage at her own weakness, Isabel shoved furiously at fitzAlan's broad shoulder with one hand and brought the other up and around with the full force of her arm behind it. The slap landed against the side of his head with a crack that echoed around the room. Her wrist felt as though she'd broken it, but she didn't wait to find out. Taking advantage of Guy's momentary stupefaction, she wriggled out from under him and leapt off the bed, everything forgotten but the need to escape from something she dared not put a name to.

Panicked, angry and perilously close to tears, Isabel sprang for the door.

She had not taken more than two steps before fitzAlan caught her. Both arms wrapped her in a bruising hold, and when her mouth opened her scream was smothered by his hand.

'Quiet!' he spat, ignoring her futile attempts to push his hand away.

It was like trying to push a fully harnessed plough horse. Isabel abandoned the attempt and fought to regain her control instead.

As if sensing that she had given up fighting *him* for the present, fitzAlan released her immediately, frowning down at her distraught face. 'You'll have the guard in here if you continue with that racket,' he growled. 'Was that your plan? To have me accused of assaulting you? Were you going to provide the Countess with a legitimate excuse for murder?'

The last word was like a pail of cold water dashed over her. Rage and panic at her muddled, turbulent emotions vanished. They were replaced by a chilling mental picture of Edmund as she had last seen him. Saints have mercy, she was making an appalling mess of everything.

Tears of desperation sprang into her eyes. 'No. *No*! Oh, please, you must believe me. I was outside the chapel when I heard them. . .the Empress and my lord Sheriff. . . 'Twas such a strange place to. . .but Matilda

said she would have you killed and. . .I didn't wait to
hear more. . . Oh, please. . .'

'God, not tears as well, you little traitor.'

'I'm *not* a traitor,' she protested huskily, roughly
swiping at her face with her sleeve. The tears stubbornly
continued to flow, but, driven by fear, intent on making
fitzAlan believe her, Isabel ignored them. 'I hate this
place. 'Tis true that I came to warn you, but also to beg
you to take me with you.'

Something flickered in his eyes before they went hard
and cold again with suspicion. 'I'm returning to the
Queen; your home is in the other direction.'

Isabel's gaze slid nervously away from his and back
again. 'I. . .can't go home.'

'Why not?'

'You heard the Empress earlier. My brother holds
our castle for Matilda and sent me here to serve her. He
won't take me back.' Oh, Edmund, forgive me.

Guy stood still, glittering eyes narrowed on Isabel for
a long, tense minute. There was something wrong with
her story. Something he felt but couldn't pinpoint. It
sounded plausible enough on the surface, but. . .

'All right,' he said at last. 'You've warned me. I'll be
ready if any attempt is made on my life. As for taking
you with me — forget it. I'm not on this trip for pleasure.
You'd never be able to keep up.'

'I can ride hard if I have to,' protested Isabel. 'My
lord, please —— '

'No, damn it!' he broke in roughly. 'What in God's
name would you do in Winchester? What's left of the
town is full of soldiers and Flemish mercenaries. . . 'Tis
no place for a woman. Hell! Why am I even discussing
it?' Guy added disgustedly, turning away from her.

'Do you think the soldiers here are any different?'
cried Isabel on a sob of despair. 'I can't stay here.
I *can't*!'

'Don't be ridiculous.'

Isabel heard the impatience in his voice and fear lanced through her. He was standing there as if he'd dismissed her already. In another moment she would find herself on the other side of the door, facing disaster.

Whirling suddenly, she grabbed up the candle burning near the bed. 'Look,' she cried, holding the light close to her bruised cheek. She wondered crazily if she should thank Matilda for inflicting the injury.

FitzAlan glanced over his shoulder, turning fully when he saw the ugly discolouration along her cheekbone and the narrow line of dried blood where she had been cut by a ring. Whoever had struck her had come perilously close to her eye.

'Who gave you that?'

'The Empress, and only because I refused to cower at her anger. If she discovers that I've been here, I'll be killed.'

'She doesn't have to discover it,' he retorted in exasperation. 'Damn it, girl, I can't take you with me.' There was a short silence. 'Where's your father, for God's sake?' he demanded tersely.

'Dead.' The answer came out baldly, unemotionally. Her face went blank, but this time Guy saw the effort it cost her to regain that air of remote calm, and her eyes still held a mute appeal that stabbed him to the heart.

God, how could she have such an effect on him? First he'd been crazy enough to subdue her with a kiss which, though it had begun in anger, had aroused a need for her so hot and instant that it had stunned him more than her slap, and now this.

Furious at the strong wave of protectiveness that washed over him, despite all his suspicions, Guy bit out a curse that, in normal circumstances, he wouldn't have dreamed of using in the hearing of a woman.

He saw Isabel flinch, but she continued to hold his

glowering gaze, oblivious to her dishevelled hair, mussed clothing and the tear-stains glistening on her bruised cheek. Guy cursed again, silently this time. It was extremely likely that she was pleading with him to escape so she could lead him straight into a trap which would result in accusations of spying or some such thing. If he wasn't careful he would find himself in the dungeon — or dead.

And yet, to his utter disgust, he wanted to believe her, to believe that her fear and distress were as genuine as her outrage at his slighting advances. He did believe in that. Her slap had had real anger behind it. His head was still ringing. But any woman would have reacted with anger to his insults, he reminded himself, especially if the barbs he'd slung at her were accurate and she was trying to convince him otherwise. If he wanted to survive — or retain his sanity — he would do better to get rid of the wench. By the Saints, Matilda herself had warned him!

'I must be out of my mind,' he heard himself say instead. 'All right, I'll take you to Winchester, but you'll have to get out of the castle on your own and meet me on the road tomorrow.'

Isabel's eyes widened in renewed dismay. 'But. . .I can't do that,' she protested. 'Not alone. I —— '

'Why not?' Guy asked inflexibly. 'You had the guts to come in here alone. Why so insistent that we leave tonight? Unless there's a party of soldiers waiting for us somewhere along the route. Is that it? Am I to be killed in this mysterious attempt to escape?'

That final question was too much. Isabel replaced the candle on its spike and slumped down on to the bed in despair. 'Why won't you believe me?' she whispered pleadingly. 'I came to warn you, not to lead you to your death. I swear it on the blood of Christ Jesu.'

FitzAlan didn't move for a moment. Then he strode

over to the table and picked up the ale jug standing there. Splashing the liquid into a goblet, he carried the drink back to the bed and shoved it brusquely into Isabel's hand.

'Here, drink this,' he ordered gruffly. 'I'm assuming, of course, that 'tis not poisoned.'

This cynical aside went right over Isabel's head.

He waited until she had obediently taken a few sips of the ale, before propping one knee on the bed beside her and jerking her face up to his. 'You really believe Matilda would have me killed — tonight?'

'Aye!' Isabel answered fervently, and closed her mind to her conscience. 'You don't know her. She — '

'I know what she's capable of. And you would go against your family? You realise what that means? You'll cut yourself off from them completely.'

'I know that.'

FitzAlan held her face still a moment longer, staring down into her eyes. 'Very well,' he continued softly. 'We leave tonight. I'll take you to Winchester and let the Queen decide what to do with you. But listen well, Lady Isabel de Tracy. . .' His fingers tightened with a menacing precision that kept her absolutely motionless. 'You'll obey my every order. And if you've betrayed me, if I find my head in a noose, I swear to God yours will be right there along with it. Understand?'

His grip relaxed enough to let her nod.

'I understand,' she whispered. And suddenly, despite fitzAlan's merciless vow of retribution, a fatalistic calmness descended on her, bringing a return of the cool impassivity that had served her so well in the past. What was another threat, after all? If she failed in her task she would probably be killed anyway, after first watching Edmund die.

When fitzAlan stepped away from her and sat down on a nearby chair, hooking one booted foot over his knee and regarding her with grimly assessing eyes, her mind was clear once more, ready with the plan Matilda had outlined.

'We can leave in an hour or so when everyone is asleep. I know a way through the keep that will take us out near the stables and the postern. The gate is guarded, but there is only one sentry, and no one guards the stable so you should be able to get your horse out.' She paused, regarding fitzAlan with slight misgiving at the expression that crossed his face. He didn't appear overly impressed with the scheme. In fact, he now looked downright sceptical.

'One——' he cocked a thumb '—when you're trying to creep out of a castle *no one* is asleep. Two——' a finger joined the thumb '—I know another way through the keep that will take us out to a side-gate which, if we're lucky, won't be guarded. . .

'I've been in this part of the country before, remember,' he broke off to explain at Isabel's surprised stare. 'I examined this place years ago.'

He went back to counting objections off on his fingers before she could reply. 'Three, horses tend to make a considerable noise when they're disturbed late at night, and four, if the stable lads didn't hear us every sentry in the bailey would. Matilda is no fool; this place is well patrolled.'

Isabel looked at him. 'Do you have a better idea?'

FitzAlan lifted a derisive eyebrow. 'Co-operative little wench when you get your own way, aren't you.' It wasn't a question. 'First, we leave right away——'

'Right away? Are you mad?'

'Probably. Now shut up and listen.' He ignored the affronted expression that crossed Isabel's face at this sardonic rejoinder, and continued. 'Getting outside the castle isn't a problem. I'll leave you in the ditch near the gate I know of and go back for my horse.'

'But——'

FitzAlan scowled heavily, and Isabel subsided again.

'If I go openly to the stable no one's going to question it. 'Tis only furtive behaviour that draws attention. The stable boys and sentries won't know I'm not supposed to leave until tomorrow. I can ride out of here quite safely.'

'What about me?' she asked in a small voice.

'We'll have to ride double. Once I'm across the drawbridge and out of sight I'll circle around and pick you up. Thank God there's no moat,' he tacked on matter-of-factly. 'Although if it's still raining the ditch won't be too comfortable. Still, you'll be safer right under the wall until we have to make a run for it.'

But Isabel wasn't concerned with her own safety. The thought of Guy walking into the stable as calmly as you please, asking for his horse and riding out in full view of the entire garrison was utterly nerve-racking. She determinedly erased the alarming pictures from her mind.

'Don't worry,' he said sardonically, as if privy to her thoughts. 'I'll get you to Winchester, my lady. That is, if you're tougher than you look. You're going to have to leave in the clothes you're wearing, and 'twas damned wet and cold out there when I arrived earlier.'

Isabel almost laughed. He was worried about the *weather*? She might have been housed in Gloucester Castle for three years, but before that. . .

No. She wouldn't allow herself to think of the past. Except to be thankful for the strength it had given her.

'A shower of rain won't kill me,' she retorted, as that derisive eyebrow lifted again in mocking challenge at her apparent hesitation.

The eyebrow quirked further, but fitzAlan merely rose to his feet and reached for the pack on the floor beside the bed. 'In that case,' he said blandly, 'we only have to worry about the guard outside my door.'

CHAPTER THREE

'HE PATROLS the gallery,' Isabel explained quickly, not bothering to ask how Guy knew the sentry was there. 'We can slip out when he has turned the corner. But the entrance is on the other side of the keep,' she added worriedly.

'Aye, as far away as possible from this room,' fitzAlan agreed ironically. 'But it doesn't matter. We're going down the north-west staircase and past the garderobe passage.'

'Doesn't that. . .doesn't that lead to the dungeons?' Isabel asked cautiously.

Guy flattened himself against the wall and opened the door a crack before answering. 'Aye,' he murmured absently. 'The passage we want runs right past them.'

He closed the door again and looked at Isabel. 'There are grilles high up in the walls, so whatever happens don't make a sound or we'll be in a cell so fast your head will spin.'

He didn't wait for an answer, but strode forward to snuff out the candle, then edged the door open again. In the dim light from the gallery Isabel saw that all traces of mockery had vanished; his profile was grim and hard, the look of danger very pronounced. She heard the regular tramp of the sentry's boots against the floor. He passed down the gallery, the sound growing fainter.

'Stay close behind me,' ordered fitzAlan, his voice a mere breath in her ear. 'And go on my signal—*now*!'

Isabel knew that that progress through the castle was destined to become part of her nightmares. She was still trembling half an hour later, as she huddled beneath a small gateway, trying to keep her footing on the wet grass of the embankment.

The descent of the empty turret staircase had been uneventful enough, but the garderobe passage had seemed to her anxious gaze to teem with a constant flow of traffic. Had everyone chosen that night to drink more than they could hold? she had wondered dementedly. And then, instead of hiding until the passage was clear, fitzAlan had given her a shove and told her to wait in the last cubicle.

'Just act as you usually do when you have to visit the privy,' he had instructed, with a grin that Isabel could only describe as fiendish.

That had been bad enough, but worse was to come.

The sconces burning in the passage had at least provided some light, poor though it was. The narrow staircase that had been revealed when Guy had removed a grille from the wall of the tiny chamber had been so black that Isabel had forgotten her embarrassment at their surroundings. Only her determination not to betray weakness in front of fitzAlan had enabled her to grit her teeth and step into the seemingly bottomless pit. She had thought longingly of the candle left behind in Guy's chamber, but had known better than to mention it.

FitzAlan had replaced the grille and taken her hand. For guidance, Isabel knew. There was no comfort in the hard, impersonal touch of his fingers. Well, that was all right, she'd decided. The man had escape on his mind, not dalliance. The absurd thoughts had got her as far as the foot of that horrible stairway, then she had felt the level floor of another passage beneath her feet. The darkness had been unrelenting.

Isabel shuddered at the memory and wrapped her arms about her waist. She couldn't stop shivering, but whether it was caused by cold or the strain of waiting

until fitzAlan won free of the castle she didn't know.
She didn't doubt that he would find her. She had
discovered that he possessed the eyesight of a cat. How
else could he have got them out of the keep? Disorien-
tated by the smothering blackness surrounding them,
she herself had completely lost her sense of direction —
until they had been midway along the passage.

A constant eerie keening sound, which she had been
only vaguely aware of until then, had suddenly risen to a
blood-chilling shriek, before being abruptly cut off. A
loud clanging, accompanied by a rough, shouted curse,
had answered the shriek, and Isabel had known they
were passing the dungeons. She had immediately closed
her mind to all thought, not even realising how tightly
she had been gripping fitzAlan's hand.

Moments later he had led her up a short stairway,
through the heavily bolted door at the top, and out of
the building, and Isabel had recognised the alley leading
to the wash-houses and pressing-rooms, which lay
between the towering keep and the curtain wall.

And now here she was outside the gate used only by
the laundresses. It was indeed unguarded, apart from
the sentry patrolling that section of the wall, since there
was no bridge across the ditch, and the land on the other
side dropped gradually to meet the swiftly flowing
waters of the Severn.

In fine weather the steep, grassy embankment was a
colourful patchwork of clothes and sheets spread out to
dry. Isabel wondered why she hadn't thought of using
the laundry gate herself, before she realised that it
would have been kept locked. That thought then raised
the interesting question of how fitzAlan had managed to
open it — and the door leading up from the dungeons.

She was still pondering on this mystery when a low
whistle came from the other side of the ditch. At the
same moment, the moon appeared briefly from behind

its cover of cloud and Isabel saw the indistinct shape of a horse. She plunged instantly down the slippery incline.

The rain had stopped. Guy knew it would make hard riding easier, but any noise they made would no longer be muffled by the downpour. He had waited until the sentry reached the tower at the end of his beat, knowing, after watching the man from the bailey, that the guard would pause to exchange a few words with another man-at-arms before they separated to retrace their steps.

He estimated that Isabel would have about one minute to negotiate the treacherously wet embankment, cross the ditch, and scramble up the other side. Less, if the men weren't feeling talkative at that particular time. Then they had an open patch of land to cross before reaching the shelter of the woods about a hundred yards away.

It was risky — the sentry would be sure to hear their horse as it picked up speed — but crossing the dangerous waters of the Severn at night was riskier, and would point them in the wrong direction for Winchester. Guy could only hope that Isabel was quick and that the sentry wasn't inclined to shoot at an unseen target.

He heard a splash and a muffled gasp, and grinned faintly. She had reached the ditch. In his experience women did not like getting their feet wet and muddy, and were apt to have plenty to say on the subject. Well, she'd badgered him to let her come along; she could take cold, muddied feet and be thankful it wasn't worse. He rather hoped she would complain so he could point out that incontestable fact.

Isabel didn't even notice her wet feet as she encountered the pools of water left by the rain. The last one had caused her to slip and she had jarred her already sore wrist by flinging out a hand to save herself. Gritting her teeth, she climbed the far slope towards the point where fitzAlan waited, ignoring the throbbing ache.

'Here,' he said softly, as she reached the summit.

The moon scudded across a gap in the clouds again, just as Guy reached down to haul Isabel up into the saddle before him. Barely giving her time to find her balance within the circle of his arms, he spurred the horse towards the beckoning trees.

The animal responded at once, quickly lengthening its stride into a gallop. Almost immediately a confused medley of sounds followed. Isabel heard a yell from behind and above them, swiftly running feet, and then a sinister rush of air. An instant later she felt fitzAlan's arm jerk and slacken about her.

'You've been hit,' she cried in horrified comprehension.

'Shut up,' he grated through clenched teeth. 'Just hang on and shut up.'

'We have to stop and get that arrow out of your arm.'

It wasn't the first time Isabel had said the words. In fact she'd been repeating them every mile or so. She didn't know how far they had come from Gloucester, but surely after an hour at a steady gallop they had put enough distance between themselves and the castle to halt for a few minutes.

It wasn't only the pain fitzAlan must be enduring that worried her. The longer the arrow remained in the wound, the greater the danger of infection. Especially with the rough treatment it was being subjected to. And it was beginning to rain again. That was all he needed, Isabel thought. A chill on top of an arrow wound.

'If your arm festers you might lose it,' she pointed out, desperate enough to try shock tactics. After all, he was a warrior. They tended to need two good arms. 'Perhaps even die,' she tacked on for good measure.

He muttered a curse that Isabel thought it best to ignore. 'Worried that you won't make it to Winchester on your own?' he asked unpleasantly.

'I'll make it,' she answered, refusing to rise to the bait. 'But you won't with an arrow sticking out of you all the way.'

'God! *Women*! Think, you little idiot. 'Tis more than likely that we've got a party of Matilda's soldiers after us. Hell, I should have remembered that she makes a habit of greeting emissaries with violence.'

'I think 'twas more in the manner of a farewell,' Isabel murmured, and then wondered if she was growing light-headed after the events of the night. However, levity would not help her to convince fitzAlan that they were not being followed. 'What would be the point in chasing us?' she demanded reasonably. 'If the rain gets heavier there won't be any tracks to follow, and, even if there were, 'tis too dark to see them.'

There was a moment of silence. Then, sighing slightly, Guy reined in the horse. Before he could change his mind, Isabel slipped to the ground.

He dismounted also, his left arm held stiffly by his side. Beneath the trees where they stood it was too dark to see much, but Isabel could feel the tension in fitzAlan's body and knew his arm must be hurting terribly. Her own body flinched at the thought.

'I can't reach back far enough to pull it out cleanly.' Guy's voice, tight with frustration at his own helplessness, came to her out of the darkness. 'You'll have to do it. And for God's sake don't swoon before you've finished the job.'

'I'm not the swooning type,' Isabel bit out.

'Thank the saints for small mercies. Get a cloth out of my pack, and be ready to press it to the wound as soon as the bolt comes clear.'

Isabel obeyed, suppressing various retorts. This was

not the time to object to his tone. She had to pull the arrow out. Their very survival might depend on it. And if he was still alert enough to be insulting, his wound might not be so bad after all.

'It will be easier if you sit down,' she suggested, gently feeling for the place where the arrow protruded. He sucked in his breath when she found it.

'For once I agree with you,' he murmured, sinking to the ground.

'I'll try not to hurt you too much,' she said. 'But 'tis difficult in the dark.'

'Just do it,' Guy muttered. 'And don't waste any time with a fancy bandage. We have to keep moving. Even if we're not being followed, Matilda's men hold most of the castles in this part of the country. I want to win past Malmesbury tonight before——'

He broke off, clamping his teeth together. The damn thing was in deep, he thought, as Isabel's little hand closed around the shaft of the arrow. He was probably going to start bleeding like a pig the instant the barb was out, and he only hoped——

His thoughts were abruptly cut off by a blinding flash of pain. His whole arm seemed to be afire, a searing contrast to the cold sweat he felt break out on his brow. Then he felt a cloth being held against the wound. The pressure only added to the fiery torture. 'Are you satisfied now?' he growled. 'Can we be on our way?'

'I hope this is clean,' Isabel muttered, again ignoring his temper, knowing pain was causing him to lash out like any wounded animal.

'Never mind. Just bandage the thing and be done with it.'

'You can't mean to keep riding,' she protested, firmly winding the cloth about his arm. 'You need to rest, and your arm should be washed and tended properly.'

'And just how do you propose to do that?' The

question was savage. 'Do you see a convenient castle near by?'

'Then we'll just have to stop at the first one,' Isabel declared. 'At least I'll be able to see what I'm doing.'

'Stop at the first one?' he repeated disbelievingly. 'Do you think they're going to have a sign out, telling us which side they're on?'

'There must be a village somewhere,' she insisted, tying a final knot and stepping back. Her foot nudged the discarded arrow and, unthinkingly, she bent to pick it up. 'Where are we anyway?'

Guy rose slowly to his feet. 'Heading towards Winchester,' he replied unhelpfully. 'Get on the horse.'

'Very well,' sighed Isabel, obeying only because she knew they had to find shelter, and there was none where they stood. She stuffed the arrow absently into Guy's pack, gathered up the reins, and mounted. 'I can afford to wait. At the rate you're going, you'll probably swoon before too long.'

'I'm not the swooning type,' snapped fitzAlan, quoting her own words back at her. 'So don't count on it.' He mounted behind her and ruthlessly removed the reins from her hands.

Isabel sighed again as the horse moved off at his signal, breaking easily into a canter. Now she'd made him angry again.

An hour passed in silence, and then another. The horse had gradually slowed as it tired, until the animal now moved forward at a resigned walk.

We must be well past Malmesbury by this time, Isabel thought. But the fortress there was an outpost, virtually surrounded by enemy castles. It would be miles yet, probably another day of travelling, before they reached safer country, and even if fitzAlan stubbornly insisted that he could travel the horse wouldn't go forever.

And the weather had grown steadily worse. With the

disappearance of the moonlight, they had had to abandon the forest and find the road. It was easier to follow in the darkness, but exposed them to the full force of the wind and rain. The relentless downpour had soon saturated the cloak Guy had wrapped about them. She wouldn't have to worry about his wound, Isabel decided. They were both going to die of exposure.

'Or lung rot,' she grumbled aloud.

'What?'

His deep voice after miles of silence made Isabel jump.

'Nothing,' she answered. 'I was just. . . Why are we stopping?'

'There,' Guy said very quietly, as the weary horse plodded to a standstill and let its head droop against the driving rain.

Isabel peered ahead. At first she only saw the dark shape of the forest beside the road, then as her eyes adjusted to a faint lifting of the gloom a narrow laneway appeared between the trees.

'Do you think it leads to a village?' she whispered.

'Perhaps. 'Tis too narrow a road to be guarded by a castle.' FitzAlan seemed to hesitate for a moment, then turned his mount on to the barely discernible path. 'The horse needs to rest,' he said, as though in explanation.

And so do you, thought Isabel. But she didn't dare say it.

A quarter of a mile further on the lane widened out into a small clearing in the trees. Several small huts stood in a roughly circular pattern, as dark and silent as the rest of the countryside.

'What are we going to do?' asked Isabel, still whispering. 'Knock on a door and ask for shelter?'

'No need,' returned fitzAlan aloud. 'The doors are all open. Look. The place is deserted.'

He was right, Isabel realised, staring hard at the black

hole that marked the entrance to the nearest hut. Glancing around at the rest, she could see that none of the small hovels was secured against intruders. The doors were all wide open, and one hung drunkenly from its rawhide straps. It must be almost dawn, she thought absently; an hour ago she had not been able to see a thing.

Guy urged the horse over to the largest of the mean shelters and dismounted. The second his cloak was gone, Isabel was buffeted by the heavy rain. She slipped hurriedly out of the saddle, and then had to grab for it when her legs threatened to buckle. She was numb with cold, and bone-weary.

FitzAlan was fumbling in his pack. 'Here,' he said, producing his flint. 'Go inside and see if you can find a light. I have to tend to my horse.'

Isabel eyed the inhospitable rectangle of darkness in front of her. 'What if there is someone in there?' she asked warily.

'Then we can spend what's left of the night discussing the lousy weather with them,' was the disagreeable reply to this nervous question. 'Use your head, woman. If the villagers were driven out today, the rain would bring them back. They wouldn't spend a night like this in the forest with women and children to think of.'

Isabel wanted to ask why not. After all, fitzAlan hadn't seemed to worry about exposing *her* to the elements. Why would peasants be more considerate of their womenfolk? Unfortunately another possibility occurred to her which drove the question of chivalry out of her mind.

'They might all be dead,' she whispered.

To her surprise he answered this quite gently. 'There would be bodies out here as well as inside if there had been a massacre. They wouldn't all have been killed in their beds. Go on, you're starting to look like a drowned kitten.'

Charming, thought Isabel indignantly, as she cautiously felt her way into the hut. How could he tell what she looked like in the darkness? Though dawn was approaching, he had only loomed as a huge shadow to *her*.

'Eyesight of a cat,' she muttered aloud, then immediately uttered a pained yelp as she bumped into a rough-hewn table. Her hand skidded across the wooden surface and collided with a small round object. A bowl, she decided, exploring with fingers that were almost too frozen to feel anything, with something inside it that felt like a tiny lump of candlewax — and a wick.

'Saints be praised,' she murmured. But, of course, there was nothing on which she could strike the flint. A fireplace? No, a peasant's hovel wouldn't have such a thing, but surely a fire would have been needed for cooking?

Dropping to her hands and knees, Isabel crawled gingerly forward across the earthen floor, clutching the candle-bowl. Despite fitzAlan's assurances that she wouldn't encounter a corpse, she held her breath with trepidation every time she swung her free hand in a groping semicircle. At last she felt stones. A small circle of them, enclosing a heap of cold ashes and dried leaves.

Within seconds Isabel had a twig alight, its crumbling leaves quickly shrivelling in tiny flames, but with fire enough to light the candle. However, her heart sank when she examined the bowl more closely. The wick lay almost flat in a perilously small amount of wax. She had to find something else before its feeble light expired.

Shielding the flame carefully from the draught sweeping in through the open door, Isabel glanced about the single room. It was small, but seemed surprisingly well stocked for a peasant's shack. The table stood to one side of the doorway with a stool beside it. Another stool lay on its side some distance away. On the other side of the stone circle, against the wall, a wide bench for sleeping was covered with a thin woollen blanket, and high up on another wall a shelf had been fashioned, hand-made and crooked, but functional nevertheless, and holding an assortment of objects and jars that drew Isabel at once.

Her spirits rose considerably at the sight of an uneven blob of wax. She had seen such lumps before. Whoever had lived here had been given the remnants of used candles and had melted the stubs down to make a crude light. Which meant, she reasoned thoughtfully, that there was a castle or town near by where one of the vanished occupants of the hut had probably been employed.

She decided against mentioning this little fact to fitzAlan. He would probably insist on leaving again. And she refused to go another step until his arm was properly cared for, Isabel vowed, as she dug a small hole in the top of the misshapen lump with her thumbnail. She carefully poured the melting wax around the wick into the larger candle, and balanced it in the bowl.

'There,' she said to herself, replacing the bowl on the table and feeling inordinately pleased with the result. 'My lord fitzAlan is not the only one who can be useful.'

But the lonely sound of her own voice in the emptiness of the hut immediately made Isabel wonder why Guy was taking so long. He'd had time enough to get ten horses under shelter. Had he collapsed? Should she venture out to search for him?

A mental picture of fitzAlan lying senseless out in the rain sent Isabel hurrying to the door. Guy met her on the threshold, only just managing to avoid knocking her over. He dropped his pack, unbuckled his sword and propped it against the wall, then turned to rake Isabel with eyes as sharp as the wicked-looking blade behind him.

'Going somewhere?' he queried interestedly.

'We'll need wood for a fire,' returned Isabel with aplomb, not about to admit that she had been worried about him.

That piercing blue gaze made a comprehensive sweep of the room and fixed unerringly on an untidy pile of wood in one corner. 'I think the dry stuff will be better, don't you?' he asked smoothly.

Taking Isabel's disconcerted silence for assent, Guy turned and pushed the door closed. The abrupt cessation of the draughts blowing into the room was a welcome relief, although Isabel was so chilled by now that she was conscious of no great change in the temperature. They had to have warmth immediately. Her gown was almost wet through and water dripped from her long hair to the floor. FitzAlan didn't look any drier, she thought critically, his blond hair darkened with rain, his tunic drenched, and his boots squelching with every step.

'I'll build a fire,' he said, not mentioning the light Isabel had managed to produce.

She made a face at his back, but her expression quickly changed to concern when she caught sight of his arm. The rough bandage was saturated, and not only with rain.

'You're bleeding,' she cried. 'Leave the fire for the moment. Let me tend to your arm.'

'It's been bleeding on and off all night,' he responded coolly. 'Another few minutes won't make any difference, and we're both soaked.'

He took the candle from the table and bent over the fireplace, setting the twigs ablaze. The sudden warmth, meagre though it was, drew Isabel like a magnet. She held her frozen hands to the flames as Guy fed the fire

with more kindling before placing a log from the
woodpile on to the blaze.

'It looks as if they were interrupted at their meal,' he
remarked, righting the overturned stool and using it to
indicate a soiled trencher and several dusty earthenware
mugs on the table. He pulled the table closer to the fire
and draped his cloak over it to dry, but his movements
lacked the usual lithe, co-ordinated strength Isabel had
hitherto seen in him, and she noticed that he wasn't
using his left arm at all.

'Here,' she said gently, pushing forward the stool he
had set down. 'Sit near the fire and let me bandage your
arm properly.'

'In a minute. Get out of that wet gown.'

The brusque command brought her widening eyes up
to his.

'There's no need to look at me as though I'm about to
rape you,' he barked impatiently. 'I didn't ask you to
strip to the skin.'

Isabel went completely white. Even in the dim,
flickering light cast by the fire Guy saw all the colour
wash out of her face. He wondered what the hell was
wrong with her now, but it was becoming strangely
difficult to think clearly. And the cramped hut was
becoming too damned hot.

Stepping away from the fire and dismissing the odd
behaviour of his charge, Guy removed the makeshift
bandage and his sodden tunic and undershirt. The fact
that he could barely move his wounded arm didn't
improve his mood. When he turned back to drape the
garments alongside his cloak, and saw that Isabel was
still clothed and beginning to shiver visibly with cold, his
precarious patience snapped.

'Strip!' he roared.

She flinched once, then started to obey, unfastening

the ties at the neck of her gown with shaking fingers. Guy watched her through dangerously slitted eyes.

There was no lecherous anticipation in his expression, however, Isabel realised. He was doing it to punish her. For not immediately obeying him, or for her very presence? she wondered briefly, then gave a mental shrug. What did it matter? She had survived this indignity before; she could survive it again.

And her hesitation hadn't even been caused by the grim memory his words had stirred up. Common sense had already told her they had to get out of their sodden clothes, but, for an unexpected instant, the sight of fitzAlan half naked, the firelight burnishing tanned skin over strong muscle and bone, had made her suddenly, acutely, aware of the differences between them. The differences between male and female; between hard masculine power and yielding feminine softness. He was so much bigger than her. So much stronger. He could force her to do anything. And yet the vulnerability she felt seemed strangely *inward*—as though danger lay within her own body, and not in the raw strength of the man before her.

Shaken off balance by her startling thoughts, Isabel glanced away, stepping out of her gown and hanging it over the table. She sent up a brief prayer of thanks that her shift was still dry, although it could hardly be described as a significant covering. The once fine linen had thinned and shrunk with frequent laundering, with the result that the garment only reached just past her knees and did little to hide the curves of her body.

She could still feel fitzAlan's eyes on her and flushed slightly, steeling herself before she could look at him again, and fully expecting a remark that was sure to be unpleasant at best. She wasn't disappointed.

'You don't have to play the shrinking virgin for me,'

he mocked. 'I'm sure you've stripped willingly enough for the men who have enjoyed your favours in the past.'

Quick resentment surged through Isabel, deepening the colour in her cheeks. She let it build, momentarily forgetting the dangers in arguing with him. Right now there was more danger in the strange, yielding weakness that had just taken her by surprise. 'You don't know anything about my past,' she cried. 'I've n ——'

'Don't bother with the usual outraged denials,' he interrupted scornfully. 'You knew what to expect when you came to my room tonight. What's more, I could have had you. I felt your response. If you hadn't decided to retaliate for my plain-speaking, you would have been willing to pay the price for my escort to Winchester.'

Another affronted retort rose to her lips, but bewildered honesty forced Isabel to choke it back at the last moment. He was right in a backhanded sort of way. The Empress had ordered her to do whatever was necessary in order to leave with fitzAlan, and if she hadn't been so angry and confused that she had forgotten the threat to Edmund she would have complied.

But an odd sense of hurt washed over her at the scornful sound Guy made at her silent acquiescence. Ridiculous, she knew. He wasn't to know the truth, and yet, against all reason, she wanted him to believe in her innocence. Fool, she chastised herself, angrier than ever. Wishes would not help in this situation. Let him believe what he liked.

Isabel lifted her chin, pride and defiance turning her eyes a stormy grey as she stared back at fitzAlan coldly.

'If we had more time I'd take you up on that challenge you're issuing, my lady,' he growled, in a voice that had gone dark and soft. 'But, until we do, you can make yourself useful by binding up this hole in my arm before I give you the pleasure of bleeding to death.'

His death, give her pleasure? A sudden spasm of pain

pierced her heart, subduing her anger. She quickly suppressed it. She would not allow his insults to touch her. She would not care what fitzAlan thought of her. He was a callous brute, and if she didn't need his protection on the journey to Winchester she wouldn't care if he bled to. . .

But she couldn't finish the thought. Despite her outrage and hurt, Isabel knew she *did* care if fitzAlan lived or died.

Turning away, she determinedly refused to acknowledge why. Exploring that path would take her to the edge of a precipice over which she did not wish to step. Instead she would tend his arm, make sure she did not become a hindrance by falling ill herself, and refuse to acknowledge his barbed remarks. She knew how it was done. You just made your mind very cold and distant. You retreated to a place where harshness or cruelty couldn't touch you. A place where you felt nothing.

Only. . .this time it was not so easy.

She had drawn back from a direct confrontation again, Guy realised. He was beginning to recognise the signs. Her face was remote and serene; her eyes showed only calm resolve as she began to inspect the jars on the shelf.

'What are you looking for?' he snapped, perversely unwilling to let her resume her cool composure. He kicked the stool further away from the fire and sat down. The action didn't seem to stop the room from spinning. Guy wondered vaguely when he'd first noticed the wavering movements of the walls.

'Ale,' she answered briefly, turning with a jug in her hand and sniffing experimentally. 'It smells a bit stale, but there's no wine so it will have to do. Come closer to the fire.'

'I'm not cold,' he said shortly, bending to unwind the thongs from his boots.

The words caused tentacles of fright to curl around Isabel's stomach. He should have been as frozen as she was herself. Blessed Mother, was he feverish already? She looked at Guy more closely. He did appear flushed and his eyes held a strange glitter. And she had nothing, Isabel remembered. No herbs, no clean linen, no water. Unless. . .

Searching through a scattered pile of utensils, she found an empty pail, opened the door, and shoved it outside. Water, at least, could be obtained, she told herself sternly, before the frightening sensation of help-lessness got the better of her.

'Leave the door open a little. 'Tis like a bread oven in here.'

Isabel ignored the curt order. 'You have a slight fever, I think,' she replied with the quiet firmness she would have used towards any sick person. 'I'll have some water for you to drink soon, but you must keep warm. Now sit still and let me see to your arm.'

'Aye, my lady,' he responded with mocking compli-ance. But Isabel saw genuine humour flash briefly in his blue gaze.

She turned her attention to his injury, relieved to see that he was now losing very little blood, and that although the area about the wound was reddened and irritated the edges of the gash where the arrow had entered were not jagged, which would have delayed healing.

She was about to report this piece of good news when fitzAlan took the ale jug from her, and, before she could protest, tilted it to his lips for a healthy swig. He then up-ended the rest over his wound. She heard the air hiss between his teeth at the bite of the liquid.

'That should clean it,' he grated, his teeth still clenched. He tossed the jug aside and reached for the discarded bandage with his good arm. 'What does it look like?'

'I was about to tell you,' retorted Isabel, 'before you applied your own method of healing. It looks clean enough, but don't be surprised if your fever gets worse after that primitive treatment. It should have been washed with water and then a salve applied.'

'Do you see one?' he asked sarcastically, shoving the soiled cloth at her.

Isabel eyed it with disfavour. 'No,' she admitted, unabashed. 'But that doesn't mean I'm going to add to your foolishness by tying that filthy rag over the wound.'

Ignoring the suddenly bright gleam in his eyes, she bent and grabbed the hem of her shift, tearing the flimsy material easily until she had enough for a bandage.

'Foolishness?' Guy repeated with a derisive laugh. 'You think there's been *anything* that makes sense about tonight? I still haven't decided if you're really afraid of Matilda, or whether you have some other reason for leaving her.'

Isabel refused to answer. She finished tying the bandage, stepped away from him, and indicated the bench. 'You'd better rest if you want to be well enough to travel tomorrow,' she suggested coldly.

FitzAlan stood up, immediately looming over her in the confines of the hut. Even the fact that he staggered slightly didn't lessen his menacing impact on Isabel's senses. 'I intend to rest,' he agreed, an unexpectedly devilish smile crossing his face. 'With you.'

Isabel reminded herself that he was mocking her, that his wickedly attractive smile didn't affect her one bit, and that keeping her own expression politely aloof wasn't at all difficult. It was less easy to convince herself that the thought of lying down on the bench with fitzAlan, wth hardly a stitch of clothing between them, didn't scare the wits out of her.

'I am going to dry my hair,' she announced, pleased that her voice sounded so calm and resolute. 'Then I am going to fetch some water. Then I am going to sleep by the fire.'

'You're damn well going to sleep with me,' he countered bluntly, disregarding this comprehensive schedule. 'So I can keep an eye on you. Don't worry,' he tacked on sardonically at her rebellious expression. 'Your questionable virtue will be safe enough. I've a feeling I'm going to need two sound arms for the task of taming you, my lady Isabel. 'Tis something I shall look forward to.'

'You'll have a long wait,' flashed Isabel, and immediately cursed herself when fitzAlan grinned again. How did he manage to ruin all her fine resolutions to remain cool and distant? she asked herself. She had never found it difficult before. It really wasn't fair. First the man insulted her, and now he seemed to be taking a perverse delight in taunting her.

Taking a deep, steadying breath, she tried to reason with him. 'My lord, I am not such an idiot as to go fleeing into that downpour. How far, indeed, do you think I would get alone? Believe whatever you like of me, but please —'

Her assurances fell on deaf ears. Not giving her a chance to finish, fitzAlan's good arm shot out and snagged Isabel about the waist. She was lifted against his bare chest as if she weighed no more than a feather, the shock of his warm skin and the slight roughness of short, curling hair against her palms rendering her abruptly speechless. Taking a step back, he flung the blanket aside, cursing aloud as the movement wrenched his arm, and lowered them both to the hard bench.

By the time Isabel realised her position, it was too late to do anything about it. She was trapped between fitzAlan's solid body and the wall at her back. And

when she opened her mouth to protest at this treatment
she saw that her objections would have to wait. He had
turned on to his stomach, flung his right arm over her —
to make sure she didn't escape, Isabel assumed indignantly — and fallen instantly asleep.

CHAPTER FOUR

ISABEL wished she could find the oblivion of sleep as easily, but though her body ached after the unaccustomed hours in the saddle her mind refused to rest. The hard bench under her wasn't conducive to restful slumber either, although she had known worse beds. No, it was not discomfort keeping her from sleep. She was too on edge, too nervous, too aware that their shelter was easily accessible and fitzAlan hurt.

She turned her head to study him, close beside her. Very close. She could see the dark gold lashes feathering his broad cheekbones, and the tiny lines radiating out from the corners of his eyes. His face looked slightly less hard in repose, but, even sleeping, he was still intimidating. That aura of compelling strength remained. Despite his wounded condition, Isabel had the distinct impression that to awaken fitzAlan would be dangerous. Rather like rousing a sleeping wolf, she thought fancifully, remembering her earlier comparison. Only a fool would risk doing so. A sensible person respected the sleeping beast and crept away.

So why did she want to stay? Why did she wonder if the wolf could be tamed?

Her eyes drifted from his face to the smoothly muscled shoulder near her cheek. Aye, dangerous. The arm lying across her was relaxed and heavy, but Isabel knew it could become an iron band, trapping her in an instant.

Her breath caught as a strange little *frisson* of excitement slid from her throat to her toes at the thought. The sudden sharp urge to lift her hand, to test the strength of that broad shoulder with her fingers, was almost irresistible. Isabel trembled, half afraid, half shocked, at such shameless, hitherto unknown longings. And yet still unwilling to creep away, still wanting to arouse the sleeping wolf, wanting. . .

What? she asked herself almost fearfully. To feel that firm, beautifully drawn mouth on hers in tenderness rather than anger? To know the meaning of the weakness that had sapped the strength from her limbs when she had seen him half stripped earlier? To lie in his arms?

Isabel stared at Guy's face, her heart beginning to pound. Had she run mad? Had she not already decided that five and a half years of girlhood dreams bore little resemblance to the harsh warrior beside her? That a fleeting encounter in the past, no matter how romantic, had no place in the bleak present? Of course she had.

He was no different from the other men she knew. Perhaps not as brutal, although she had no doubt he could be if the situation warranted, but definitely arrogant, intimidating, ruthless. At best he did not trust her. In truth, he seemed to dislike her intensely. And if he knew of the wanton pictures chasing one another through her head his insulting opinion of her would no doubt be confirmed.

He was not to know that those pictures appalled her, that she had never imagined herself capable of such thoughts. On the contrary—she had sworn never to marry, never to expose herself to the mercy of a man's rough or abusive treatment. For years she had turned a calm, expressionless face on the world—quiet, distant, not even blatantly cold, because that would have been a challenge to some men. She had learned how to protect her emotions and thus her body.

So why couldn't she erase from her memory the image of fitzAlan, tall and strong and golden in the firelight?

Powerfully, overwhelmingly male. He had looked almost. . .*primitive*, she thought. And she had *felt* primitive. As though she had been nothing more than a vulnerable female creature in the presence of her mate.

A five-year old memory did not explain *that* feeling.

Isabel wrenched her eyes away from fitzAlan and glared at the wall. She must be very tired to give room to such feeble-minded notions. She would go to sleep. No one would be abroad in this weather. They were safe enough for the present.

Clinging to this assurance, Isabel listened to the rain beating down on the other side of the wall and refused to think about her peculiar reactions to fitzAlan any longer. Tomorrow, when she was rested, she would be her sensible self again. In the meantime, there were far more practical things to consider. She would retrieve the pail soon, she promised herself, wriggling into a more comfortable position on the wooden bench. And the fire would need another log.

Her movement seemed to disturb fitzAlan. He shifted restlessly and Isabel raised herself cautiously to peer at his bandaged arm. No matter what else she thought of him, she could not ignore his wound.

There was no blood on the bandage, but as she glanced across the broad sweep of his back Isabel realised suddenly how close Guy had come to being killed. A few more inches to the right and the shot would have been fatal. The knowledge made her shiver.

Frowning thoughtfully, she pulled the thin blanket over them both and lay down again, her mind now busy on another track. Had the sentry panicked at the sound of a galloping horse and fired off a lucky shot, or was there a more sinister design?

The disturbing question brought the scene in Matilda's chamber flashing into Isabel's mind, and the odd looks exchanged between the Empress and her

men. She had sensed the undercurrents in the room at
the time, but had been too tense and afraid to take
much notice. But now. . .she had to wonder. Had she
been used for a purpose other than the stated one? Had
Brien fitzCount's aim been to appease Matilda by killing
Guy while he was apparently escaping, sooner than
allow the Empress to murder her guest out of hand?
Guy himself had suspected as much, she remembered.

Isabel shook her head. It didn't make sense. Why go
to all the trouble of providing her with information
about Rainald, which she could easily have related to
fitzAlan? No, that wasn't right either. Matilda would be
sure that any knowledge Isabel possessed was safe as
long as Edmund lived. That silent communication had
come with the mention of her brother's name, after all.

For a few minutes longer Isabel tried to sort out hard
facts from vague suspicions, with little success.
FitzAlan's misgivings had aroused her own unease
about the Empress's true motives, but she was growing
too sleepy to reason it out now. The warmth of the small
hut was finally melting the frozen ice in her veins, and
the ceaseless rain had become a distant cradle-song.
Even the vague awareness of her assorted aches and
bruises no longer had the power to keep her alert.

Unknowingly nestled against Guy's shoulder, Isabel
slept.

There was heat and gentleness and safety. And she was
floating.

Floating? That was strange, thought Isabel drowsily.
She must be dreaming, but surely she had only just gone
to sleep. From a vague distance she was aware that the
rain continued unabated, but it couldn't touch her. She
was so deliciously warm. Surrounded by warmth.
Enfolded, sheltered, protected by warmth.

Her lashes fluttered, but it was too much of an effort

to open her eyes. She just wanted to sink back into the dream and give in to the lovely floating sensation. The gentle caress of warm lips pressing her eyelids closed seemed part of the fantasy. So did the low, husky whisper accompanying those feather-light kisses.

'That's it, sweetheart. Just relax and let me love you. Don't run away this time. Not this time. . .'

Run away? How could she? Isabel wondered hazily. You couldn't run away if you were dreaming. . .at least if you did 'twas only part of the dream. . .not real. . . Somehow it seemed very important to make that clear.

''Tis only a dream. . .' she whispered, almost inaudibly.

'Then dream with me, darling girl. Stay with me. You always disappear. Don't disappear. . . I need you so. . . I've needed you. . .' The words faded as those warm lips closed gently but firmly over her mouth.

The dream shifted with startling speed. Suddenly Isabel was no longer floating, she was falling instead, the sensation so swift and unexpected that she flung up her hands to save herself, and found them clinging to the source of the heat above her. It didn't help. She continued to fall. Her head was spinning, she couldn't breathe, and when she clung tighter the kiss changed, as though keeping pace with the dream. Warm gentleness became heated demand. Against the hard, insistent pressure of Guy's mouth, Isabel's lips parted and a whimper of surrender sounded deep in her throat. But that was all right, she thought vaguely. She could surrender because it was her knight kissing her. She wasn't sure just how she knew that. But it didn't matter, did it? Because this was only a dream. Wasn't it?

She couldn't think properly. Her mouth was being taken with a possessive intensity that obliterated thought and left only sensation. It was almost terrify-

ing—and yet wildly exciting. It felt so real. Surely
dreams weren't *this* real?

Still drugged with sleep, struggling to free herself
from her half-dreaming state, Isabel's eyes snapped
open just as Guy released her mouth. She stared
dazedly up into a wild, glittering gaze that held her
helplessly captive.

'I'm not——' she tried to say, but his mouth
descended on hers again, quick and hard.

'Don't talk,' he commanded hoarsely. 'Whenever I
speak, you vanish.' He groaned and held her closer.
'Whenever I touch you, you leave me. . .Isabel. . .
Isabel. . .'

He lowered his head to bury his mouth against her
neck. His lips were fiercely hot, melting every bone in
Isabel's body, despite the dawning knowledge fighting
its way up through the mists of sleep still clinging to her
brain.

Didn't it hurt his arm to hold her like this? she
wondered distractedly, but then another tremulous
whimper escaped her as the hand holding her against
him moved to cover her breast. The heat of his caressing
fingers through the thin linen of her shift made Isabel
gasp. He was burning her. And the fire went straight to
a place deep inside her body that she hadn't even known
existed until this moment. Then her breath was lost
completely when Guy's mouth left her throat and closed
hotly over the tender peak cupped in his hand.

She had never known such deliriously exquisite sensations, never known that one could feel like this and
still want more. The pleasure was so intense that Isabel
thought she was going to swoon. A soundless cry parted
her lips and her body arched, instinctively seeking his,
but when his hand lifted to unfasten the neck of her shift
and she heard a sharp, tearing sound a shaft of fear

lanced through the delirium, wrenching her abruptly into full wakefulness.

'No! Wait——'

'Don't stop me,' he pleaded thickly. 'God, Isabel, please don't stop me. I don't care if 'tis only a dream. I——'

'But it isn't,' she cried, frantic now as her words brought home the enormity of what was happening. ''Tis real!' She pushed against fitzAlan's massive chest, her fear escalating into panic when she saw the hot, unfocused glitter in his eyes. Suddenly the significance of the warmth surrounding her exploded on to her consciousness. Her hands slid up to his shoulders, his skin dry and hot to her touch.

He was burning up with fever, probably not even fully aware of what he was doing or saying.

'My lord. . .' she quavered, trying to form a plea in her mind.

His eyes went hard, though the fiery heat remained undimmed. The combination was frightening. Mother of God, how was she to get free of him? He was between her and the edge of the bench and was half lying over her anyway, imprisoning her between his arms. One long, heavily muscled leg had been thrown over hers, pinning her beneath him. She would never be able to fight him off physically. She was trapped.

'Are you going to refuse to pay the price, after all?' fitzAlan grated harshly.

Isabel's eyes flashed back to his face. Surely he hadn't been using that tone with her a moment ago? Bewilderedly she struggled to remember the words Guy had been muttering, but they had been lost in the half-sleeping state which had dulled her mind, and, later, barely heard over the unfamiliar demands of newly awakened desire. All she could recall with any certainty was the tender, soothing voice in a dream that was rapidly becoming a nightmare. Oh, why had she fallen asleep?

'I didn't. . .you can't. . .you're out of your mind with fever,' she stammered wildly.

'I'm out of my mind, all right,' he snarled. 'Out of my mind for wanting a traitorous little witch like you. But once I have you, by God, that will be the end of it!'

'No! You don't know what you're saying. You don't know what you're doing.'

FitzAlan laughed unsteadily. 'Oh, I know what I'm doing, little deceiver. Don't worry, I know what I'm doing. Before I'm finished you'll want me as much as I want you.'

'I won't. I'll fight you,' she cried in instant denial, wondering in despair if she could actually bring herself to hurt him to save herself. She might have to, Isabel decided, as he laughed again and his hand drew aside the neck of her shift, exposing the delicate lines of her throat and shoulders. 'Would you rape me?' she choked, twisting aside in an attempt to avoid his seeking mouth.

But she felt his lips, hot and hard, caress the soft skin he had bared. 'It won't be rape, sweetheart,' he murmured against the side of her neck, and, with bewildering suddenness, his voice was a soft murmur again. 'Do you think I would hurt you, my lovely girl? Not you, Isabel. Never you.'

Blessed Mother, should she try another appeal while he seemed more gentle. . .?

The thought never had a chance to become action. Isabel had one quick glimpse of the fire smouldering in fitzAlan's eyes as he lifted his head, then his mouth came down on hers in a kiss of such male dominance that she went completely limp. The yielding weakness was total, sapping her will and her strength.

He was right, a distant voice in her mind whispered

mockingly. He wouldn't have to rape her. She was his. She had always been his. She might fight him, resent him, even hate him for condemning her on Matilda's word alone, but she couldn't deny his need or her longing to satisfy it. She had never felt like this before in her entire life, knew she would never feel like this for any other man. On some deep, primitive level, sensed earlier when she had gazed at him across the fire, she belonged to him.

But at what price?

The silent question was as instinctive as her moment of surrender, hardly a conscious thought, but it was enough to wrench Isabel back from the precipice. Enough to remind her of the consequences of submitting so easily to a man who despised her.

'No!' she sobbed aloud, when fitzAlan freed her mouth to rain kisses across her face and into her hair. The word was barely more than an anguished gasp, but Isabel felt strength begin to seep back into her. That instant of frightening acceptance was pushed violently aside, buried deep, deeper than her memories of a carefree childhood, deeper than the terrifying nightmare that had followed.

'I won't let you do this,' she panted, pushing at fitzAlan's shoulders. Her desperation was now so great that she momentarily forgot his wound, striking out at him blindly. 'You already hate me. You won't make me hate myself!'

There was no answer. Not even a movement to show that fitzAlan had heard her fierce protest. Gasping for breath, Isabel managed to twist her head away from him and look around.

He was out cold, his body a dead weight on hers, his face buried in the tangled skeins of her long hair.

During the countless terrifying minutes before she managed to wriggle free and scramble off the bench,

Isabel neither knew nor cared whether it was she or his fever that had caused fitzAlan's loss of consciousness. She was too grateful for the reprieve. Her head smarted painfully where several strands of hair had been wrenched out by her violent struggles, the fragile material of her shift had torn further, and she was shaking uncontrollably and unable to stand upright. But she was free.

Heedless of the rough dirt floor, Isabel dragged herself over to the fire and crouched beside it, crying with mingled fright and relief. The racking sobs didn't last long; she was too afraid that fitzAlan would recover and come after her. But when she brushed her hair out of her face and peered cautiously over at the bench Guy lay in the same position, completely unmoving. If it hadn't been for his harsh, laboured breathing, Isabel would not have known that he still lived.

Her breath caught on another sob. Holy saints, the nightmare wasn't over yet. But fever, at least, was an opponent she could fight, and action would stop her from thinking. She would *not* think. She dared not!

Rising unsteadily to her feet, determinedly keeping her mind on what she needed to care for fitzAlan, Isabel opened the door of the hut. Daylight struck her eyes, momentarily blinding her. Then, realising that she was getting wet, she grabbed the pail and slammed the door shut again on the incessant rain.

The noise aroused fitzAlan. He muttered and stirred, flinging his wounded arm out, but his eyes remained closed.

Isabel crouched against the wall, watching him as though he were in truth the wolf her imagination had conjured up, and waiting until her fluttering pulse had steadied before moving again. Only when Guy had been still for several minutes did she cross to the bench and set the pail down. Her heart sank at the sight of fresh blood on the bandage, but she set about unwinding the strip of linen, praying that she had not opened up fitzAlan's wound too badly in her frantic efforts to escape. Praying even more fervently that, when he awoke, he would remember nothing of his fever-induced passion.

And it must have been the fever, Isabel decided a long time later, when she at last had time to sit down and rest. She knew, of course, that men were driven by lusts of the flesh, desires that they satisfied with little or no regard for the females they wanted, but, strangely enough, she would not have considered fitzAlan to be a man to lose control of himself for that reason. Especially with a woman for whom he felt nothing but contempt. He seemed too strong, too self-contained. And his reputation for honour was apparently widespread enough to have reached Gloucester.

But what did she really know of him? Isabel asked herself broodingly. As Adele had pointed out, even men of integrity could behave differently when it came to women. The thought depressed her, but she told herself it was only weariness. She was exhausted; more so because of the alarmed way she had sprung out of reach whenever Guy had become restless, than from the number of times she had sponged him down in an attempt to cool his fever. Though he appeared no longer bent on seduction, nor even aware of her seeming absence, Isabel knew she was no match for his strength. He could have hurt her badly without meaning to.

When the burning heat in his body had at last broken, she had concentrated on his arm, washing the wound constantly by setting a bowl outside to catch the clean rainwater and then replacing it with the pail, changing the two receptacles again and again. Her whole body ached, but the treatment seemed to have worked. Guy was now sleeping more naturally, and his skin felt only slightly warm.

But though tiredness dragged at her mind and body, Isabel couldn't relax. The passing hours brought other tasks in their wake. She was hungry, and there was fitzAlan's horse to check also, she remembered, reaching for her dress. It was still damp, though not uncomfortably so, and Isabel quickly pulled it over her head. After ensuring that the fire was safe and that Guy was still deeply asleep, she crossed to the door and slipped quietly outside.

The daylight, overcast and grey though it was, made her blink after the dimness of the hovel and caused her to hesitate while she got her bearings. The village was so small that it could hardly be described as such. There were only three huts and a couple of three-walled structures that Isabel had taken for huts last night. They were piled high with branches and logs, and the very old remains of a bonfire lay a few yards away.

Of course, she thought, still clinging to the dubious shelter of the doorway. Charcoal burners. They would live here while they gathered the leafless branches of the surrounding trees and prepared their charcoal for winter use in the local castle or town. At this hour the little clearing should be abustle with activity, huge mounds of logs being erected, smoke from the fires rising into the misty air.

Isabel glanced warily around at the silent forest, seeing nothing but dripping trees, ablaze with the autumn colours that even the dismal weather could not dim. Piles of fallen leaves carpeted the forest floor with gold, and the stillness was broken only by the steady rain. Whoever had been here had long since gone.

The air smelled clean and fresh after the smoky little hut, and she took a deep breath, feeling her spirits lift. In that moment, despite the grim task awaiting her in

Winchester, she savoured the knowledge that she was
free of Gloucester Castle with its dark atmosphere of
frustrated anger and intrigue. Few there would miss her,
she knew. Adele. Richard Fiennes, perhaps. But they
would soon forget. She had been a silent, remote
member of the household, retiring into the shadows as
much as possible, quickly forgotten.

The whicker of Guy's horse interrupted her thoughts,
and Isabel hurried across the clearing to the hut where
the animal was tethered. It was a big grey, strong but
fleet, built for speed. Isabel remembered the huge black
warhorse fitzAlan had ridden before and wondered
what had happened to it.

'Do you know?' she asked the grey. He flicked his
ears at her and snorted politely.

'You're a lot friendlier than your master,' Isabel
informed the horse. 'And you carried us both very
bravely last night.' She stood stroking the animal and
murmuring to it for a moment longer before glancing
around the hut.

There was evidence here, too, that the owners had
left hurriedly, or been driven out. A mouldy lump of
unidentifiable food lay on a table amid a pile of crumbs.
The food was so hard that even the small denizens of the
forest had left it alone. Isabel sighed and decided she
was going to remain hungry for a while longer.
FitzAlan's horse was better off, she saw. Guy had
obviously carried a small bag of grain in his pack and
had left some with the animal. And he had water, as
well, since the thatch roof was leaking badly in several
places. Isabel gave the grey a last pat and made sure the
door was securely closed before speeding back through
the rain to her own shelter.

FitzAlan slept on, she noticed thankfully. Quickly
stripping off her gown, which had become soaked again,
she sat down by the fire and began to comb through her

wet, tangled hair with her fingers, holding the strands to the blaze to dry.

He had been watching her for a long time before she realised he was awake. Watching her and wondering. Wondering about her reasons for leaving Gloucester. Wondering why he had agreed to take her.

Her face was tilted, half turned towards him, as she dried the back of her hair. The bronze strands hung over her arm like a curtain, a silken backdrop for her delicate features. Her lashes were dark crescents against skin flushed rosy by the firelight. Not even the fading bruise high on her cheekbone detracted from her beauty; she only looked more fragile. Breakable.

But Isabel had plenty of spirit, Guy reminded himself, ruthlessly stamping down on the protectiveness the sight of her always seemed to arouse in him. She was no helpless, timorous female. Look at what she'd faced in the past twelve hours. Very deliberately Guy went through the list.

Whether or not her warning was genuine, she had come boldly to his room to ask for his escort to Winchester. She had fought him off like a veritable wildcat when he'd slung a few well-deserved insults at her, and then had had the gall to deny she had turned traitor, although her brother held his castle for Matilda, and God only knew what she, herself, had done for the Empress. If Isabel had hated the situation as much as she claimed to, she could have refused to serve Matilda and sought refuge in a convent.

What else? Ah, yes. While another woman would have had hysterics all over him because of the rain and his wound, Isabel had had enough presence of mind to realise they could not be followed in such inclement weather. She had unflinchingly wrenched the arrow out of his arm as if 'twas all in a day's work, and had argued with him all through the operation and while bandaging his wound later. And when she hadn't been arguing she had been calm, efficient, distant. . .

Exactly as she was now. Not raising her head, nor even starting, at the sudden clamour of birds squabbling out in the clearing. She was absorbed in the feminine ritual of drying her hair, as though there were no danger in their situation, as though she had not a care in the world.

Would a mere slap from an enraged mistress send such a woman fleeing from the shelter of Gloucester Castle?

Not unless there was another damned good reason for her flight, Guy concluded grimly. But as soon as he cursed himself for being taken in last night by Isabel's distress, two insistent memories shook his belief that it had been an act put on for his benefit: the way she had clung fiercely to his hand when they had passed the dungeons, her grip almost painfully strong, and the stricken expression on her face when he had ordered her to strip.

Try as he might, he could not get those two incidents out of his mind. They nagged at him. They didn't tally with the cool, distant woman he was looking at now. And other memories, fragmented and vague, began to torment him. Of Isabel lying soft and pliant in his arms, her slender body pressed to his. Of a burning hunger that only she could appease. Then of cool hands moving over him with teasingly light caresses, but quenching some of the fire, taking away the heat. Had he dreamed all that?

Guy found his gaze moving slowly over Isabel as if her body held the answers to the questions in his mind. The shift didn't hide much. With the fire behind her, he could see the shadowy curve of her breasts through the thin material, and its ragged hem now only reached to mid-thigh. Her legs were curled to the side, slender with dainty ankles curving to small, arched feet. There was something about those little feet, Guy thought suddenly, trying to pin down the memory. Then it came to him. They were supposed to be muddy.

'You've washed your feet,' he rasped abruptly. Somehow it came out sounding like an accusation.

Isabel's head came up like a wary animal scenting the air, but her face was swiftly wiped of all expression. 'They were dirty,' she returned calmly.

An instantaneous, violent urge to shake that remote calm, to see emotion in those serene, fathomless eyes, surged through him at her cool reply. And while he was about it, Guy told himself savagely, he had better discover what little plot Isabel had in mind once she reached Winchester. Knowing Matilda, the girl could have been sent to do anything. And he was helping her to do it!

But she hadn't complained about her dirty feet.

Even more annoyed by that intrusive thought, Guy scowled furiously as Isabel rose and took a beaker from the table, filling it with water from the pail. She didn't seem in any hurry to resume her clothing, he thought cynically, considering her initial reluctance to shed the dress. Indeed, her pose by the fire had been that of the consummate temptress, and yet. . .there it was again, the feeling that something didn't add up.

He watched her graceful movements as she came towards him and tried to shut his mind to the sight of her bare limbs. She looked both vulnerable and infinitely desirable, and he didn't know which was more disturbing — or more dangerous.

'You must be thirsty,' Isabel murmured, proffering the beaker.

Still frowning, Guy took it and downed the contents in one gulp. 'My mouth feels like the bottom of a dried-up moat,' he grumbled, handing the roughly crafted mug back to her.

Isabel refilled the beaker, then hoisted the pail and replaced it by the side of the bench. She didn't exactly replace it with a thump, but she saw fitzAlan glance at her before he sat up cautiously. Let him wonder about her mood, she thought, refusing to feel contrite. Obviously she wasn't going to get any thanks for nursing him. Then she remembered that he had been wounded because of her.

"Tis the aftermath of your fever,' she explained shortly. 'You were. . . I tried to get you to drink, but. . .'

The explanation faded into silence when Isabel recalled the way she had spilled water all over her patient because she'd been so nervous of him. Even discussing the subject of last night made her nervous. So far fitzAlan showed no sign of remembering what had happened between them, seeming to be concentrating all his formidable will on remaining upright. She hoped such mundane matters would keep his mind occupied for a good while, because, if he ever discovered how helplessly she had responded to him, Isabel knew she would die of humiliation.

'I'm afraid water is all we have,' she muttered, clutching at the first diversion that occurred to her. 'I couldn't find any food here or in the other huts.'

'You've been out?'

Her chin lifted. 'Aye. To check on your horse and look for something to eat.'

FitzAlan downed another drink, his lowering gaze on Isabel the whole time. The slight pallor beneath his tan and the white bandage high on his left arm did nothing to detract from the air of menace about him. The danger might be controlled, beneath the surface, but it was there nevertheless. Isabel wondered if he knew how

intimidating he could be with just a look, and decided
fitzAlan was fully aware of his effect on her. Determined not to betray her uneasiness, she turned away.

Instantly his free hand shot out, preventing her
escape. She couldn't quite suppress a gasp of pain as
those long, powerful fingers wrapped around her swollen wrist. Immediately his grip shifted to her hand, but
he didn't release her. His intent gaze dropped to her
arm, his firm mouth curling sardonically.

'The price of retaliation,' he mocked. 'You should
have thought twice before avenging a few unpleasant
truths, my lady.'

'I care not for the hurt if it indeed avenged your
insults, my lord,' Isabel retorted. 'I would do it again.'

'Would you?' Guy's half-smile broadened into a grin
that held arrogant masculine assurance and an equally
arrogant challenge. His thumb began to stroke the
inside of her wrist. 'Then next time I'll try to be more
gallant.'

'There will be no next time,' Isabel got out, desperately trying to keep her breathing steady while she
struggled unavailingly to free her hand. She knew Guy
could feel the sudden acceleration of her pulse, but she
could do nothing to stop the traitorous throbbing. That
stroking thumb was sending shafts of heat straight up
her arm with every heartbeat.

'You think not?' he murmured, watching her efforts
to escape with the lazy, slightly curious air of the
predator who knew his victim was helpless. Then his
eyes flashed to her face, their piercing regard anything
but lazy. 'You were willing to tolerate my touch last
night. In fact, sweet traitor, you clung to my hand as you
would to a lover.'

Isabel froze, the insulting term scarcely heard. She
stared apprehensively into fitzAlan's eyes, searching
beneath the gleaming mockery for a sign that he was

beginning to remember the events of the night. Then she realised he was referring to their escape and drew in a shaky breath of relief. 'I don't like the dark,' she managed, then wished she'd had the sense to keep her mouth shut.

Utter surprise crossed fitzAlan's face. Whatever he had expected her to say, it was obviously not that. 'You're afraid of the dark?' he echoed in patent disbelief.

'I didn't say that,' denied Isabel quickly, clinging to her dignity as best she could under the growing amusement in her tormentor's expression. 'I just don't like it.' She gave another tug at her hand.

FitzAlan ignored this attempt to free herself, as he had all the others. His amusement faded, to be replaced by narrow-eyed speculation. His next words, dropping gently into the tense silence, shook her tottering composure even more.

'Hmm. I suppose that answers one question. Now for the next—why is your shift torn?'

How many questions did he have? Isabel wondered agitatedly. She had to swallow hard before she could speak. 'I. . .I needed a clean bandage for your arm. Do you not remember?'

'Your shift is torn at the neck,' Guy elaborated, his voice even softer than before.

That gentle tone meant danger, Isabel thought, mesmerised by the way his eyes bored into hers. She suddenly knew how a rabbit felt under the hypnotic stare of the hawk.

With a final effort that she felt in every nerve of her body, she jerked her hand from his and turned away to the fire. 'I. . .I tore it outside. On a branch.'

Guy knew at once she was lying. But why? Why lie about such a trivial thing? Another hazy memory floated tantalisingly at the edge of his mind. Warm skin, as soft as silk against his mouth. Memory — or dream?

'Oh?' he murmured, watching her. 'That's a relief. I thought I might have done it, since you had trouble getting me to drink when I was out of my senses.'

Not even the crackle of the fire and the pelting rain could disguise Isabel's quick gasp. She whirled to face him, braced for further interrogation, her arms wrapped defensively across her waist. Then hesitated, unsure, at the waiting stillness in fitzAlan's body. The air was suddenly thick with unspoken questions.

He was engaging in a war of nerves with her, Isabel realised at last, but he didn't remember. She stared back at him, unable to speak, terrified of betraying the slightest clue that might jolt his memory, but conscious of a heartfelt sense of gratitude for the fever that had kept her so busy during the morning hours. FitzAlan might suspect that something had happened between them, but he didn't know for sure.

Trembling with relief, she bent quickly to add another log to the fire, using the small task to break the heavy silence. "Tis fortunate we have the fire, isn't it?' she remarked in a hopelessly breathless attempt at chattiness. 'Since we're stuck here until your. . .I mean until the rain stops, and —'

'Wrong both times,' he growled behind her, frustrated anger plain in his voice. 'We leave again in the morning, rain or no, even if you have to tie me to my horse. Which reminds me — is he dry enough?'

Isabel turned to look at fitzAlan before answering. She was not very much surprised to see him on his feet and opening the door, but when he swayed and put a hand on the wall to steady himself she was unable to prevent her own hand going out towards him. It was quickly snatched back when he shot a black look at her.

'Your horse is fine,' she retorted, annoyed at that

moment of weakness. 'But you're not. At least sit down
until you feel stronger.'

'I'll feel stronger a damn sight faster if I move around
a bit,' he threw at her in a voice little better than a snarl.
'And when I do, my lady, we'll get back to that
interesting little conversation we were having.'

The door slammed shut behind him.

CHAPTER FIVE

ISABEL'S shaking legs got her as far as the bench before she collapsed. She felt as if she'd already been questioned on the rack, and fitzAlan hadn't even tried to force any definite answers out of her. But he would when he returned.

The thought sent Isabel scrambling into her gown again, as though the garment might afford her some protection. Somehow it seemed easier to dress while Guy was absent. No doubt he would have made a nasty remark, and she didn't need to hear any more of them.

When he returned, however, fitzAlan made no comment on her clothing nor demanded any immediate answers. He was looking a little pale and the lines of strain around his mouth betrayed the pain his arm was giving him. 'You're right,' he said shortly. 'Not a crumb of food in the place. But there are some strips of salted meat in my pack.'

'Oh.' Isabel gave a nervous little laugh. 'I didn't think to look in there.'

She was conscious of fitzAlan's sharp glance at her sudden murmur of laughter, then he sat down heavily on the bench, wincing at the jolt to his arm, and gestured towards the bulky pack by the door. 'Go ahead.'

Isabel didn't need a second invitation, quickly finding the meat and dividing it between them. But, despite her hunger, she took as long as possible over the simple meal, desperately trying to stave off the moment when they would have nothing to do except talk or sleep. She doubted she would ever sleep again while fitzAlan was in the immediate vicinity, but the prospect of remaining awake and having to keep her mask of aloof composure in place was daunting indeed. The questions she had feared earlier seemed to be taking physical shape in the shadowy corners of the room, phantoms waiting to trap her if she dropped her guard for so much as a second.

And yet the waiting silence was almost more than she could bear. When the lonely howl of a wolf carried to them through the forest, Isabel jumped, glancing at the door as if she expected to see the beast standing there.

FitzAlan rose and moved his sword nearer to the bench, where he could lay his hand on it quickly. ''Tis not four-footed predators we need worry about,' he observed, and Isabel knew he had seen her nervous reaction. 'I dare say we're safer here than in Gloucester. At least for tonight.'

The shadows moved imperceptibly closer.

'My. . .father. . .once told me. . .a wild animal will not venture near a fire,' she stammered. Anything to keep the conversation simple and unthreatening.

FitzAlan promptly turned it around. 'Tell me about your father,' he commanded abruptly. 'When did he die?'

She withdrew immediately, retreating into her corner of the bench, her face expressionless but for the suspicious sidelong glance she sent him. 'Why?'

Guy's brows rose. 'Why not?' he countered. He continued to watch her for a moment, then murmured, 'I liked him.'

Isabel looked back at the fire, her tense muscles easing a little. 'He had many friends,' she said softly. 'They all liked him.'

'So how did Hugh die?' he persisted when she didn't say any more. 'In battle?'

Alarm pulled her body taut again. Another quick guarded look told her he was still watching her. Why was he so interested in her father? Why did he have to ask all these questions? Perhaps if she flatly refused to give any details. . .

'There was a fight,' she confirmed shortly. ''Twas a long time ago. My father was killed. I would rather not speak of it.'

FitzAlan's brows drew together. 'What would your ladyship prefer to discuss?' he enquired with heavy sarcasm. 'The exact nature of your work for Matilda, perhaps? Is it possible that bolt in my arm should have been through my heart?'

She flinched. 'If that had been my purpose I would not have tended your wound,' she faltered, hoping he couldn't hear the tremor in her voice.

'Oh, really? Should I thank you?'

Her eyes widened, lifting to his face. FitzAlan was leaning back against the wall, seemingly at ease, but his eyes were narrowed and the muscles of the forearm braced over his raised knee were rigid. Despite the warmth of the fire, Isabel began to shiver. This was not the almost idle interrogation he had started earlier, but something darker, something dangerous. He had been angry before, he was angry *now*, but this time. . .this time he was *using* it, controlling it. Isabel's trembling increased as she saw what was happening. He was using a very real emotion, cold-bloodedly, deliberately, to taunt and intimidate.

Just like all the rest, she thought bitterly. Just like every other man. Was brute force and intimidation all they knew? Resentment flickered within her, a tiny flame, not yet warm enough to banish the chill of fear, but steady. ''Twas little enough payment for taking me to Winchester.'

'And do you always pay your debts?' The question was soft with hidden menace.

'If. . .if I can.'

'Hmm. A pity I didn't collect when I had the chance. Your skills might have been. . .interesting.'

Isabel felt all the blood drain from her face. Merciful Jesu! He had remembered. The wolf had cornered his prey and was now moving in for the kill. She could almost feel the fangs at her throat, and knew the real cause of the choking sensation was fear. And she was so tired of being afraid. So tired of having to be careful. So tired of being the target of insults. So *tired*.

She stared into fitzAlan's hard, relentless eyes, and behind her fear that tiny flicker of resentment flared into sudden blazing life with the force of a rage as hot as his was cold. Rage at a fate which prevented her from screaming and railing at him for so misjudging her, rage at him for playing this cat-and-mouse game with her, rage at herself for letting him get away with it. She could not let him throw last night in her face. This time she had to fight back or be utterly shamed.

It occurred to her far too late that in a contest between fire and ice there could be only one victor.

'You seem to have your own particular talents, also, my lord. Getting us past two locked doors, for instance.'

To her surprise he allowed the diversion. ''Tis easy enough to pick a lock when you know how.' His eyes scorned her. 'You should learn the trick of it. ''Tis a useful accomplishment for ladies who come creeping into a man's chamber late at night.'

'Is that so?' Isabel snapped. 'Well, I am happy to say that my acquaintance does not run to thieves, so ——'

'No,' he shot back, his voice suddenly harsh. 'Only traitors. Tell me, how does the Countess pay you?' He looked her up and down disparagingly. 'Obviously not with gowns. Is it your brother who reaps the rewards? Do you whore for him rather than for Matilda?'

Isabel gasped, jerking back as though he had struck her. For a stunned moment she couldn't believe what she had heard, then she leapt to her feet, dark eyes blazing from an ashen face. 'You know nothing!' she spat, her voice shaking with such fury that the words were barely coherent. '*Nothing*! You. . .' She choked on a raggedly indrawn breath and had to stop, fighting for air.

FitzAlan stood up and took two slow, measured paces towards her, until she was forced to tilt her head right back to look up at him, or retreat, which she refused to do. Blue eyes, as light and as frozen as ice, stared into hers before his glance moved slowly downwards, deliberately insulting. Isabel's hands clenched into tiny fists at her sides as she struggled against the waves of savage anger threatening to sweep her beyond caution. He saw the movement and laughed. It was the final straw.

'Who is the traitor here?' Her voice rose on a note that betrayed how near she was to breaking-point. 'Stephen swore a sacred oath to recognise Matilda as Queen. As you probably did yourself. So tell me, my lord, just who is the traitor here?'

The laughter was wiped from fitzAlan's face instantly. 'I swore no oath to Matilda,' he grated. 'And Stephen was released from his promise by the Church ——'

'Aye, on the condition of other promises, which he then proceeded to break,' she cried recklessly.

She saw fitzAlan's eyes narrow to glittering slits, his jaw lock tight with fury. His hands lifted to her shoulders as though he would shake her, but clenched and fell back as he controlled himself. Isabel found her gaze fixed in unwilling fascination on one white-knuckled fist. No wonder he had laughed at hers, she thought distractedly. If he ever hit her with that, he would probably kill her.

'Well,' he stated with deadly quiet. 'Now I know exactly where your loyalties lie, my lady Isabel.'

Her eyes flew back to his face. 'No,' she whispered,

going pale again with fright as she remembered what she was supposed to be doing. Rage drained out of her with numbing speed, leaving her empty and cold. 'No. I only meant——'

'I know what you meant,' he dismissed contemptuously. 'And if anger loosens your tongue I'll also find out what you mean to do in Winchester. Pretend to sell yourself to a higher bidder, no doubt.' He gave a short laugh. 'You won't be the first, but what do you think to offer the Queen? False information? We'll get the real thing out of you soon enough and you won't see a farthing for it.'

'*No*! I. . .' Tears clogged her throat and she had to stop, fighting them back. What had she done? She had only meant to defend herself, but it had come out all wrong. And now her flash of temper had probably endangered Edmund. FitzAlan could prevent her from seeing the Queen. . .confine her somewhere in Winchester. . .

'I. . .only intend. . .to serve the Queen. . .' she faltered huskily, her eyes pleading with him.

The plea shattered his control as her anger had not done. The words were barely out of Isabel's mouth when fitzAlan grabbed her arms with bruising strength.

'*Damn you, don't lie to me*!' he roared, shaking her hard. Her head snapped back. An involuntary cry escaped her lips at the force of his grip. Far from relenting, his fingers tightened even more, nearly lifting Isabel from the ground.

The room started to spin. Her eyelids fluttered and she went deathly white, but she fought back the dizzying sensation, her hands coming up to brace herself against fitzAlan's chest while the world righted itself. She would *not* faint. She had to think of Edmund. But the only coherent thought in her head was an awareness that fitzAlan's heart was pounding violently against her palms and his hands seemed to be shaking almost as much as she was.

Then, as her eyes lifted to his, he shoved her roughly away from him, wheeled about, and slammed out of the hut.

Isabel dropped to the floor where she stood, one hand gripping the edge of the bench. The firelight caught the tiny scar on her finger and a long, whimpering sound of anguish filled the hut. Her head fell forward to rest on her fingers. Fool! she moaned in silent despair. *Fool*! Had the past taught her nothing? Had she not learned the futility of striking back? Why had she fought him? Why had she uttered one word? And why did it tear her apart because it was fitzAlan who had said those terrible things to her?

Why did he feel as though he had just run his sword through the heart of something small and desperately struggling for survival?

Guy leaned back against the hut door, dragging the cold night air into his lungs, and tried not to think of the anguish in Isabel's white face, of the tears drowning her luminous grey eyes. He should be satisfied that he'd succeeded in destroying her calm façade. He should still be inside, keeping up the pressure until he forced the truth out of her. But instead he was feeling torn apart by his own emotions.

God, he'd never felt such savagely conflicting sensations. *Never*! He had seen her passionate anger and had wanted to kiss her senseless, had heard her lie to him and had wanted to shake the truth out of her, had almost caused her to swoon and had wanted to hold her close and tell her he wouldn't allow anything to hurt her again — all in the space of about half a minute.

And what did he have for it? *Nothing*! Oh, yes, he knew she was afraid of the dark. Wonderful! Very helpful! He was standing here on the other side of the door, knowing nothing of Isabel's plans. Hell! He didn't even know what had happened last night, although he was damned sure something had to make Isabel so nervous of him. She had been wary and guarded before, but not jumpy — not with that purely *feminine* type of nervousness.

His thoughts skidded to a halt. There it was again. That nagging doubt, the feeling that something was missing in the woman she was supposed to be. It wasn't reasoned. It wasn't logical, or even safe. It was sheer gut instinct. And that wasn't all.

Guy pushed himself away from the hut and strode across the clearing to make sure his horse was secure for the night. The anger in him slowly dissipated as questions raced through his mind. Isabel hadn't searched his pack. By design or in innocence? She hadn't taken his horse and left him when he'd fallen into a stupor last night. Because he was hurt, or because she needed his protection? There was passion in her, showing itself in anger, yet she fought to control it. And if she was not always cold and distant, what had made such a detached, unemotional mask necessary in the first place?

Questions!

He wondered suddenly what he would find when he returned to the hut. His cool, scheming enemy, or his hurt, fragile. . .

He found Isabel crouched by the fire, staring into the flames. She still looked pale, but she got slowly to her feet, watching him carefully.

Guy pushed the door shut, studying the uneasy expression in her eyes. 'We have to let the fire die out tonight,' he said quietly. 'We needed it to dry off, but now 'tis dangerous if we're near enough to a castle for the smoke to be noticed. If 'tis known this place is abandoned, someone might investigate.'

Her eyes widened a little, as though in surprise, then she nodded, glancing aside to the table and indicating the misshapen light with a hand that shook slightly. 'I think there may be a castle or. . .or town. . .quite close. The candle. . .'

Guy found his eyes following the gesture. Such a little hand. And she sounded. . .defeated. He felt a sudden piercing need to reach out, capture her hand and pull her into his arms. God's blood, why did she have to look so damned vulnerable? And tired. The bluish shadows beneath her eyes made the eyes themselves look enormous. For the first time he wondered how long his fever had lasted, and how much sleep Isabel had got the night before. Enemy or not, she had nursed him.

'Come,' he said, deliberately keeping his voice low and even. 'We have a long ride ahead of us tomorrow. 'Tis time to sleep. You'll be more comfortable on the bench with me and we'll be warm enough under that blanket and my cloak, even without the fire.'

Isabel heard the words, but they sounded all wrong. Almost too afraid to hope, she repeated them in her mind. Had she been mistaken earlier? Did he still have no memory of the previous night? Oh, Holy Mother of God, let it be so.

'The hut will stay warm for a while yet,' she ventured, despising the timid note in her voice, but powerless to disguise it. 'I won't be cold.'

'Maybe not,' fitzAlan answered, and then an unexpected smile suddenly transformed that hard, handsome face. 'But I will.'

Isabel could only gape up at him. He had smiled at her. After his rage and sarcasm, he had actually smiled at her. In that fleeting instant she had seen the soldier of her dreams. For some inexplicable reason her mind went completely blank.

Then the smile was gone. 'Come on,' he said more roughly, apparently regretting his good humour.

Once again Isabel didn't get a chance to argue, even if her brain had been working. In seconds she found herself arranged carefully within the circle of fitzAlan's good arm, her head cradled on his shoulder, and the blanket and cloak wrapped snugly around her. He made a surprisingly comfortable pillow, she thought bemusedly. And at least they were both fully dressed this time.

'Relax,' he murmured in her ear, a thread of amusement in his voice. 'I'm in no condition to attack you tonight.'

Isabel went even more rigid.

'Jesu! I've felt drawn bowstrings less tense than you.'

'I'm sorry,' she whispered, and immediately cursed herself for apologising. At this rate she might as well give him a blow-by-blow description of the last time they had shared the bench, and save him the trouble of remembering. Idiot! You've been given a reprieve. Say something harmless.

'Perhaps one of us should stay awake in case ——'

'Go to sleep,' he interrupted gruffly. 'We're safe enough for another night.'

This time she didn't answer. Guy lay still, trying to ignore the softness of her body against his, trying to ignore the urge to stroke her tension away. He knew only too well where *that* would lead. He should concentrate on his relentlessly aching arm instead. The only trouble with that idea was that Isabel was impossible to ignore. With every breath he inhaled the warm, womanly scent of her, and, as she gradually began to relax, *his* body began to tauten.

In an effort to distract himself, Guy considered all the questions about Isabel he was beginning to amass.

Questions to which there were too few answers. But there was still time. Isabel needed his protection as far as Winchester, and if he didn't have those answers before they arrived he would keep her under restraint until he unlocked every secret she possessed. And his feeling of intense satisfaction at this conclusion was only because he was finally clear-headed enough to make some sort of decision. It had nothing to do with the soft, seemingly defenceless girl lying in his arms.

But, almost of its own accord, his mouth brushed across her silky hair and his arm tightened fractionally. 'Go to sleep, Isabel,' he murmured again, and this time his voice was gentle.

Outwardly Isabel obeyed, relaxing further into the warmth of their makeshift bed, lying docile and still beside him. But she didn't sleep. Instead she gazed into the dully glowing ashes of the dying fire and remembered a wild, enchanted garden and a tender, handsome soldier who had awoken her to approaching womanhood with one gentle kiss and a rose.

There was no sign of tenderness in the man who tossed her up into the saddle the next morning, but, seeing him now in the full light of day, Isabel was forced to concede that he was still handsome. If one liked that uncompromisingly masculine type of good looks, she thought, trying to tell herself she did not.

But she couldn't resist studying fitzAlan as he secured his pack, her eyes moving over his fair head, the strong planes of his face, the hard line of his mouth. With his long blue cloak fastened across his shoulders, his injury was hidden and his height emphasised. He looked powerful and tough, and yet Isabel found herself noticing that his lower lip was slightly fuller than the upper, and that his mouth quirked at one corner, hinting at a sense of humour.

Then fitzAlan mounted behind her and she was immediately aware of the unyielding strength of his body against her back, the restrained power in his hand on the reins. She forgot about hints of sensitivity or humour. He was too big, she told herself. Too overwhelming, too hard.

She thought back to his anger last night. The prospect of a man of fitzAlan's size ever losing control, no matter what the cause, was enough to make any sane woman run for the nearest convent. But instead, for a dizzying instant, as he wrapped his cloak about her, Isabel found herself savouring a delicious sensation of feeling small and infinitely fragile, enclosed within his arms.

Utterly dismayed, she wriggled forward a little, trying to put some distance between them.

'Be still, for God's sake,' growled his deep voice above her. 'Do you want to ruin my horse's back?'

Isabel sighed and subsided. She didn't bother to answer. FitzAlan would only snap at her anyway, as he had been doing from the minute they had risen in the half-light of a chilly grey dawn. Clearly his gentler behaviour when he'd returned to the hut last night had been an aberration. All she had done this morning was suggest that she bathe his wound again before they started out, and he had refused with a complete lack of gratitude or even common courtesy. Recollecting his churlish behaviour, Isabel wondered how she could be attracted to such a man even for a moment. As for his arm, she decided, it could just fester and drop off as far as she was concerned.

Fortunately the rain had ceased some time during the night. A weak sun shone through the dispersing clouds, sending misty rays of light dancing through the trees and turning their necklaces of raindrops into sparkling gems. A cool but bright autumn day promised, and at any other time Isabel would have enjoyed the ride. However, silent contemplation of the passing forest tended to pall after several unbroken miles of it. She finally admitted to herself that even the risk of another snub was preferable to her growing anxiety about what lay ahead.

'Could we not travel safely on the road now?' she asked cautiously, as they forded yet another stream. She felt fitzAlan glance down at her and resolutely kept her face to the front.

'Possibly, if 'twas Stephen you were fleeing from. Matilda tends not to yield what she considers her property so easily.'

''Twas *your* life the Empress wanted,' she murmured. Sudden curiosity overcame her caution and she glanced up at him. 'You've met her before, haven't you?'

'Aye.' FitzAlan's eyes narrowed thoughtfully on her face. 'When she landed in England two years ago. I was among her escort to Bristol when Stephen made the idiotic mistake of allowing the Countess to join her half-brother.' His tone made it clear the job was not one he had enjoyed.

'You said Matilda repaid gallantry with ill treatment,' Isabel remembered.

'Stephen can be too generous for his own good,' fitzAlan said tersely, 'and is all too prone to listen to well-meant but foolish advice. He's easily swayed.' He hesitated, then gave a short laugh that held no humour whatsoever. 'Incredible how a man of such undoubted physical courage can be so unsure of himself in other ways.'

But you are not like that.

For one ghastly second Isabel thought she had spoken the words aloud. 'Physical courage?' she questioned hastily. She wouldn't put it past fitzAlan to read her mind.

'Aye. Stephen is the most fearless man I've ever seen

in battle. The odds were against us from the start at
Lincoln — and he knew it. But even when he was
surrounded he continued to lay about him with his
sword, and then with an axe when his sword broke, until
he went down from a blow to the head. 'Twas the same
gallantry that prompted him to send Matilda to her most
powerful supporter, instead of keeping her isolated at
Arundel. Reckless, foolhardy, but it inspires men to
follow him. 'Tis not a gift the Countess possesses.'

'But there are men who consider her beautiful,' Isabel
remarked, and in the next instant could have bitten her
tongue out. What had possessed her to make such a
statement? *And* with a faintly questioning intonation
that fitzAlan would have to be deaf to miss. Feeling hot
colour rush to her cheeks, she quickly turned away
again, but not before she had seen the sardonic amusement gleaming in his blue eyes. She braced herself.

'Surely you know men are blind to other women when
you are present, Lady Isabel.' The words were uttered
with devastating sincerity.

They were immediately followed by a stunned
silence. Isabel stared fixedly ahead of her, wondering if
she had heard aright. She had expected mockery, and,
judging by the unnatural stillness she felt in fitzAlan's
body, he had *intended* to mock her. What had
happened?

'I've no time to waste on Matilda's beauty or lack of
it,' he said shortly after a moment. ''Tis her fortitude
and determination which bear watching. She is harsher
than Stephen and won't be deflected.' He paused, then
added dispassionately, 'Had she been born a man, those
traits would have made her an excellent ruler.'

Isabel's eyes widened in surprise. She had to make a
determined effort not to look back. 'That is very
generous.'

'I may wish destruction on the King's enemies ——'

his voice was still clipped ' — but that doesn't blind me to
their good qualities.'

The russet and gold forest blurred suddenly before
Isabel's eyes. Did fitzAlan hate her so much, then? she
wondered. Did he consider her to have no good qualities at all, to be so scornful of her? He had judged her
without question, but could attribute fortitude and
resolution to Matilda despite the Empress's glaring
faults.

Isabel blinked her tears away furiously. She could not
be so generous. Not to the haughty woman who used
helpless people as pawns in her ambitious games. She
remembered Edmund, little more than a child, grave
and courteous, thanking the Empress for her hospital-
ity. And she remembered the answer he had received.
She thought of the task awaiting her in Winchester, and
the consequences of failure. The words were out before
Isabel could stop them, despair and bitterness giving
them a stark finality that was absolute.

'She is arrogant. . .and cruel!'

And that was what he got for testing her, Guy told
himself disgustedly. Five little words that only raised a
whole pile of other questions. He would have the
answers, though, he vowed grimly. And before he had
to spend many more sleepless nights like the last one. A
good thing they'd be in Winchester tonight. . . Wry
humour put a slight quirk in his mouth. Another night
like the last, with Isabel in his arms, would try his
control to the limits. And if he wasn't in control, how
could he expect to control *her*?

Two sleepless nights, Isabel brooded as the silence
remained unbroken, was not conducive to good sense.
She felt as though control was slipping away from her in
some obscure way. FitzAlan could not have made his
opinion of her clearer, and yet for an insane moment
there, shaken by his reasoned judgements of Stephen

and Matilda, she had been tempted to confess the truth
and beg for his help.

She must be going mad. He probably wouldn't believe
her, and, in any event, what could he do? Turn around
and make for Tracy Castle? Alone? Edmund would be
killed the instant they appeared at the castle gates. What
was the alternative? To toss Rainald into prison when
they reached Winchester? There were sure to be other
spies reporting to Matilda; Brien fitzCount had said as
much. Again, Edmund's life would be taken. She simply
couldn't risk it.

But as the day lengthened into afternoon the argument lurched back and forth inside Isabel's head until
she could no longer think straight. Weariness and
hunger were also taking their toll. When they crested a
wooded hill shortly before sunset and saw cultivated
fields stretching down towards a small village in the
distance it took all her will-power not to beg that they
stop there for the night.

FitzAlan reined in his horse just before the trees
thinned out. 'The Test,' he said, pointing past her to the
silvery flash of sunlight on water beyond the village.
'There's another ford south of here, and then
Winchester, about nine miles yonder.'

Don't cavil at another nine miles, Isabel ordered
herself. If fitzAlan were alone, he would be in
Winchester by now. I won't ask if we can rest. I won't
ask if we can buy some food from that village. I
won't. . . She suddenly realised that fitzAlan had turned
his horse back into the forest, along a parallel course
with the river, but out of sight of the small hamlet.

'Why are we going this way? That village looked
harmless enough and your horse must be thirsty.' There,
she hadn't actually *asked* for any favours.

FitzAlan jerked his head back at the settlement.
'Men-at-arms,' he explained succinctly. 'Four of them.

Probably only collecting rents or some such thing, but it will be better if they don't lay eyes on you. Besides, I want to reach Winchester before dark.'

Isabel was still vaguely wondering if chivalry or haste was behind fitzAlan's decision to ride on, when the choice was abruptly taken out of his hands. The horse had barely stepped on to the gravelly riverbed at the edge of the ford when it stumbled, almost falling to its knees. The animal plunged to a halt, snorting and tossing its head nervously as water sprayed into the air around them.

Guy was out of the saddle instantly, backing the grey out of the river and examining its hoofs. Isabel heard him mutter an oath.

'What is it?' she asked anxiously.

'Chalon has picked up a stone.' He lowered the horse's left foreleg and came back to lift Isabel to the ground. 'I can get it out, but it will take a moment. Hold his head, will you?'

Isabel picked her way carefully over the rough bank, the cramped muscles in her legs protesting at the exercise, and took the reins. While fitzAlan hefted the grey's hoof and set to work, she glanced about, absently patting Chalon's velvety muzzle.

It was peaceful by the river. Two swans glided majestically past and ripples spread over the breeze-ruffled surface as a fish captured an unwary insect which alighted above it. On the other side of the ford the trees grew almost to the water's edge, appearing shadowy and dim as the sun moved slowly westward. The air was growing cooler with the approach of evening.

Chalon whickered softly, as though recalling her attention, and Isabel murmured soothingly. 'What happened to your other horse?' she asked on a sudden impulse. 'The black one.'

'Romulus?' FitzAlan released the grey's leg and

glanced back. In the light of the setting sun his eyes glittered like blue ice.

Too late Isabel heard the unspoken admission in her question.

'I still have him,' Guy said. She had watched him leave all those years ago, he thought. She had not seen him arrive at her home, since she had not known who he was when they had encountered each other in the garden — but she had seen him leave. From some hidden vantage-point she had watched him that morning, while he rode away with the image of her in his mind and his —

'If you've finished petting my horse we can be on our way,' he rasped abruptly, annoyed at the direction of his thoughts. 'I'd like to ford the river before dark if it won't inconvenience your ladyship too greatly.'

''Twas not my fault we had to stop,' Isabel snapped back indignantly, the peace of the afternoon ruined for her. The sooner she was free of such a boorish escort, the better, she thought angrily, taking a hasty step forward.

She shouldn't have moved so quickly. The riverbank rushed towards her with dizzying speed as the stiffness in her legs caused her stumble and lose her balance on the uneven ground. But even as she flung out a hand to save herself she was whisked off her feet and pulled into the secure haven of fitzAlan's arms.

Isabel gasped at the strength of his grip, her senses reeling as she fought a wild impulse to melt into the crushing pressure of his embrace. He was so *strong*. It should have frightened her — she felt so weak by comparison — but instead she wanted to cling, to soften, to yield. Appalled, she pushed back, but the movement only succeeded in pressing her lower body more closely to fitzAlan's hard thighs. His reaction was immediate and unmistakable.

Isabel froze, staring into those glittering eyes only inches from her own. They seemed to have darkened, smouldering in a way that sent hot and cold chills chasing each other through her body. Suddenly she *was* frightened. Her heart was beating somewhere in her throat and she felt giddier than ever.

'Please,' she whispered, forcing herself not to struggle, hardly breathing in her attempt to remain still. 'Please let me go.'

For a nerve-racking minute Isabel thought fitzAlan would ignore her plea. Then with excruciating slowness he relaxed his hold, allowing her to back away a pace. She was still imprisoned within his arms, but they no longer kept her clamped against him. FitzAlan shifted one hand to the nape of her neck, holding her still, while that probing gaze seemed to penetrate the very depths of her soul.

He was watching her, Isabel thought perplexedly, with the single-minded intensity of the hunter. She felt helpless. She could not look away, could only gaze back at him, wondering what he sought.

'Hell's serpents, lads! Look what we've found here. More booty for our lord.'

The loud, coarse voice ripped through the quiet air with shocking force, like a dagger through silk.

FitzAlan's head jerked up. One glance at the mounted soldiers emerging from the trees was enough. Uttering a low, violent oath, he grabbed Isabel's arm and yanked her behind him, drawing his sword at the same time. In that moment it didn't matter who or what she was. She was threatened, and the primitive male instinct to protect what was his brought his entire body to battle-readiness within seconds.

CHAPTER SIX

MEN-at-arms. . .four of them. . .better if they don't see you. The words echoed in Isabel's head as she clung to Chalon's saddle, where fitzAlan's shove had sent her, and watched the four soldiers size up the situation.

It didn't take long. Like a wolf pack scenting easy prey, they dismounted and spread out. Three of them moved forward, swords unsheathed, while the fourth held their horses, grinning evilly and calling encouragement to his fellows.

"Twill be a good day's work if we can bring in this prize, lads. A wealthy lord to fleece and a tasty little wench for us to play with.'

'You'll have to go through me first,' warned fitzAlan, his voice low with menace.

Isabel couldn't see his face, but she could feel the murderous ferocity emanating from him. The foremost of the advancing men hesitated, a flicker of doubt crossing his rough features as he considered the size and strength of his victim. FitzAlan moved a pace to meet them, his free hand unfastening his cloak. He flicked the garment around his left arm and brought his sword up in a sweeping arc.

'Come on,' he snarled. 'Which of you vermin wants to be the first to burn in hell?'

Isabel gaped at him, horrified. Had the fever turned his brain? He was one against four — and already wounded — and yet he stood there deliberately inciting the men to fight. As if they needed encouragement! His aggression was going to get them both killed.

'We're on the Queen's business,' she cried, in a desperate bid to avert disaster.

The soldiers' attention shifted to her immediately. One of them laughed, his eyes gleaming with anticipation. 'You could be on th'devil'sh businesh, for ought we care,' he slurred.

'Shut up, you little fool!' hissed fitzAlan. 'He's drunk.'

He was right, Isabel realised, watching the soldier lurch forward another step. Her eyes moved swiftly to the others. Were they in a like condition? Would it slow them down or make them more vicious?

'Stay with the horse,' ordered Guy, without taking his eyes off his opponents. 'Use him as a shield if you have to.'

Isabel barely heard him. Sick with fear, she watched helplessly as, at a shouted signal, the three rushed at fitzAlan in a concerted attack that looked like succeeding through sheer weight of numbers.

Then, in a movement so fast that Isabel had to replay it later in her mind to sort everything out, fitzAlan flung his cloak over the drunk on his left and brought his sword slashing through the air to slice through the arm of the man on his right. The soldier howled in agony and staggered back, dropping his own weapon to clutch at the gaping cut that had opened his arm to the bone.

Ignoring him, Guy let the impetus of his powerful swing carry the blade onwards to clash violently with the sword of the third soldier. Steel met steel with a force that sent a nearby flock of birds shrieking into the air. The man reeled under the shock of the blow, his blade wavering briefly. That instant of unguardedness was long enough for fitzAlan. His sword plunged into the exposed chest before him, aimed unerringly at the heart. The man was dead before he hit the ground.

Jolted abruptly out of her paralysis by this drastic

reduction of their adversaries, Isabel suddenly became aware of the curses of the fellow untangling himself from fitzAlan's cloak. His struggles had brought him to within reach of Chalon's powerful hindquarters, and Isabel didn't hesitate. Pulling on the reins with one hand and pushing the big horse with the other, she backed him straight into the drunken lout just as he flung the cloak aside. He went down immediately, yelling and cursing afresh.

Already unnerved by the fighting, Chalon lashed out, catching the soldier a glancing blow before the man could roll free of the deadly, flashing hoofs.

FitzAlan swung about, ice-blue eyes blazing. A grin of unholy amusement slashed across his face. 'Good girl,' he said. 'Keep him busy.'

He's enjoying this, thought Isabel incredulously. But there was no time to enlarge on the idea. The fourth man had abandoned their horses to his wounded companion and was launching himself into the fray. He came in on Guy's unprotected left side, swinging a long pike, clearly hoping to cripple his opponent with the advantage of the weapon's longer reach. The solid oak staff caught Guy a brutal blow on his wounded arm.

Isabel screamed, almost feeling the agony of the blow in her own body. She saw fitzAlan stagger back, his face whitening with pain. The soldier swung again, this time aiming for the head. FitzAlan hurled himself forward in a low tackle, the pike whistling harmlessly over him. It flew through the air to land some distance away as both men went down with a crash that shook the ground.

Isabel heard the sounds of the ensuing fight only vaguely. Her scream had startled Chalon and she now had her hands full trying to control the plunging, frightened horse, realising with a renewed surge of alarm that he was much too strong for her. The threat of

Free Books Certificate

Yes Please send me FREE and without obligation 16 specially selected Mills & Boon Romances, together with my FREE teddy and mystery gift. Please also reserve a special Reader Service subscription for me. If I decide to subscribe, I shall receive 16 superb Romances every month for just £28.80, postage and packing FREE. If I decide not to subscribe I shall write to you within 10 days. The FREE books and gifts will be mine to keep in any case. I understand that I am under no obligation whatsoever. I may cancel or suspend my subscription at any time simply by writing to you. I am over the age of 18.

11A3R

FREE TEDDY

MYSTERY GIFT

Ms/Mrs/Miss/Mr _____

Address _____

_____

_____ Postcode _____

Signature _____

Mills & Boon
Reader Service
FREEPOST
P.O. Box 236
Croydon
Surrey CR9 9EL

NO STAMP NEEDED

mps MAILING PREFERENCE SERVICE

the soldiers was momentarily forgotten as she struggled to keep her footing and prevent the animal from bolting.

There was a sharp crack behind her, then a shout. 'Get the girl, Raoul. Hurry! Use her to disarm the bastard.'

At the same moment Chalon side-stepped, dragging Isabel with him. She lost her hold on the saddle. Her flailing hand slipped down to the pack, wrenching its cords open, just as cruel fingers seized her arm. There was a flash of steel. Hardly aware of what she was doing, driven by the blind instinct to fight for her life, Isabel grabbed at the falling object. It was in her hand when the soldier jerked her roughly around and pulled her against him.

Everything seemed to stop. Time stood still. The leering triumph on her captor's brutish features changed to a rigid mask of surprise. Isabel stared into muddy brown eyes, frozen with terror herself.

Then the eyes glazed, the sweaty, grasping fingers slid from her arm, and the man crumpled to the ground.

How very, very quiet it was. She wondered why she hadn't noticed the quiet before now. The birds had settled again. Even the breeze had died away.

'Isabel?'

She frowned, not wanting anything to intrude on the peacefulness.

'Sweetheart? Are you all right? Did he hurt you?'

The insistent, questioning voice wasn't going to leave. Isabel wrenched her gaze from the limp body at her feet. She found that muddy brown eyes had been replaced by alert blue ones. FitzAlan's eyes. She felt life begin to flow back into her limbs. *What* had he called her?

'Are you hurt?' he repeated, running his hands over her arms.

Isabel's eyes followed his progress downward. Nausea

rose in her throat, threatening to choke her, when she saw the bloodied arrow clutched in her hand. With a stifled cry, she dropped the bolt, stepping back on legs that were suddenly made of water. If she hadn't cannoned into Chalon, now standing quietly, she would have fallen.

'Did I kill him?' she whispered, her face pale as she stared at the weapon. With seeming irrelevancy she remembered stowing the arrow in fitzAlan's pack when she had pulled it out of his arm. What had made her do that? she wondered.

'Not intentionally,' replied Guy drily. 'The fool ran straight into it when he attacked you. Come on, we've got to cross the ford and get away from here before ——'

'I *did* kill him,' Isabel whimpered, not even hearing this terse advice. 'I killed a man ——'

'*Listen to me*!' FitzAlan's voice was rough with barely controlled impatience. 'We don't have time for this. I'll get the Bishop of Winchester himself to absolve you if it'll make you feel better, but first we have to get there. Now *move*!'

The barked command finally registered. Isabel dragged her eyes away from the ground and stared at fitzAlan. The first thing she saw was the fresh blood staining his sleeve. 'Your arm. . .'twas struck. . .'

''Tis well enough for now. Come on, up with you.'

'The other man. . .the one you wounded. . .' Isabel murmured, her mind still working only sluggishly, although she managed to grasp the saddle when she found herself sitting in it. Grey eyes still clouded and wide with horror, she glanced along the riverbank as though seeking the remaining soldier.

'He forgot about his bleeding arm long enough to get on a horse and run,' fitzAlan said grimly, retrieving his cloak and swiftly re-tying the pack. 'We don't know how far he has to go, but you can be sure others will be back for the horses. So we're leaving right now.'

How could he be so calm and practical? Isabel asked herself as fitzAlan swung himself into the saddle behind her. Her own body and mind still seemed to be moving in slow motion, and she had a wild urge to—what? Laugh? Cry? Scream? She wasn't sure just how she felt, but she retained enough control to know that she couldn't give in to shock in front of fitzAlan. She had to push it aside, forget it. Because his mockery or contempt on top of everything else would devastate her.

But when Guy urged Chalon into the shallow water of the ford, she looked back again, as though compelled, to the bodies behind them. ''Tis very different, isn't it?'

Guy flicked a glance down at her, his eyes narrowed and intent. 'What is?'

'Killing someone,' Isabel whispered, her voice a mere thread of sound. ''Tis very different from seeing it done.'

For a while there was silence between them. Isabel listened to the sound of Chalon's steady hoofbeats, finding a vague comfort in the monotony of the noise. It had almost lulled her mind to blankness when she felt fitzAlan's arms close tightly about her with the utmost care, bringing her nearer to the warmth of his body. As though he feared she might break, Isabel thought wonderingly.

'You had to do it, Isabel. He might have killed both of us,' Guy said very gently. 'Remember that.'

She had been wrong, Isabel discovered. Wrong to fear fitzAlan's impatience or scorn. It was his unexpected kindness that caused her jaw to clench suddenly in an attempt to stave off the hot tears scalding her eyes.

So he *could* be tender.

The thought crept into her mind and lingered. Isabel forced herself to dismiss it. In that direction lay a hope too fragile to be exposed — even to herself. It was more likely that fitzAlan did not want a distraught woman on his hands. With the way she was shaking he probably thought she was about to fall to pieces at any moment.

"Tis only reaction setting in, Isabel told herself sternly, trying unavailingly to control the tremors rippling through her body. You're safe now. Safe!

She fixed her burning eyes on the road ahead of her and tried to believe her own words. A solitary tear trickled down her cheek and was quickly brushed aside. She would *not* cry. She would *not* be weak. They would be in Winchester soon. She had to prepare to meet the Queen, plan what to say. . .

But nothing came to mind. The orders she had been given whirled about in her brain in disordered, meaningless circles. If only she weren't so tired. If only she could sleep.

'You need to rest,' murmured Guy's deep voice. 'We'll stop here.'

Isabel stared blankly ahead. Had he read her mind? The thought didn't bother her. Such was her exhaustion that she would not have cared if her traitorous purpose was emblazoned across her face for him to see. She had no idea where they were, had not even noticed that night had fallen. They must have been riding for a long time, but there was no sign of a large town, only a solitary light shining ahead. Then she vaguely remembered fitzAlan saying something about circling around to approach Winchester from the north in case of pursuit.

'Where are we?' she asked listlessly, not really caring.

'An inn near Winchester.' Guy dismounted and lifted Isabel out of the saddle, keeping his arm around her. 'The gates of the city will be closed by the time we arrive, and won't be opened until morning. We might as well spend the night in some comfort.'

As he led her towards the wood-and-thatch building by the roadside, Isabel contemplated another night in fitzAlan's company. She felt strangely detached about it. In fact, nothing seemed quite real. She was so tired. So terribly tired. Perhaps that was a good thing. She would probably fall into slumber tonight if the devil himself were to share the room with her.

But the dreams came when she was tired. What if —— ?

Guy's fist hammering on the door of the inn broke into Isabel's rambling thoughts. She could hear footsteps approaching and the sound of a bar being lifted. A strange sort of inn, she reflected, to be barred to customers. But it all came to her from a distance.

'Who is it?' demanded a suspicious male voice from the other side of the door.

'Travellers needing shelter for the night,' fitzAlan called back. 'We were on our way to Winchester but have been waylaid and robbed.'

'Robbed! Saints have mercy! Wait just a minute, sir; I'll have the door open directly.'

The muffled exclamations of horror continued, accompanied by the sounds of another bar being removed and the rattle of a key. Under cover of the noise Guy's voice was a soft murmur in Isabel's ear. He spoke just as the door opened.

'You're my wife.'

Wife?

Wife!

'*What*?' Isabel squeaked, wrenched forcibly out of her apathy. Before she could say more, she was confronted by a flaring rushlight held in the hand of a wiry little man who peered into their faces.

'Save us! You have your lady with you, sir. And only the one horse and that small pack. . . Thieves! Rogues! But enter, enter, my lord, my lady, and welcome.

Walter! Here, you scoundrel, take my lord's horse and mind you care for him properly.'

Confused by the light in her eyes and the constant chattering of their host, Isabel found herself ushered into the house before she could correct the man's assumption that she was fitzAlan's lady. A rosy-cheeked, motherly-looking woman, as small and wiry as the innkeeper, bustled forward, adding her exclamations to those of her husband.

'Robbed, did you say, my lord? Aye, the roads are not safe for anyone these days. You poor child,' she added without drawing breath, turning her attention to Isabel. She urged her into the centre of the room, where a bright fire burned. 'Come, my lady, sit by the warmth. I swear you are frozen to the bone. Lucky you were to escape with your lives, let alone your horse. But you'll be safe enough here. We keep the door barred tight.'

'Aye,' agreed her husband. 'A fine thing, is it not, sir? That a man cannot keep an open house for the benefit of travellers such as yourselves.'

'Never mind your gossip now, Thomas,' exhorted their hostess. 'Fetch up some ale, while I put the broth back on the fire. My lady looks pale nigh unto death and you stand there gabbling like a half-wit.'

'A loose tongue to match a loose brain, eh, Thomas?' chuckled a third voice from the shadows beyond the fire. 'I don't know why Dame Sybil puts up with you.' The speaker came forward. He was a youngish fellow, dark of hair and eyes, and modestly clad in a plain green tunic over buff-coloured leggings.

An apprentice or pedlar, Guy judged, removing his cloak. Glancing about the big, lofty room, he saw an elderly merchant snoring gently in a corner, hands folded over his well-rounded belly. Two younger men, serfs by their garb, and most likely travelling with the merchant for his protection, sat at a nearby table nursing ale-cups. They looked up incuriously for a moment, then went back to their talk. An open door opposite gave a glimpse of rows of barrels, and next to it a short flight of wooden stairs led to another door above the store-room. Probably the landlord's private solar, he thought. The place looked clean and secure, the yokels doltish but harmless.

Guy sat down on the bench next to Isabel, casting a quick glance down at her. She looked confused, almost dazed. He carefully draped his thick woollen cloak over her shoulders, wryly conscious of the indulgent smile on the face of their hostess. No doubt the woman thought him a concerned, doting husband. Only Isabel knew that the arm he kept around her was more in warning than attentiveness.

He noticed the shrewd examination Dame Sybil gave them, and hoped she would believe that Isabel's worn gown and his stained raiment were the clothing of impoverished nobility. Their lack of baggage was easily explained away by his tale of robbery, as was his wound. This thought had no sooner crossed his mind than the good dame noticed his bloodstained sleeve.

'Holy Mother save us!' she exclaimed, shocked into abandoning her broth. 'You've been hurt, my lord. Ralf, instead of lolling there mouthing insults, fetch my pot of salve from the pantry and —'

'Later, perhaps, if you would be so good, mistress,' interposed Guy firmly. 'My lady needs food and sleep before anything.'

Sybil favoured him with a keen stare, but obediently turned back to the fire. 'A few more minutes will make little difference,' she agreed, seizing a knife and cutting several thick slices from a loaf of bread. 'Food you shall have, and your poor lady looks asleep on her feet. You shall have our solar, my lord. 'Tis but a simple place, but you will be comfortable and private there.'

'But. . .we can't take your bed,' objected Isabel
faintly, although she wondered why the thought of
sleeping in a bed with fitzAlan seemed worse than
sleeping with him on a bench. 'A pallet by the fire will
be——'

'Hush, my love,' admonished her supposed husband.
'Dame Sybil is a better judge of what you need.'

If Isabel had had the energy she would have wiped
the solicitous smile off his face. As it was, she had to be
content with glaring at him, subsiding beneath the
Dame's amused chuckle. What was the use of arguing?
If she denied fitzAlan's story so she could have the solar
to herself, she would become lost in a morass of other
lies and explanations, and her mind wasn't clear enough
to cope with such a task. Besides, Isabel comforted
herself, as she concealed her ringless left hand in her
skirts, she would never see these people again anyway.

'Don't think you've talked your way out of Sybil's
ministrations,' Ralf warned fitzAlan, stretching his legs
out before him. 'She won't rest until she's seen to your
arm. How did it happen?'

'There were four of them,' Guy answered briefly.

'Four?' exclaimed Sybil. 'Against one? Cowards!'

'You've come lately from Winchester, my friend?'
fitzAlan enquired of the younger man.

'Aye, my lord. Ralf the pedlar, at your service. I was
in Winchester for St Giles' Fair last month——' he
paused and shook his head '—but 'twas a poor showing
this year, half the town still needing to be rebuilt, and
the other half with scarce two farthings to rub together.
As for those Flemish mercenaries of the Queen's, they
were as likely to wreck the stalls as buy from them. I'm
hoping for brisker trade on the road.'

'You'd do better to stay put,' argued Dame Sybil,
pouring a thick savoury broth into two large bowls as
Thomas returned from his foray into the cellaret with a

tankard of ale in each hand. She passed one of the heavy dishes to Isabel, whose cold, shaking hands nearly dropped it.

Instantly Guy steadied the bowl. 'Easy, sweetheart,' he murmured, the note of concern in his voice causing fresh tears to gather in Isabel's eyes. She knew he was only pretending for the benefit of their audience. Why did she have to respond so to his gentleness? Even the thought of sharing a bed with him didn't seem so threatening when he was being kind. She *wanted* to be held in his arms, to feel safe. If only for this one night.

Forcing back the tears, she watched Dame Sybil take a warm stone from the fireplace to put between the sheets of the bed. The small kindness nearly overset her again. Had she lived with fear and harshness so long, Isabel wondered, that even ordinary thoughtfulness from strangers undermined her strength? It had started with fitzAlan battering at the wall of indifference she had erected between herself and the world, and now every little thing seemed to hinder its rebuilding.

Fortunately Sybil came bustling back, distracting her, armed with clean linen, warm water and a pot from which wafted an ominous odour. Isabel wrinkled her nose. Thomas and Ralf both groaned.

'Sheep fat,' pronounced fitzAlan, looking amused at these reactions.

'Aye, mixed with healing herbs,' confirmed Sybil. ''Tis of my own making. Take no notice of these weak-stomached creatures, my lord. This will heal your arm in a trice.'

'I know,' he agreed. 'But will my lady allow me to share her bed tonight if I smell like an unwashed ram?'

Isabel nearly choked on a mouthful of broth. How could fitzAlan say such things so naturally? He spoke as if they had been married for years, and could joke about sharing a bed. It was bad enough that they were deceiving these innocent, kindly folk — did he have to do it so well? There was a sinking sensation in the pit of her stomach, as though she was falling deeper into the morass of lies. What had he said about getting the Bishop to absolve her sins? At this rate they would both need no less a person than the pope!

And the wretch knew what she was thinking, Isabel realised, as fitzAlan threw a wicked grin at her under cover of the good-natured ribaldry from the other three. Oh, why did he have to look so irresistibly handsome when he smiled like that? Why was it so difficult not to smile back?

And when he stood to strip off his tunic and shirt to have his arm attended to, why did he have to look so big and strong? So like the protector of her dreams.

'Now, my lord, hold still, if you please,' commanded Dame Sybil, obviously not a female to be overawed by a man twice her size. 'This bandage is stuck fast, but 'tis clean enough, thank the Saints.'

Isabel felt herself blushing, but either fitzAlan took pity on her or his arm was hurting too much, for he made no comment on where the bandage had come from. Thomas stood by holding the bowl of water and looking anxious.

'Sybil's right, you know, Ralf,' he said. 'If thieves have taken to the roads you're likely to end up with a hole in you like. . .' He paused enquiringly.

'FitzAlan,' Guy murmured.

'I dare say thieves are no more frequent on the roads than in the town,' argued Ralf, saving Guy from further introductions. 'There was plenty a cutpurse at the fair. A man had to keep his money close. Not to mention a sharp dagger in case of attack.'

'Of what use is a dagger against four?' demanded Thomas gloomily.

'These weren't common thieves,' corrected fitzAlan.

His keen eyes went from Thomas to Ralf. 'They were soldiers.'

'Soldiers, you say, my lord?' Thomas looked unsurprised. 'Aye, 'tis easy to believe in these woeful times. But whose?'

FitzAlan shrugged, earning himself an impatient cluck from Dame Sybil, who was trying to separate the bloodstained bandage from his arm with as little pain to her patient as possible.

'There's been no trouble in these parts,' Thomas continued, stroking his jaw thoughtfully. 'And further afield — well, 'tis only rumour. You recall what that minstrel told us some weeks back, Ralf? Where had he come from?'

'Further east,' supplied Ralf. 'There've been villages looted, men killed, women carried off — the usual tale of barons who do as they please while the King is helpless. I can't remember this particular fellow's name. Eudo. . .' Ralf broke off, shaking his head.

'What matter the name?' put in Dame Sybil. ''Tis all of a piece. Travellers stripped of their possessions and disappearing into castle dungeons, never to be heard of again. Towns pillaged and burned, crops razed to the ground, even Holy Mother Church defiled and mocked. There's no law anywhere in the land, nor will be until King Stephen is free and that woman packed off back to Anjou.'

She paused to examine Guy's arm, bending to sniff at the healing gash. 'No poisoned flesh,' she announced. ''Tis badly bruised, but a good, clean wound, my lord. You heal quickly, if I may say so.'

'Aye,' agreed fitzAlan non-committally. 'My thanks, Dame Sybil.'

'And mine,' added Isabel, finishing her broth and coming alive under the beneficial effects of warmth and food. She could act the loving spouse as well as fitzAlan, she decided, succumbing to a rare mischievous impulse to repay him for his earlier comments. 'He would not let me tend it properly before, stubborn man that he —'

FitzAlan took instant revenge by leaning forward and silencing her with a slow, gentle kiss. Stunned, Isabel could only sit there, ensnared by the caressing warmth of his mouth. And something else — a strange, almost seeking touch that made her tremble inside. By the time he drew back she was blushing, and completely incapable of further speech. She felt as though all her bones had melted and that everyone knew it.

Dame Sybil earned her everlasting gratitude by suggesting that it was time she retire. Unfortunately her attempt at a dignified exit was ruined by fitzAlan murmuring in a perfectly audible voice that he would not be long in joining her.

Cheeks still aflame, Isabel scurried up the stairs after her hostess, trying to ignore Dame Sybil's chuckles and the three grinning male faces behind her.

'If you give me your gown, my lady, I will have it brushed for tomorrow,' the kind woman offered, ushering Isabel into a tiny chamber containing a bed and a low stool. Sybil gestured to a wooden rod protruding from one wall for the hanging of clothes. 'I would lend you something of mine, were it not for the fact that everything I own would be indecently short. But if you sit here a moment, I will comb out your hair, and you may keep the comb. The brutes must have ripped the coif from your head to leave your hair so tangled. Ah, 'tis a sorry pass we are come to when a lady is robbed of the clothes on her back.'

'You are very kind,' murmured Isabel. She hadn't given a thought to her lack of coif; her mind was too occupied with trying to think of an excuse for remaining in her gown, and failing dismally. She handed it over, silently cursing fitzAlan for calling her his wife. Why couldn't he have said she was his sister — or even a cousin?

'You'll be going to join the Queen, I suppose,' remarked Sybil chattily, drawing the bone comb through Isabel's long hair. 'Poor, gentle lady. How she must fret for the King. Fortunate you are to have your man with you, my lady. Although 'tis easy to see that he could not leave you behind, nor take his eyes off you for a moment. You are not long married, I warrant.' She chuckled again.

'Not long,' repeated Isabel weakly. Not leave her behind? Not take his eyes off her?

'I knew it. And a strong, lusty young husband he must be, too.' She smiled and wagged the comb at Isabel. 'Oh, no need to colour up, my lady, when 'tis merely we women gossiping. You wouldn't think it to look at him now, but my Thomas was just such a one. Not so big as your man, but he was a comely-looking lad in his day, and kind of heart. We are fortunate, you and I; 'tis a rare combination in a man.'

'Aye,' agreed Isabel, bemusedly struggling to reconcile the description 'kind of heart' with her image of fitzAlan.

The mental exercise proved impossible. Arrogant, aggressive, autocratic. Those were the words she would choose, she decided vengefully, after Dame Sybil had tucked her into bed and returned to the hall. *And* mocking. Embarrassing her like that in front of everyone. Her cheeks burned again as she remembered the kiss and her utter submission to it. He hadn't even used force, holding her with nothing more than the subtle movement of his mouth on hers.

Turning over, Isabel pummelled the straw-filled pillow into a more comfortable shape. She was a weak fool — the pillow received another thump — imagining things when he had only been intent on silencing her.

Thump! Thump! Just as she had imagined that concerned endearment after the fight on the riverbank. She
must have been dreaming.

No! Don't think of that! Dreams were dangerous.
Better to remember that he had called her sweetheart
tonight, and it had been as much a sham as his kiss. If
she weren't so tired she would be angry with him, except
that it was difficult to remain angry with a man who had
saved her life.

Isabel laid her cheek against the abused pillow and
her eyelids drooped. No, she couldn't remain angry with
fitzAlan. She might tell herself he was arrogant and
aggressive, but she could not suppress another little
voice whispering that those very qualities went hand in
hand with others that drew her irresistibly — courage,
strength, utter dependability.

And, briefly glimpsed, in a place she longed to reach,
there still lay tenderness.

He heard the whimpering first.

Not really whimpers, Guy thought, holding the
candle higher as he entered the solar so he could see
Isabel more clearly. The sounds were those of a person
weeping and trying desperately not to be heard. She was
crouched in one corner of the bed, against the wall, her
knees drawn up, hands over her face, oblivious to his
presence.

Guy put the candle down on the stool and reached
across the bed. He'd been expecting something like this
since Isabel had killed the soldier. She had been on the
verge of hysteria then; add to that a day of travelling,
with him pushing Chalon as fast as the horse could go
carrying a double weight, plus the previous day's ten-
sions, and it was a wonder she hadn't given in to it. But
then he should have known that her courage was equal
to the task of remaining calm until she was alone.

A tiny shaft of surprise jolted through him at the realisation that, this time, he had imputed courage to Isabel's stoic control instead of calculated coldness. However, before he had time to dwell on the thought, another stronger jolt shook him when his fingers grasped her wrists and he pulled her hands away from her face. An icy chill slid up his spine, causing the hair at his nape to rise.

She was completely unaware of him. Her eyes were wide open, but they stared straight ahead, gazing in anguish at sights he couldn't even begin to imagine. Her soft lower lip was caught between her teeth, stifling the sobs that shook her body intermittently. She made no attempt to prevent him from taking her into his arms, gave no sign that she knew of his presence.

What had happened to her, to cause such torment to visit her in sleep? It had to be more than the trauma of the afternoon. As Guy gathered Isabel close to him, her words at the ford flashed into his mind. It was different, she had said. Killing someone was different from seeing it done. At the time he'd thought she was referring to his slaying of the two men-at-arms. But now he had to wonder what other deaths she had witnessed, what other acts of brutality.

And what was happening to *him*, that he felt torn apart, rent violently in two, at the sight of her agony?

This was no act. Though rigid with tension, she was totally acquiescent in his arms, still asleep, and gripped by God knew what nightmares. An unaccustomed feeling of helplessness washed over him. He didn't know whether to wake her, or even if that was possible if her sleep was so deep that she could crouch in a corner, weeping, and not wake herself.

Before he could decide, a shudder passed through Isabel's body and her lashes fluttered closed. He felt her lips move, warm against his throat. 'So dark,' she whispered. 'So dark.'

'No, sweet,' he answered very softly. 'The candle still burns.' He had hoped to waken her gently, but she drew in a small gasping breath. The little hand resting against his bare chest was suddenly ice-cold. Guy drew back so he could see her face. Her eyes were open again, but heavy-lidded now and dazed, unfocused. She was clearly exhausted and barely awake.

'What —— ?'

'Sssh,' he soothed, folding her closer as protectiveness flooded him. ''Tis all right, sweetheart. Go to sleep. You're safe now.'

'Safe?' It was a small, disbelieving whisper. She lay limply in his arms, those cloudy, fathomless eyes gazing up into his. Her next whimpered, broken words cut him to the heart.

'Where. . .were. . .you?'

Guy almost flinched. Did she know who was holding her? Were those words meant for him? She was looking straight at him, but. . .

Then her lashes closed once more, and Guy knew there would be no answers tonight. Her body relaxed against him in sleep and his arms tightened, supporting her instinctively. God, she was soft. Soft and small and hauntingly lovely. And he ached. Not only his injured arm, but his whole body throbbed with wanting her. He wanted to press his mouth to her softly parted lips and taste the sweetness within, he wanted to push aside the loosely tied neck of her shift and let his hand savour the warmth of her flesh, he wanted to lay her back on the bed and hold her against him as he had at the river-crossing; he wanted *her*.

With a careful movement at odds with the set grimness in his face, Guy shifted position so he could hold Isabel more comfortably. There would be no sleep for him tonight. Sleep was impossible while she lay in his arms like this, completely vulnerable. And twice as impossible while an insistent question, as tormenting as any nightmare, began to beat at his brain.

Despite all the evidence against her, despite her own words, her betraying silences, had he been wrong about Isabel from the start?

CHAPTER SEVEN

ISABEL awoke slowly, reluctant to abandon the warmth and safety of her snug nest of blankets. She had felt like this once before, and recently, she thought with sleepy vagueness. Secure and warm. Protected. Safe — with fitzAlan.

FitzAlan!

Full awareness and memory returned in a blinding flash. She remembered everything. *Everything*! Oh, not the details of the dream, but that didn't matter. The nightmare had once been real and the spectres visiting her in sleep were always the same. No, the picture tormenting her mind was of herself waking in fitzAlan's arms and *staying there*. Worse, she had fallen asleep again, cradled to the warmth of his body, after asking him why he hadn't rescued her!

Isabel almost groaned aloud. How was she ever going to face him again? He knew of her weakness. What was he going to do? What questions would he have this time?

She lay very still for a moment, trying to think. It was very quiet in the solar. Dared she hope that fitzAlan had already risen, giving her time to resume her protective mask? Holding her breath, Isabel slitted one eye open to encounter the crude, bare wall of the inn solar only inches away. She glanced down, to discover she was hugging the very edge of the mattress. Which meant that there was a lot of bed left to investigate before she knew if it was safe even to turn around. Listening carefully for any sound that might indicate fitzAlan's presence, she stretched out a cautious foot, ready to withdraw it immediately if she encountered so much as a hint of him.

Nothing. Exploring further, Isabel decided she was alone. Both eyes opened and her breath rushed out in a small burst of relief as she rolled over on to her back — and her heart slammed to a stop.

FitzAlan was sitting on the stool by the bed, back propped against the wall, arms folded across his chest, long legs stretched out in front of him, his brilliant light eyes fixed on her from under half-lowered lashes. Isabel wondered how long he'd been sitting there — intent, watchful, waiting. For a fleeting instant she felt as though she had woken to find herself in the lair of a dangerous wild animal. The wolf's lair, she thought. And he had her trapped.

Seeing that she was awake, fitzAlan sat forward, resting his forearms on his thighs, his eyes never leaving her face. 'Did you sleep well?' Somehow he made the softly growled question sound incredibly intimate.

Isabel swallowed nervously, pondering her answer as if the fate of the kingdom rested on it. Could she pretend not to remember last night? Would he believe her? People did forget dreams. FitzAlan had done so himself, except that his had been caused by fever and. . . Oh, blessed Saint Elizabeth, help me.

Not trusting herself to speak, she nodded.

'Good. How do you feel today?'

'Why?' The suspicious query slipped out before she could stop it. Isabel could have bitten her tongue when she saw one corner of fitzAlan's mouth kick up.

'You've endured a great deal, especially yesterday.'

'Yesterday?' Her eyes shifted to his mouth, staring in fascination as the smile deepened. Then, abruptly realising what she was doing, she wrenched her gaze back to his. 'Aye, yesterday!' she exclaimed accusingly, seizing on the distraction when his words finally got through the strange fog in her brain. 'I thought we were going to be killed, and you *enjoyed* it!'

The smile vanished, leaving fitzAlan's face shuttered, almost brooding. 'Action of some kind was long over-due,' he muttered cryptically.

What did he mean by that? Another vivid picture, this time of herself standing by the ford in fitzAlan's arms, insinuated itself into Isabel's mind. She had a distinctly uncomfortable feeling that he was not referring to the fight which had followed that little incident. And if he thought she had endured a great deal, why hadn't he mentioned her nightmare? Where was the barrage of questions she had expected?

A discreet tap on the door reminded her that they were not alone, thank the saints. She made a belated grab for her wits while Guy rose and went to answer the summons, exchanging a few murmured words with whoever was on the other side of the door.

When he turned back into the room Isabel saw he had her gown in his hand. He stopped a pace or two away from the bed and regarded her with an unexpectedly teasing glint in his eyes. Another smile played about his lips as he held out her dress.

'Time to rise, my lady wife.'

Not while he was standing there daring her with his eyes, Isabel vowed silently. She sat up, clutching the blankets to her breast and feeling faintly ridiculous when she recalled her lack of modesty in the hut. But everything seemed different this morning. Waking up to that penetrating ice-blue gaze was enough to throw *anyone* off balance for the rest of the day. Nor did she understand this new playful mood of fitzAlan's. The quick shifts from concern to curtness to mischief were confusing. And that lurking half-smile was doing pecu-liar things to her pulse-rate.

'I am not your lady wife, my lord,' she pointed out as

coolly as possible. 'And I do not intend to entertain you by dressing while you watch.'

FitzAlan tossed the gown carelessly on to the stool, where it promptly slithered to the floor. Isabel opened her mouth to protest at this cavalier treatment of her clothing, only to shut it again in alarm when he took a step forward and leaned over her, bracing his hands on the mattress and trapping her between them. She stared up into his blue eyes, trying to conquer the urge to scoot further up the bed. Apart from the need to preserve some semblance of pride, she knew such a retreat would cause her to lose her hold on the blankets.

'This new-found modesty is very admirable, sweetheart, but a little out of place when you've just spent the night in my arms.'

Isabel's eyes closed for a despairing second. She clutched the blankets even more tightly. 'I know we had to share a bed, thanks to your lies,' she corrected, valiantly trying to stave off the dreaded interrogation.

It didn't come. Instead, fitzAlan leaned an inch closer. 'For all I knew, the inn could have been full. You may not think so now, little one, but you were safer as my wife.'

Isabel turned her face away. 'That's a matter of opinion,' she muttered beneath her breath. Then, afraid he might have heard, she added waspishly, 'You mean you suspected I might run away. 'Tis what you thought in that hut, if you recall.'

'Then, perhaps,' admitted fitzAlan. 'Not now.'

This brief reply threatened to bring the argument to an abrupt halt. The distant sounds of the inn door being opened for the day sounded unexpectedly loud in the silence.

'Let me see your eyes.'

The low, husky command sent a shiver down her spine. 'No,' she whispered stubbornly, keeping her head to the side. She would not look around. Not while he remained so close that she could feel his warm breath against her cheek. But then, as the silence lengthened and fitzAlan still didn't move, curiosity got the better of her. 'Why?'

'Your eyes don't lie, sweetheart.'

Sweetheart? *Little one*?

Slowly, as though pulled towards him against her will, Isabel obeyed. And was instantly caught, imprisoned, by the warmth of his gaze. His eyes were like blue flames, she thought, drawing her irresistibly into his fire. She had forgotten all about her dream and its consequences.

'I thought so,' he murmured. 'I saw it before, and felt it last night when I kissed you. Something missing.'

'My virtue, I suppose,' snapped Isabel, fighting a losing battle against the treacherous weakness creeping over her. He was so big. So warm. She was melting inside. How could she feel like this when he wasn't even touching her?

FitzAlan's eyes burned fiercely into hers for another second, then he straightened, stepping back. 'The innocence I saw five years ago is gone,' he said calmly, 'and one day you're going to tell me how it happened. But that isn't what I meant.' His expression gentled and he gave her a slow smile filled with a conviction that was very male and utterly sure. 'Real experience hasn't taken its place.'

Isabel was so stunned that she nearly fell back on the pillows. Still gripping the blankets as if they were a lifeline, she stared back at fitzAlan, completely speechless.

He reached out a big hand and touched her cheek fleetingly with the backs of his fingers. 'Our breakfast is ready. I'll settle up with Master Thomas while you dress.'

And he was gone, leaving Isabel to gaze blankly at the wooden panels of the door while she cudgelled her brain, trying to decide what had caused such an astounding about-face. Surely not one brief nightmare. She remembered uneasily that he hadn't said a word about it. Perhaps he hadn't understood her last night. She had been all but asleep and possibly incoherent. But that left only one alternative—that fitzAlan was beginning to trust her. That he believed her story.

A quick rush of hope surged through her, only to be instantly squashed when Isabel remembered the treacherous reality behind the truth. She felt sick. Of what use was the truth, she asked herself bitterly, when it could so easily be turned against her? Aye, she had told fitzAlan that she wanted to leave Matilda—but the Empress had planned her escape. She had denied his accusations of betrayal—but would spy on the Queen. She might have saved fitzAlan's life—only to use him.

Of what use was the truth?

The truth was sometimes very simple, Guy decided, as he led Chalon over to the open doorway of the inn. Isabel had grasped the opportunity of his presence to escape from Gloucester.

Of course that didn't alter the fact that de Tracy had changed sides. Nor did it remove the niggling suspicion that Isabel was hiding something. Whenever her family had been mentioned she looked as guilty as hell. But he could handle that. She was not responsible for the actions of her male relatives. The real problem lay in convincing her that he could be trusted with her secrets.

Guy grimaced, remembering the way he'd been treating her. It wasn't going to be easy. However, he didn't have time now for self-reproach, nor to wonder why Isabel's seeming betrayal had cut so deeply that he had instantly thought the worst of her, had immediately accepted Matilda's word though he'd known how vindictive and spiteful the woman could be.

Isabel's personal integrity had been there in her clear gaze all the time, if he'd been thinking with his head instead of with his emotions. Integrity, combined with wariness, pride, and the kind of stoic endurance that accompanied an understanding of suffering, a loss of innocence that went as deep as the soul. But Guy would have staked his own soul on the fact that Isabel had never lain with a man.

The knowledge sent a fierce surge of possessiveness through him, which almost translated itself into violent action when he saw Isabel emerge from the inn with Ralf hovering attentively over her. The younger man's voice carried clearly across the small space separating them.

'Dame Sybil mentioned that you have no ribbon to fasten your braid, my lady. You will honour me beyond measure if you accept so small a token from one who is your humble servant.'

Guy's fist clenched involuntarily, but, fortunately, common sense reasserted itself. Much as he wanted to pound Ralf into the mud, he contented himself with sending the fellow a narrow-eyed glare which brought a look of respectful caution to the pedlar's usually cheerful countenance.

'You're very kind —— ' Isabel began uncertainly.

'But there's no need to throw away your wares for nought when business is so poor,' Guy interjected bluntly. He produced a penny, nicked at the side to denote its present value of a half-penny, and tossed it to Ralf.

The young pedlar cast him a wary glance and apparently decided on practicality over valour. He pocketed the coin.

Isabel, however, drew breath to argue. Before she

got a word out Guy seized her gently by the shoulders
and turned her around, so that he stood between her
and Ralf. He felt her jump slightly when he slid his
fingers beneath her braid. She started to move away,
lifting a hand to stop him. 'I can ——'

A careful tug on her hair silenced her. 'Keep still,' he
murmured, and bent to drop a warm kiss on the tender
nape of her neck before tying the ribbon. He had to take
a deep breath to stop himself tasting the delicate spot
again.

Isabel felt the kiss clear down to her toes. A dismay-
ing number of seconds passed before she could even
move. And then, as though determined to keep her in a
state of confusion, fitzAlan startled her again. Instead
of lifting her into the saddle first, as he had always done
before, he mounted Chalon, turned the horse in a tight
circle to present its left flank to Isabel, and extended an
imperative hand. One booted foot was thrust out for her
to use as a stirrup.

Isabel stared at that strong hand for several seconds
before lifting her gaze to fitzAlan's face. Piercing blue
eyes, full of masculine command, gleamed down at her.
She went very still, the sensation of being poised too
near the edge of a precipice sweeping over her again.
This was no mere offer of assistance, she saw. FitzAlan
was asking—no, *demanding*—something from her. It
was there in the challenging tilt of his head, in the
assertive reach of his hand. She had never felt the force
of his personality more strongly.

Yet he was giving her a choice, Isabel realised
suddenly. And it was not the option of walking behind
all the way to Winchester. He was sitting far enough
back in the saddle for her to mount without his help if
she wished to. He might demand, but he was not going
to force her.

That last thought prompted Isabel's decision. Placing her hand in his, she prepared to mount.

Something fierce blazed in his eyes for an instant. She saw the muscles in his thigh brace to take her slight weight, then his long fingers closed over hers, such overwhelming possession in his grip that Isabel gasped, suddenly, inexplicably, afraid, and tried to pull back.

It was too late. She was pulled upwards with startling velocity, the sensation of flying through the air causing the world to tilt so precariously that she found herself clinging to fitzAlan like a drowning woman. She stared into the handsome face so close to her, aware of his powerful body against hers with every fibre of her being, and all she could think of to say was a trembling, 'Does this mean your arm is better, my lord?'

He grinned down at her. 'Much better, sweetheart. Thanks to Dame Sybil's potion.' He nodded in the direction of the inn.

A tide of crimson flowed into Isabel's face when she hurriedly disentangled herself from fitzAlan and saw that Ralf had been joined by Sybil and Master Thomas, who had come to the inn door to wave them off. Ducking her head, she busied herself arranging her skirts comfortably, fighting embarrassment and wondering how she could have forgotten all about their audience.

And she had also forgotten the stern lecture she had given herself earlier, she thought despairingly. The lecture had kept her mind occupied all through breakfast, and had contained a great deal of sound advice on the best method of dealing with fitzAlan, which had not included embracing him as if he were in truth her husband. But with those powerful arms enclosing her she couldn't seem to remember a word of it. Indeed, she had scarcely enough presence of mind to return Sybil's bright smile and bid farewell to the genial innkeepers.

Surely fitzAlan had not held her so close yesterday? She was practically draped all over him. She should move away, or at least sit forward, but the horrifying part was that she *liked* it. His arms were strong, his body muscled and hard. Her blood seemed to flow swifter, hotter, in response. She felt soft and vulnerable, scared and—*excited*. Obviously she was losing her mind.

As Chalon responded to Guy's signal to start, Isabel tried to remind herself of fitzAlan's arrogant judgement of her, his mockery, his taunting insults, the frightening force of his anger. Not to mention his probable reaction should he discover the truth.

She repeated the list again. And a third time. Nothing changed. Instead, her stubborn mind persisted in remembering the unexpectedly lighter side he had shown at the inn. Her body persisted in leaning into his warmth, seeking his strength—almost as though it knew something she did not. Even her skin seemed to recall the touch of his hands, strong but tender.

The last sensation was unnerving to say the least. It was not until they had rounded a bend in the road, and the echoes of Master Thomas's good wishes had long since died away, that Isabel managed to pull herself together enough to recall her resolution to put fitzAlan at a safe distance—and keep him there. She had a task to carry out. A task which made her his enemy, not—

'Did you have to behave so churlishly with Ralf?' she burst out, saying the first thing to enter her head. 'He was only trying to help.'

'He was drooling all over you.'

Everything else was promptly pushed to the background. Isabel turned her head to stare up at fitzAlan incredulously. 'He was not!' she denied. 'How can you say such a thing?' Indignation showed clearly on her expressive face. 'Ralf isn't a *dog*! "Drooling", indeed!'

'Listen, my little innocent, I know what was in Ralf's mind.'

'By our Lady,' exclaimed Isabel, quite exasperated. 'He's only a pedlar.'

'That doesn't make him less of a man,' countered fitzAlan. 'Another smile like the one you were giving him and he would have been fastening that ribbon himself. And I don't want another man's hands on you,' he added in a soft growl that sounded incredibly dangerous.

'Really, my lord.' The protest came out weakly and Isabel strove to inject some firmness into her voice. It was difficult when she could hardly speak at all, but she couldn't let a statement like that go unchallenged. 'You do not have the right — '

'You gave me the right when you accepted my protection, sweetheart.'

'Don't call me that,' she said crossly, aware that she was becoming side-tracked. She should be firmly denying his claim to *any* rights where she was concerned, not arguing about his habit of using unsuitable endearments. 'Ralf meant no harm, and, in any case, there is no need to keep up the pretence that we're married.'

FitzAlan smiled down at her. 'I'll kill any man who touches you, Isabel. You had best keep that in mind.'

He might as well have knocked all the breath out of her body. The shocking contrast between fitzAlan's smile and the stark violence in his words turned Isabel's legs to water. She had to grip the saddle to prevent herself pitching forward on to the road.

What was happening here? Why this sudden show of possessiveness? It didn't make sense. Nothing made sense today. Even if Guy believed her tale, surely he couldn't change his opinion of her so completely? He had seemed to hate her, but now. . .

Now it was too late, Isabel reminded herself miserably. She could not let him get close to her. Already she was terrified of what lay ahead. How could she cope if fitzAlan was starting to like her? She must keep him away, keep fighting him, because as long as she fought with him she and Edmund were safe.

'There's no need to look so worried,' he observed softly, yanking Isabel back to the present. 'I know you would not behave dishonourably.' He lifted one hand to her mouth and gently freed her lower lip from between her teeth, soothing it with a stroking, caressing movement of his thumb.

Isabel's mouth went dry. She hadn't even been aware of gnawing on her abused lip. Now it tingled under fitzAlan's touch. Her whole body tingled. She couldn't speak, could not even think while his thumb was brushing back and forth across her mouth like that. His touch was feather-light and yet deeply compelling. She wanted to part her lips and ——

No!

Terrified that he would guess her wanton reaction to the heart-stopping touch of his hand, Isabel jerked her head away. FitzAlan slid his fingers into her hair, exerting just enough pressure to force her face back up to his.

Isabel knew her heart had ceased beating because now it shuddered into action again, racing so fast that she began to feel faint. She was unable to meet the intense look in his eyes, and her lashes fluttered wildly against her cheeks. His mouth was so close. Was he going to kiss her? A wild thrill of anticipation shot through her, shocking, frightening, exciting.

'Easy,' fitzAlan murmured, his voice like dark velvet. His hand slipped down to encircle her throat.

Did he think she was a horse that needed soothing? Isabel wondered, half angrily, half hysterically. His hand felt so warm, so strong, pressed against the frantic pulse beneath his fingers. She swallowed and knew he must be able to feel the betraying movement. What was he doing to her? *Why* was he doing it?

Then all coherent thought fled as fitzAlan's hand lowered further. His right arm was suddenly rigid, holding her still, at the same moment as that warm, strong hand brushed across the upper curve of her breast.

The contact lasted barely seconds. Isabel had scarcely felt the fiery rush of blood to her cheeks, the quick involuntary swelling of her flesh, before fitzAlan wrenched his hand away, transferring the reins from the other as if that was the only thing that would prevent him from touching her again. His free arm tightened further, pulling Isabel hard against him.

'Hush,' he whispered against her hair, although she had made no sound. ''Tis all right, sweet, 'tis all right.'

Still shocked, utterly shaken at his action, Isabel forgot all thought of fighting him. Turning her heated face into his chest, she shrank into fitzAlan's embrace, her hands clinging to his tunic for support. She was vaguely aware of the irony of seeking safety from the man who threatened a danger far greater than any she had ever faced, but she pressed closer — needing him, wanting him, longing for him to hold her forever.

A minute crawled by. The intensity of the moment was almost more than she could bear. FitzAlan's heart thundered against her cheek and his body was strung as tightly as her own, the arm around her like iron. Isabel started to shake, fear for Edmund maintaining its clutch on her mind, and an increasingly urgent desire to trust fitzAlan tearing at her heart.

Then a shudder went through him and his arm relaxed. She felt him glance down at her.

'You don't have to be afraid, Isabel,' he murmured softly. 'Tell me what troubles you. Trust me.'

'What do you mean?' she faltered, trying to summon the will-power to move. She wondered if fitzAlan had noticed that Chalon, taking advantage of his master's unusual inattentiveness, had stopped and was investigating a bush by the side of the road.

'I want to know why you left Gloucester,' stated fitzAlan. His voice was still gentle, but the iron will behind the question was unmistakable. 'The Countess of Anjou can't hurt you now. All you have to do is tell me the truth.'

For several seconds Isabel remained absolutely still. Then as the meaning of Guy's actions sank into her brain she pushed herself back, glaring up at him and quite unaware that her hands remained splayed against his chest.

'The truth!' she exclaimed, too hurt and angry to remember that he still had every reason to be suspicious. 'Is that what this little scene is about, my lord? Did you think I would fall straight into your arms, confessing everything?'

'I don't know,' Guy replied, a strangely crooked smile curving his mouth. 'Will you?'

'Why, you conceited, arrogant. . . I don't have anything to confess!' Isabel cried, her voice rising. She was so furious that she forgot that he had first asked for her trust. The humiliating knowledge that those tender, ardent caresses—indeed, his every action since she had awoken this morning—had been coldly calculated shattered her fragile composure in seconds.

Oh, how could she have let herself be so easily tricked, so eager to believe that he had changed? How could she have responded so instantly? And how dared he use such a method, and then have the gall to ask if it would have succeeded?

'I am not so easy a conquest!' she stormed. 'Does that answer your question, my lord? And you won't get any more answers out of me just because you started to. . . started to. . .'

'Make love to you,' fitzAlan supplied. There was an oddly grim note in his voice now, and all signs of humour had vanished.

'Love had nothing to do with it!' shrieked Isabel, almost beside herself with rage and shame. Suddenly noticing the position of her hands, she snatched them back, thrusting aside fitzAlan's supporting arm. Far from wanting him to hold her, she now wished to get as far from him as possible. Without stopping to think, Isabel leapt from the saddle.

The road was hard. She landed awkwardly, falling to her hands and knees. Small stones bit into her palms and an involuntary cry escaped her lips, to be quickly followed by another when fitzAlan's hand grasped her elbow. She had forgotten how fast he could move — he must have been off Chalon in seconds — but as soon as he hauled her to her feet Isabel began to struggle, swinging her free arm up.

Her hand was caught and held before it was anywhere near its target.

'Not this time, you little vixen,' he grated. 'Calm down before you hurt yourself again.' He started brushing the dirt from her hands.

Isabel tried to yank them free. 'I'm not hurt,' she spat. Then immediately ruined the effect of this proud statement by adding, 'You tried to use me,' in a choked, husky voice that betrayed all too clearly where the real hurt lay.

FitzAlan gave a short laugh and released her. 'Then perhaps we're even, my lady.'

Isabel stared up at him, momentarily silenced, her eyes stricken. She wanted to cry out in protest against his charge, but her throat was too tight to allow the words to escape.

FitzAlan made a slicing gesture with his hand. 'Isabel, I didn't mean that,' he began quickly. 'I only wanted. . . Oh, *hell*!' He turned away, raking his hand through his blond hair.

It looked more silver than gold on this dull, overcast day. How could she notice such a trivial detail when her vision was impeded by tears? Isabel asked herself. Worse still, she longed to reach up and smooth the ruffled disorder caused by his impatient gesture. She really was losing her reason. How else could he have the power to make her feel this way — angry and hurt and yearning?

Then fitzAlan turned back to her and the serious, searching expression in those piercing light eyes banished reason of any description. Isabel was very much afraid he was looking straight into her heart. Before she knew what she was going to say, the words were tumbling out, tripping over each other in her nervousness.

'I didn't use you like *that*. I couldn't. . .I've never. . . This morning you said you knew. . .'

'I do know,' he said swiftly. 'Isabel, I do know. I didn't mean to hurt you.' He lifted his hand to her face and caught an escaping tear-drop on the tip of one finger. 'Please don't cry,' he murmured. 'Why should you trust me, indeed, when I'm so clumsy with you?'

'I. . .I know I am in your debt,' Isabel stammered. His gentleness had her utterly confused. Was this wry contrition yet another ruse to weaken her defences?

He shook his head, still stroking her cheek softly. 'There are no debts between us, little one.'

With a supreme effort of will Isabel swallowed the lump in her throat and forced back her tears. Her mind raced like a deer before the hunter. Did she dare trust fitzAlan? He had claimed to believe in her innocence, but had not apologised for misjudging and insulting her.

He had started to caress her and had been enough in control to ask questions. Could a man feign desire to obtain the information he wanted? She didn't know, but she thought it might be possible.

Why did that conclusion hurt so much? The suspicion that fitzAlan might have cold-bloodedly used kindness, then seduction, for his own ends almost felt like a betrayal. But wasn't she about to betray *him*?

Isabel went cold. She stepped back, shivering slightly when fitzAlan's hand fell away from her face. Where had that question come from? It was the Queen she had to betray. Not fitzAlan. It couldn't be fitzAlan. It would destroy her to have to choose between Guy and her brother.

Sweet lord, what was she thinking? FitzAlan meant nothing to her. She was confusing him with her old dreams. And she could not sort out her brain while he stood less than a foot away, watching her with eyes that gave away nothing of his own thoughts. She had to get to Winchester. Then she could decide what to do. She wouldn't think beyond that.

'We had best be on our way, my lord,' she managed in a barely audible voice. 'Before we become objects of interest to the passing traffic.'

'There is no passing traffic,' he contradicted, frowning at her. 'Isabel. . .'

But, even as he spoke, two black-robed monks driving a small donkey-cart crested the hill ahead of them. Four men-at-arms rode alongside, and bringing up the rear was another monk herding a flock of sheep and goats. The Benedictines nodded genially as the procession clattered past.

FitzAlan looked after them, a wry smile slowly replacing the frown. 'I stand corrected, my lady.'

And, despite everything, a shaky smile tugged at Isabel's lips also. She couldn't help it. The prosaic sight of monks going about their everyday business, just when she needed them, was irresistible. But the smile lasted less than a heartbeat and vanished entirely when she saw that fitzAlan continued to watch the small party until it disappeared from view.

'What is it?' she asked, following the direction of his gaze.

He shrugged quickly. 'Nothing. I was just thinking there might be something to that tale Ralf told last night, if the monks need an escort to move their flocks.'

It was Isabel's turn to frown. A dim memory teased the back of her mind. She hadn't really been listening to the talk last night, but there had been — what? A word? A name? She shook her head, strangely uneasy, then the vague feeling that she had let something important slip through her fingers faded away when fitzAlan turned back to her. His eyes made a swift study of her face, before he cast a glance at the sky.

'Come. 'Tis beginning to look like rain again. The sooner we reach Winchester, the better.'

He spoke with such calm practicality that Isabel felt her resolve harden. She had been right not to trust him. Surely if that tense moment had affected him at all he would not sound so cool and distant now as he reached for Chalon's reins. He pulled the grey's head out of a bush and gestured to Isabel to mount. Without assistance this time. Isabel told herself she didn't care. She didn't need his help. She would rebuild her defences and cope alone, the way she had always done.

Guy led Chalon back on to the road, casting another searching glance up at Isabel's closed face. She had managed to squeeze herself into such a small space in the saddle that there was practically room left for *two* men. Two days ago the sight would have amused him. Now it only increased his determination to find out what had made her so wary, so controlled.

But her trust would not be easily won. He was going to have to move with extreme caution. Not a pace he usually favoured. Especially when he knew he could push aside her doubts by making love to her. The urge to do just that was almost overpowering, but he wanted Isabel to come to him willingly, not because he had taken advantage of her innocence.

Unfortunately the discovery that he could make her respond to even his lightest caress was enough to make the ride into Winchester a damned uncomfortable one. He might be able to force his mind to forget the way she had felt in his arms. His body was another matter.

Swinging himself into the saddle, Guy turned Chalon's head towards Winchester and began to consider the various means whereby he could ensure that Isabel belonged to him while he was giving her the time she needed.

CHAPTER EIGHT

WINCHESTER. Seat of England's rulers since before the coming of the Conqueror.

Isabel stared up at the royal castle high on its hill overlooking the town and wondered what the grim stone fortress would mean to her. Pennants fluttered in the breeze, indication that the Queen was in residence. A little distance away the spire of the old minster soared towards the clouds. Several shorter spires surrounded it, like chicks around a mother hen.

So many churches. How would she find the right one?

Anxiety fluttered deep inside her stomach, like thousands of tiny moths, but then they rode in through the north gate of the city and the clamorous bustle of the narrow, crowded streets assaulted her senses. It was like entering a whole new world, thought Isabel. She gazed, wide-eyed, at the first large town she had ever visited, for Matilda had not permitted her the freedom of Gloucester.

The noise was deafening. Street vendors called out the merits of their wares, shouting each other down in the hope of attracting customers from the goodwives who were out doing the morning marketing. The shrill tones of their voices mingled with the bawled instructions of a master mason, whose men were engaged in repairing the spire of a nearby church. Across the street a merchant cursed vociferously, shaking his fist aloft, as slops hurled from an upper room landed a scant inch in front of him.

Chalon picked his way nervously among the throng, tossing his head and splattering mud over the feet of

165

more than one unwary pedestrian who was too slow to get out of the way. Nobody seemed to mind, thought Isabel. Or, if they did, they knew better than to remonstrate with the grim-faced man behind her.

An unexpected pang lanced through her as she realised that after today fitzAlan would no longer stand between her and the rest of the world. She stifled it immediately, straightening her spine. Once she met the Queen she would not need fitzAlan's protection. She had managed without it before; she would do so again.

They turned into a quieter street where open shutters gave a view of craftsmen bent over worktables placed at the front of their shops to catch the best of the morning light. Silversmiths, goldsmiths and moneyers seemed to abound. One fellow was haggling with a customer over the price of a heavy silver buckle.

'Why do they all wear yellow?' queried Isabel, noticing the bright clothing along the entire length of the street.

'They're Jews,' fitzAlan told her. ''Tis their colour.'

'Jews? But do they all live here in the one street?'

'Aye. 'Tis near the castle since they're under the King's protection.'

'Why is that? Don't the townspeople like them?'

She felt fitzAlan shrug. 'Sometimes there's trouble.'

His voice had become more terse with each of her questions, and now his brief reply caused Isabel to fall silent. She wondered uneasily what was in his mind, but at that moment the main gate of the castle came into view and, as they started across the drawbridge, a new wave of apprehension assailed her.

Several buildings, showing signs of the recent siege, lay within the walls of the bailey, which was dominated by the huge stone keep built by the Conqueror. A whole street of houses had been demolished to make way for the edifice looming above her, Isabel vaguely recalled hearing. But then William had had to build the castle because he had permitted the defeated Harold's widow to remain in her own hall. Which just went to prove, she reflected, that there were two sides to every situation. Unfortunately, this conclusion didn't make her feel any better.

A loud hail from across the compound broke into her thoughts. With a start, Isabel saw that they were in the midst of the busy activity that characterised every large household. She watched, round-eyed, as several men-at-arms, pikes in hand, marched by on their way through the gate, and tried not to imagine herself a prisoner in their charge. Nearer, a plump, important-looking individual was tallying the stores being unloaded from a recently arrived wagon, and from the armoury came a steady clanging as the blacksmith hammered the dents out of the shield of a knight, who stood by watching.

And striding across the bailey towards them was a tall, dark man of about fitzAlan's age, dressed in businesslike chainmail and armed with both sword and bow.

'Guy! I expected you yesterday. How the devil did the Empress's messenger pass you? And you travelling across country. I would have thought ——'

The words were broken off abruptly when the man saw Isabel sharing the saddle with fitzAlan. Keen hazel eyes under black brows widened incredulously, before sparkling with a quick mischievous gleam. 'By every saint in the calendar! I don't believe it. You've been side-tracked by a woman. Wait until Joanna hears about this!'

'Put a gauntlet in it, Simon,' recommended fitzAlan, his apparent imperviousness to this gleeful threat restoring Isabel's stomach to its proper place. Although why it should have plummeted to her feet at the mention of the unknown Joanna, she could not have said.

'What's this about a messenger?' Guy continued tersely. 'And what are you doing here? Is the Bishop with the Queen?'

'Well, 'tis nice to see you, too,' replied his friend indignantly. 'Aye, the Bishop's within. The man won't step foot outside his castle without myself as escort, so I have to kick my heels until his business with Queen Matilda is done. I might as well move into the place.'

FitzAlan dismounted and reached up to lift Isabel to the ground. He made no attempt to present her to the other man, however, apparently so deep in thought that he seemed to have forgotten her very existence. Isabel didn't know whether she was relieved or affronted. All of a sudden several unpleasant consequences of spending a large amount of time alone with fitzAlan, without so much as a spit-boy for chaperon, rose forcibly to her mind. Unless Guy came up with an acceptable explanation, the entire Court would be gossiping about them. And she was supposed to remain inconspicuous.

Their companion cast them exactly the sort of curious glance Isabel had just been anticipating. 'As you may guess, his Grace's business is to do with the fellow who rode in here yesterday morning. I swear he must have ridden from Gloucester at the gallop to arrive before you. What's going on?'

'The Countess is covering her tracks,' murmured Guy. 'I can even tell you what her message says.' He looked thoughtfully at Isabel. 'So your warning was genuine also, my lady.'

'What warning?' demanded Simon instantly. 'What tracks? Will someone tell me what is going on?'

'Later,' returned fitzAlan brusquely. 'I have to see the Queen at once, and privately. Give me about ten minutes, then bring Isabel into the hall, will you?'

Before either of his listeners could reply to these curt instructions, fitzAlan shoved his reins into the other man's hands and strode off towards the forebuilding without another word. They continued to watch in stunned silence as Guy ran up the stairs and disappeared through the doorway, then turned to look at each other.

Isabel could not think of a single thing to say. The only words in her head were aimed at fitzAlan and they were quite unrepeatable. So much for explanations! Did he think she was invisible? And how dared he leave her standing out here in the bailey like a. . .like a *serf*?

Her escort seemed equally speechless, but he recovered first. 'Uh. . .Guy met you on the road?' he queried delicately, with obvious caution.

Isabel shook her head. She would never forgive fitzAlan for putting her in this position, she promised herself. Her scowl was furious enough to cause her companion to revise his original opinion.

'No, of course not,' he murmured hastily. 'I'm Simon de Villiers, by the way. Um. . .Isabel, is it?'

'Lady Isabel de Tracy,' pronounced Isabel clearly, finally retrieving her voice. If fitzAlan expected *her* to explain everything, he could cope with the truth, she decided angrily. It would be worth a little temporary gossip to see how he did it. 'My lord fitzAlan agreed to give me his escort from Gloucester. Unfortunately, in times such as these, a lady must accept whatever ill-mannered protection is available at short notice.'

A grin appeared unexpectedly on de Villiers' face. 'Guy can be a little abrupt,' he agreed. His bemused gaze shifted to the keep again. 'But I must say I've never seen him quite so ——'

'Rude?' suggested Isabel. 'Arrogant? High-handed?'

De Villiers made a noise in his throat that sounded suspiciously like smothered laughter. 'Something like that. I'll have to introduce you to my wife, Joanna. I seem to have heard her use several similar words when describing her brother.'

'Your wife is Guy's sister?' asked Isabel, in her curiosity not even noticing that she had used fitzAlan's given name.

De Villiers eyed her keenly. 'Aye. In fact, she's staying at Ashby Chase. 'Tis safer for a woman than Winchester at the moment.'

The wistful note in this last remark produced a slight smile from Isabel. 'You miss her.'

'Aye.' De Villiers grinned disarmingly. ''Twould not be so bad if I could get some work done so I could visit her now and then, but there's little chance of that with the Bishop running to the Queen every five minutes.' He heaved a sigh, which was instantly belied by the droll look in his eyes. 'On the other hand, if she were here I wouldn't get any work done at all.'

Isabel nodded, although her mind was only half on the conversation. The knowledge that fitzAlan had a family had come as a strange shock. He had seemed so solitary, so self-reliant. Again she realised how little she knew of him. Why, he, too, could have a wife somewhere. . .even children.

A black depression descended on her at the thought.

'No,' de Villiers said gently, with a shrewd glance at her face. 'He isn't married.'

'Oh. . .' If surprise hadn't made it impossible for Isabel to prevaricate, her quick blush would certainly have betrayed her. 'How. . .?'

'I've seen women look after Guy like that before.' He hesitated, looking uncomfortable, and appeared to pick his words carefully. 'Forgive me, Lady Isabel, if I trespass, but you seem to be alone here. Don't depend too much on fitzAlan. He will stay for no woman.'

'I take your concern most kindly, sir,' Isabel responded politely, if a little coolly. Hadn't she already given herself that very same advice? 'However, I can assure you I am in no danger of succumbing to my lord fitzAlan's rather blunt charms.' She thought of the way Guy had left her just now without a word of reassurance or explanation. 'No danger at all,' she muttered grimly.

'Aye, well——' de Villiers' expression was a comical mixture of relief, guilt and boyish appeal '—I'd best take you inside. I don't know why we're standing here for all these fools to gape at. Here boy. . .' An imperious wave of the hand summoned a serf to take fitzAlan's horse, and with another apologetic smile de Villiers began to guide Isabel over to the castle forebuilding.

'What makes you think I am alone here?' she asked him, relenting a little as they mounted the stairs. After all, he had meant well, and he certainly had better manners than that. . .that. . .

'If you had family or friends in Winchester, Guy would have taken you straight to them,' de Villiers answered, more at ease now. 'But no need to fear the Queen won't make you welcome, my lady. She's a kind soul. Not like that she-wolf in Gloucester. You're well out of that den.'

Isabel shivered suddenly. They had passed out of the daylight into the comparative dimness of the castle interior. She didn't know if it was the lessening of daylight, or Simon's mention of the Empress, but in a matter of seconds her entire body had become ice-cold, her hands and feet almost numb. The huge fire roaring in the hall beyond the small entrance chamber warmed her not at all. Indeed, the blaze did little to counteract the wintry draughts blowing into the room through the unshuttered windows, some strong enough to stir the heavy tapestries covering the stone walls.

Despite this chilly inconvenience, however, the place was crowded with people who all seemed to be talking at once. No one appeared interested in a new face,

Isabel was relieved to see. She was just one of the many
petitioners waiting for an audience with the Queen or
her sheriffs. Trestles were being set up along both sides
of the room, but only a few sombrely dressed ladies
were seated, the rest of the company apparently prefer-
ring to mill about in the centre of the hall.

Broken snatches of conversation wafted around
Isabel's head as she followed de Villiers around the
perimeter of the room, interspersed with the thunk of
wooden trenchers as the servants set places for the
midday meal.

'And I told him the mud in the high street was an
absolute disgrace. The bridges are meant to be kept in
good repair. My best shoes lost forever, and the fellow
only laughed. Wait until the Sheriff hears of this, I
said. . .'

'Not there, you dolt. The finger-bowl goes on the high
table. How many times. . .?'

'That hospital is nothing but a place for layabouts.
Aye, the lepers and beggars must have somewhere to
go, but why does it have to be on my front doorstep?
The Bishop started the hospital; let *him* live
alongside. . .'

'They say Stephen is failing. Not that anyone would
repeat that to the Queen, but. . .'

The sound of the King's name sent another wave of
ice water rushing through Isabel's veins. Her limbs
began to feel heavy; it was an effort to walk. She was
glad when de Villiers paused beside a colourful tapestry
depicting a hunting scene, to indicate fitzAlan crossing
the room towards them.

Somehow at the sight of him all her anger seemed to
vanish like the wisps of smoke wreathing up the great
chimney near by. Isabel found her eyes clinging to him,
his height making it easy for her to watch his approach.
She could not look away. He moved through the crowd

with that long, prowling stride, the aura of leashed danger about him causing other men to make way automatically. Aye, he was big and tough and sometimes he frightened her, but in a world that had suddenly become alien and dangerous he was her only security. She wanted to run to him, to feel his arms close about her, to forget treachery and deceit and the choice that was coming inexorably closer.

'The Queen will see you in her private solar,' he said without preamble when he reached them. 'Her counsellors will have some questions for you, then Matilda will speak with you alone.'

Isabel barely heard him, but she nodded. The voices buzzing all around them echoed in her ears. She felt as though she was going to be sick.

FitzAlan must have seen something in her face, because he took her hand briefly, his fingers tightening ever so slightly around hers in a gesture meant to reassure. 'I won't leave you,' he murmured. Then, louder, 'You'd better come too, Simon.'

'Did you think I was going to be left behind?' responded de Villiers cheerfully, his bright, interested gaze going from one to the other. 'I wouldn't miss this for the whole of Christendom.'

FitzAlan sent him a look that would have pierced armour at a hundred paces.

His brother-in-law remained unscathed. Grinning unrepentantly, he strode ahead and rapped on a door at the far end of the hall. A gruff male voice bade them enter.

And in that instant the harsh reality of her task hit Isabel like a blow to the head. The choice lay before her. No longer was it a plan calmly discussed from a safe distance. No longer was it something she could think about later. It was here. It was now. It was *real*. There was no going back.

Hands tingling with fear, hearing only the thundering of her heart, Isabel stepped over the threshold to confront the wife of the man who had once come to her aid, and whom she must now betray.

She couldn't do it. Even if fitzAlan had not been involved, Isabel knew she would have to find another way to save her brother, because she could not deceive the anxious, sweet-faced lady who was gently explaining her new duties.

'And I shall look forward to having you read to me, my dear, while you are with us. My ladies find it a sad chore since reading Latin does not come easily to them, and after a day spent poring over official parchments my own eyes ache so.'

Barely making sense of the murmured words, Isabel responded with a weak smile. It was the best she could do. The last hour had left her mentally exhausted.

The minute she had entered the room a grim, tense atmosphere had fallen over the Queen's solar. It had not been lessened when William of Ypres, the surly Flemish commander of the royalist army, had begun to question her extensively about the size and strength of the garrisons at Gloucester and Bristol, the state of the Empress's exchequer, the loyalty of her supporters, and whether Geoffrey of Anjou was planning an invasion of England to help himself to the throne by right of his wife.

With fitzAlan, de Villiers and a chastened but still influential Bishop of Winchester listening to every word, Isabel had answered as best she could in the hope that by doing so she might appease her conscience.

It hadn't worked. For one thing, she knew very little of the Empress's plans and had sensed Ypres's disappointment in her replies. He had also been extremely suspicious and had made no secret of it. In fact, if

Matilda's messenger hadn't carried a letter to the Queen explaining the 'unfortunate misunderstanding' that had resulted in Isabel's 'ill-considered' flight from Gloucester with fitzAlan's assistance, she was quite sure William of Ypres would have clapped her into prison until he had verified her story for himself. And when she realised that the messenger giving credence to her tale no doubt served the dual purpose of informing Rainald of her presence, Isabel felt wretched indeed.

Worse still, she had seen almost immediately that it would be the easiest thing in the world to listen for information. The two ladies in attendance on the Queen had been banished to a corner of the solar, where they sat talking quietly, half hidden by a carved wooden screen, but only the slightest effort would have been needed for either of them to overhear the interrogation going on by the fireplace.

It seemed that no obstacle at all stood in the way of the Empress's plans — unless Isabel were willing to sacrifice Edmund.

When the intensive questioning was at last over, fitzAlan had left with the other men, looking as stern and thoughtful as the dour Fleming commander. As she watched him leave, without so much as a glance in her direction, such a feeling of desolation had swept over Isabel that she had almost cried out. And now, battered by guilt and indecision, desperate half-formed schemes jostling themselves about in her head, she could scarcely summon the wit to listen with a show of attention to the Queen.

'But carrying on the business of the realm is the least I can do while the King is so wretchedly confined,' Matilda concluded.

'At least the Empress has agreed to the exchange of prisoners, madam,' faltered Isabel. She sat on a stool beside the Queen's high-backed chair, her hands

clenched tightly in her lap, eyes fiercely studying the fur-
trimmed hem of Matilda's crimson robe.

The warm colour suited the Queen, she thought,
daring a fleeting glance upwards at the softly rounded
face framed by a white veil. A simple gold circlet held
the veil in place, beneath which guileless blue eyes
shone with a gentle womanly strength. Between Matilda
the Queen and Matilda the Empress there was a world
of difference, Isabel reflected. This Matilda had shown
herself to be as resolute and intelligent as her cousin and
namesake in Gloucester, but had forgotten neither
compassion nor patience.

Isabel's eyes fell as guilt racked her again.

'Aye. And for that we owe you our thanks,' acknowledged Matilda, unwittingly turning the knife in her
listener's heart. 'If the Countess of Anjou had not been
so anxious to correct any false impressions we may have
had about your arrival the negotiations might have
dragged on indefinitely. The King's release is the last
thing she must desire.' The Queen sighed wearily. 'I
fear my cousin will never relinquish her claim, since she
is fighting for a position that she considers to be her
son's heritage as well as her own.'

'But surely an anointed king cannot be put aside,'
murmured Isabel.

'Not put aside, perhaps,' agreed Matilda, 'but never
given any peace while a rival cause serves the purpose of
every malcontent in the realm. Even a king cannot
please everyone, though, Our Lady knows, Stephen
tried. 'Tis why loyalty such as my lord fitzAlan's is so
appreciated. You did us a great service in warning him
of the threat to his life, Isabel. Why, even William was
forced to admit that his doubts about you were
groundless.'

Isabel shook her head. 'I cannot blame him, madam.

He has your safety at heart.' The words were almost whispered.

Matilda laughed unexpectedly. 'You mean he is a rough, unmannerly soldier who you feared would bring out the thumbscrews. But you answered his questions very well. I am sure William no longer thinks you've been sent here to poison my wine, or whatever dark thoughts he was harbouring.' She leaned forward and patted Isabel's hand. 'You must not mind his unpolished ways, child. The Flemings are not famed for their courtliness, but William's loyalty to Stephen is as beyond question as fitzAlan's. And as your own has proved to be.'

Every word flicked Isabel like a whip. No torture devised by William of Ypres could be worse than this, she decided, still not daring to raise her head. Oh, what was she to do?

'But I can see you are still troubled, my dear,' observed the Queen kindly. 'Can you not tell me what it is? Something you could not mention before the men, perhaps?'

Again Isabel looked up, into clear, sympathetic eyes that seemed to offer understanding and infinite tolerance. Her lips parted — trembling — as she hovered on the brink of speech. Here was her opportunity. All she had to do was tell the truth and she would be free. Free of guilt. Free of the fear of discovery.

And Edmund would die.

If only she had time. Time alone to think. Time to plan. *Time*. . .

The glimmering of an idea flashed into Isabel's brain.

Stammering, feeling her way, she prayed for inspiration. 'Perhaps they would not understand, my lady, being men and accustomed to. . .' She hesitated, took a deep breath, and plunged on. 'You see. . .yesterday. . . there was a fight, and ——'

'Ah, so fitzAlan explained,' interposed Matilda. 'But surely the soldier's death was by his own evil hand, Isabel. I will never believe you killed a man purposely, and nor will our most merciful Lord. A dreadful experience, to be sure, but you must put any thought of blame from your mind.'

'And so I would, madam, if I could but confess,' suggested Isabel tentatively. 'I even know of a priest. . . at St Mary's Church. . . I once knew him. . .' Her voice died away as she resisted the urge to cross herself against the lie.

Matilda looked doubtful. 'I don't know, child. Not that I would prevent you from confessing,' she added hastily. ''Tis just that the town is no place for a lady at this time. My own confessor would absolve you, but he has taken alms and clothing to the hospital and, if I know Father Selwyn, will no doubt spend some time there, helping out. . .'

'Perhaps an escort,' hinted Isabel, worried that Matilda was going to suggest she wait for the good father's return. 'A serf, or maid, or some such person.' The rider was tacked on as hurriedly as Matilda's had been. The last person she needed was fitzAlan, but an attendant of humble rank wouldn't matter, if it helped her to obtain permission to go into the town. And she sensed that the Queen, a deeply pious woman herself, did not like to deny her new lady's apparent need for immediate absolution after killing a man, albeit accidentally.

A flicker of hope stirred to life, although it was accompanied by a shiver of horror, as Isabel saw the evil hidden once again behind the truth. The conspirators at Gloucester could not have planned the soldier's death, of course, but still she shuddered. It was a chilling thought that the very circumstances she was using for her own purpose accorded only too well with the Empress's schemes.

Matilda's face had cleared. 'Of course,' she exclaimed. 'A maid. I was going to arrange for one to attend you anyway.' Suddenly animated, she clapped her hands to summon her ladies.

It was odd that she would have her own servant, Isabel mused vaguely. This was a very different place to Gloucester, where the Empress's ladies were virtually servants themselves, but in the flurry of introductions and orders for a place in the ladies' chamber to be made ready for her Isabel forgot about comparisons. Nothing seemed quite real. It was as though she had become two people. A shadowy image of herself stood there, nodding and smiling shyly, while the real Isabel remained in the cold, lonely place she had inhabited for so long and grimly decided that the first step was almost accomplished.

The Empress would receive word that she had made contact with Rainald, which would stay her vindictive hand for a while. If she could then convince Rainald that it might be a few days before she was granted another opportunity to meet him, and if she could discover how many spies the Empress had in Winchester, the precious time gained might be used to save Edmund. She was not sure, yet, how that might be accomplished, but at least she would have won a reprieve. And then——

'Lady Isabel will be staying with us for a short time. Pray you, Judith, pick out a likely girl to serve as her maid, and, Eleanor, fetch some of my gowns. She must look her best for my lord fitzAlan.'

This jerked the real Isabel back to the Queen's solar with a vengeance.

'But madam, I am here to serve you,' she began, belatedly hearing these commands. Matilda was speak-

ing as though she was a guest, she realised, startled.
And what did fitzAlan have to do with gowns?

'And so you shall, child.' Matilda barely paused in her
instructions to voice the smiling assurance. 'Don't forget
a cloak, Eleanor. The red woollen mantle with the hood
will be the most suitable, I think.'

Isabel could only watch helplessly as Lady Eleanor
was set to scurrying back and forth between the solar
and the Queen's wardrobe. Gown after gown was
brought out and held up to her. And when Matilda
finally pronounced in favour of a close-fitting robe of
soft, unbleached linen, worn under a blue velvet over-
tunic, laced at the sides to show the garment beneath,
and trimmed with soft grey vair, her protests had quite
died away. What girl could resist the lure of the first new
clothes she had possessed in years? At Matilda's insistence she tried on the gown then and there, even
forgetting her tattered shift until her old dress was
whisked away.

'Merciful saints!' uttered Matilda. 'You can't wear
that! Quick, Eleanor, fetch a clean shift at once.'

The door shut behind the hapless Lady Eleanor again.

'I needed something to bind my lord fitzAlan's arm,'
explained Isabel weakly, feeling compelled to offer an
apology for the indecent state of her underclothing.

However, Matilda didn't appear unduly shocked,
despite her horrified exclamation. 'So he said. 'Twas
regrettable, of course, though you obviously had little
choice but to abandon modesty when the need was so
imperative. And no need to fear that anyone outside
this room will learn of it, my dear. FitzAlan is a man of
honour, and would never let the slightest hint of gossip
touch you.' She smiled at Isabel. 'Tell me, child, what
do you think of him?'

This unexpected rider took Isabel by surprise. 'What
do I think of him, madam?' she repeated, nonplussed.

'Why. . .I. . .I. . .don't know. I hardly know him. That is, we were together only a short time, and. . .' She stopped, aware that she was stammering like an idiot, and yet quite at a loss. Words didn't seem able to describe the confusion of her feelings for fitzAlan.

'My lord fitzAlan gave me his escort to Winchester,' she tried again, cautiously. Was the Queen about to warn her in much the same way as Simon de Villiers had done? She was beginning to wonder if fitzAlan was in the habit of leaving languishing females behind him wherever he went. 'There was nothing more between us than that. I mean, we didn't. . .he didn't. . .' she faltered, not at all sure she was telling the exact truth.

'Faith, child! I know that,' expostulated the Queen. 'I merely wished to know if you. . .well, if you like him.'

'Like him?' echoed Isabel. Could anyone apply such a bland, woefully inadequate word as 'like' to fitzAlan? she asked herself bewilderedly. He had made her angry, afraid, excited. She had felt alternatively vulnerable and safe with him. But *like*?

Isabel found herself staring at Matilda's kindly face, completely at a loss.

'I see I have you thoroughly perplexed,' the Queen said, laughing. 'Forget I asked, my dear. I am sure Lord fitzAlan is more than capable of conducting his own affairs without any well-intentioned assistance from me.'

The return of Lady Eleanor with a pile of fine linen shifts scarcely registered with Isabel as a rapid succession of images flashed through her mind: fitzAlan confronting the Empress with that cold, relentless logic; wounded and feverish in the hut, but still in control of both her and the situation; swinging his sword with savage, deadly grace at the ford; leaning over her at the inn this morning; holding her. . .

'Of that I have no doubt, my lady,' she muttered, determinedly quelling that last thought. 'But why ——'

''Tis nought, my dear. Merely, I have a great kindness for fitzAlan and would see him happily. . . But I go too far and too fast,' Matilda broke off to amend hastily. 'Think no more of it, I pray you, except ——' she paused in the act of motioning Isabel behind the screen, and this time her smile was one of pure feminine conspiracy '—do not dismiss him as another rough, unchivalrous soldier, Isabel. He has known little but fighting these last few years, but I think, with the right woman, he could be as gentle and tender a knight as any girl could wish for.'

It was fortunate, Isabel decided, that the screen shielded her from curious eyes as she changed her shift. She could feel heat searing her cheeks, and a strange trembling seemed to have seized her hands, making her fumble with the ties at the neck of the garment. What had fitzAlan told the Queen? What was Matilda telling her?

Nothing made sense any more. Words and pictures spun around behind her eyes with a speed that made her head start to ache. Edmund. . .Rainald. . .fitzAlan. . . the Queen. . .de Villers' advice. . .what to choose. . . whom to trust. . .whom to believe. . .

Weak and dizzy, Isabel slumped against the wall, wishing she did not have to move. The images swirled and danced in her head like figures around a maypole. Voices echoed in her ears.

'*It won't be forever, Isabel. One day I'll be old enough. . .*' '*He'll be waiting at the church for you, every day for an hour between noon. . .*' '*Why should you trust me, indeed. . .?*' '*as gentle and tender a knight. . .*' '*He will stay for no woman. . .*'

She could not bear it. She had to clear her mind. She had to think only of the next few hours. She had to be calm and distant just once more. Just one more time, Isabel told herself, straightening, just enough to get through the meeting with Rainald. Especially, she must not think of fitzAlan.

'Ah, here is Judith and your new maid.'

The Queen's voice came from a great distance. Her maid. Another person to whom she must speak, at whom she must smile, with whom she must pretend.

Stepping from behind the screen, Isabel schooled her features into an expression of remote serenity. From that cold, emotionless void she watched herself speak kindly to the young girl introduced as Ellen, thank the Queen for her great kindness, beg to be excused from dining in the hall on the grounds of wishing to find her priest as soon as possible, and resolutely put all thought of fitzAlan out of her mind.

After all, he had left without a word to her. His task was done. He had delivered her safely to Matilda. There was no reason for him to see her again.

He was waiting for her in the hall.

The instant she saw him, leaning with careless masculine grace against the wall, Isabel's throat tightened. His head was bent slightly, listening intently to Simon de Villiers, who was speaking rapidly, and he was frowning. The frown gave a ruthless edge to his handsome face, as though the leashed danger in him had moved nearer to the surface, was more visible. She wondered what the two men were talking about.

Then fitzAlan looked up and saw her, and the hard look of danger vanished. A smile flashed into his vivid blue eyes, warming them instantly. Isabel felt the barriers around her heart shake. Not yet, she told herself desperately. Not yet! She had to meet Rainald first, she had to gain some time for Edmund, she had to——

'All right?'

Isabel blinked, coming back to her surroundings with
a start. Simon had disappeared into the crowd still
milling about the hall, and fitzAlan was standing before
her. He had asked her something.

'Are you all right?' he repeated.

When Isabel only nodded silently, he glanced at
Ellen, hovering behind her new mistress. 'Where is my
lady housed?'

Ellen dropped an awed curtsy, rounded eyes gazing
up at him over the pile of red woollen mantle in her
arms. 'In the ladies' solar in the south tower, my lord.
We were on our way there.'

'I will escort Lady Isabel.' A quick smile softened the
brief statement. 'Run ahead and make ready for her.'

'Aye, sir.' Flushed and eager, emboldened by
fitzAlan's smile, Ellen prattled on. 'The Queen has said
that my lady shall have a place in the bed. No mere
pallet for her, and——'

FitzAlan gently stopped the excited flow. 'That is
excellent. . .' He paused interrogatively.

'Ellen, sir, if it please your lordship.' The girl curtsied
again before scuttling off down a nearby passage.

Everyone from the Queen to the servants thinks he's
wonderful, thought Isabel, and a flash of awareness
rippled through her. A sense of urgency, of impending
loss, of. . .

But fitzAlan spoke again before she could pin down
the feeling.

'I believe you and Simon exchanged some rather
uncomplimentary views about my deplorable manners.'
His blue eyes twinkled down at her with sudden,
unexpected mischief and he offered her his arm. 'Allow
me to make amends, my lady.'

'Oh. . .' Confused, flushing as though she had been
found out in some guilty action, Isabel tentatively let

her fingers rest lightly on fitzAlan's arm. Heat flowed over her, turning her bones to water. When he started down the corridor Ellen had taken she was surprised that her legs still functioned.

'The thing is,' he murmured, sending her a smile that managed to be wicked and appealing all at the same time, 'I'm so used to trusting Simon completely that I forgot you didn't know him at all.'

How could she resist him when he was like this? No woman could, Isabel thought. The combination of sheer male power and boyish devilment was too seductive. She glanced up at him, feeling oddly shy, almost as though she were meeting him for the first time with no doubts, no mistrust, between them. 'I think I understood that,' she whispered, admitting, 'I trusted him, too.'

It was the truth, she realised. Though she had been angry with fitzAlan, she would not have blurted out the bare facts to just anyone.

'I hope that means I'm forgiven.'

'Of course,' Isabel managed. Her pulse fluttered. Even barely touching him, she could feel the taut power of the muscles beneath her hand. His strength was compelling, drawing her closer until their bodies almost brushed with every step. The resulting sensations had the strangest effect on her thinking processes, she discovered. She didn't even seem capable of taking note of where they were going. They had reached a short flight of stone steps leading down to an open door, and she had no idea of how they had arrived there.

FitzAlan stopped just out of earshot of the room, his free hand covering Isabel's before she could remove it. 'I have to leave you now,' he said. 'Tell Ellen to bring you something to eat. I don't want you dining in the hall unless I can accompany you, and I'll be busy at Wolvesey Castle with Simon until this evening.'

'As you wish,' Isabel replied vaguely. She was so busy absorbing the knowledge that fitzAlan would be safely occupied for the rest of the day that she only belatedly heard the possessiveness behind his instructions. Looking up, she saw his brows lift in amused surprise at her meekness, and added hurriedly, 'But I must attend the Queen some time, my lord. You need no longer feel an obligation——'

He stopped the words with a gentle finger against her mouth. The finger was removed almost immediately, but not before Isabel had felt the throbbing pulse against her lips. She could not have spoken if her life depended on it.

''Tis no obligation, sweet lady,' he said very softly. 'You are under the Queen's protection now—for a little while.' Gazing down into her eyes, he raised her hand to his lips and pressed a lingering kiss into the soft palm before releasing it. 'Until this evening,' he said huskily, and turned to go back the way they had come.

Isabel stared after him, gripped again by that frightening sense of loss. She watched fitzAlan walk away from her and saw him walking out of her life, saw the final destruction of a young girl's dream that her mind had rejected and yet her heart could not relinquish. She didn't understand it. She had made the right decision to first appease Rainald. Why this terrible fear that it could all go horribly wrong, that a dream was all she would ever know?

Without giving herself time to think, Isabel called out Guy's name, and began running after him.

He stopped halfway down the passage, whirling about to meet her. Even in the dim light of the narrow corridor Isabel saw the flash of some powerful emotion in his eyes. Unaware that she had called him by name for the first time, she halted, still some feet away, gazing at him uncertainly.

'I just. . .I wanted to thank you. . .' she began, not really comprehending why she was so reluctant to let him go. Then, as Guy reached her in one long stride, it no longer mattered. This was her knight. The man who had fought for her, who had killed to protect her. If he wanted to claim her, she was his. For this brief moment in time nothing else mattered. Lifting her hands to his shoulders, she raised herself on tiptoe and brushed her lips across his cheek.

His arms closed around her instantly, fiercely possessve as he pulled her against him. Isabel didn't have to wonder this time if he was going to kiss her. Intent blazed from his eyes, tautened the strong lines of his face. His mouth descended on hers, hungry, demanding, almost frighteningly rough in his unhidden need.

Overwhelmed by the force in him, trembling with the intensity of her own response, Isabel parted her lips, whimpering in feminine submission and an equally feminine fear of the total surrender he was wrenching from her. Instantly he gentled. One hand came up, cradling her face as he slanted his mouth over hers, softening the demand and yet deepening the kiss with a tender seduction that was as devastating as his initial urgency.

When he lifted his head minutes later Isabel was completely helpless in his arms. She clung to him, dazed, her heart pounding, her breath coming raggedly from between slightly swollen lips, her legs barely supporting her. Her lashes fluttered open to meet fitzAlan's darkened eyes mere inches away. The stark desire in his face threatened to take what strength she had left, nor did he make any attempt to hide the blatant response of his body to that consuming, passionate kiss, continuing to hold her so tightly that she could feel him with every part of her being, could still taste him inside her mouth.

Then very slowly he put her a little away from him,

his hands holding her steady until he was sure she could stand alone. He drew in a shuddering breath. 'Don't ever doubt that I want you, Isabel,' he said, his voice so hoarse that the words sounded as if they were torn from deep inside him. His eyes burned into hers. 'Don't ever hide from me.'

He put out his hand, as though he would touch her again, then turned quickly and walked away.

The hectic flush on Isabel's face gradually faded as she watched fitzAlan leave. She was still trembling, tiny aftershocks of excitement tingling inside her. If he had set out to prove that the passionate interlude on the road this morning had been genuine on his part he had certainly succeeded. In his arms all her doubts on that score had been obliterated.

But men wanted women all the time. It didn't mean anything. How could she have forgotten that? Isabel moved restlessly as bitter memories engulfed her. She had forgotten the dreadful price her own sisters had paid for that male greed and self-interest. As in that night in the hut, she had been conscious only of fitzAlan and the wild sensations he aroused in her. And she had not been half asleep and dreaming this time.

Isabel put her fingers to her lips. Her mouth felt soft and pliant; her lips still throbbed. She wanted to tell herself that fitzAlan had taken her by surprise again, but she could not. And he had not been brutal or selfish. He had sensed her fear of yielding to a man's passion and had reined in his desire immediately. Nor could she get his last words out of her mind. 'Don't ever hide from me'. Was she a fool to hope there had been a deeper meaning in that fierce command?

Impatience, knife-edged and turbulent, gripped her body. She wanted it over with. She wanted it done. Until she met Rainald she could not think of a future, with or without fitzAlan. Somehow she must discover the extent of the threat to Edmund's life. And tonight. . .

Sudden resolve flowed over her, calming her, restoring her strength. Tonight she would see fitzAlan again. He would be with her. Tonight she would tell him everything.

CHAPTER NINE

'ARE you sure the Bishop's castle is at the other end of town?' Isabel asked Ellen for about the tenth time. She picked up her skirts to avoid a particularly noisome pool in the road and wished they could move more quickly.

FitzAlan and Simon de Villiers were the only people in Winchester who knew her, but she still could not banish a feeling of trepidation at being on the high street in broad daylight. She had to resist a constant urge to glance back over her shoulder to make sure they were not being followed, although she had given fitzAlan enough time to be well ahead of her before starting out.

Ellen halted at a short wooden bridge, one of many which spanned the streams dissecting the main road through the town. 'Aye, my lady. Look, you may see it past the abbey.' The girl pointed eastwards, where a brightly coloured pennant could just be seen beyond the abbey's spire.

As the two girls stood there, Isabel dubiously eyeing the rickety-looking structure at her feet, a wagon rumbled to a stop behind them, filled with women. One raggedly clad individual shouted an incomprehensible greeting, cackling shrilly when Ellen quickly pulled Isabel away so the cart could proceed over the bridge. The driver yelled an order for silence over his shoulder and flapped his reins.

'Your pardon, my lady,' apologised Ellen, 'but we don't want those dreadful creatures following us all the way down the street.'

'Who are they?' Isabel whispered, eyes round with curiosity.

'Harlots,' replied Ellen repressively, waiting until the wagon was some distance ahead before stepping on to the bridge.

'But why are they in that cart? Where are they going?' Isabel persisted. The women had been crammed together like animals, she thought.

'Every few months they're rounded up and driven from the city,' explained Ellen. 'It doesn't seem to matter, though. They always come back.'

Isabel was silent, unable to share Ellen's seeming indifference to the women's fate. She knew all too well by what circumstances a woman could be forced into using her body as a means of ensuring survival for herself or her family.

She shivered as a stray gust of wind whistled around the corner of a side-street, averting her eyes from the shadows cast by the encroaching house frontages. The upper storeys of the dwellings leaned out over the street, giving them a drunken appearance, and the dim caverns beyond the light of the high street seemed to Isabel to mirror the dark side of this city of churches. Evil behind the truth everywhere, she thought.

'Here we are, my lady.' Ellen's voice broke into her grim reflections. 'The church of St Mary.'

Isabel looked at the small stone building in front of her, then glanced up and down the street. It was almost deserted. A group of people were gathered at a mill two blocks away. Opposite, the fields of the abbey stretched to its grey stone walls. Several young boys were racing each other across the open expanse, leaping and shouting, and from the abbey itself the voices of monks chanting the noon office rose on the air. No one was near enough to accost her or wonder about her presence. The hour had been well chosen.

Drawing in a deep breath, Isabel pushed open the door. 'Wait here for me,' she said quickly to Ellen as the other girl began to follow her. She slipped into the church before her maid could protest.

Peace and quiet surrounded her. As her eyes adjusted to the muted light, Isabel saw that the walls had been limed to the height of a man, and that the windows were glazed, shutting off all sounds from outside. Rows of simple wooden benches drew her gaze towards the altar, where candles burned beside a tall, plain wooden crucifix. The place was empty, but for a cloak-shrouded figure bent over a rosary to the right of the door, and a man sitting alone in the front row. The latter turned his head as the door shut behind her, coming to his feet and raking her with a glance that was both sharp and insolent.

The church was tiny. Only a few steps brought him to within feet of her. He was short but built like a bull, with a thick neck and heavily muscled shoulders. Isabel wiped her suddenly damp hands on her gown. 'Rainald?'

'Lady Isabel.' His voice was harsh, uncultured, the slight emphasis on the 'Lady' definitely mocking. 'Torold's description didn't do you justice.'

Isabel went to speak again, but he motioned her to silence, his eyes going to the figure shuffling towards the door. Enveloped by the cloak, it was impossible to tell if it was male or female, but the worshipper had evidently finished praying. The door whispered shut.

'Probably just an old peasant,' Rainald said, 'but 'tis better to be careful. You have news for me?'

'Not yet,' she whispered, and cleared her throat. She had to be firm. 'We only arrived today and——'

'We? You mean Lord fitzAlan? Is he a danger to us?'

'No.' Isabel swallowed nervously. 'I don't think he suspects me any more.'

'You don't *think*?' Rainald's small black eyes narrowed maliciously. 'You had better make sure, lady, or I send a message direct to Tracy.'

'No, please. . .' She stopped. Pleading would not work with this creature. She must be firm. 'I'll co-operate. But I'll need some time. I can't leave the castle every——'

Her halting explanation was cut off short. Behind her the door crashed open, flung against the wall with a force that rattled the windows and sent the candles flickering wildly. With a half-stifled cry, Isabel spun about.

And there, framed in the open doorway, long legs braced apart, blazing eyes flashing from her to Rainald and back again, stood fitzAlan.

For a moment there was utter silence. No one moved. At the edge of her vision Isabel could see Ellen peering fearfully around fitzAlan's arm. There was another man behind her, a stranger.

Then very slowly fitzAlan advanced into the church. Isabel could see the tension in his body, feel the waves of fury vibrating from him. The very air seemed to be alive with his anger. How had he caugbht her so quickly? She had been sure he had already left the castle before she and Ellen had ventured into the town.

The useless question had no sooner formed in her mind when Rainald moved. The instant fitzAlan was free of the doorway he was through it, shoving Ellen roughly to one side and racing into the street. The man standing beside Ellen moved to go after him, but fitzAlan turned on him.

'*No!*

'Let him go,' he added more quietly. 'He won't get far. I've sent orders for the gates to be watched while Simon's men round up the rest.'

Round up the rest? It sounded like the harlots, Isabel

thought hysterically. Then wondered what she was thinking of. They didn't need her. Edmund did!

Jolted into action, she sprang forward and grabbed fitzAlan's sleeve, almost shaking his arm in desperation. 'You can't let him go,' she screamed. 'You ——'

'*Quiet!*' FitzAlan turned on her, flinging her off as if she carried the plague. 'Not one word out of you!' he roared. 'Not one word!'

The savagery in his face was such a horrifying contrast to his recent ardour that Isabel shrank back in terror, stumbling over one of the benches. She half fell, half collapsed against it, unable to stop the tears of fear and anguish pouring down her face.

Failed. . .failed. . .failed. The word repeated itself over and over in her head like a death knell.

FitzAlan ignored her. Glancing back at the young man waiting in the doorway, he gestured impatiently to Ellen. 'Take this girl back to the castle,' he ordered tightly. 'And wait for me there.'

'Aye, sir.' Casting an unreadable look at Isabel, the boy obeyed, taking Ellen by the arm and urging her away from the church. Isabel could hear her maid's protesting voice fading into the distance.

'Get up!'

It was fitzAlan, looking down at her with eyes that ripped her heart into pieces, speaking to her in a voice so hard that the words were like blows. Where was the man who had held her — kissed her. . .?

'You don't understand,' she pleaded, nearly sobbing with despair. 'My brother ——'

FitzAlan reached down and yanked her to her feet. 'Your brother?' he snarled, his grip merciless. 'Are you going to tell me that he holds his castle for the Empress and won't take you back?' He laughed mirthlessly. 'My God, you're good, I'll give you that. Even after what I just learned I couldn't believe you've been lying to me since we met — that I was coming back to ask you ——'

He bit off the next words with an oath and pushed her away. Turning, he reached the church door in two steps, grabbed it, and slammed it shut. There was so much enraged violence in the action that Isabel knew she had missed being hurled across the church by that powerful arm only because of fitzAlan's self-control. Her terrified eyes gazed at him as she stood with his back to her, both hands braced against the door, staring at the ground between his feet.

'Ask me what?' she quavered. Anything was better than the terrible silence that had fallen.

He turned around slowly, moving like a man in pain. That last ungovernable action must have hurt his arm, she thought distantly.

'I had my answer before I entered this church,' he bit out. A muscle jerked in his tanned cheek. 'There was an old peasant in here when you arrived, was there not?'

Isabel's lips parted. She couldn't speak, but the answer was there in her horror-stricken eyes.

A mirthless smile, more like a grimace, twisted fitzAlan's mouth. 'Aye, you saw him. More to the point, he saw you. Heard you greet a known spy by name and heard him acknowledge you.' His voice had roughened, growing harsher with every word, but now it dropped to a flat monotone. 'You left your maid in the street to no purpose, my lady.'

'You know Rainald,' Isabel murmured dully. It wasn't a question. What use were questions now? He had told her the one thing of importance, even if nothing else made any sense. She and Edmund had been doomed from the start.

'We know him. And the rest. A cosy little nest of vipers sent here by that bitch you serve. That peasant was one of Simon's men. We've been watching them for weeks.'

'And now?' As if she didn't know.

'They'll be hanged.'

'Hanged,' Isabel repeated almost to herself as she worked it out. 'The Empress will hear nothing, and. . .' Her eyes lifted to fitzAlan's. 'You don't know what you've done,' she whispered brokenly, tears running unheeded down her cheeks. 'Edmund. . .'

The name seemed to act on fitzAlan like a goad. His right hand shot out and snapped around Isabel's arm. All feeling left the limb, but she didn't struggle. Perhaps the rest of her body would become lifeless, too. Then she wouldn't have to see or hear. . .

'Don't use your brother's name to save your neck,' he grated in a voice she barely recognised. 'God's teeth, no wonder you were so convincing when you said you'd go against your family. You were already estranged from them!'

'What? *No*! I ——'

'No more!' he roared suddenly. 'No more, God damn it!'

She sobbed, more in confusion now than anything else. 'But ——'

'Do you need to see the proof that 'tis over before you'll stop lying to me?' he cut her off to demand. 'Do you?'

Not waiting for an answer, fitzAlan flung open the door and almost dragged Isabel into the street. Two passing merchants stared at them in surprised disapproval. She scarcely noticed. All she could think of was Edmund, her young brother, her childhood playmate, her companion and strength during the endless months of darkness. Would they tell him why he was going to die, or just run him through? Would he know that she had failed him?

Her eyes blinded by scalding tears, Isabel stumbled after fitzAlan, the punishing pace he set almost causing her to fall several times, only his vice-like grip on her arm keeping her upright. She heard the thud of his boots on wood and was distantly aware that she was once again within the walls of a castle. Minutes later, Edmund's image was replaced by Simon de Villiers' startled face.

It was strange that she could see Simon so clearly, thought Isabel, because everything else seemed lost in a hazy mist. She had a vague impression of a small room, of stone walls and light from a narrow window falling on to a table. FitzAlan's brother-in-law sat there, sorting through piles of official-looking documents. At their abrupt entrance he rose to his feet, surprise and concern crossing his face as he glanced from her to fitzAlan.

Without uttering a word, fitzAlan jerked Isabel roughly forward, at the same time riffling through the parchments scattered over the table.

'Guy? What in the name of —— ?'

For all the notice fitzAlan took of him, Simon might not have spoken. 'Look at that,' he snarled at Isabel, yanking a parchment from the pile and thrusting it under her nose. 'Look at it well, my lady.' Releasing her at last, he stepped back.

A blurred jumble of markings swam before Isabel's vision. Why couldn't she see properly? The fine mist at the edges of the room seemed to be drifting closer, enveloping her in its clinging tendrils. Isabel squeezed her eyes shut for a second. When her lashes lifted she found herself looking at a name. It was quite clear, quite distinct, quite unmistakable. *Edmund, Baron de Tracy*.

Fearful, utterly unaware now of the two men near by, she let her eyes move slowly up the document, seeing other names but only vaguely noting that she was scanning a list of some sort. Her gaze came to rest on the inscription at the top of the page. For an aeon of time the words meant nothing. Then Isabel read them one by one.

> Killed at Lincoln, in this year of our Lord, one
> thousand, one hundred and forty-one,
> fighting on the side of God and King Stephen.

The words blurred again as the strange mist returned, thicker this time. Had fog suddenly permeated the room? She couldn't see anything at all now, and there was an odd buzzing sound in her ears. Isabel turned around slowly. Someone was with her, but she wasn't sure who it was.

She took an uncertain step forward, one trembling hand outstretched—then pitched headlong into infinite blackness.

'Jesu, Guy, what the hell have you done to her?'

FitzAlan glared at his brother-in-law over Isabel's unconscious body. He hadn't been able to prevent himself from catching her when she fell, and now the feel of her, cradled helplessly against his chest, sent shafts of agony through him. And rage. He'd never known such fury before. Rage at her, at himself for wanting her, at a war that had turned her into his enemy.

'I made her face the truth,' he grated, laying Isabel down on a bench by the door.

Simon threw a puzzled glance at the disordered pile of documents on his table. 'What truth?'

Guy's hands flexed as he stood looking down at Isabel. 'She told me her brother held his castle for the Empress, that he had sent her to Gloucester, that she was estranged from him.' The words were low and clipped, as though it hurt him to speak. "Twas the truth, all right, but in reverse. De Tracy was loyal to Stephen; *she* served Matilda.'

'De Tracy?' Simon strode over to the table and picked up the parchment on top of the pile. 'Killed at Lincoln last February,' he read aloud. 'On our side.' His eyes met fitzAlan's icy gaze. 'I suppose this is what you meant when you told me there was something wrong, and rushed off. I don't remember anyone of that name, but you know what a shambles everything became after Stephen was captured. God alone knows who was there. Are you sure there's no doubt?'

Guy gave a mirthless laugh. 'That innocent face took you in as well, did it? I'm not surprised. 'Tis her stock in trade. Matilda very kindly warned me herself.' He whirled suddenly and struck the wall with his clenched fist. '*God*, why didn't I *listen*?'

'Does it matter?' asked Simon, looking surprised. 'Obviously you've put a stop to her activities.' When fitzAlan didn't reply, de Villiers glanced down at Isabel's unconscious face and muttered, 'Hard to believe, isn't it? How did you find her out?'

'The man you've had watching Rainald the Tanner. I met him on his way back here to report. . .' Guy stopped, an abrupt movement of his head indicating Isabel. The bitter, humourless smile pulled at his mouth again. 'The peasant disguise was good.'

De Villiers nodded absently. ''Twas safer. What are you going to do? Let her hang with the rest?'

FitzAlan's quickly indrawn breath sounded shockingly harsh in the still room. Simon's brows drew together. He watched his friend watching Isabel and his hazel eyes slowly widened as he took in the tightly drawn stillness in the other man's body, the white-knuckled fist still clenched against the wall.

'By the Holy Rood,' he said softly. ''Tis her, isn't it?

The girl you told me about years ago. You wrote to her father when we were in Normandy with Stephen in '37, after he granted you the barony, and got a letter back saying she was already betrothed, about to be wed.'

'Drop it, Simon.'

'But——'

'*Drop it!*'

'You fool!' De Villiers refused to back down, even when fitzAlan turned a look of fury on him. 'This might not be her fault. If her husband is one of Matilda's——'

'*She's never been married, damn you!*'

The explosion of sound pierced Isabel's unconsciousness. Shouting, she thought confusedly. We're under attack again.

Then the past vanished into the receding mists. The present returned—with brutal, stunning clarity. Edmund had been dead for months and she hadn't known it.

Grief tore through her, constricting her heart, but hard on its heels raced anger, fierce and implacable. Matilda had known of Edmund's death and had deliberately kept that fact from her. It was so very simple. The look that had passed between the Empress and Brien fitzCount was all too plain now. He had been warning Matilda, reminding her that she could still threaten Edmund's safety to ensure Isabel's obedience. She had been used—cold-bloodedly, callously used.

And fitzAlan—so ready to believe her guilty. So ready to condemn her. He had not asked her one question, had not given her one chance to explain. Still half dazed by shock, lashed by rage and a deeper pain she told herself was grief for Edmund, Isabel forgot the fleeting moments when fitzAlan had shown her tenderness despite his suspicions, forgot that he *had* asked for the truth. She remembered only his accusations and her helplessness against them. He had scorned her honour,

but she had more than all the rest, Isabel thought
bitterly. Including fitzAlan. She had been right not to
trust him, for he seduced with soft words, with heat and
passion and false promises of safety. There *was* no
honour in this world of fighting and hatred and betrayal,
a world that had taken everything: her family, her
home, her freedom.

Her anger flared higher, searing, blazing, white-hot.
She opened her eyes.

FitzAlan and de Villiers were glaring at each other
across her, but as she made a move to sit up Isabel saw
the scowl fade from Simon's face and he reached down a
hand to steady her. She didn't even acknowledge his
presence. In that moment of bitterness and pain she
despised everyone. Pulling her arm from Simon's grasp,
disdaining any assistance, she stood up. They would not
take her pride as well.

FitzAlan's eyes were like daggers, but Isabel faced
him unflinchingly. 'I am your prisoner, my lord. You
have already judged me and found me guilty. Will you
be my executioner as well?'

'Don't tempt me,' he grated through set teeth, reaching out to wrap powerful fingers around her wrist. His
voice was as hard and controlled as her own, but the
white line about his mouth betrayed the fury still lashing
him.

Isabel saw it and didn't care. Let him hate her. Let
him kill her. Nothing he did could hurt her now. She
lifted her chin in a gesture that deliberately exposed the
vulnerable line of her throat. Stormy grey eyes chal-
lenged him, proud and scornful.

De Villiers cleared his throat. 'I think we should all sit
down and——'

'Shut up, Simon.' FitzAlan wrenched his gaze from
hers, yanked the door open, and thrust Isabel outside
with barely leashed violence. He glanced briefly at his

brother-in-law. 'Don't say anything about this to a soul. I'll speak to you later.'

'Well, of course not, but. . .'

De Villiers was left talking to the air, a very thought-ful look on his face as he leaned against the doorway and watched fitzAlan stride across the bailey, towing Isabel behind him.

She wouldn't say anything, vowed Isabel, gritting her teeth against the agonising pain in her side. She would not beg fitzAlan to slow down.

The return journey through the town had been uphill most of the way; her legs were trembling and her breath was coming in short, uneven gasps as the castle gates came into view, but she would not protest. She would fall and make him drag her the rest of the way first. The thought had no sooner entered her mind when she tripped over the first slat of the drawbridge and fell to her knees before she could save herself.

FitzAlan stopped immediately, turning hard, relent-less eyes on her. He retained his hold on her wrist but made no move to pull her to her feet. Isabel reached out and grasped the heavy chain attached to the drawbridge, fighting for breath and the strength to drag herself upright. She was acutely aware of fitzAlan standing over her, powerful and dangerous, as though waiting to crush any sign of defiance or rebellion. To her dismay, hot tears burned her eyes in frustration at the physical weakness that kept her kneeling in such a submissive attitude at his feet for several more seconds.

'Save your tears, my lady,' he advised, the cold mockery in his voice bringing humiliated colour into Isabel's face. 'You have no more need of such tricks.' His grip tightened on her arm and Isabel found herself upright again.

For some strange reason she couldn't seem to relin-

quish her hold on the chain and braced herself for the
wrench she was sure would follow when fitzAlan started
towards the castle gates. It didn't come. Instead, the
arm he held captive fell back to her side as he loosed
her, and he stood staring into the distance, his face set
in grim lines. The silence seemed broken only by the
sound of Isabel's laboured breathing.

'Why?' fitzAlan said at last. His voice was low and
controlled, but his hands were clenched at his sides and
his glittering eyes would have frozen hell-fire.

Isabel stared up at him, too distraught to answer
immediately. Indeed, she was not even sure what he was
asking.

'Was your betrothed Matilda's man?' he went on, still
in that frigid tone. 'Did he even exist or was he an
invention to put me off? Were you so enamoured of the
woman that you remained with her after your father was
killed?'

He turned blazing eyes on her and his voice suddenly
roughened. 'Why, damn you? Was the Countess such a
gentle mistress that you would risk your life for her?
That you would continue to lie to me after everything——?' He broke off abruptly, his mouth tightening
into a thin, angry line.

Isabel shook her head in bewildered denial. Her chest
still heaving, she drew in a gasping breath. 'Betrothed?'
she managed, and immediately fell into a helpless fit of
coughing which sent another stab of pain through her
stomach.

Holding her free arm against her cramped side, she
struggled to regain control of herself. She could hear
fitzAlan firing more questions at her, sensed his rage
was slipping out of control again, but could only flinch
from it. Her own anger had been vanquished, leaving
her defenceless, by that gruelling uphill climb. It took
energy to sustain that degree of emotion, she dis-

covered, and what little she had left was directed at
physical recovery.

'What a talent. That look of innocence. No wonder
you were so useful to the Countess.'

That registered. Remembering past insults, Isabel
finally looked up, into a steely-eyed glare that was like a
sword-thrust to her heart.

'My God! You can even look stricken to order. But it
won't work this time, my lady. You seem surprised.
Remember when I ordered you to strip in that hut? I
looked at your face that night and thought—Jesu! What
does it matter? You must have lost count of the number
of men who have seen your charms.'

Isabel went cold. Her trembling increased, but this
time the violent tremors were caused by the fresh wave
of anger which surged through her. He was just like the
rest. Believing what he wanted to believe. Seeing what
he wanted to see. Never looking beneath the surface.

She released the chain and straightened, taking a
quick step towards him. 'You want the truth?' she cried
shrilly. 'Then have it! You're right. I *have* stripped
before. In front of a whole company of soldiers! Right
down to the skin! Is that what you wanted to hear? Is it,
my lord?'

Half blinded with rage, hardly knowing what she was
doing or where she was going, Isabel went to brush past
him. FitzAlan's hand shot out, his long fingers clamping
around her arm. He jerked her back to face him and
Isabel couldn't repress a sharp cry of fear at the violence
in his eyes. He looked as if he hated her.

When an incongruously cheerful voice spoke from
somewhere behind her, she went absolutely rigid with
shock.

'Saints be praised! Just the two people I wanted to
meet.'

Isabel saw the same shock replace the ferocity in

fitzAlan's face a second before his gaze flashed to a point beyond her. His hand slid downwards, holding hers in a grip that was suddenly unbreakable. And yet he wasn't hurting her, she realised shakily. Still feeling more than a little unbalanced, she glanced back over her shoulder.

Ralf the pedlar stood in the centre of the drawbridge, a pleased smile stretching from ear to ear. 'I thought I'd have to comb the whole town for you,' he began jovially, coming forward. Then, as his sharp eyes took in the unnatural stiffness of the other two and their frozen expressions, he groaned with mock-consternation. 'Oh, no! Don't tell me I've interrupted a marital squabble. Well, never mind. . .' He grinned even more broadly. 'I'm told 'tis a symptom suffered by all newly. . .'

The rest was abruptly swallowed on a nervous gulp, the grin vanishing, when fitzAlan's eyes turned glacial. 'You were looking for us?' he demanded, his tone not encouraging Ralf to waste any more time in pleasantries.

'Aye, my lord,' confirmed the pedlar with extreme sobriety. 'About an hour after you left us this morning a party of soldiers arrived. Nasty-looking lot. They had orders to search every village in the area, but they didn't take anything. Master Thomas said they must have been looking for people, not things, and thought you should be warned, so. . .' A deprecating shrug completed the explanation.

'That was very good of you,' whispered Isabel, rather surprised that she could speak at all. Her breathing had returned to normal and the terror that had seized her when fitzAlan had turned those savage ice-blue eyes on her had receded somewhat, but her limbs still felt shaky and she found it difficult to properly comprehend what Ralf had said. She felt fitzAlan glance down as she spoke and carefully kept her eyes lowered, not risking even a brief look at the pedlar.

'Was anyone hurt?'

Ralf shook his head. 'A few bruises, my lord. Nothing to speak of, and the mess can be cleaned up. Dame Sybil took her ladle to one of the soldiers when they started shoving their swords into the mattress, but they only laughed and pushed her outside until they'd finished.'

'She was fortunate,' muttered fitzAlan grimly. He pulled a small leather bag out of his tunic and counted out several coins. 'This should help repair any damage those louts caused. Convey my thanks to Dame Sybil and Master Thomas and my apologies for bringing trouble upon them.' He handed Ralf the money. 'And take something for yourself; you must have lost a day's trading to chase after us.'

Ralf ventured a tentative smile. 'You are most generous, my lord. I'll guard this well.'

'You'll need an escort,' nodded fitzAlan. 'I'll arrange it.'

''Tis not necessary, sir,' interposed Ralf hurriedly. He gestured to the castle behind him. 'While I was enquiring for you I fell in with a party of men who are heading in my direction shortly. 'Tis only the last mile or so I'll have to travel alone and 'twill be dark then. I'll be safe enough.'

'Then I'll wish you Godspeed.' Clearly fitzAlan considered the pedlar capable of looking after himself. And, equally clearly, Ralf was only too anxious to be on his way before the hostilities he had interrupted broke out again. He left without any further references to the pitfalls of early married life.

Isabel watched him vanish beneath the barbican and felt as though she had been abandoned to face the enemy without weapons or protection. The shield of cold indifference, the sword of anger, had both been snatched from her by Ralf's warning. Instead of worrying about what fitzAlan might do to her after her last defiant outburst, she could only think that he might be in danger.

'Will they come here, do you think?' The frightened question was out before she could stop it.

FitzAlan looked down at her. His face was shuttered now, stern and remote, his light eyes cool and expressionless. He still held her hand. 'I'm taking you to Ashby Chase.'

'What?' Isabel's brain reeled at the abrupt statement. Did he think *she* was endangered? Why should he care? A cell awaited her, and certain death — unless she could throw herself on the Queen's mercy.

'Don't you understand what's happened?' he demanded. 'Ralf thinks we're married.'

Isabel was beginning to feel dizzy. 'What does that matter?' she asked bewilderedly. ''Tis those men who ——'

FitzAlan dismissed the soldiers with an impatient gesture. 'Do you think Ralf deals only in ribbons and such trifles? He spreads gossip faster than a travelling minstrel, and too many people here know I don't possess a wife — yet.'

There was an appalled silence. Isabel jerked her hand from his, holding it out as though to ward him off.

'Would you rather hang?' he queried harshly, correctly interpreting the horrified comprehension on her face.

She flinched, her head moving slowly from side to side, but more in denial of what was coming next than in answer to his question. 'No,' she got out, her lips barely parting to allow the words to escape. 'I won't. I'll speak to the Queen. You can't deny me a proper trial. I'll ——'

'You're not going anywhere near the Queen,' he

interrupted with brutal finality. 'Removing you from her vicinity is the least I can do after bringing you here to betray her.'

'I didn't. . .' But the protest was a hopeless sigh, almost inaudible. If fitzAlan heard it he gave no sign, just continued to watch her with narrowed, implacable eyes.

'Why are you doing this?' she cried out suddenly, completely unnerved under that ice-cold stare. 'You don't. . .you can't wish to marry me.'

'Wish?' His eyes went even harder. 'You think I wish it to be known that I brought a traitor here?'

Isabel stared at him. ''Tis your own reputation you want to save, not mine. . .or my life,' she accused, her voice trembling. 'Do you think me a fool? You won't even have to marry me. Ralf won't talk — why should he? With that purse on him and those men after us, he'll keep silent. All you'll do is imprison me in your castle.'

'If I have to,' he agreed with a cool arrogance that utterly appalled her. 'But we will be married, my lady. There's one thing you've forgotten. Your brother's death left you heiress to Tracy Castle, and I intend taking it for the King.'

Isabel felt as if he'd slapped her. She actually staggered back a step. She went hot then cold, she couldn't seem to think, and something hurt deep inside her. The sheer unexpectedness of the pain stole her breath. Instinctively she tried to retreat, shrinking within herself, desperately seeking that distant place where she was beyond hurt, but fitzAlan spoke again, pulling her back to awareness with terrifying ease.

'Who holds it for the Empress?' When Isabel only continued to gaze up at him blankly, he added impatiently, 'The castellan — who is he?'

'I. . .I don't know,' she stammered, only now realising the implications in his question. She had been too numb, too bewildered, to think beyond the fact of her brother's death. Too much had happened in too short a time. She hadn't thought about the situation at Tracy, had not even wondered how Edmund had managed to escape his gaolers to join Stephen at Lincoln.

And then, as she looked into fitzAlan's eyes, she saw something else. Once again, her own words had damned her.

'Well, at least you don't deny 'tis the Empress's men who hold Tracy.' His voice was quiet and held a world of bitterness. 'How soon after the boy's death did you hand it back?'

Isabel couldn't answer. Tears welled in her throat, blocking the passage of either protest or plea, and only years of hard-won control prevented her from giving way to them in front of fitzAlan. That, and the last vestige of pride left to her, because somewhere in her mind grief for Edmund was being overshadowed by a silent warning.

She had to get away. She had to run from fitzAlan before he damaged her beyond recovery.

A sudden clatter of hoofs brought her back to an awareness of their public surroundings. FitzAlan, also, glanced around. As a solitary horseman went by, he stepped in front of her, partially shielding her from view, then grasped her arm and propelled her swiftly across the drawbridge and into the castle in total silence. Isabel followed helplessly.

Pausing only to send a page running to fetch her maid, fitzAlan marched her all the way to the ladies' solar, deliberately avoiding the crowded hall. 'When Ellen gets here, tell her to pack your things,' he ordered curtly, throwing the door open. 'We leave as soon as I've spoken to the Queen.'

Mercifully the room was empty. Isabel went past him without a word or look. She had no intention of obeying him, but she wasn't going to argue. Let fitzAlan believe her cowed and defeated, so he would leave her alone to think.

'And don't think of leaving,' he added, echoing her thoughts in a way that sent an icy shiver down her spine. Again she wondered if he could read her mind. 'I intend posting a guard outside this door.'

One second later the latch clicked shut with ominous softness.

Guy took two steps away from the solar door and had to stop. His hand went out to the stone wall to brace himself. It was shaking, he noted distantly, dragging air into his lungs. Every breath was agony. His chest hurt and he felt sick, as if someone had just kicked him in the gut. Every muscle in his body was knotted with unbearable tension. A pulse throbbed painfully in his temples.

'Isabel,' he whispered achingly. A tiny echo sighed back at him.

A full minute passed before he could move again.

CHAPTER TEN

'I WILL never marry him! *Never!*' Isabel hurled the pile of blue velvet across the bed and snatched her old grey dress from Ellen's slackened grasp.

'But my lady, Lord fitzAlan is with the Queen now. If she permits it — and why should she not? — then ——'

'Ellen, I *can't* marry him.' Isabel paused in the act of stepping into the worn garment and met her maid's worried brown eyes. 'I can't marry a man who hates me ——' her voice wobbled dangerously but she quickly brought it back under control ' — who believes me to be a traitor, without a single question or. . .or. . .'

The last word refused to emerge as a little voice reminded her that fitzAlan *had* asked why, out there on the drawbridge. Would he have listened to her then, if she had not flung that furious retort at him before they were confronted by Ralf? She would never know now.

Biting hard on her lower lip, Isabel brushed away a traitorous tear. He'd deserved it, she told herself, deliberately fanning the flames of anger again as she tugged her gown over her shoulders. Hauling her all the way from the Bishop's castle at a pace he must have known was impossible for her to keep up with, until she'd had no breath left with which to explain. She would not cry over such an overbearing, ill-tempered brute. She would not shed one tear! And she would not meekly wait around to be married to him!

'I know he was very angry,' ventured Ellen, shuddering at the memory. 'But surely my lord fitzAlan would not wed you if he truly thought ——'

'He doesn't wish to wed me. 'Tis his honourable

reputation he's worried about. And he thinks to hold Tracy Castle for the King, now that my brother. . .' But Edmund's death was still too raw a wound, still too painful to discuss. Unable to continue, she gestured to Ellen to fasten the ties at the back of her gown.

The girl obeyed, sympathy in her eyes as she gazed at her mistress. 'That woman should be imprisoned for life,' she grumbled. 'To let you find out in such a way. . . She must be every bit as cruel as they say, my lady.'

'I hated her and made no secret of it,' Isabel said softly. 'It probably amused her to keep me there, unknowing, continuing to act as her lady-in-waiting, having to obey every order, every whim. And then my ignorance became useful. But I am not ignorant this time,' she added, determination hardening her voice. 'And I won't be used again.'

Ellen looked doubtful. 'What can you do, my lady? If the Queen orders the marriage, you must obey.'

'Not if I can't hear the order,' Isabel muttered grimly. 'And I don't intend to be here to listen to it.'

'Not be here? But what. . .how. . .where will you go? Is there someone in Winchester who might help you?'

Isabel thought briefly of Simon de Villiers and as instantly dismissed the notion. He owed loyalty to fitzAlan by ties of friendship as well as family, and would return her to his brother-in-law before she could blink. And there was no one else, except. . .

'Ellen, is Ralf still here? The man who was asking for us?'

Ellen's jaw dropped. 'My lady, you aren't thinking of running off with a *pedlar*?'

'No,' agreed Isabel, her sudden hope dying as the inevitable consequences of this course of action sprang to mind. 'FitzAlan would think of him, too, and Ralf's life wouldn't be worth a straw.' She took a couple of paces across the room, thinking hard. 'Where did those women go? You know, the poor creatures in the wagon.'

Ellen forgot herself so far as to sit down plump on the bed. 'You wouldn't,' she uttered in horrified accents. 'My lady, you *couldn't*! 'Twould not be decent, 'twould not be safe!'

'But he'd never think to look for me in such company.'

'I'll tell him,' averred Ellen, bouncing to her feet in her agitation. 'I swear I will. You don't know those women. They. . .' She hesitated, seeming to grope for words, then waved a hand wildly at Isabel's dress. 'You think your gown old and shabby, but they would rip it from your body because 'tis better than the rags they wear. And then they'd throw you to whatever man happened to be passing for the money you'd earn for them.'

Isabel knew her face had whitened; the pictures conjured up by Ellen's speech awakened all her most terrifying memories. But if she let fitzAlan carry her off and marry her she would be completely powerless against a man who despised her. She had to get away.

'I can't marry him,' she repeated softly, despairingly. Why couldn't the other girl understand? Ellen had been so sympathetic earlier, had believed at once in her innocence when Isabel had told her what had happened.

'There is my father's alehouse,' murmured Ellen hesitantly, unable to resist the desperation in Isabel's eyes.

'Oh, Ellen, the very place. Would your father object, do you think?' The words tumbled over each other in her eagerness. ''Twould only be for a day or so while I try to get a message to the Queen. Once I speak with her, tell her the truth, she will surely not force me to this marriage.'

'My father needn't know who you are,' said Ellen. 'But, my lady, consider. 'Tis not the sort of place you are used to, and we still have to get there. 'Tis a mile or so outside the town, past the meaner suburbs to the east. There is only the one room and the customers are rough. They're as likely to ——'

'Is it meaner than a dungeon so dark that you can't see your hand in front of your face?' The low question cut through Ellen's objections like a scythe through dry hay. 'Is it meaner than a place so foul that you can't bear to touch your own skin except to brush off the things crawling over you?'

Ellen shook her head, her eyes enormous in her startled face.

'Then help me,' begged Isabel, holding out an imploring hand.

'If my lord ever finds you here, scrubbing tables, *my* life won't be worth a straw,' muttered Ellen two hours later, as she wielded a brush with more energy than accuracy. 'I wish you would not do that, my lady. 'Tis not seemly.'

Isabel pulled her hands out of a wooden bucket of sudsy water and dried them on her gown. 'He won't harm you, Ellen. I only said that about Ralf because he's a man, and for some strange reason fitzAlan seemed to think. . . But never mind that,' she added hastily. 'And you must remember to call me Isabel.'

'It doesn't feel right, my lady,' protested Ellen. ''Tis all very well putting on your old gown and pretending to be a serving-girl so we could pass that dolt at the solar door. You don't have to do the work as well. Look at your hands, pray.'

'They've looked worse,' retorted Isabel drily. 'Truly, Ellen, I would rather do something to earn my keep. Your father has been so good allowing me to stay, and ——'

'He doesn't know your true station, remember,' interposed Ellen, lowering her voice and glancing over at one of the tables, where her parent was enjoying a tankard of his own home-brew. 'He's too busy preening himself on acquiring the prettiest serving-maid for miles around. It worries me, my lady. Word spreads, and some of the clods who come in here would sell their own mothers for profit. Soon this place will not be safe for you.'

"Tis only until I can find someone to convey a message to the Queen, begging her to see me.'

'If you would let me ——' began Ellen.

But Isabel shook her head quickly. 'No. I've told you. He knows you were with me and may have set someone to watch for you.'

'Probably that impudent squire of his,' agreed Ellen, a scowl marring her usually placid features. 'You never saw anything like the way he marched me back to the castle earlier. You would have thought I was under arrest.'

'Just like his lord and master,' muttered Isabel, seizing a broom and attacking the mouldy rushes on the floor. 'But I'll see you don't suffer for this, Ellen. I'll tell the Queen I ordered you to accompany me.' She hoped she could keep that promise.

Ellen took the broom from her. 'If it comes to that I can always use the excuse that Father needed me,' she answered calmly. 'But what about you, my lady? You say I can't go, and Father — well, look at him; can you see him being taken to the Queen's presence?'

Isabel turned to contemplate her host. Ellen's father, Jack, had greeted his daughter with the testily expressed hope that she had not left the safe position at the royal castle that he had gone to considerable trouble to obtain for her. Having been reassured on this point, he had grudgingly accepted Ellen's explanation that she had been given leave to visit him to see how he was coping alone, and had promptly put his daughter and her companion to work. His own duties appeared to be limited to joining his patrons in a drink whenever he was thirsty, which seemed to be often. Long, unkempt hair, several missing teeth, and a nose that looked as if it had met more than one fist in its owner's lifetime did nothing for his general appearance.

Isabel had to admit he was not messenger material, but she was beginning to question the wisdom of her panicked flight from the castle. She hoped fitzAlan would begin his search for her on the road to Gloucester; he might even think she had sought shelter with Dame Sybil, but the hope was a weak one. He knew Ellen was with her and was perfectly capable of tracking down their whereabouts. And here she was, trapped outside the city without money or the means to get a message to Matilda.

'If I had some token to send with him. . .' she thought aloud.

'Father would still be questioned,' Ellen reminded her. 'With King Stephen imprisoned, the Queen is more closely guarded than ever. They'd want to know who sent him. If he says his serving-maid he'll be laughed at; if he tells the truth ——'

'He'll be forced to lead fitzAlan straight back here,' finished Isabel despairingly. 'Oh, Ellen, what am I going to do? I thought perhaps one of the customers might take a message, but. . .' Her voice died away as she glanced anxiously out of the unshuttered window.

Hearing the stamp of hoofs that had alerted Isabel, Ellen came to stand beside her. 'Soldiers,' she announced, peering out. 'They'd be on foot if they were looking for you, I think, but perhaps 'twould be safer to get behind the counter. 'Tis darker in that corner.'

Isabel hurriedly took Ellen's advice, retreating to one

side of the room, where a rough table near the fireplace served as a bar. Several barrels stood behind it, the shelf above them holding crude wooden tankards. She shrank into the furthest corner just as the door was pushed open, thankful that Jack had not yet seen fit to light the sconces against the shadows of late afternoon.

Three soldiers entered, calling loudly for Jack and seeming to fill the room. Two of the men flung themselves down on a bench, scabbards clattering, while the third strode forward, kicking Isabel's abandoned bucket out of his path. Water spread across the floor in a greasy stream, mingling with the pile of filthy rushes. The fetid odour of damp refuse filled the air and the soldier made a disgusted face.

'Faugh! This place stinks!' He reached down and hauled Jack off his bench. 'Come on, Jack, you lazy rogue. On your feet. 'Tis rent day and we want a drink as well.'

'Aye, 'tis thirsty work collecting rent,' one of the others called out. He seemed to find the remark hilarious, because he broke into raucous laughter.

The fellow still holding Jack by the scruff of the neck grinned and shook his victim with casual contempt. 'The wench at the last place didn't want to pay up,' he explained with a leer. 'Said she didn't have the money, so we had to persuade her.' He scratched obscenely at the front of his tunic. 'Thirsty work, like Hal said.'

'What do you say we let your girl do likewise, Jack?' queried the man named Hal. 'About time she helped out like a dutiful daughter.' He gave another coarse guffaw.

'I'll pay in coin like I always does,' growled Jack, but his eyes flickered uncomfortably towards Isabel for a second.

His captor followed the direction of his gaze. 'Well, well.' He released Jack and took a step in Isabel's direction. 'What have we here? A new wench, by the Rood.'

Ellen darted past him to join Isabel behind the table. She snatched up three tankards and filled them with ale, her movements swift and practised. 'Here.' She slapped the drinks down. 'Father, get the rent money.'

Isabel, backing further into the shadows, dared to breathe again when the soldier went to pick up the ale-cups. His eyes were still fixed on her, but she knew he could see little in the dark corner. Perhaps they would down their drinks and leave. She saw Ellen's father reach behind one of the barrels and draw out a small sack.

'Not so fast.'

The softly spoken command came from the third man, who had remained silent until now. He was slightly different from the others, Isabel saw, watching him with apprehensive eyes. His voice was more cultured and he was cleaner, his black hair close-cropped and his beard neatly trimmed. 'Let the girl bring the drinks,' he ordered, lounging on the bench at his ease.

The man near the table snickered and rejoined his companions, snatching the sack out of Jack's hand as he passed.

Isabel glanced uncertainly at Ellen.

'You'd better do it,' her maid whispered. 'They've never. . .hurt me, but try not to protest if they touch you. It'll only make them worse.'

Isabel nodded and gritted her teeth. Picking up the drinks, she crossed the room and set them down on the trestle, careful to keep her face turned away from the window. The two men-at-arms leered but promptly buried their noses in their cups. The other picked up his drink and took a long swallow, watching her over the rim of the tankard. She started to turn away.

'I didn't say you could move, slut.'

Isabel froze.

'What's your name?' he asked, casually tossing back the rest of the ale. He held the cup out to her.

Trying not to let her hand shake, Isabel reached out to take it. As quick as a striking adder, the soldier's fingers fastened around her arm. She was yanked off balance to land on her knees in front of him. 'I said, what's your name?' he repeated menacingly.

'She's my cousin, Isabel,' said Ellen quickly, moving from behind the table. But when Hal lowered his tankard and glared at her she halted, uncertain.

'Your cousin?' The quiet voice turned sardonic. 'You hear that, Jack? We never knew you had a niece. Never knew you had brother or sister, in fact.' The man shook his head in mock-reproach. 'My lord likes to know everything about his tenants, Jack. He's not going to be pleased that you've kept this little morsel to yourself.'

'She's no niece o'mine,' grumbled Jack, shrugging helplessly when his daughter turned a horrified look on him. 'Just a friend of me girl's. But 'ware how you treat her. She's from the castle. The royal castle,' he added for emphasis.

'Interesting,' mused the soldier. He narrowed his eyes at Isabel, who looked up at him, frightened but desperately trying to keep her wits about her. She had to hold on to her control. If she stayed quiet and calm he wouldn't hurt her.

'Lately come to Winchester, have you, girl?' Not waiting for an answer, he stood up and dragged Isabel closer to the window. She barely had time to struggle to her feet before cruel fingers tangled in her hair and her face was jerked up to the light. Frowning, he studied her for a moment, then, with an impatient curse, yanked the ribbon away and unwound her braid. Her eyes watered when her hair was pulled so roughly, but she refused to make a sound.

'Long, dark hair. . .young. . .beautiful,' he murmured thoughtfully. Then, much louder, 'How did you come to Winchester? From where? Were you with a man? Where is he now? Did he abandon you here?'

Calm! She had to stay calm. The rapid fire of questions was deliberate, she knew, designed to scare her into blurting out the truth. She had seen the technique used before — don't give the victim a chance to think of a convincing lie. It was almost working, too, but his insistence on a supposed escort kept her mind clear by sheer instinct alone. There was no time to question her motives; she just knew she would never mention fitzAlan to this man.

'Is he coming back?' The soldier gave her hair another painful jerk. 'Answer!'

'I don't know what you mean,' Isabel choked breathlessly. 'There's no man.'

His eyes bored into hers for another nerve-stretching minute, then he seemed to relax and accept her answer. He smiled and the hand in her hair turned caressing. 'That's very sad. No man. We'll have to see if we can mend the situation.'

'I don't want no trouble,' put in Jack uneasily. 'I've paid me rent; you've no right —— '

'Then leave if you don't want to watch.' The words were uttered with such chilling disinterest that Isabel's stomach turned over and her legs started to tremble. Already cringing under the hand in her hair, she suddenly felt terrifyingly weak. She watched the other two men get to their feet, matching expressions of anticipation on their coarse features.

'This one's mine,' Isabel's captor drawled. He hadn't taken his eyes off her once. 'But you can have the other if you didn't get enough at the last place.'

The whole room seemed to explode in seconds. An

enraged roar rent the air as Jack leapt forward. 'I'm a free man,' he bellowed. 'You've no right——'

A resounding crack cut him off when one of the men-at-arms grabbed a bench and swung it. The rickety wood splintered under the impact and Jack crumpled, blood welling from a gash on his forehead. Ellen screamed and was instantly seized by the other man, who, laughing at her wild struggles, began to force her down to the floor.

Isabel didn't see anything else. Without any warning whatsoever, the man holding her swung his foot back and kicked her legs out from under her with a careless, emotionless violence that wrenched a panic-stricken scream from her throat. She sprawled flat on the hard wooden floor, her cry abruptly silenced as all the air rushed out of her body. Before she could recover he was upon her, his ale-scented breath almost making her retch when his mouth crushed down on hers. She felt the sharp edge of his teeth trying to force her lips apart and tasted blood.

Choking with revulsion, Isabel tried to fight him, but her own fear made her helpless. She couldn't see, couldn't breathe; her entire body was immobilised by the weight of her attacker. He shifted slightly, tugging at her skirts, and she got one arm free. She heard him grunt as her nails raked across his face and he pulled back, releasing her mouth. She gulped in a lungful of air and forced her eyelids open. Hard black eyes gleamed down at her. His fist clenched and drew back. He smiled, a smile that was neither gloating nor excited, but almost inhuman in its utter coldness. The fist began to descend.

Isabel screamed again, twisting her head from side to side, catapulted brutally into panic-stricken hysteria. Almost senseless with terror, she wasn't even aware that her screams went on and on. Nor did she see the sudden eruption into the alehouse of two more men.

Her assailant's fist was stopped in mid-air. Less than a second later he was jerked up and around to meet a devastating punch straight to the jaw. The nauseating sound of breaking bone was immediately followed by a crash as another blow to the side of the head dropped him like a stone.

Strong hands grasped Isabel's arms. Uncomprehending, she renewed her struggles, her screams weakening to rasping sobs. She was pulled to her feet and managed to aim a kick at her attacker that didn't have a chance of connecting. She sobbed harder.

'Isabel! Stop it!' Powerful hands shook her hard. '*Stop it!*' roared fitzAlan.

She stopped fighting, blinking up at him through a mass of tangled hair, her eyes wild, her breath coming in convulsive gasps. 'Guy,' she whispered.

He didn't answer. Backing her up to a bench, he pressed her down on to it and left her. Not until she had been sitting there for several minutes did Isabel realise that no sound at all had come from her torn and bleeding lips. She put a shaking hand up to her mouth, her eyes falling on Ellen, who was kneeling by the fireplace, clutching the tattered edges of her dress together over her breasts and watching her father anxiously. FitzAlan bent over Jack as he began to stir.

Isabel's gaze skittered nervously past them to the two men-at-arms, now held at the end of a very businesslike sword attached to the hand of the young man she had seen with Guy at the church.

'We didn't know they'd run away before you'd finished with them,' one of the soldiers was grumbling sullenly. He eyed the sword-point warily before peering past it to the body on the floor. 'You've killed our Baron's knight over a couple of alehouse wenches. He isn't going to like that.'

'I doubt he's dead,' said fitzAlan coldly, getting to his

feet. He glanced contemptuously at the unconscious man. 'But he'll make sure the next wench he fancies isn't another man's property. As for your Baron, whoever he is, tell him. . .' He stopped short, his eyes moving swiftly to Isabel.

She had risen and now stood staring at him, trembling visibly and feeling as if a puff of wind would knock her down again. In frightening contrast fitzAlan looked tough and completely immovable, and bigger than ever in the confined space of the alehouse. His mouth was set hard and his eyes were filled with a cold rage that was all the more dangerous for its very restraint.

And he had spoken of her as though she were no more than a female to be used and then discarded.

'No,' she whispered, her voice still painfully hoarse. 'I'm not —'

'Be quiet!' he snarled at her.

But Isabel was too distressed to heed him. 'I won't go with you!' she choked. 'I won't ma —'

The distraught protest ended in a sharp cry as fitzAlan's open hand flashed out, striking her cheek with enough force to whip her head to the side. The silence that followed was finally broken by a nervous laugh from one of the men-at-arms.

FitzAlan turned on him immediately. 'Get out of here, and take that filth with you.'

Isabel stood as if turned to stone, her face still averted. He had actually hit her this time, she told herself dazedly. *Really* hit her. Strange, her cheek wasn't even stinging, just slightly warm. He hadn't hurt her, and yet pain overwhelmed her with battering force. She felt as though she was dying inside.

Why? Despite the threats, the insults, the accusations, had she thought he would never physically strike her? Had her dream hero been so deeply embedded in her heart that her mind had never stopped believing in him? She had thought he could do nothing more to her, but he had. Oh, dear God, *he had*! She had thought she knew suffering, but she had not. Loneliness and fear and grief had never been like this. The loss of her family, the futile years of servitude, even Edmund's death — none of it had hurt like this.

There was sound and movement in the room, but Isabel heard and saw nothing. Dreams and reality had collided in her shocked mind with stunning force, sending her hurtling over the edge of that invisible precipice, and the fall had broken her into a thousand agonising pieces, like brittle shards of glass that could never be whole again.

Moving very, very slowly, she wrapped her arms around her waist and sat down on the bench. It didn't matter what fitzAlan did to her now. It didn't matter what happened to her. Nothing mattered any more — except the truth that was breaking her heart.

She loved him.

'My lady?'

It was Ellen, looking a little pale but seemingly recovered. A homespun woollen mantle was fastened across her shoulders, hiding her torn dress.

'Come, my lady, 'tis time to go.'

Isabel rose obediently, allowing her maid to drape a vaguely familiar red mantle over her own shoulders. She didn't know where they were going, nor did she care. She followed Ellen outside, not thinking, not feeling.

Horses whickered restlessly, held by a small urchin who watched Isabel emerge from the alehouse with round, inquisitive eyes. Quite a crowd had gathered, lured by the fight and the presence of gentry in such a squalid neighbourhood. The sibilant hiss of a sword being drawn sounded behind her and instantly the crowd dispersed, melting away into the shadowy alleys off the street.

'You'll ride with me, mistress,' ordered a brusque voice. 'The grey is for my lady.'

''Tis Will, my lord's squire,' Ellen whispered in Isabel's ear. 'He has enough sauce for a king's fool, but impudence I can stomach so long as I don't have to ride something that big on my own.'

Reins were put into Isabel's hand. She felt a firm grasp on her arm and a second later she was on Chalon's back. Will made sure she was secure, then lifted a nervously protesting Ellen on to his own horse.

'Hush your tongue, mistress,' he ordered impatiently. 'I'm not going to drop you.'

Their voices faded into the background as Isabel's eyes came to rest on the third horse. A big black. Romulus. His head came around, brown eyes alert as fitzAlan strode out of the alehouse, ducking his head to negotiate the doorway. He made straight for the big warhorse, mounted, said something to Will, and started along the street.

He hadn't come near her, hadn't even glanced in her direction.

It was Will who leaned over and smacked Chalon's rump, sending the horse after fitzAlan. Tossing a coin to the ragged urchin, he brought his mount alongside Isabel, not speaking, but clearly ready to offer assistance should it be needed. She sensed the long look he directed at her, but continued to stare blindly ahead.

Time passed. Vague pictures swam before Isabel's eyes: a cobbled section of street where children ran heedlessly between the horses' hoofs, the high walls of the city on her left, then fields to either side of the rutted road. Somewhere along the way they were joined by Simon de Villiers and several men-at-arms, but Isabel scarcely noticed. Unable to hide physically, she had simply closed everything off, shrinking from further pain like any wounded creature.

The numbing stupor got her through the next few hours. Through the long ride, through the noise and confusion when they reached their destination, through the hurried ceremony that followed almost immediately, during which she moved and spoke when so directed like one in a trance. Until, finally, there was night and blessed silence, and she was alone with no one to witness her pain. She lay in a huge, curtained bed and felt the ice around her heart begin to melt, her mind begin to function again.

Very carefully, as though testing a raw wound, Isabel thought about her present situation. She was married to a man who believed her to be a traitor and a spy, a man who had stood beside her during a ceremony that bound them for life and had not once looked at her, nor touched her except to push a heavy, engraved ring on to her finger.

Isabel raised her left hand and peered at the ring in the dim light cast by the clock-candle burning near the bed. There were faint etchings in the gold, but she couldn't make them out. Her eyes lifted to the candle. Its flame had sunk well past the midnight mark. Would he come to her bed? He had desired her once, and now she was his wife. Did he still want her? Had his desire been completely destroyed by hatred?

Isabel whimpered softly. She curled up in a tight ball as though to stop herself from breaking apart. The solar. Look at the solar, she ordered herself. Tapestry-hung walls, flames dancing in a fireplace, a table and chair between the two window embrasures, an enormous studded chest and a smaller one near it, and sheepskin rugs. Warmth and comfort, even luxury. She felt so cold. Would he come?

Think of the other people she had seen. FitzAlan's

sister, Joanna, serfs and soldiers, a wizened yet bright-
eyed old man who had welcomed her profusely, a priest
intoning Latin. But her mind's eye saw only one face,
one man. He had married her. She was his wife. Would
he come?

Isabel lay very still, her muscles so rigid with tension
that she doubted she could have moved anyway. Her
eyes watched the flame of the clock-candle sink ever
lower. She watched until dawn, until utter weariness
overtook her without her being aware of when she slept.

He never came.

'Now, my lady, you must eat something.'

Isabel didn't respond. It was a foolish suggestion of
Ellen's anyway, she reflected. She would be sick if she
tried to eat.

'You've been sitting there the whole morning in
nothing but that flimsy shift, just staring through the
window at all that water. 'Tis not right. Lady Joanna
will think you don't like her.'

That got her attention. She even felt a twinge of
amusement. Isabel turned her head. 'You sound just
like my old nurse, scolding me for not playing with my
cousin whenever she stayed with us.'

A look of relief replaced the frown on Ellen's face.
'Thanks be to the Blessed Virgin. You're with us again,'
she muttered beneath her breath. Then, raising her
voice, 'I don't think Lady Joanna expects you to play
with her, my lady, but she has been asking if you are
feeling more rested. She knows you've been
through. . .a difficult time.'

A difficult time, mused Isabel. A small ironic smile
curved her lips. 'Is that what he told them?' she
murmured, glancing out of the window again.

The prospect that met her eyes was strangely comfort-
ing. Beyond the placid waters of a small lake, a golden

forest of trees stretched as far as the eye could see.
Ashby Chase. Her new home. An island fortress surrounded on three sides by a deep moat which emptied
into the lake situated on the eastern side of the keep. It
was a pretty setting. The late morning sun was beginning
to break through the clouds. It glinted on the water,
reminding her of fitzAlan's eyes. Isabel's hands
clenched in her lap.

'My lord said that he'd brought you from Gloucester,'
volunteered Ellen, setting a trencher of bread and fruit
on the table, 'where you'd been held since your father's
death. But you heard all that yesterday, my lady.'

She hadn't, but there was no need to tell Ellen that.
Instead Isabel laughed shortly, a bitter little sound that
held pain. 'If he only knew. 'Twas near enough to the
truth.'

'Well, no need for you to fear captivity again,' stated
Ellen in bracing tones. 'An entire army could drown
trying to get into this place. For myself, I think the moat
alone would have been quite enough, but I dare say one
gets used to the feeling that we might all sink.' She
pulled up a chair and patted it invitingly. 'At least
swallow some milk, my lady. Lady Joanna mixed a little
wine and honey with it, and she'll be disappointed if you
don't try it.'

'I don't suppose anyone would live here if there were
any danger of sinking,' replied Isabel, ignoring the rest
of Ellen's speech. But she rose and walked over to the
table, moving stiffly because of muscles chilled from
sitting in the stone window embrasure for so long.

'My lord's sister seems a sweet lady,' Ellen chattered
on, pouring the warm milk into a goblet. 'And my Lord
de Villiers obviously adores her.'

Pain slashed through Isabel again, clutching at her
heart. It left her so weak that she had to put a hand out
to the table before she could sit down. She tried to recall

her impression of Joanna in an effort to distract herself, thinking back to their arrival. A lovely girl, not much older than herself, she thought, with fitzAlan's silvery-fair hair, her beautiful face gentle and anxious as she hurried from the keep to greet them. She had smiled uncertainly at Isabel and had started to say something, but then Simon had put his arm around her waist and had led her away, his head bent over her fair one, his expression tender. Joanna had looked up at him, open adoration in her glowing sapphire eyes.

The memory became too painful. With a shaking hand Isabel picked up the goblet. Maybe the milk would wash down the lump in her throat. Her gaze followed Ellen as the girl moved about the room, straightening the crimson velvet bed curtains, placing another log on the fire. Draped across the carved wooden lid of a nearby chest were the clothes given to her by the Queen. Isabel wondered when fitzAlan had found the time to pack up the garments. And he'd had Chalon ready saddled for her, also. Had he been so sure of finding her at the alehouse?

'Ellen, your father!' she exclaimed suddenly. 'Is he all right?'

'Aye, my lady.' Ellen grimaced wryly. 'Father has a hard head. My lord offered him a place here in case those men cause any more trouble, but he refused.' She shrugged philosophically. ''Tis the only life he's known — keeping an alehouse. He'd miss it.'

'But what of yourself?' Isabel asked softly. 'Your place with the Queen. I never thought. . . How selfish I was —'

'Never say so, my lady! The Queen knew I would accompany you here. She ordered it. Besides, you were not yourself and who could wonder at it? After so many shocks I was surpised you could stand up at your own wedding.'

'My wedding.' The whisper hung in the air. It still didn't seem quite real. She was a wife and yet not a wife. Even saying it aloud didn't help. 'I'm married.'

'Aye, my lady,' agreed Ellen placidly. 'Not an hour after we arrived. And what a stir it caused, too,' she added, quite as though Isabel had not been present. 'There were tongues wagging a plenty, I can tell you, at such a hasty wedding, but they were soon stilled when my lord announced he was leaving immediately, and — '

'Immediately? He's *gone*?' Isabel shoved her chair back so quickly that it almost toppled over. FitzAlan wouldn't. . .*surely* he wouldn't. . .leave without seeing her? Did he intend everyone in the castle to know he did not want the wife he had married in such a hurry? Did he intend to ignore her completely?

Then Isabel saw Ellen's stunned face and realised that her maid, at least, did not know she had spent the night alone.

'I thought my lord must have told you,' the girl said, still looking confused. 'He's leaving today. The siege engines have gone already.'

'Siege engines?' repeated Isabel slowly, sinking back on to the chair as understanding flooded her. 'That's why Simon had so many men with him. The Bishop must have given him leave to help fitzAlan. They're going to capture Tracy Castle. No matter how long it takes.' And a siege could take weeks, she knew. Weeks in which an attacking force could be rallied and sent against the besiegers.

Springing to her feet again, Isabel snatched up her gown. 'Quickly, Ellen, help me dress. I have to see him.'

Ellen hurried forward automatically. 'But my lady,' she almost wailed in obvious puzzlement. 'My lord said you were to rest today. What do you mean to do that cannot wait —— ?'

'Help him,' said Isabel, heading for the door before Ellen had her gown properly fastened.

She was through it before her maid could draw breath to protest.

CHAPTER ELEVEN

THE tower stairs were lit only by narrow window slits cut into the ten-foot-thick walls at irregular intervals, but Isabel didn't hesitate. This was no time for doubt and despondency and moping in solars. The pain would return, she knew, cruel and cutting, but pride and hurt meant little compared to the fear that she might never see fitzAlan again. No matter what it cost her, she could not let him leave without trying to speak to him. She could no longer hide from the truth she had faced yesterday.

She loved him. She loved fitzAlan. And it was not the five-year-old image of a man that she loved, but the man he was now. Arrogant, strong, passionate, proud—she loved him. He might never know of her love, might never want it, but she was his wife. He would know that her loyalty was his.

Filled with equal parts dread and determination, Isabel careered down the staircase, trying to remember the way to the hall and bailey. Her soft leather shoes made little sound on the stone steps and she was so lost in her thoughts that she didn't hear other footsteps coming as rapidly towards her. The last arrow slit had just flashed past when a large shadow loomed on the wall in front of her. Unable to stop, she collided heavily with the man ascending the stairs, only his strength and quick reflexes preventing them both from tumbling the rest of the way.

When the tower walls swung back into focus Isabel found herself clutching a chainmail tunic, quite unaware of the metal links cutting into her palms as she gazed straight into the ice-blue eyes of her husband. His hands held her slender arms in a grip that hurt, and his mouth was only inches away from her own. For a mindless second, forgetting everything but the warmth and strength of him, Isabel swayed closer.

'What were you trying to do? Break your neck?'

Her head snapped back. The harsh question was like another slap in the face. Her teeth sank into her bottom lip, biting back a cry, and she winced. It was still tender from the soldier's abuse, but the pain helped her fight back incipient tears. What had she expected? she asked herself mercilessly. A concerned enquiry about her health? Just concentrate on what you have to say.

'I had to see you,' she whispered, unable to speak any louder under a look that was as stern and forbidding as she had feared. 'To tell you —'

A loud clatter of arms from below interrupted her. FitzAlan half glanced back over his shoulder. 'We can't talk here,' he said curtly. 'Go up to the solar.'

When Isabel hesitated his mouth crooked in a faint reflection of the wry half-smile she remembered. 'Where did you think I was going?' he asked, turning her around and giving her a little push.

Now doubting that she would be able to speak at all, Isabel began to climb the stairs, acutely aware of fitzAlan behind her every step of the way. She tried to pull her scattered thoughts into some sort of order, but all she could do was wonder if the cold, level gaze he had given her betokened indifference or anger. What was she going to face when they reached the privacy of the solar? What was he going to do to her for running away?

Her imagination promptly sped through a catalogue of punishments which ranged from an hour in the stocks to a beating. She had just got to incarceration in a convent for the rest of her days when they arrived at the top of the stairs.

Ellen was hurrying out of the solar. Isabel stepped back so she wouldn't bump into the girl and instantly cannoned into fitzAlan instead. The heat of his body scorched the length of her back. He felt very solid and very big. She shot into the room as though pursued by demons, not even hearing Ellen's murmured, 'I'll return later, my lady.' Behind her the door closed with a decisive snap.

Isabel walked over to the window and stared out, not seeing a thing. Her mouth went dry, her heart raced, and her legs shook. The past few days seemed to hang like a heavy stormcloud over the room, seething with half-truths and suspicion, misunderstandings and mistakes. She wanted to explain, but didn't know if fitzAlan would listen; longed for gentleness, but was braced for anger.

When fitzAlan spoke right at her shoulder she nearly leapt a foot into the air.

'Your gown isn't fastened,' he murmured, his voice soft and deep. 'And. . .'

Isabel didn't have to look around to know he had caught sight of her over-tunic, still reposing on the chest. A tide of red flooded her cheeks. Now he would know that she had rushed out of the solar, half dressed, to find him.

Wheeling about, she parted her lips to say something — anything — to distract him, and not a word came out. He was standing less than one pace away, so close that her swift movement caused her gown to brush across his hauberk, catching on a metal link. He glanced down at it.

How could a man dressed in chainmail move so quickly and silently? she asked mutely, watching as he took the soft linen in one big hand and carefully freed the material. She had a sudden unnerving vision of those long fingers moving as gently over her flesh, and bit her lip again on a shiver of awareness.

FitzAlan's gaze immediately flashed to her mouth, his eyes darkening so abruptly that Isabel's knees went weak. This time heat suffused her entire body. She had to sit down, she thought, looking dazedly around for a chair. Before she fell down.

'Don't. . .' he began, then bit off the rest, his hand clenching on the fabric he still held. Isabel prayed he couldn't feel the trembling in her limbs.

Then, with a rough exclamation that made her heart jump, fitzAlan jerked his hand away and strode over to the chest. 'Put that on,' he ordered, picking up her over-tunic and throwing it at her.

This didn't seem the time to remind him that he had seen her wearing considerably less. Isabel obeyed, watching in trepidation as he paced over to the door, then back to the fireplace. There he halted, staring down into the flames, but his stillness had a taut, barely restrained quality that kept her heart beating much too fast, and though he seemed totally absorbed in the glowing fire Isabel sensed he was aware of her every movement. Clutching the velvet bliaut to her, she waited, nervous chills replacing the heat of a moment ago.

FitzAlan looked up, his gaze locking with hers. 'You wanted to see me?'

'Aye,' she managed. 'But. . .don't you want. . .? Aren't you angry. . .?' She stopped. What was the matter with her? Since when had fitzAlan needed encouragement to show anger? That fleeting, intense look had addled her brain as well as scrambled her insides.

His face never changed expression. 'You wanted to see me?' he repeated evenly.

Isabel gulped on a mouthful of air. It suddenly occurred to her that total disregard of her escapade was a very subtle punishment indeed. And effective. She felt as guilty about running away as if she had just robbed a lame beggar of his last groat.

'You're leaving for Tracy,' she stammered at last.

It wasn't a question, but he nodded, his eyes narrowing slightly.

'There's a way into the castle. You won't need your siege engines.'

FitzAlan was silent for so long that Isabel wondered if he thought she was lying. She was just about to speak again when he said, 'If you mean undermining, it takes too long. I presume serfs are still living there and I'd rather break in than see innocent people die of hunger while ——'

'I didn't mean undermining.'

He frowned. 'What, then?'

'Against the south wall of the bailey there's an empty dovecote. Some of the stones in the wall are loose. If you can pull them out you can make a hole big enough for a man to get inside. He could open the postern and ——'

'While we're being fired upon from above? I think not.'

The interruption was sardonic, but Isabel merely shook her head, intent on finishing before he cut her off again. 'One or two men wouldn't be seen. 'Tis where ——' her breath caught and she glanced away, flushing slightly ' —where the pleasance used to be. 'Twas a wilderness years ago and will be more so now. If you created a diversion, drawing their attention elsewhere. . .'

She fell silent again, unable to tell if the mention of the garden had aroused similar memories in fitzAlan's mind.

'Quite the little strategist,' he murmured. Then, before Isabel could decide how to take *that*, his gaze sharpened. 'You said *if* we can pull the stones out. Don't you know if they'll move?'

'They did once. Edmund and I loosened them enough, but. . .'twas a long time ago.'

FitzAlan took a step towards her. 'After your father was killed?'

'Aye.' Her voice dropped and went toneless. Just for a moment the solar slid away and she was back at Tracy Castle. 'We couldn't lift them. Edmund was too young, and I wasn't strong enough. And then. . .'twas much too late.'

'You and Edmund?' Guy asked very quietly.

But Isabel blinked, pushing the past and the question aside. Her hand made a tiny movement of finality. 'That's all.'

'Is it?'

She looked up, almost fearfully. Now he was going to yell at her.

'There's a lot I don't know, isn't there, Isabel.' He made it a statement.

'I. . .' She didn't know what to say. Hope flared within her so strongly, so quickly, that the force of it frightened her. She could only nod mutely, her hands gripping each other so tightly that her fingers went numb.

'And I don't have time to hear it,' he muttered, more to himself than to her.

She was so tense now that her muscles were beginning to quiver. 'Must you go today?' she breathed.

Guy moved suddenly, taking another swift step towards her, his blue eyes glittering, and Isabel promptly lost her nerve, jumping back out of reach. He must not touch her. If he did she would break down completely and beg him to hold her, beg him not to

leave her. 'I. . .I mean, your arm is scarce healed,
and——'

He had stopped the instant she retreated, halting in
the middle of the room. The fierce glitter vanished,
leaving his eyes cold and distant. ''Tis best that I go
now.'

The clipped remark choked off the rest of her sen-
tence and her hopes. Despair engulfed Isabel in a
swamping wave. Her shoulders drooped and she turned
her face away, staring at the floor, hardly able to listen
when fitzAlan continued speaking.

'After Stephen was captured I swore to serve the
Queen until his release, to obey her commands as I
would the King's. She wants me to take Tracy immediately, before the Empress realises no word has reached
her from Winchester and enlarges the garrison.'

'The Queen,' repeated Isabel dully, only hearing the
words 'obey' and 'command'. 'Of course. She ordered
you to marry me.'

For the first time a note of impatience sharpened his
voice. 'Damn it, stop looking as if I've just hit you again!
I know you didn't want to marry me, but 'tis not as
though I'm forcing myself on you!'

And we both know that force wouldn't be necessary.

For a minute Isabel thought she'd said the words
aloud, or that fitzAlan had. They seemed to whisper
through the room, mocking her.

''Twas you who didn't want to marry me,' she cried,
trying to drown out the tormenting echo. She met his
eyes defiantly, but she was shaking. Perhaps he was
right to go, she thought despairingly. Perhaps the time
spent away from him would help her regain some
control over the wild emotions roiling inside her.

She was lying to herself. She would be only half alive
without him.

'I have to leave,' he said in a surprisingly gentle voice.

'While I'm gone, Isabel, think on this. I could have told the Queen about your meeting with Rainald. You would have forfeited Tracy Castle immediately, and 'twould have been granted to me to hold for the King. I didn't have to marry you to get it.'

Isabel had gone very still, almost forgetting to breathe. She couldn't worry about breathing when she had to understand what fitzAlan was saying. And what he was saying seemed to be in direct conflict to the hurtful reasons for their marriage he had given her on the drawbridge yesterday. Had she misunderstood him? But if that was so. . .

'What *did* you tell the Queen?' she asked in a suspenseful whisper, her eyes clinging to his.

He shrugged, watching her as closely. 'Little enough. She's too busy making arrangements to leave for Bristol to worry about us. She and Prince William will be hostages in place of the King. When Stephen reaches Winchester safely, the Earl of Gloucester will be released and his son detained. When the Earl arrives in Bristol, Matilda and the prince will be allowed to go free and Gloucester's son likewise.'

'It sounds complicated.'

'Exchanges of such important prisoners usually are. Runaway ladies are soon overlooked by comparison.'

Her eyes fell. He had dashed her down again. Just when she thought they were starting to talk more naturally. What was she supposed to think? If he truly believed there was more to her actions, if he had married her to protect her life or reputation, why couldn't he spare a few insignificant minutes to listen to her now? It would take him three days to reach Tracy with a small army and cumbersome siege machines slowing him down—what did one hour more or less matter?

'Well. . .well, then——' her only recourse seemed to

be in stiff formality '—I wish you Godspeed, my lord, and. . .and success in your. . .that is. . .' Her lip quivered and she stopped dead, willing herself not to cry.

Guy appeared to hesitate for a second, those intense, light eyes burning into hers. His jaw clenched. Then he turned abruptly and strode to the door.

'My lord!'

He stopped, his hand on the latch. 'What?'

The tone wasn't encouraging, but desperation spurred her on. If she did nothing else, she had to explain the one half-truth that, to her distraught mind, was the most damaging. 'What I said to you. . .on the drawbridge. . .about stripping for. . .for a whole. . .'

FitzAlan released the latch and turned slowly to face her. Quite suddenly he looked extremely dangerous.

Isabel hurried on while she could still speak, almost slurring the words in her nervousness. ''Twas the truth. . .but 'tis not what you think. 'Twas not done willingly. . . We were all forced. . .all of us. . .men and women alike. . .old and young. . .exposed to mockery. . .but that was all. They didn't. . .didn't. . . I was still very small. . . They thought I was a child like Edmund. . .but the older girls. . .'

She stopped and tears came into her eyes. 'I'm still a maid. Please believe that, at least,' she finished brokenly, not caring now if he saw the naked pleading in her eyes.

''Tis a lie that is easily disproven,' he said coolly, but the ferocity was gone from his expression.

'I know.'

Very slowly, fitzAlan came back to her, gazing down at her face for a long moment. His ice-blue eyes seemed to touch her every feature, one by one. Isabel held her breath as his hand lifted. Gently, so very gently, his fingers wrapped around the back of her neck, warm beneath her hair. Holding her still, he bent down and brushed his mouth against the cheek he had struck. For an infinitesimal second his lips parted slightly and lingered.

'We'll talk when I get back,' he murmured against her skin. 'God keep you, lady.' Then he was gone.

Isabel stood alone in the solar. 'Guy, I love you,' she whispered after him. And in her heart she allowed hope to blossom into fragile life again. He had not said that he believed her, had only touched her for that fleeting moment, but she knew what she had felt. The powerful hand, holding her so carefully, had been shaking.

'Two days,' sighed Isabel, sealing a small jar of dried herbs and laying it aside.

An answering sigh came from the fair-haired girl standing next to her. 'I know. Already it feels more like the two weeks Guy promised. But remember, we swore not to count the days, Isabel. Why, I won't even mention Simon more than ten times today.'

'Well, that's once,' murmured Isabel sceptically, and grinned at her new sister-in-law. The light-hearted expression still felt strange to her, but she was getting used to it.

Joanna grinned back, her serene beauty sparkling into the quick, unexpected mischief that Isabel had seen in fitzAlan.

In the two days since the men had been gone the girls had become close friends, beginning from the moment Joanna had knocked timidly on the solar door soon after Guy had left. Isabel had opened it, taken one look at Joanne's over-bright eyes and trembling mouth, and had promptly burst into tears herself.

The next several minutes had been spent, as Joanna put it, enjoying a good weep on each other's shoulders. They had finally calmed down, smiled sheepishly — albeit damply — at one another, and Joanna had

demanded the whole story, from Isabel's meeting with
Guy right down to their arrival at Ashby Chase.

Isabel had told her, unable to deny herself the relief
of letting the truth out at last. To her considerable
surprise Joanna had been entirely on her side.

'Don't tell me what that brother of mine is like,' she
had said fervently. 'One look from those eyes when
someone had displeased him and we'd all be walking
around on eggshells. I don't wonder you couldn't bring
yourself to tell him what was happening. But he's not
always like that,' she had assured Isabel hastily. 'Guy
can be very gentle. Amazingly so for such a big man. I
remember the time I found a wounded falcon. . .'

And Joanna had launched into the tale, thereafter
regaling her fascinated listener with other stories of
fitzAlan's past. Isabel had consumed the tales the way a
starving person consumed food and drink, and had
demanded more.

''Tis only fair to my poor Simon,' protested Joanna
now, laughing. 'I swear my tongue is worn out with
stories of Guy's exploits. And now this latest one. Two
weeks to march over a hundred miles, capture a castle
and march back? He must be going to take your advice,
Isabel. A normal siege can take forever. Look at this
place. Impregnable.'

''Tis not Tracy,' Isabel agreed. 'My maid is still
wondering whether she ought to learn to swim. With the
drawbridge raised 'tis the only way out of here.'

'Or in. Guy told me not to lower the bridge for
anyone except the villagers until he gets back.
Although, these days, no one with any sense leaves their
drawbridge down.'

Isabel tried to stifle a pang at the thought that Guy
had left instructions for their safety with his sister and
not his wife. She was being too sensitive, she told
herself. Joanna had been living at Ashby Chase for

many months and the serfs knew her well. She could see one now, hurrying through the herb garden to the little hut where they worked.

It was the elderly reeve, Fulk. As he drew nearer Isabel tensed suddenly. He looked pale and alarmed, even frightened. She touched Joanna's arm in warning, feeling the other girl stiffen as she, too, glanced through the open door.

'Nothing can have happened to them this soon,' Joanna whispered, crossing herself. 'Fulk, what is it? 'Tis not. . .?'

'No, my lady. . .ladies,' he corrected himself breathlessly, skidding to a stop just inside the door. 'Your husband and my lord are safe, I presume. Not but what 'tis trouble enough that they must needs be gone, leaving us with this madman on the other side of the moat. But it might be nought. Perhaps he's got the wrong place.'

'Got the wrong place?' Joanna looked at Isabel as if hoping for enlightenment. 'Madman?'

'Aye, madman,' asserted Fulk, nodding vigorously. 'He accuses my lord of injuring one of his knights who was trying to recapture a runaway slave, and says he won't budge until he receives compensation. I said I would fetch an answer and he smiled as though he knew my lord is not here, and replied that my lady would do as well, in fact better.'

'He *must* be mad!' exclaimed Joanna. 'Do you mean to say the fellow is going to besiege us because Guy hit one of his men who was about to. . .? That is to say. . . Good heavens! You don't think he means Ellen, do you, Isabel?' she amended hurriedly, remembering that no one at Ashby Chase knew of Isabel's sojourn in the alehouse.

'Jack is a free tenant,' Isabel managed to reply, a shivery premonition of danger beginning to creep along her nerves. Something was very, very wrong here, and the feeling that, somehow, she knew the cause was overwhelmingly strong.

'Then he can sit there until Guy comes back,' Joanna pronounced. 'When he'll regret ever leaving his castle. You may tell him so, Fulk. And then ignore him.'

'And so I would, my lady. Let him shout himself hoarse out there, I'd say, but there's more.'

'What?' asked Isabel. The inner tremors grew stronger.

'His men have rounded up the children from Ashbrook—'tis one of my lord's villages a mile or so from here,' he explained when Isabel made a small querying sound. 'I don't know why, but I don't like it. Why all of them if he's searching for one slave?'

'That doesn't make sense,' Joanna agreed. She turned puzzled eyes on Isabel again. 'If his quarrel is a personal one he might try to starve us out before Guy comes home, but. . .does he mean to take village children hostage? Their ransom would hardly make it worth while.'

'Did he give a name?' Isabel whispered, holding Joanna's sapphire gaze as though the guileless, open sincerity within would ward off the evil moving closer. But she knew. She knew before Fulk spoke. She knew the rebel baron who had been ravaging the countryside, the man whose name Ralf had been unable to recall. She knew and fought against knowing.

'Eudo de Raimes.'

Joanna's startled face jolted Isabel into the realisation that it was she who had spoken, not the reeve.

'Fulk?'

'Lady Isabel is right, my lady. 'Tis the name he gave.'

'Isabel? Do you know him, then?'

'I know him.' A chill calm enveloped her, a sense of inescapable fate. 'He is the man who murdered my father and sister when he attacked Tracy Castle, who made my other sister's life such a hell that she killed herself rather than endure it any longer, and who then would have forced me to wed him in her place.'

'Mother of God,' breathed Joanna. 'What happened?'

'Our priest managed to get a message out to the King, who sent Miles, Sheriff of Gloucester, to rescue us. He took us to Gloucester since Edmund was too young to hold Tracy alone, and then the Empress landed in England, the Sheriff went over to her almost immediately, and we were prisoners once again.'

'And Guy knows nothing of this? No, of course he doesn't. We'll have to send someone after him. Thank the saints a messenger will travel faster. . .' She paused when Isabel shook her head. 'Don't worry, Isabel. I know we've only a small garrison left, but he can't get in and you're hardly a runaway slave, no matter what de Raimes intended in the past. Besides, he may not know about you; his purpose may be nothing more than he says.'

'He knows. I don't know how he guessed 'twas me with Ellen the other day, but he swore vengeance three years ago when he was banished to his smaller estate and forced to hand Tracy to the Sheriff of Gloucester, and he doesn't forget.'

'Well, if he thinks we're just going to hand *you* over, he can think again,' stated Joanna fiercely. 'And so I shall tell him.'

She marched out of the hut, eyes sparkling with unaccustomed wrath. Isabel and Fulk hurried after her.

But even Joanna's courage was shaken at the sight and sounds that confronted them when they mounted to the walkway at the top of the curtain wall.

Across the broad, still water of the moat stood at least a dozen mounted soldiers, more than enough to overcome the serfs, since most of them would have been at work in the fields. The sound of high-pitched wailing from the woods indicated that the village women were being held there, out of sight but close enough to hear what was going on. But the most blood-chilling sight of all was the man who sat his horse a little apart from the others. Before him, almost under his horse's hoofs, knelt four or five small children, bound together and obviously terrified.

'Holy Saint Peter save them,' cried Joanna. 'They'll be trampled.'

Her clear voice carried easily to the waiting horseman.

'An interesting alternative to hanging, my lady,' he called back. 'But my business is not with you. Ah, I thought so.' He nodded once in satisfaction as Isabel stepped away from Joanna and stood apart. 'Lady Isabel de Tracy. I am rarely mistaken.'

'In this instance you are sadly at fault, my lord,' retorted Joanna. 'This is my sister, Lady Isabel fitzAlan.'

'I can get a clear shot from here, my lady,' murmured a young soldier near them. 'While he's stewing over that information.'

'No!' protested Isabel quickly. She turned to Joanna. 'De Raimes's men are. . .are. . .' She couldn't think of words bad enough to describe them. 'He deliberately picks the most brutal, the most savage. . . The children would be killed immediately. The women, too.'

Joanna nodded. 'Do nothing,' she instructed the man. He lowered his bow reluctantly. The other men stationed along the wall returned grim faces to the tableau below.

''Tis me he wants,' Isabel continued. 'And he knows we're helpless.'

As though he had heard the low-voiced conversation

on the wall, de Raimes cupped his hands around his mouth and shouted again. 'One name or another matters not. Your surrender for the life of these brats, Isabel. I'll even withdraw my men to assure your so-called sister that I don't want her brother's castle. She can lower the drawbridge for you, then raise it again without hindrance. You have until that cloud above you moves past the sun, then I string this peasants' spawn from the nearest tree. One by one.'

'Dear God,' whispered Joanna, glancing at the sky. They only had minutes. 'How does he expect to get away with this? 'Tis against every code of honourable warfare. Doesn't he care for his soul, or his own life? If he kills those poor children, Guy will kill *him*.'

'Guy is at least three days away,' said Isabel with dreadful calm. She hadn't bothered to look up. There was no alternative to surrender, and she knew it. 'Plenty of time for de Raimes to lock himself into his keep. He'll do it, Joanna. I know him. He won't stand back and negotiate a time to allow us to summon help. The man is evil. Vice is his pastime. He'll hang those innocents in front of us all unless I go to him.'

'You can't! There must be something we can do. Our archers are top marksmen. If——'

'What of the men we can't see, my lady?' broke in Fulk grimly. 'Those in the woods. If we attack, they would have their instructions.'

An angry murmur of frustrated agreement sounded along the wall. Isabel knew that some of the men had wives in those woods.

'Oh, dear God, why didn't I call the villagers into the castle?' Joanna wrung her hands in despair, beginning to weep.

Isabel flung her arms around her sister-in-law. 'You weren't to know this would happen,' she cried. 'No one could have foreseen this.'

'Aye,' nodded Fulk. 'We're in country loyal to the King and my lord didn't expect trouble. Least of all from a creature like that, lost to all decency and proper codes of conduct. Evil, indeed. Don't blame yourself, lady.'

'Fulk is right, Joanna.'

'But that doesn't help you,' sniffed Joanna. She glanced skyward again, where a brighter haze was appearing at the edge of the cloud, and made a sound of mingled anger and helplessness, clutching Isabel tighter.

Isabel gently disengaged herself. 'Tell them to lower the drawbridge, Joanna.' She turned to look out over the battlements again and raised her voice just as the sun broke through. 'We accept your terms. Tell your men to stand back. I will come out.'

And so this is how it ends, she thought minutes later as she walked with steady steps across the wooden planks. There would be no chance to tell fitzAlan the truth, no chance to discover how he felt about her, no chance at life and happiness. Joanna had vowed to send a message to Guy as soon as they were out of sight. She had agreed, had even reassured her sister-in-law that de Raimes was unlikely to kill her immediately. But in her heart Isabel had known it was too late. She would die by her own hand before the man she was approaching so unflinchingly had the chance to dishonour fitzAlan's name by using her for his amusement.

And if there was any justice remaining in this world, she would take de Raimes with her when she left it.

CHAPTER TWELVE

THE most frightening thing about Baron Eudo de Raimes, Isabel decided several hours later, was that he didn't *look* vicious, or even particularly dangerous. He wasn't a tall man, nor strongly built. Rather he was not much taller than herself and almost comically rotund. In fact, she thought, tonsure his greying hair and put him into a plain robe and he would have passed for a tubby, somewhat benign-looking monk.

Until you looked into his strangely colourless eyes. Then you saw evil — soulless, malevolent evil.

But Isabel would not permit herself to do that. Instead she glanced about the small chamber off the hall into which she had been ushered, thanking whatever saint had been responsible that de Raimes was apparently going to keep her to himself. It wouldn't last, of course. She knew his methods. Sooner or later his men would take their turn with her. If she was lucky, she would be dead before they had their chance.

The room was dim, lit only by rushlights high up on the walls, and furnished sparsely with a trestle, some chairs and a bed. She would not permit herself to look at that either.

'A cup of wine, my dear Isabel? Meat will be on the table shortly, but perhaps a refreshing draught before-hand. We'll drink a toast.'

'To your early death,' returned Isabel coldly. She might be light-headed with fear, but she would not give this vile creature the pleasure of seeing it.

De Raimes laughed, but the sound had a nasty ring to it. 'Dear me, I can see a lesson in manners will be called

249

for. Just a small one, not too painful. I enjoy spirit in a woman until I'm ready to crush it. Your sister Alice was sadly lacking in that respect. She became quite boring, indeed.'

Rage erupted inside Isabel. She felt hot blood shoot straight to her head, making her temples throb. 'She had spirit enough to fling herself from the tower to be free of you. That took more courage than you'll ever possess. And don't think I'll hesitate to do the same.'

The falsely affable mask slipped for a second, then de Raimes was smiling again. She remembered that avid, anticipatory smile. It sickened her.

'A fitting end, perhaps, to go like her,' he responded blandly. 'After all, Alice did sacrifice her virtue for you and that grubby brat of a brother—Edward, was it?'

'Edmund,' enunciated Isabel through gritted teeth.

'Aye, Edmund. Well, I will surely keep your desires in mind, Isabel. I might even throw you over the battlements myself when I've finished with you. Or mayhap 'twould be more pleasurable to watch it done by another. An interesting question. And there is a knight here who would be happy to accept the task. A small reward for having to live the rest of his days with a deformed jaw, thanks to your husband.'

'The rest of his days will be counted on the fingers of one hand when Guy hears of this,' Isabel spat. 'As will yours.' But her voice quivered on the last word as she remembered the cold, dispassionate violence of the man in the alehouse. She had not one, but two enemies to face, and didn't know which was more terrifying.

De Raimes' smile broadened. 'Oh, I think not. You haven't looked around, Isabel. Did you not notice the gatehouse?'

She had. Isabel repressed another shudder. The entrance to de Raimes' castle was a death trap, no less. A long, narrow corridor of stone with a portcullis at each end, it was designed to render an invading force helpless once they had entered its confines, when both grilles would be dropped. The men within would then be fired upon through holes in the roof, picked off like pigeons in a cote, Isabel had thought when she had ridden through it earlier.

'Only a fool would risk that gatehouse,' she said, turning a haughty shoulder on de Raimes. 'And my husband is no fool.' She took a few steps about the room, hoping the movement successfully concealed her dread.

Her captor chuckled. 'Perhaps not, but he's a man of unusual strength and courage. Such men are inclined to be reckless.'

Isabel stopped her pacing about the room and looked at de Raimes in surprise.

He laughed. 'I've seen your husband before, my dear. So has Boisson, the man he struck the other day. At Lincoln, to be precise. Aye, I was there. Really, your surprise is most unflattering. I swung my sword a time or two before retiring from such a dismal cause.'

'Ran away, you mean.'

'Hmm. You appear to be as reckless as fitzAlan.' De Raimes' voice lost some of its smooth mockery. 'We'll see how far it takes you when you watch him try to clear the gatehouse the way he charged through a whole company of men that day, sword flashing right and left, trying to get to the King. He was fortunate to get away with his life, but sooner or later his luck will run out.'

Isabel smiled. 'A man of strength and courage, indeed,' she said softly. 'Thank you. I will treasure the memory you've just given me.'

De Raimes' eyes narrowed as her meaning sank in. 'Why, you little bitch!' he said softly. 'You——'

The door opened. A serf hesitated apprehensively in the entrance. 'Your supper, my lord.'

'Well,' barked de Raimes, turning on the man, 'come in, fool! Do we have to starve while you hover there?' He glared back at Isabel. 'Very clever, my lady, but over-hasty. You give yourself away.'

'How so?' Isabel heard herself ask the question but her attention was suddenly drawn to the servant setting food and trenchers on the table. A loaf of bread was plunked down not far from her. And a knife. Its blade gleamed dully in the shadows.

'You love him.' De Raimes nodded as her head jerked back to him. 'And you can't have been married long. The last I heard you were still in Gloucester with the Empress Matilda, so, whether fitzAlan loves you also or has yet to lose interest in your pretty face and form, he will come for you. I shall enjoy watching you observe his futile efforts to save you.'

'You're mad,' she whispered in horror. 'Revenge I can understand. You swore to destroy my father and take his castle when he refused your offer for Alice — 'twas evil, but no worse than many another who coveted another man's property. But why the rest of us? Why fitzAlan?'

De Raimes shrugged carelessly and picked up the lid of a warming dish, inspecting the food beneath it. He waved the servant away. 'Get you gone. And don't come back until I call for you.

'Why the rest of you?' he repeated as the man departed. 'I swore to destroy the house of de Tracy, Isabel, not merely your father. Revenge is never sweet unless 'tis thorough. Hugh de Tracy refused me his daughter as if I had less worth than the slave who cleans out the garderobe tunnel. As for fitzAlan. . .did you think killing three of my men would go unnoticed? He was recognised.'

'So they were your soldiers at the ford,' Isabel realised.

'Of course. And the description of fitzAlan's lady I found most interesting.' He replaced the lid of the dish and came to stand beside her, staring at her with malicious eyes. 'Did you think I had forgotten how you smuggled that message out of Tracy, forcing me to lose almost everything? I've been waiting a long time, watching the roads, asking about new arrivals in the large towns. There was a slight chance the girl at the ford was you, and Boisson had orders to keep his eyes open while he was collecting rents. The fool was careless, of course, but then he didn't expect to find Lady Isabel de Tracy in a flea-ridden alehouse. However, when he recovered his senses your name was all I needed. After that a visit to Jack proved most enlightening.'

'What did you do to him?' she whispered. She couldn't meet that cold, unblinking stare.

'Not a lot, unfortunately. His bluster turned to co-operation quite soon. 'Tis how I learned that you'd been at the castle. Some discreet enquiries there yielded the information that fitzAlan was about to take Tracy, leaving his new wife at home. Amazing how far a little coin will go. The only thing I couldn't discover was how he managed to get you out of Gloucester and marry you after all. The man must be extraordinarily persistent. I thought I had put him off rather neatly four years ago. The tale will make very interesting hearing.'

'I don't know what you're talking about, but even if I did I wouldn't tell you anything.'

'Ah, I can see you will prove much more rewarding than your sister. But remember, Isabel, if you dislike your present position, that once I offered you honourable marriage. A brief moment of madness, I admit. I must have been drunk.'

'Honourable marriage? To you? She looked at him at last, with such obvious disgust that de Raimes' face darkened. 'The very state of holy wedlock would have been defiled.'

'Keep going, madam,' he grated through set lips. 'You will only make things more painful for yourself later, and more pleasurable for me.' Suddenly his hand moved, fastening around one slender wrist so tightly that Isabel's bones cracked. Her eyelids flickered, but she made no other sign. He laughed softly. 'Aye, very pleasurable, but first we'll eat, while I describe some of the activities you can look forward to. You shall learn the delights of anticipation, my dear.'

With surprising strength he jerked Isabel forward, releasing her just as abruptly. She hit the edge of the table with bruising force, her upper body sprawling over its surface. Her splayed arms sent the dishes clattering.

De Raimes made an annoyed sound with his tongue. 'How very clumsy of you, Isabel. I think you should serve my meal first as penance. On your knees. That may begin to teach you your proper place.'

Isabel hadn't moved. A fierce, terrified elation raced through her veins as her eyes fell on the knife only an inch away from her hand. Her fingers closed over the handle, the half-raised posture of her body shielding the movement from de Raimes. It had to be now. This might be the only chance she would have. She would stab de Raimes and then turn the blade on herself. A quick end, rather than torture and rape at the hands of those barbarians in the hall.

It was true, she thought distantly as her muscles tensed. One's whole life did flash before one's eyes at the moment of death. Oh, Guy. . .*Guy*. . .

'This is all you'll get from me,' she cried, coming up and around with a swiftness born of wild desperation.

He was closer than she had expected. Her hand was still at table height. There was no time to raise it and draw back for a stabbing blow. With the swing of her arm, the knife flashed through the air, light dancing off its foot-long blade. It caught de Raimes low in the body, slicing across and downwards.

Apart from the soldier at the riverbank, which had been accidental, Isabel had never attacked anyone in her life. Her reaction paralysed her. She hadn't expected her stomach to churn, her throat to close up, at the sound of ripping fabric and flesh. Sickened, she staggered back, her trembling hand almost dropping the weapon. For a moment she couldn't believe she had actually struck, then she stared in horrified fascination at the dark red stain spreading diagonally across de Raimes' belly and down to his thigh.

He looked down also, appearing as horrified as she. His hand clutched at his groin. 'You've cut me,' he said, as if not quite believing it. Blood welled between his fingers. 'You vicious little bitch,' he roared suddenly. 'You've damned near castrated me. Guards! *Guards,* damn it!'

The door burst open. Men rushed into the room. Belatedly Isabel remembered what else she was supposed to do. She tried to lift her hand, but the knife now seemed as heavy as a sword. For some reason she could only move with nightmarish sluggishness, while everyone around her tore past with dizzying speed.

Someone knocked the knife from her hand. Another man flung his arm around her throat and held her, pulling her slightly off balance so she couldn't struggle. His free hand wrenched her arm around, cruelly forcing it up against her back. The rest crowded around de Raimes, who had staggered to a chair. Isabel watched it all in a daze, barely conscious of the pain of the soldier's grip.

"Tis not deep,' said a nervous voice. A man in the long robe of a clerk or scribe bent over the injured baron. 'A glancing blow, but will take time to heal. 'Tis a sensitive spot, my lord.'

'I know that, damn you,' snarled de Raimes, his face pale and sweating. 'Just bind it somehow so I can get on my feet and deal with that slut.'

'Leave her to us, my lord,' growled a voice in Isabel's ear. We'll take a slice out of her own sweet flesh.' He jerked her arm higher.

A gargled sound came from the doorway and every eye turned that way. The man who stood there was dark with coal-black eyes. One side of his jaw was swollen and bruised, his mouth almost invisible. The swelling made it impossible to discern his expression, but it was easy to see that the lower half of his face would always be grotesquely twisted.

Isabel felt her blood freeze. She almost passed out with terror. There would be no mercy for her now. When de Raimes had exacted his revenge he would hand her over to his knight, who would complete her destruction. She didn't need to listen to the words when she could read her future in their eyes.

'No. You'll have your turn, but Boisson and I have a score to settle with the bitch first.' De Raimes' breath hissed out and he cuffed the man working over him. 'Clumsy fool! Watch what you're doing.'

'Your pardon, my lord, 'tis awkwardly —— '

'Get on with it!'

''Tis done, my lord.' The man shuffled back a few paces, bent almost double. 'But I must beg of you, my lord, not to move impulsively. You should be laid on your bed for several days at least.'

'Several days? Aye, 'twill serve.' Deadly eyes went to Isabel's ashen face. 'You'll learn the pleasures of anticipation, my lady, where you can do no damage. We'll see how much fight is left in you after some time in the dungeon. Mayhap you'll prefer the company down there.' He gestured to the man behind Isabel. 'Let her go.'

She staggered and almost fell when the man obeyed. Her left arm hung uselessly at her side, agony tearing through it from shoulder to wrist as the circulation returned. Someone grabbed her elbow, thrusting her out of the room, and she cried out with the pain, then clamped her teeth into her lip. She tried to think, but waves of agony kept washing over her, dulling her mind. Dimly she was aware that de Raimes was being carried by two men, that she was being prodded and pushed down a flight of stairs.

It could have been hours or minutes later that Isabel found herself staring into a dark pit. More stairs led downwards. Hadn't she seen something like this once before? she thought vaguely. She had been with fitzAlan and —

'Your quarters, my lady,' purred an evil voice at her side. 'You'll find they are an improvement on the last place I provided for you. This time you will have light, the better to see your company.'

A soldier went ahead of her, holding a rushlight. It flickered over stone walls, glinting on darker, shinier patches here and there. At the foot of the stairs he shoved the torch into a wall sconce, pushed Isabel further into the gloom, and retraced his steps. The air was bitterly cold and still, with the peculiar lifelessness that pervaded closed-off places. It smelled of rotten straw, damp and an overpowering stench that caught in her throat, almost choking her.

'When I've recovered you'll be released, Isabel,' de Raimes called down to her. 'Think about what will happen to you when that times comes. Remember how your sister Constance died.'

Just before the trapdoor slammed shut, cutting off de

Raimes' harsh laughter and the additional light from above, Isabel saw an indistinct lump in one corner.

The lump didn't move. How long she stood there, just as immobile, staring at the bundle of rags, Isabel never knew. As her eyes adjusted to the darkness she saw that the dungeon was a fairly large open area, the light from the sconce barely reaching the furthest walls. A row of darker rectangles indicated smaller cells along one side. Water dripped somewhere. In several places it ran down the walls. Panic licked at the corners of her mind. Blackness, the dank chill, the faint rustle of tiny creatures in the darkest corners — it was terrifyingly familiar, threatening her very sanity.

'This isn't the same as before,' she whispered to herself, still frozen to the floor. 'You have light. If anything moves you can see it coming.' Her gaze shifted to her fellow prisoner. 'And 'tis not Edmund, but 'tis human company.'

She took a tentative step forward and then another. The stench grew worse, making her gag, but it was not until Isabel was standing over the motionless form that she realised why. She was alone in this dreadful place after all. Death had long since claimed her companion.

Thunder woke her out of a fitful sleep. Isabel started up, bewildered, as the low rumble faded away. Had she been dreaming? Thunder could not penetrate the layers of stone above and around her.

Rubbing a weary hand over her face, she tried to estimate how long she had slept. Beyond the small cell the light from the sconce was barely discernible. Soon she would have to use the last of the rushes. That meant three nights, she thought. Three nights she had been imprisoned here — the last one without food or water, since the guard had not come at his usual time.

At first she had been surprised when a flask and a

chunk of bread had been tossed down to her that first
night, until she had remembered that de Raimes did not
want her dead just yet. For a while she had considered
starving herself, but one thought made her force down
the bread and drink the water. She had been given a
chance of survival. Every day she spent in the dungeon
meant that fitzAlan came closer.

The knowledge had steadied her. With a strength
Isabel had not known she possessed she had beaten
back panic and calmly taken down the rushlight, dividing the rushes into smaller bundles to conserve the light.
She could do nothing about the cold or the slick damp
that covered the walls, but she had gathered as much
straw as she could and had made a bed in the driest of
the cells. By sheer force of will she ignored the sounds
of pattering and gnawing near the body in the corner.
And she looked for a way out, though she knew there
was none. It passed the time.

Today, however, de Raimes had obviously stopped
the food and drink. Fear coiled inside her. Perhaps he
was planning to weaken her before she was released
from the dungeon. He must be very sure that his fortress
was safe from fitzAlan.

'But it isn't,' Isabel whispered, getting stiffly to her
feet. 'He'll find a way in. You have to believe that. You
have to.'

Her voice echoed eerily in the cold air and she
shivered, chafing some feeling into her frozen hands.
She had to be strong. Joanna's messenger would have
reached Tracy by now. She could survive another day or
two — even in the darkness. She would not think of her
dry mouth or her empty stomach, or the clammy chill of
the dungeon that had seeped into every bone in her
body. She would not think of the pitiful remains in the
corner. She would keep busy. While she still had light

she would continue to search for a way out; she
would——

A distant explosion of sound scattered her thoughts
like leaves in the wind. It was followed by another,
much nearer, and then a third, the echoes becoming one
continuous thundering roar that seemed to go on forever. Isabel stood as though chained to the floor, her
heart galloping out of control like a runaway steed as
she tried to make sense of the unholy din.

It was too soon to be fitzAlan, she told herself, reason
overwhelming her first impulsive hope. And no storm
made that much noise. Unless de Raimes' castle was
falling down by itself, he was under attack from someone, and if no one came for her she could be buried
alive, forgotten, trapped in the darkness until death
overcame her.

Shaking with terror, Isabel put a hand to the wall in
an attempt to hold on to something solid, only to have it
scoot across the slimy surface, almost throwing her to
the ground. Her frightened cry was smothered by yet
another explosion that shook the stones next to her and
sent a dozen small creatures streaming out of the dark
corners and across the floor, their high-pitched squeaks
audible even above the shattering reverberations
assaulting her ears. Beyond the doorway the dim light
flared suddenly, illuminating the fleeing rats with an
unearthly orange glow. Tiny red eyes gleamed at her for
a moment before disappearing.

She cried out again and thought another voice
answered. Holy saints, was she losing her mind? Isabel
froze, straining to hear.

'Isabel!' This time the yell reached her over the crash
of falling masonry.

'Guy!' she screamed, starting forward. She trod on
something soft and screamed again.

'*Isabel*!'

He sounded closer. Isabel stumbled out of the dark cell into a scene that made the priests' descriptions of hell seem tame.

Where part of the roof and the top of one wall had been there was a jagged, gaping hole. Dust still swirled above the pile of stone and rubble on the floor below it, creating a hazy curtain behind which red and orange flames danced and writhed like living things. The staircase had all but been buried under the collapsing wall.

'Guy,' she called out again, looking wildly about her. Then she saw fitzAlan, halfway down the steps, almost unrecognisable with sweat-darkened hair, his face streaked with dirt and dust. Isabel started to run towards him just as another block of stone came away from the wall, hurtling downwards. It tore the sconce from its bracket before crashing to the floor, sending debris flying in all directions.

Isabel fell back, flinging her hands up to protect her head. She felt a sharp blow to her arm and gasped, retreating further. Through the cloud of dust she saw fitzAlan sheath his sword and crouch at the edge of the stairway. Putting his hand to a crumbling step, he vaulted down to the ground and landed running.

His hand reached for her as the whole building seemed to shudder under another asssault. 'Come on,' he shouted, urging Isabel towards the stairs. 'This place is about to fall apart.'

She followed blindly, stumbling over the shifting piles of stone blocking the stairway. Her foot caught and she wrenched it free of its shoe, clinging to fitzAlan's hand all the while as he half led, half pulled her upwards. Through eyes watering from smoke and dust Isabel saw daylight and the castle entrance and knew they had reached the guard-room. They were halfway across it when an enraged, strangled shout came from behind them.

'*FitzAlan!*'

She knew that distorted voice. Boisson had been waiting for them.

Guy whirled. Isabel saw his face go taut an instant before he whipped an arm around her and dived for the floor, taking her down with him. As soon as they hit the ground he rolled, shoving Isabel beneath him.

'Stay down,' he rasped.

The clang of a sword blade ringing on the stones where she had just been standing made the order unnecessary. Isabel flattened herself, only risking a glance over her shoulder when she felt Guy's weight lift off her.

He came up off the floor in one swift, powerful lunge, slamming the full force of his body into Boisson and driving him back towards the dungeon before the man could gather himself for another swing. The heavy two-handed sword fell with them, sliding along the floor as the two men wrestled each other in a deadly silence broken only by the sound of fists meeting flesh and their hoarse breathing.

Isabel watched in horror. She had seen Guy fight before at the river crossing, but then he had been quick and efficient. In this encounter there was no time for swordplay or skill. It was bloody, primitive, brutal. Both men were fighting for their lives. She saw Guy jerk back to avoid a slashing blow to the throat, then they closed again, rolling right to the edge of the treacherous stairway.

Isabel cried out. She couldn't see who was on top. The smoke was too thick. She was too far away. Sobbing, gasping for breath, she began to crawl across the floor. She had not moved more than a few inches when one of the men broke free, his fist smashing downwards. His opponent's head snapped back over the edge of the drop and was still. And at last Isabel saw who it was.

She collapsed on the floor again, not moving as fitzAlan got to his feet. Her eyes studied Boisson. He didn't look dangerous at all now, she thought, lying there like a mummer's puppet flung down with its limbs every which way and the head at an odd angle. Her gaze lifted to fitzAlan's face. Now *he* looked savage, his eyes still glittering with deadly ferocity. There was a raw graze across one cheekbone. Blood ran from a cut on his jaw.

He hunkered down beside her just as a flaming beam from the ceiling crashed to the ground only inches away. Isabel didn't even flinch.

'He recognised you,' she whispered. 'At the alehouse.'

'Did he?' FitzAlan slid one arm around her shoulders and the other beneath her knees. Very carefully he lifted her into his arms. 'We have to get out of here, darling. 'Tis quicker if I carry you. Trust me.'

She wondered why he was speaking to her in such a quiet, gentling tone, then realised how stiffly she was holding herself. Her hands were splayed across his broad shoulders as if she would push him away, and for some reason she couldn't seem to relax them.

'I'm sorry,' she managed. Even her teeth were clenched tight; she could barely speak. 'I don't know what's wrong with me.'

He held her closer. 'It doesn't matter.'

Then suddenly there was cool air on her face and light that hurt her eyes. And a familiar voice speaking to fitzAlan.

'Guy! Thank the lord you found her.'

Isabel looked around. As abruptly as it had become paralysed, her tongue was loosened. 'Hello, Simon. You've got a black eye.'

De Villiers' hazel eyes shot from her face to fitzAlan at the bright greeting. One brow went up.

'Shock,' said Guy tersely. He handed her over to Simon. 'Get her away from all this smoke. I'll be with you in a minute.'

'Place is about to collapse,' agreed Simon. 'Come on, little sister.'

'That wasn't very nice of him,' protested Isabel as Simon strode off with her. She cringed at the too cheerful sound of her voice. What was wrong with her? First her unnatural stiffness with fitzAlan, and now this. She couldn't seem to stop talking. 'He's always leaving me with you. Not that I don't like you, Simon, but you would think if the man goes to all this trouble to rescue me he could at least stay around afterwards.'

'He'll be back. Guy swore to bury de Raimes under his own keep and he's going to see it done.'

'Very thorough,' she approved with an abrupt about-face. 'I want to watch. I'm the last of my family and I have to watch. He killed my father, you know. And my sisters. And who's to say that Edmund wouldn't be alive today if. . .?' The dreadful spate of words at last dried up. It was followed by a strange feeling of detachment, as if she'd suddenly gone somewhere else.

De Villiers' shrewd eyes scanned her face. 'Then we'll watch,' he said. A few yards further on he stopped at the edge of a grove of trees. Several horses were tethered there. 'It shouldn't be long now,' Simon continued, setting her down on the grass. 'We've been bombarding the place since dawn.'

Isabel looked back up the slight incline to the castle. Sounds of fighting could still be heard from the far side of the bailey, but it was easily apparent that de Raimes' men were outnumbered and outclassed. And the castle itself no longer provided any defence at all. Flames shot through a window high up in the keep. Half the gatehouse was missing.

The cause of the wreckage was not hard to find. A

hundred yards away two great mangonels had been set up. Even as she watched, the arm of one was released, propelling a huge boulder through the air with terrific force. It soared over the wall and hurtled into the side of the keep, enlarging the hole already there. A second rock followed immediately and a wide, jagged crack appeared in the wall.

'Great shot!' exclaimed Simon. 'Right into his foundations.'

'There's so much damage,' murmured Isabel, sinking to the ground.

''Twas built on marshy land, fortunately for us,' Simon told her. 'Not like Ashby Chase, which is built on rock, with the lake and moat put in later. A few years of storms with plenty of rain would probably have undermined this place anyway. Once the foundations go, the rest follows.'

'That's why the dungeon was so damp.' The words were a soft murmur, almost to herself, but Simon heard them.

'De Raimes kept you in a dungeon?'

Isabel nodded.

'God's teeth! A good thing Guy didn't know that before he st. . . I mean, before he killed the bastard.'

Isabel looked at him. 'How?' she asked serenely.

De Villiers hesitated.

'Do you think I'll grieve over the manner of that monster's death, Simon? How did Guy kill him?'

'No, you're too damned calm,' he muttered. 'Well, I'll tell you, but remember that we didn't know what we were going to find when we finally broke in. Hell, getting here was bad enough. We practically grew wings and flew. One look at the gatehouse told us that way would be suicide, so we launched a full-scale attack to distract them from you and get Guy over the wall. It worked, but I thought he was going to lose his mind when we found de Raimes locked in his solar and you were nowhere to be seen. The coward choked out that you were still alive and hadn't been harmed, but it didn't save his neck. Guy strangled him.'

Isabel's gaze went back to the crumbling keep. 'And now he's going to bury him.' She wasn't shocked at fitzAlan's actions.

'Aye.' Simon actually shuddered. 'He didn't even give de Raimes time to grab a weapon. 'Twas vengeance, pure and simple. I've never seen Guy like that. In battle he's unstoppable, but I've never seen him kill a man in cold blood before.'

'Not vengeance. Justice.'

Simon nodded, looking uncommonly solemn. Then he stiffened. 'Look! There it goes.'

There was a shattering roar. Before Isabel's awed eyes one entire side of the keep plummeted to the earth, leaving the interior exposed. Burning timbers crashed to the ground, to be extinguished in the billowing cloud of dust.

'Guy,' she cried, starting up.

'Don't worry. He'll be here.'

Isabel sank back to the grass, beginning to shake. The crash had jolted her out of her odd tranquillity. Somewhere deep inside her a tightly coiled tension was unravelling with frightening speed. She was starting to feel her bruises. One of her feet throbbed rather painfully. She seemed to have lost a shoe, and her dress was not only dirty but torn in several places.

She wasn't the only one. There was a girl sitting next to her who was barely recognisable as female. Her dark hair was a wild, half-damp tangle, her face and hands begrimed with a black substance that had the most awful smell. It reminded Isabel of the dungeon.

It was a full minute before she realised that she was looking at a reflection of herself in the polished metal

shield that Simon had propped against a tree to protect
her from any stray arrows.

'Oh, Mother of God, look at me!'

The sharp, high-pitched cry brought Simon's head
around. 'What's wrong?'

'*What's wrong*?' Isabel's voice soared. She stumbled
to her feet, wiping her hands uselessly on her tattered
dress before holding them out. Her nails were torn and
rimmed with black, as filthy as the rest of her. 'Look at
me!'

For the first time de Villiers seemed to notice the state
she was in. He grinned. 'Don't worry about it. Look at
any one of us. We're not dressed for a Court feast-day.
What's Joanna going to say about my eye?'

'Oh, Simon.' Isabel smiled back waveringly through
suddenly brimming eyes. 'You know Joanna will be
overjoyed to see you in any condition.' She burst into
tears.

'For God's sake, Simon! I thought you were looking
after her. What the hell. . .?'

At the sound of his brother-in-law's furious voice
Simon looked vastly relieved. 'She was all right until a
minute ago,' he protested. 'Cool as a nun's kiss. Then
all of a sudden——'

'Never mind. I shouldn't have left her, but I thought
she didn't want. . .' FitzAlan broke off, reaching out to
grasp Isabel by the shoulders.

She shrank away from him, covering her face. '*No*!
Don't touch me!'

'Oh, God. Isabel. . .' Ignoring her frantic protests,
Guy took her wrists and pulled her hands away from her
face. 'Sweetheart, don't be afraid of me, *please*. No one
is ever going to hurt you again, I swear it.'

With one glance from the weeping girl to fitzAlan,
Simon turned and strode back up the hill towards the
castle. Neither of them saw him go.

'I'm not,' Isabel sobbed, trying to pull away from fitzAlan. ''Tis de Raimes. . .what he did. . .'

Guy's face went white. He looked as if she'd hit him. 'Christ Jesu! Did he rape you? Did any of them?' His fingers tightened on her wrists. 'Isabel, tell me!'

'No!' she cried, momentarily ceasing her struggles. 'Do you think I wouldn't have died before they could dishonour you so?'

'Never mind my bloody honour!' he exploded, pulling her closer. 'I'm concerned about you! What did that bastard do to you?'

'He threw me in a dungeon.' Isabel started to cry again, shuddering sobs racking her body. 'There was a corpse in there and rats, and the rushes were almost used up. It was going to get dark and I'm so filthy and cold and —'

'Dear God. Come here, darling. Stop fighting me. Hush now. Hush, sweetheart.' Taking no notice of her feeble attempts to bat his hands away, Guy pulled Isabel into his arms, holding her tight, murmuring to her, soothing her.

After a long time the tears stopped. Isabel remained very still for a minute, thinking about how much worse she must look with red-rimmed eyes and tears mingling with the dirt on her face. 'You can let me go now,' she sniffed into his mail-clad chest. 'I've probably got fleas all over me, or worse, and I'm not crying any more.'

'No, but you're. . . Stop shaking, damn it! It's tearing me apart.'

''Tis. . .'tis the cold,' she stammered. Had her mind gone, or had she really heard that tormented note in his voice?

'I know. I know, sweetheart.' He folded her closer, his voice a deep, gentle murmur again.

She must be imagining things, Isabel decided. His kindness must have gone to her head, but she would not read too much into it. Now that the nightmare of her captivity had receded somewhat in the safety of his arms, she suddenly remembered, with painful clarity, the way they had parted, the truth still unspoken between them. He still thought her a traitor. He still thought her his enemy.

'I really am all right now,' Isabel insisted quietly, keeping her face lowered. She tried a tentative push against his chest. A mountain wouldn't have felt more solid and immovable. 'I'm sorry I made such a spectacle of myself.'

FitzAlan simply shifted his hold and lifted her off her feet. The beginnings of a smile lurked deep in his eyes, setting Isabel's heart racing when she ventured a glance up at him.

'Little idiot,' he said very softly. 'I'm never going to let you go again.'

CHAPTER THIRTEEN

ISABEL had clung to those words all the way home, wrapped snugly in fitzAlan's cloak, held fast in his arms. Every time she had protested that she could ride alone and was not fit to be near anyone until she'd had several baths he had laid his hand over her mouth and told her to hush.

Isabel had eventually hushed. It was so sweet to be held thus, to feel so cherished and protected. For a few precious hours she had savoured the sensation, and had determinedly closed her mind to the thought that only the most hard-hearted man would not have offered comfort in her present condition.

Torches were already flaring on the castle walls when the first wagons carrying the dismantled mangonels rumbled across the drawbridge. Men surrounded them, asking questions, full of their own tale to be told. And Joanna had sped down the outer stairway, crying and joyous at once. She had embraced Simon, patting his face and exclaiming over his bruised eye, and had then flown to Isabel, taking her in her arms and weeping over her enough, so her husband had said, to raise the level of the lake.

Joanna would have drawn Isabel indoors then, but fitzAlan would not permit her to walk. Her carried her up to the solar and delivered her over to the care of his sister and Ellen, leaving her with a look in his blue eyes that clearly said *later*.

And now later had come. Isabel was sitting on a stool by the fire, dressed in a filmy shift borrowed from Joanna, a mantle over her shoulders for extra warmth, when the door opened and he was there, tall and strong, the sconce lights gleaming on his fair hair. He had obviously cleaned up also, and shaved. The heavy chainmail was gone; he wore a long dark blue tunic, embroidered with silver thread and loosely belted at the waist. Soft knee-high boots, fashioned of calf-hide for light indoor use, were laced about his leggings. His white linen undershirt was open at the throat, drawing Isabel's gaze upward.

Vivid blue eyes glittered in his tanned face. Shadows cast by the open door slanted across the strong lines of nose and jaw, softening the hard line of his mouth. The graze along his cheekbone somehow managed to emphasise the tough, assured air he wore so easily.

Realising how she was staring at him, Isabel quickly looked back at the fire, leaning sideways a little so that her still-damp hair fell forward, partially shielding her face. She saw Joanna glance up when fitzAlan remained standing in the doorway.

'Guy? Is something wrong?'

There was a long pause, then he came into the room. 'No, nothing's wrong.'

There was an oddly arrested note in his voice. Isabel wondered what he was thinking, then Guy spoke again and the question was driven out of her mind.

'I'll care for her now. Go put a poultice or something on Simon's eye before he uses up all the raw meat in the kitchen.'

Joanna laughed, apparently sensing nothing amiss, and kissed Isabel's cheek. 'She's been through a terrible ordeal,' she told her brother severely, drawing Ellen out of the solar with her.

Guy shut the door after them. 'Does she think I need reminding?' he muttered.

Isabel didn't answer. She heard the key turn in the lock and a fear that was just short of primitive assailed her. She was suddenly far too aware that they were alone and wouldn't be disturbed until morning, too aware that the man whose overpowering masculine strength filled the room was her husband and had certain rights, too aware that the last frail layer of her protective façade had been shattered forever when she had wept in his arms and let him comfort her.

The utter vulnerability in loving a man who seemed to retain his formidable control no matter what the situation, while she fell apart, was terrifying. She felt exposed, raw. As if she stood naked before him, her very soul bared. Nowhere to hide. Defenceless.

'Isabel.'

The softly murmured name was like a hand stroking over her flesh. She started to tremble deep inside, a nervous quivering that was beyond her control. The tremors increased when fitzAlan crossed the room and hunkered down beside her stool.

He reached out a hand and brushed her hair back over her shoulder. 'You're hiding from me,' he accused gently, watching the cool silky strands cling to his long fingers. 'I asked you not to.'

'That. . .' Her voice sounded rusty, as if she hadn't used it for a long time. 'That was before. . .'

The caressing hand stilled and withdrew, but not very far. His forearm rested across one thigh, his fingers only inches from her own. 'Before I frightened you into running away from me.'

Isabel shook her head. She stared at their hands, hers slender, small-boned and delicate, his so tanned and strong. She remembered how he had killed de Raimes. He could break her.

'Why deny it? 'Tis the truth.' He was looking down, too, Isabel saw, risking a fleeting glance through her lashes. Without warning, his hand lifted to cover both of hers. 'You're afraid now. I can feel you trembling.'

Trembling and weak, she thought. Weak with a love that I can't speak of until you know the truth. Trembling with the fear that you might not believe in the truth or my love.

When she didn't respond, Guy removed his hand and reached into his tunic. 'I have something for you,' he said casually, producing a small wooden box. It was fashioned of sandalwood, beautifully carved, and no larger than was needed to hold a psalter. In fact, as Isabel knew well, that was exactly why the box had been made.

Guy placed it on her lap and stood up. 'I believe you gave that to the priest at Tracy for safekeeping when you were sent to Gloucester. He said you treasured it beyond any other possession.'

Her fingers touched the carved lid, trembled, and withdrew. Then all at once understanding dawned. Her eyes flew upward, looking at him for the first time. 'The priest. . . You know. . . I didn't think you'd had time to take Tracy. . .you came back so soon—'

'I should never have left you,' he burst out, startling her. 'God, Isabel, if anything had happened to you, if he had. . .' Biting off the rest, fitzAlan reached down and pulled Isabel up and into his arms. 'Forgive me,' he groaned hoarsely. 'Forgive me, my darling. I can't stand here and not hold you. Let me do that, at least. I swear I won't hurt you, I won't do anything to frighten you; I just need to hold you, to know you're alive and safe. *Isabel*. . .' His arms tightened convulsively and he buried his face in her hair. A violent shudder racked his powerful body.

The box and her mantle fell unheeded to the floor. Shock held Isabel utterly still. FitzAlan was holding her as if he would make her part of himself, as if he could not bear to be separate from her. This man who had strangled another with his bare hands to avenge her,

who had faced danger and death without flinching, was
trembling with the need to have her as close to him as
possible.

Hope broke over her in tumultuous waves. Unaware
that she was holding her breath, Isabel slowly slid her
arms around his waist. Very gradually she leaned into
his strength, letting him take her weight. He was so
warm. Sensation after sensation assailed her. The heat
of his body, the strength of his arms, the fierce rhythm
of his heart against her cheek. Swept by an overwhelming longing to touch him, she let her hands relax,
absorbing the feel of the hard muscles of his back
against her palms.

Guy tensed the instant she moved, as though bracing
himself for resistance. Then, as he felt her soften against
him, his hold changed. It was no less intense, but
suddenly Isabel felt a gentling in him, as if he held a tiny
helpless creature in his hands and was afraid of bruising
it.

'Isabel?'

She felt the whispered question rather than heard it.

'I'm not afraid.' How could she fear this man who
cradled her so tenderly, whose much greater strength
would only be used to protect her? Who, in one swift,
unexpected movement, had let her see that he was as
vulnerable as she? 'Can't you feel?' she murmured. 'I'm
not shaking any more.'

Guy's mouth moved against her. 'I hope not,' he
breathed. 'God, Isabel, I hope not.' He was silent for a
moment, then said, very low, 'Can you forgive me? I
hope for that, too, because I don't think I'll ever forgive
myself.'

'Because of de Raimes? You weren't to know.'

She tried to raise her head, wanting to see in his eyes
what she was feeling in his embrace, but Guy cupped
her cheek, holding her still against his chest. 'For de

Raimes, for believing that bitch at Gloucester even for a minute, for losing my damnable temper and not giving you a chance to tell me the truth.'

Isabel's heart jolted. The truth. No wonder he was so conscience-stricken and gentle. He knew what had happened years ago.

Guy gave her a little shake, rocking her against him. 'I know what you're thinking,' he murmured. 'There's no need to tense up on me. Your priest only knew about the past. I knew you were innocent of any willing betrayal before I left here.'

'I don't. . . You believed in my innocence before you left?' she repeated incredulously, not sure she had got it right.

'Absolutely.'

'But. . .but. . .I hadn't told you anything.'

'You didn't have to. Once I knew you were still. . . untouched. . .only one explanation made sense: that the Countess had some hold over you.'

'Aye,' she confirmed dazedly, unaware of clinging closer. ''Twas Edmund. I didn't know he had been killed. Matilda never told me. 'Twas why I fainted that day. I don't even know how he escaped from Tracy.' She couldn't get the words out fast enough, terrified that Guy couldn't possibly believe her, no matter what he said. It sounded so unlikely.

His mouth brushed across her hair. 'Edmund knew that some of the garrison had been called to Lincoln to fight for Matilda. 'Twould have been easy enough for a determined boy to climb the wall and follow them. He wasn't confined indoors. He told your priest he was old enough to fight to regain de Tracy honour.'

Tears sprang into Isabel's eyes. 'Old enough to fight?' she choked. 'He was barely fifteen.'

'Old enough,' Guy said gently. 'But I wish I had known, at Lincoln.'

'Could you have kept him safe?'

'Maybe.' He shrugged slightly. 'That's what you were trying to do, wasn't it?'

'Aye.' Her lip quivered again, but she pressed her cheek to fitzAlan's tunic and held on to her control. '*I* was going to sacrifice our honour. After de Raimes sacked Tracy he kept us in a dungeon for three months until Alice was forced to become his mistress, and had it not been for Edmund I would have lost my mind.'

''Tis all right, sweetheart, you don't have to ——'

'But I couldn't do it,' she continued, as if he had not spoken. 'I met Rainald to gain some time, not because of Edmund. I couldn't ——'

'Betray the Queen,' he finished for her.

But Isabel shook her head against him. 'No,' she whispered vehemently. 'I told myself that, but the truth was I couldn't betray *you*.' She felt his mouth lower to her cheek and hurried on. 'I wanted to tell you the morning you left, but you were in such a hurry to be gone and ——'

'I had to leave!' Releasing her abruptly, fitzAlan pulled Isabel's arms away from him and held them, gazing down at her face as if the sight of her tormented him beyond bearing and yet he still could not bring himself to look away. A ragged laugh escaped him at the startled look in her eyes. 'You don't know why, do you, little innocent? God damn it, we were married! I couldn't stay here and not throw you on that bed and take you, again and again and again, until you couldn't hide from me any longer!'

Isabel's eyes widened even further and he groaned. 'Oh, hell, now I've frightened you again.'

'No,' she said faintly. 'I thought. . . You left me alone. . .after the alehouse. . . You didn't speak, you didn't even *look* at me.'

'Don't you know why?' he demanded, his hands

tightening on her arms. 'Mother of God, I'd just struck you. 'Twas to stop you becoming completely distraught, but I was afraid to look at you, afraid to come to you that night in case I saw fear or revulsion in your eyes.'

'Afraid?' she squeaked. '*You*?'

'You think I'm immune to fear?' FitzAlan gave another short laugh. 'Believe me, I could have written a book on the subject when Joanna's messenger found us.'

Isabel shook her head in wonderment, then, quite unexpectedly, a tentative, almost teasing little smile flickered across her face. 'You hide your feelings rather well, also, my lord.'

Guy went completely still. 'I've never seen you smile,' he said huskily. 'Until now.'

His hands slid down to hers and an expression of such intense emotion burned in his eyes that Isabel glanced away, suddenly shy and uncertain. She felt him lace their fingers together and trembled with a strange mixture of excitement and trepidation. He must feel something for her. He must, to look at her like that.

'You didn't hurt me that day,' she said softly, her voice breathless with the pounding of her heart. 'It sounded bad, but ——'

'*Sounded* bad? My God, I've heard that slap in my head ever since. Do you know what it did to me to strike you like that? To see you go so pale and still? Do you know what it did to me to see that animal on top of you, about to. . .?' He broke off, closing his eyes as though in pain.

'I thought you were angry because I'd run away.'

There was a loaded silence. When fitzAlan opened his eyes again they were a brilliant, glittering blue. His hands gripped hers almost painfully. 'I was,' he said on a raggedly indrawn breath. 'Angry with you, aching for

you——' his voice dropped and went wholly intense
'—in love with you.'

Isabel felt as though one of the mangonels had just
rolled over her. She couldn't seem to catch her breath.
If Guy hadn't been holding her, she was sure she would
have dropped to the floor. She had dared to hope he felt
more than desire, but that he loved her. . . She was
afraid to believe in so much happiness all at once.

'You hated me,' she whispered. 'When we met again
at Gloucester you hated me.'

'*No!*' He pulled her closer. 'I was angry, but I've
never hated you, Isabel. And even the anger was mainly
at myself because I couldn't stop wanting you, even
after Matilda warned me of your. . .usefulness.'

Isabel glanced away, flushing. 'She lied.'

His voice gentled. 'I know.' When she didn't move,
he freed her hands to capture her face, tilting it gently
up to his. 'Darling, I swear I started questioning her
story as early as the next day. There were so many
things that didn't add up. I began to see the nervousness
in your eyes whenever I got too close to you, and when I
kissed you at the inn I knew that Matilda had lied about
one point at least. Then, just as I was convinced of your
innocence, I discovered you'd lied about your brother
and I caught you with Rainald. Everything just seemed
to go red. I was nearly crazy with pain and rage. I kept
throwing those accusations at you, hoping desperately
that you'd deny them, explain them somehow. . .'

He dragged in another uneven breath, his eyes
moving from her brow to her mouth as though engrav-
ing every detail on his mind. ''Twas as though I'd lost
something beyond price. That day in the garden. . .you
were so innocent, so gentle, so untouched by war and
betrayal. I couldn't have you, but I carried the memory
of that day into every battle, into every stupid, meaningless council, to every siege. It gave me something to

fight for, the knowledge that there was still one uncorrupted heart somewhere, one thing pure and unchanged. You were with me everywhere.' He looked into her eyes, his own anguished. 'Can you understand that, Isabel? Losing that memory felt like losing part of myself, but I never hated you. I couldn't hate you. I love you!'

She was starting to believe him. She had to, Isabel thought. No man could speak with such passionate urgency, look at her with such naked yearning, and not mean what he was saying.

''Tis all right, sweet,' he said quickly when she didn't answer him. 'I won't rush you. I know you need time, but I had to tell you. I can't bear you to be frightened of me.'

'I'm not,' she whispered brokenly. 'Oh, Guy, how could I be frightened of you? I love you. I've always loved you.'

'Oh, God, Isabel. . .' With the swiftness of movement that always surprised her, Guy swept her into an embrace that almost crushed her. 'I love you,' he vowed fiercely, as though she might still doubt him. 'I love you! You're my life, my heart.'

For a few moments he was content to hold her, then the solar spun before Isabel's vision as she was lifted into fitzAlan's arms.

'What are you —— ?'

'Hush,' he commanded. 'We've talked enough. You need to sleep, and if I hold you any more. . .'

A small smile curving her mouth, Isabel nestled trustingly against him as Guy carried her to the bed. Throwing back its bearskin cover, he lowered her carefully to the mattress and stood looking down at her. She lay perfectly still, knowing that when the light, filmy shift settled over her body it revealed more than it hid. When his eyes returned to her face they were almost

black with desire. A spasm of nervous excitement
tightened her insides.

'I'm not very sleepy,' she whispered.

'Sweetheart. . .' Guy sat down on the end of the bed.
There were lines of tension about his mouth, but his
hand was gentle as he cradled her lacerated foot.
'You've been hurt,' he said gruffly. 'Abused and frightened and hurt. You need gentleness tonight, not a man
on the knife-edge of control.'

'I'm not afraid.'

FitzAlan's eyes flashed to her face, then very carefully
he bent and pressed his lips to the cut across her instep.
It was the most tender of caresses and yet Isabel felt a
tingling sensation shoot straight up her leg to the most
secret part of her.

The tiny sound she made brought Guy's head up. A
muscle clenched in his jaw. 'Aren't you? I frightened
you once before, that first night in the hut, and I want
you a hell of a lot more now.'

'Ohhh.' A fiery tide of colour rushed to Isabel's
cheeks. She put her hands over her face. 'You knew. . .
all this time. . . You remembered. . .'

'No,' he said, a soft laugh escaping him at her obvious
embarrassment. 'I wish I had; 'twould have given me
some hope that you might come to care for me.'

When Isabel peeped at him through her fingers, Guy
laughed again. 'I only remembered tonight when I came
in and saw you drying your hair,' he assured her, his
blue eyes gleaming with tender amusement.

Isabel lowered her hands and held them out to him in
an invitation that was as ancient as womanhood. 'I
wasn't afraid of *you*,' she murmured, her face still
flushed but glowing with love. 'Only that you would
hate me.'

His eyes shut for one second, then he moved, coming

down on the bed beside her. 'No, never,' he breathed, taking Isabel into his arms. 'Never, my darling girl.'

Isabel went into Guy's embrace without an instant's hesitation or fear or memory of the past. Here there was no brutality, no force. There was only fitzAlan, leaning over her, his eyes brilliant with love and desire, his strong arms drawing her closer. And his mouth. That beautiful, hard mouth descending on hers in a kiss that held passion and tenderness, excitement and safety.

Her shift vanished in one swift movement, but in her husband's arms she felt no embarrassment. Even when Guy left her for the few seconds it took him to remove his own clothes, his murmured words of love and praise still warmed and reassured her.

Isabel lay looking up at him, her lips softly parted and moist from his kisses, eyes heavy-lidded with love and longing. He came back to her in a barely controlled rush, gently parting her legs, his mouth and hands caressing her body in a way that made her move sinuously against him, and which wrenched a low moan of need from his throat.

The heat and strength of him that had alarmed her that first night now enthralled her. She couldn't touch him enough in return. Her fingers widened, sliding over the bunched muscles of his shoulders, down through the golden hair feathering his chest, across the ridged hardness of his stomach. But when she would have moved lower in her innocent foray Guy captured her hands with one of his and pinned them gently above her head.

'Not this time, sweet,' he said raggedly, moving over her, slowly letting her feel some of his weight and the first seeking touch of his body. 'Relax, darling,' he whispered against her mouth. 'I'll be so gentle with you. . .so careful. . .'

Isabel gasped and clung to him. She felt her body

stretching, a slight resistance, but there was no pain. And then she gazed up at him, her hands gripping his shoulders and absorbed the incredible feeling of having him inside her.

FitzAlan's eyes blazed down into hers. 'At last,' he growled, his face taut with control, his breathing harsh. 'Mine. . .at last!' He slid one arm beneath her hips to lift her against him. 'Hold me, sweetheart. Hold me *tight*!'

Isabel was already clinging to him. A strange insistent pressure was beginning to build within her. She wanted. . .wanted. . . Then, just as the pressure became almost unbearable, Guy's mouth came down on hers and he began to move.

When Isabel at last returned to an awareness of her surroundings it was to feel the gentle touch of Guy's mouth, moving over her throat in a series of feather-light kisses. Her arms were clasped loosely around his back and she lay completed relaxed beneath him. The kisses moved to her face and she opened her eyes.

Guy was gazing down at her, an expression of such tenderness in his face that Isabel felt her heart shake.

'Did I hurt you, little one?'

'Never.' Her grey eyes were luminous with emotion. The closeness she felt was more than the joining of their bodies; it was all-encompassing, and shared, for in taking her he had also given himself. 'I didn't know,' she whispered, touching his face wonderingly. ''Twas like nothing. . .'twas so. . .oh, Guy. . .'

'I know, sweetheart.' He moved to the side, kissing away her soft protest and holding her close to the warmth of his body. ''Twas like nothing I've ever felt before either. I love you, Isabel.'

'Even though I'm no longer that innocent child?' she asked suddenly, not quite teasingly.

Guy's arms tightened about her. 'I don't want that child,' he assured her. 'She was a dream I held dear, but 'tis the woman you are now that I love — sweet and true and courageous.' He held her close for a moment, then drew back so he could see her face. 'And 'twas not for the hand of a child that I wrote to your father a year later.'

'Four years ago? You wanted to marry me four years ago?'

Guy smiled briefly at her astonishment. 'Aye. Stephen had just granted me the barony, and I decided 'twas time I had a wife. I know now that my letter fell into de Raimes' hands. I was in Normandy with the army, otherwise I would have gone to Tracy to claim you. It must have amused that bastard greatly to write back saying you were betrothed. And I never questioned it.' His mouth tightened with remembered pain and anger. ''Twas stamped with your father's seal, and I just accepted it — and then flung myself into battle after battle, trying to forget you, never knowing why you continued to haunt me, until I thought you had betrayed me.'

'So that's what de Raimes meant about putting you off years ago,' Isabel exclaimed. 'Oh, Guy, if you only knew how I longed for you, how I dreamed that one day you would rescue me.'

'And instead I let you be captured and pitchforked into the same nightmare again.'

The bitter statement made her cry out in protest. 'Even if I'd told you everything, you wouldn't have known 'twas de Raimes' men at the ford. They recognised you, and described me well enough for him to start making enquiries. I didn't suspect anything until it was too late. And besides,' she added softly, lifting a hand to stroke the tension from his face, ''twas not the same as before. This time I knew you would come.'

'If I'd had to storm hell itself,' he confirmed huskily, turning his head to kiss her palm.

Isabel made a small sound of contentment and snuggled her head into his shoulder. She had never felt so loved, she decided sleepily, so cherished, so secure. Guy had given her so much. . . Her eyes snapped open.

'Oh, my psalter!' she exclaimed, coming up on one elbow.

FitzAlan quirked an eyebrow in lazy enquiry. 'What?'

'My psalter. 'Tis in the casket you brought me. I have to show you. . .' She glanced over her shoulder, spying the box on the floor near the fireplace.

'Wouldn't you rather wait until tomorrow? You must be exhausted.' He started playing with the dark hair spilling over his chest.

'Are you?'

Guy smiled up at her, a smile that held male triumph, utter possessiveness and love. Before Isabel had taken another breath she found herself on her back, gazing up at him bemusedly. 'I could go out and conquer an entire army,' he told her, bending to kiss her on the mouth.

'Just bringing my psalter will do for now,' Isabel murmured when she could speak again, revelling in the teasing intimacy of lovers that was still so new to her.

The smile turned indulgent. 'Well, if that is all your ladyship desires. . .'

Swinging himself off the bed, Guy strode across the room. Firelight danced over the powerful musculature of his body as he bent to retrieve the box. He grinned when he turned back towards the bed and saw Isabel watching him with a mixture of shyness and feminine appreciation that brought a blush to her face. 'You'll get used to it, sweetheart.'

Isabel sat up and concentrated on the small casket he placed beside her. She was trying to open it with one hand, while the other held the bearskin to her breasts, when Guy reached down and retrieved her shift. Very gently he drew the bed covering away. His eyes caressed her, then he lowered the shift over Isabel's head, tucking her arms into the full sleeves.

'You'll get used to me looking at you, too, my beautiful little wife,' he murmured, kissing the warm cheek nearest him.

Her eyes smiled shy appreciation of his understanding as she opened the box. She lifted out the illuminated psalter within and handed it to him.

Guy gave her a questioning, half-quizzical glance, but accepted the book, its leaves parting easily at his touch. Isabel, watching closely, saw him go very still as he saw what lay between the pages.

The fragile, preserved petals of a peach-coloured rose glowed softly in the sconce light.

'I should have taken you with me years ago and damn the consequences.' His deep voice held an intensity of feeling that Isabel had never imagined even in her most private dreams.

She placed her hand lightly over the rose, her eyes meeting his with an answering depth of emotion. 'I'm with you now,' she murmured. 'I'll be with you forever.'

FitzAlan covered her hand with his. 'Forever,' he echoed.

It was a vow Isabel knew would be kept for the rest of their lives.

LEGACY *of* LOVE

Coming next month

HEART OF A ROSE
Christine Franklin

Devon 1906

Patti Nevill had returned home to Devon, but knew her sister could not support her for long. But while looking for a new post, Patti succumbed to curiosity, and sneaked into the garden at Porphyry Court to look at the old roses. Caught red-handed by Sir Robert Challoner, Patti was very surprised when the end result was an offer to be companion to his sister Faye! Disturbed by her reactions to Robert, and even more by his to her, Patti reluctantly agreed, only to find herself in the middle of a mystery. . .

THE CYPRIAN'S SISTER
Paula Marshall

Regency - Leicestershire

Bel Passmore was horrified to discover, on clearing up her sister's effects, that Marianne, far from being a respectable widow, had been a courtesan with a nice line in blackmail! It was Bel's misfortune that Lord Francis Carey should arrive at that moment, bent on wresting his nephew Marcus out of Marianne's clutches! His assumption that Bel must be Marianne startled Bel – she was a vicar's daughter! – until his intemperate language roused her ire. He needed a lesson – but the consequences of Bel's impulsive actions were more far-reaching than she ever anticipated. . .

LEGACY of LOVE

Coming next month

SWEET JUSTICE
Jan McKee

California 1882

Morgan Rossiter – bitter, dark and hungry for justice – was searching for the accomplice of his brother's killer. Now he'd stumbled upon the woman his agents swore was his quarry. But could Jessica Miller be an outlaw's woman? Even Morgan himself was falling under sweet Jessica's tranquil spell.

Jessica knew Morgan was after something – and that she had a lot to hide. She'd sworn that no man, certainly no charmingly devilish stranger, would ever again win a smile from her. Whether prying Morgan was after the secret of her past or her love, it was all the same to Jessica... He'd have no luck getting either!

TORCHLIGHT
Doreen Owens Malek

Pennsylvania 1870

One look into the fires of Sean Jameson's rebel eyes, and Elizabeth Langdon knew she would forsake everything for the shattering pleasures of his forbidden embrace. Sean was bent on the destruction of all her family stood for, but Elizabeth vowed her love would triumph over the society that tore them apart.

Sean tried to keep away from the woman who represented all he could never have – but one illicit moment with Elizabeth and his hunger for her rivalled his commitment to the rebellion he led. How could he resist the daughter of his sworn enemy, when her heart spoke the language of his soul?

FOUR
HISTORICAL ROMANCES

&

TWO
FREE GIFTS!

THE 9-STEP ECOMMERCE BUSINESS GUIDE

How To Create, Find Products &
Automate A Successful Online Business

Avoid Mistakes That Cost Time & Money

GW00471902

FRANCIS OCRAN

CONTENTS

INTRODUCTION

This book focuses on providing you with a detailed, thorough guide about how to start an online business and maintain it irrespective of the obvious hurdles that you may face down the road.

Are you unsure about jumping onto the ecommerce bandwagon? You will be more certain after reading some of these inspirational stories from entrepreneurs.

WHITNEY WOLFE HERD OF BUMBLE

Whitney Wolfe Herd founded Bumble because she was in a toxic relationship in 2014 (Alter, 2021). Whitney wanted to provide a platform for people to help them meet the people they deserve. Bumble is a dating app that is pro-women and allows only women to message once a match is made.

Wolfe, with the help of ecommerce, made it possible for women to reduce the possibility of being catfished or abused on dating platforms. Bumble is now the second most popular dating platform around the world only after Tinder (Statista, n.d.).

JAN KOUM OF WHATSAPP

Jan Koum is the founder of the famous messenger app "WhatsApp." Born in a poor family in Ukraine, he didn't understand why there are no good messaging apps for the Android operating system which is popular in developing and underdeveloped countries.

Koum became determined to create a messaging app for Android, and hence, WhatsApp was invented. Within a few years, it became famous and an iOS version was also launched. He later sold WhatsApp to Facebook Inc (now Meta Platforms) in 2014 for a whopping $19 billion (Olson, n.d.).

MELANIE PERKINS OF CANVA

Melanie Perkins created a web app called Canva that can be used to easily design graphics. The thought came to her when she faced difficulties designing photos for a client meeting. When she first pitched the idea to venture investors, no one was interested in her proposal. However, she started it on her own as an ecommerce service in 2012. Canva now has 60 million customers and has extended its services worldwide (TechCrunch, n.d.).

WHAT IS THE MORAL OF THESE STORIES?

- All these entrepreneurs had a vision and used the ecommerce ecosystem to achieve their goals.
- All these entrepreneurs focused on providing solutions for the problems that could help millions.
- All these entrepreneurs had foresight and created something that can uplift society.

Ecommerce is important in today's economy because it provides a decentralized way to do business. Anyone can start an online business without worrying about the complexities usually associated with running an offline business.

HOW CAN THIS BOOK HELP YOU?

While ecommerce is definitely the future of business, it is still complex to understand for beginners. This book is designed to help you understand the objectives for a successful ecommerce business and how to begin your journey to achieve financial independence with help of the steps shared.

The ecommerce business is extremely competitive as there are so many people trying to reach out to millions of people around the world with their products and services. No matter what niche we talk about, there will always be competition. If you think that you have a groundbreaking idea, then it is well possible that someone has already had and implemented that idea.

It takes an abundance of strength and power to overcome your competitors in the current ecommerce market. However, it is important for you to remember that there are always success stories in ecommerce businesses that come from nowhere. People are still innovating and there is still a high probability for you to succeed in the ecommerce business if you understand what you are doing and are committed.

As an entrepreneur, I have experienced both failures and successes in the ecommerce industry. It is important to understand that failure is a stepping stone to success, and I am here to help you reach your goals. The book is primarily designed for beginners to create a successful business portfolio and make a mark in their niche.

This book will help you think like a true entrepreneur and will reveal the secrets of the business economy. This book is designed not just to be a guide but to be used as a resource for your entrepreneurial journey.

HOW IS THIS BOOK ORGANIZED?

A 9-step model is used in this book to help you understand the ecommerce business. Each step in this model is mentioned chronologically to help you understand the business structure and what you need to do in a logical manner. The first chapter introduces the fundamentals for the ecommerce business and from then, you will be introduced to the nine steps of ecommerce business in this guide. Chapter numbers are indicated as Step 1, Step 2... for you to easily browse through the guide.

A Quick Checklist

Before starting to learn about the secrets of the ecommerce business, answer these questions yourself.

- Why are you interested in doing business?
- Do you believe that the ecommerce business is the future?
- Are you someone who is interested in creating your own digital store for your business?
- Do you have any debts?
- What are the main goals that you are trying to achieve by doing an ecommerce business?

Embark on a thrilling and vast journey into the world of ecommerce business.

BECOMING AN ENTREPRENEUR

WHY BEFORE HOW

When in crisis, humanity always strives to find solutions. While the global pandemic has unimaginably hurt us and made us realize how important it is to have financial independence, it also increased the pace of the digital revolution and evolution. Consumer behavior has also rapidly evolved, making ecommerce a more preferable way to manage a business. With high-speed internet and complex encryption algorithms that ensure that digital transactions are safe, the popularity of ecommerce will only increase exponentially in the future.

If you are not convinced, then some of these statistics can change your mind as the growth in ecommerce in the last few years is mind-boggling (Shephard, n.d.).

- The total ecommerce market value has grown to $10 trillion in 2020. Grand View Research has predicted that the market value will increase to $27 trillion by 2027.
- Online shopping has become one of the popular trends around the world making people spend more than $4.9 trillion in 2021.
- People were usually skeptical about cross-border transfers before. But with services such as eBay improving their logistics department, there was growth of more than 20% in cross-border transfers and shipments in 2020.
- The average cart abandonment rate decreased from 80% in 2020 to 70% in 2021. While it is still not a good percentage, it reflects the fact that there are a lot of places for businesses to grow.
- There are close to 4 billion ecommerce users around the world giving a huge opportunity to scale business.

While these statistics can be overwhelming, they can provide you an insight into how great the opportunities are in the ecommerce world. To help you get a clear picture of what you are diving into, let us explore the advantages that you will have in your hands once you decide to rope into the ecommerce business.

WHY BECOME AN ENTREPRENEUR?

Fundamentally, becoming an entrepreneur is something that you do by choice but not by force. No one will force you to start a business by yourself but many can force you to do something that you are not fond of to climb the corporate ladder.

Being an entrepreneur gives you back all the freedom and happiness that being an employee has taken away. Becoming an entrepreneur can help you achieve the seven foundational blocks that we consider important for your career growth and happiness.

SEVEN FOUNDATIONAL BLOCKS

1. Believing in Something Passionately

Being an entrepreneur makes it possible for you to believe in a product, idea, or business with all your passion. There is nothing more satisfying than believing in something and building an empire around it. Entrepreneurs such as Steve Jobs and Elon Musk said that belief is something that can make you achieve the unachievable. Being a corporate employee will slowly suck your energy into believing something. On the other hand, being an entrepreneur will push you to work hard for what you believe in.

2. Continuous Learning

Doing a corporate job even though it is tough can be quite unchallenging as you spend years doing the same thing. Even if technologies improve, your learning process will constantly decrease as there will be so many people who will be helping you out. Entrepreneurship, on the other hand, is tough and challenging. You need to solve problems by yourself and hence, by solving them, you will receive skills that can help you scale your business rapidly. It makes the process more interesting and you will wake up with a smile that makes you want to do something better than yesterday.

3. Financial Independence

When your business starts to improve and gives you results, you need to no longer worry about a paycheck that you usually depend on. You can buy your dream house or take long vacations which are usually not possible when you are an employee. Financial independence can not only improve your life but also your family's. You can afford a tuition fee for your children that you wouldn't have before. Financial independence is the primary reason many choose entrepreneurship. However, remember that money shouldn't be your primary motive as it can make the process more stressful. Enjoy what you do and the financial perks will automatically follow.

4. Control

By being an entrepreneur, you will be your own boss and hence, you have more control over the decisions you make. When you are a regular employee in a corporation, you will often be controlled by higher authorities and hence, your potential may not be utilized as you want it to be. With control comes more responsibility and hence, you will be able to make decisions that can impact lives.

5. Work-Life Balance

One of the harshest reasons why many employees have a terrible experience in their professional lives is that corporate jobs don't give you enough work-life balance that you need. Being an entrepreneur can be challenging but can give you a lot of time to spend quality time with your friends and family. You will be living the life of your dreams all the while running your business.

6. Giving Back to the Community

When you start a business as an entrepreneur, you will be believing in a vision that can help people and communities around the world. Irrespective of which niche or sector you chose, the product or service you wish to develop should always make someone's life better. You will be creating jobs and hence, will be improving the community and the global economy to increase prosperity.

7. To Change the World

Ultimately, every entrepreneur dreams to change the world around them or beyond them. Every entrepreneur works intending to create services or products that can make humanity live peacefully and confidently. If you are someone who believes in creating your own destiny, all the while doing your part to change the world, then there is nothing more satisfying than being an entrepreneur.

These seven foundational blocks which are essential to be successful as an entrepreneur should have already answered your question about why you should be an entrepreneur in the 21st century. You can apply these foundational principles irrespective of whether you are trying to do an ecommerce or traditional business. The ideas are the same but the approach is different.

ENTREPRENEURSHIP POST-COVID-19

The COVID-19 pandemic is one of the most bizarre dystopian times we all have ever lived in. The two years of lockdown and travel restrictions along with individuals following social distancing have changed how businesses operate. Research says that in 2020, the percentage of business creation decreased due to the challenges caused by the pandemic (McKinsey, n.d.).

However, it is also important to remember that due to the COVID-19 pandemic, entrepreneurship and business creation have also evolved in a completely different way. Understanding these changes is critical if you want to be an entrepreneur in the post-COVID-19 business world.

Use of Digital Technology

While it is true that there was a decrease in business creation during 2020, the percentage, however, increased in 2021 resulting in the conclusion that new entrepreneurs have started to understand how to operate even with pandemic restrictions (Seal, 2022). While the first few months of the pandemic were difficult due to a lack of understanding of the resources we have, over time, entrepreneurs and businesses around the world have understood the importance of digital technology.

Digital technology ensures entrepreneurs that their businesses can continue even when it is not possible to solve problems and create solutions traditionally. Digital technology ensures that the workflow is not disturbed even when the employees are working from home.

For anyone to be successful as an entrepreneur in the post-COVID-19 world, it is important to embrace the digital world and enjoy the perks provided by it. Statistics say that the people who started their own businesses were those in economies where digital technology is adopted more (Shephard, n.d.).

Surge in Entrepreneurship

The world has always faced economic depressions and recessions. The most recent recession we faced was during 2008 when the housing market collapsed in the United States leading to a ripple effect around the world; people lost their lifelong savings and jobs. During 2008, or 1929 when the economic depression occurred, there was no surge in entrepreneurship according to the records (FDR Library, 2016). People were not ready to do business because they knew that it would not work due to the recession.

The interest in post-pandemic entrepreneurship is, however, quite opposite. The U.S. Census has mentioned that there was a more than 38% increase in business applications during 2021 (Economic Innovation Group, 2022). The applications for these businesses also extended to several sectors making it obvious that both large-scale and small-scale entrepreneurship is on the rise.

When we look at our history before the industrial revolution, people used to work more on their own instead of working in industries. While the industrial revolution has shaped our finance and technology, it, however, has taken away the freedom of the working class. The pandemic pushed the thought process of many individuals to stop depending on multinational companies for their financial independence, and hence, is believed to have created a new entrepreneurial wave (McKinsey, n.d.).

One of the other reasons that also is making people start their businesses is because of the low wages they have been receiving. Many companies are reducing wages, citing the upcoming recession (IRI, 2022), making it easy for people to become part of the gig economy and slowly clinching into the entrepreneur world.

To be precise, there is a lot of scope for being an entrepreneur after the pandemic as digital technology has developed exponentially and also due to the huge number of resources that can be accessed for product or service development. This is irrespective of whether you are part of a corporation or someone who is handling a business personally as an entrepreneur. Fortunately, the world we live in now is powered by the internet, and the decentralized technologies that are growing in popularity in recent times will only make the sentiment grow further and make it easy for entrepreneurs to start and manage their isolated businesses.

THE WORLD HAS BEEN SHAPED BY ONLINE BUSINESS

We all know Google which is our favorite and most used search engine on the web. Google's popularity first grew when the search engine was released. Google search engines' primary task was to find different web pages on the internet and query them so that users can find what they want. Google started as a small business in the garage of one of its two founders—Larry Page. Twenty years later, if we look at Google's products and services, its achievements can be hailed as an unimaginable task.

While many companies tried to develop a business model that can make it easy to find localities, businesses, or people, most of them failed due to the digital revolution they couldn't catch up to. Google's founders, on the other hand, understood the importance of the digital revolution and tried their level best to provide services for a wide range of people. Gmail, YouTube, Google Maps, and the Google Play Store are some of the many internet services that made Google a powerful multinational corporation in the world.

Google is just one example of thousands of businesses that played their part to make the internet and the world more connected. Facebook, WhatsApp, YouTube, and PayPal are some of the many services that made people connect and handle several businesses that were tough to handle before.

Dominance of the Internet Around the World

Just a few decades back, there was no trace of consumer internet in sight. Even though people owned computers, they were not able to access the advanced internet technology that we now have access to. In the last two decades, the popularity of the internet has spread all around the world, making it one of the driving forces of our economy. We now depend on the internet for everything. If you want to pay credit card bills, you need the internet. If you want to chill for some time by watching a movie, then you need the internet, and if you want to watch breaking news, you need the internet. The internet provides knowledge, entertainment, and employment for billions of humans around the world.

Web 3.0 is the next-generation web technology that is under development and has the potential to curb the power of a few multinational corporations and can extend the power to all the members of the network. This is an opportunity for people to create new ecommerce applications that can not only change their lives but also others.

The dominance of the internet has also helped us realize how entrepreneurs can make a difference in their businesses with newborn technology. Let us take a look at some of these rules that the internet changed around the business world.

1. Marketing and Advertising

Due to the internet, it is now easier for businesses to promote their products and services. While it is still possible to connect with people without the internet, it is very costly. Social media marketing has made it possible to target ads to the demographics where your targeted audience is. Innovative marketing tactics on the internet also make it possible to reach your potential customers without spending a lot of money. Google and Facebook are, right now, the pioneers in the digital advertising arena for small businesses and entrepreneurs.

2. Data

Due to the internet, it becomes easy to collect and store data. Before the internet, businesses depended on traditional paperwork to store all the details. Due to the internet, businesses can now ask for their customer's consent to get any required data and use this data further to improve the suggestions provided by their algorithms.

Technologies such as data analysis and data analytics have become popular in the industry.

3. IT

Because of the internet and the businesses that it has created, we have quickly developed our infrastructure. Before the success of the internet, computers were present for more than 50 years but there has been very little improvement over the years as both governments and businesses didn't give much thought to developing newer technologies (Our World in Data, 2018). With the success of the internet, both corporations and governments became conscious of providing resources for talented developers to create newer and more complicated technologies that can keep up with the ecommerce revolution that is happening.

4. New Products and Services

Without the internet, we would have never gotten a digital voice assistant such as Alexa. The success of the internet has made it possible for businesses and individual developers to create newer technology that makes our lives more comfortable and peaceful.

THE STORY OF IDA PAVLICHENKO

Ida Pavlichenko, CEO of PionEar Technologies, is an entrepreneur who embarked on a journey into the business world during the time the world was panicking due to the pandemic. She understood that technology can help humanity by making professional bonds and creating wonderful products. She used virtual networking along with augmented reality (AR) to expand her startup during the pandemic. Like Ida Pavlichenko, anyone focusing on ecommerce business can make use of the technology to make a mark in their niche or industry.

We discussed what it means to become an entrepreneur and the importance of being one in the modern economy. This will help you realize why online businesses are the next big thing in the financial world.

In the next section, we will focus on the first step in our ecommerce journey, looking at what ecommerce is and the positives and negatives to expect along the way.

STEP 1

LEARNING THE ROPES OF ECOMMERCE

J ust a few decades back, if someone had proposed to start a business entirely on the web, people would have laughed it off because it was considered back then as a not-so-possible way to make money. The process of creating, handling, and managing businesses has changed over time, making it possible for ecommerce to create a huge impact in the business industry. While ecommerce is now ruling the charts, its journey, however, is not a one-night success. A lot of individuals and companies have helped ecommerce grow as far as the 1960s (Miva, 2011).

While it is true that ecommerce marketplaces such as Amazon, Etsy, and eBay have made ecommerce popular with the masses, several other projects inspired entrepreneurs to use the internet as a medium to connect with their targeted consumers. This section focuses on providing information about the historical timeline related to the development of ecommerce.

HISTORY OF ECOMMERCE

The roots of ecommerce trace back to as far as 1969 when CompuServe launched as an online service provider. It was not a huge success back then but received some appreciation from the scientific community (Miva, 2011). However, it was tough to figure out how to use it, and hence, it didn't become a huge success.

The next significant achievement in ecommerce was in 1979 when a programmer named Michael Aldrich created an online electric shop and made the first electronic transaction on the internet (Miva, 2011). Within the next few years in 1982, Boston Computer Exchange expanded its business to the internet making it the first ecommerce company.

While the next decade continued without any significant improvements for ecommerce, things started to get interesting when the world wide web was introduced in 1991 and has given wide opportunities for entrepreneurs to try out. Within the next few years, several ecommerce companies such as Book Stacks Unlimited, Amazon, and eBay had risen in their ranks in the business industry (Miva, 2011).

A number of advanced search engines and social media platforms provide businesses with the opportunity to target ads based on their needs, while platforms such as Shopify make it easy to create an ecommerce business. This has led to the increased popularity of ecommerce.

THE ECOMMERCE CRASH COURSE

For learning any skill, you need to first understand the fundamentals they possess. For you to create a new ecommerce business, it is important to have a good understanding of what ecommerce is and the different types of ecommerce businesses that exist.

What Is Ecommerce?

In simple words, ecommerce refers to individuals and businesses trying to either sell or buy goods and services on the internet. Ecommerce has now extended to different types of segments and can be quickly done using laptops, smartphones, or even smartwatches. In the modern financial world, almost every product and service can be bought through ecommerce, such as books, flight tickets, movie subscriptions, or financial services (such as stock market trading and paying insurance premiums). Ecommerce is a disruptive technology that changed how businesses are handled.

Disruptive technology is something that changes how humans deal with things in day-to-day life and usually, disruptive technologies will reintroduce several new technologies along their lifecycle. For example, electricity and automobiles are disruptive technologies similar to ecommerce that have helped humanity thrive during the industrial revolution.

In ecommerce, more than one party is involved while making an online transaction and hence, there will be additional security provided for both businesses and consumers. Ecommerce itself is part of the business model that is developed to run a company completely using online technologies.

One of the major achievements of ecommerce is that it has helped businesses, especially small businesses to reach a wide range of consumers with less effort than it took for them in the traditional brick-and-mortar presence. Even large companies that have a large brick-and-mortar presence started to focus on ecommerce business simultaneously to reduce their costs and increase their profits.

While the concept of ecommerce seems simple, a lot goes on behind the picture just like the traditional business system, and hence, a lot of knowledge is required in individuals to become successful in the ecommerce industry. First of all, it is required to do a lot of research about products and services to determine which ones will be profitable for you as an entrepreneur. Once it is determined, you need to register a legal name just like how a corporation is set. Once these are done, you need to create an ecommerce website and integrate it with a payment gateway for customers to visit and order your products or services. Once the payment is confirmed, you also need to manage the logistics to ensure that the product is delivered correctly. Logistics can be automated but still, it is important to monitor for better results.

Examples

There are countless examples on the internet now that use the ecommerce model to handle their business. Amazon is probably the most popular ecommerce website because it makes it easy for individual sellers to reach out to millions of consumers around the world. Amazon has impacted the retail industry and how it does its business.

Jeff Bezos, who founded Amazon in 1994, first started it as an online book store but has quickly spread its wings looking at the response that he has received. Amazon also started to invite sellers to their platform so that their online inventory of products would grow. Amazon's revenue and sales started to increase every year as more people started to get access to the internet and are increasing their faith in digital transactions due to the improved security and verification systems. While there is still a lot of room to develop especially in developing and underdeveloped countries, Amazon is still the king of the ecommerce business (weDevs, 2022).

When we look broadly, there are three major categories that ecommerce companies usually fall into.

1. Sell Physical Goods

Physical goods are tangible products that need to be first manufactured using a strict set of principles. Once the manufacturing is completed, ecommerce can make it easy for the owners to sell these goods to their consumers. All electronics and smartphones that people order from online stores are good examples.

2. Sell Digital Goods

Not all goods are physical. For example, if someone wants to research their business, then they need to use a keyword research tool such as Semrush. This is a digital good that can be used by consumers for a fee. Digital goods require less effort than physical goods and are hence, more popular in the ecommerce arena.

3. Sell Services

Instead of tools, ecommerce can also extend to services. For example, freelance writing is a service that can be offered by veteran writers to consumers who are looking for someone to create content for their websites.

WHAT ARE THE TYPES OF ECOMMERCE BUSINESSES?

Ecommerce provides flexibility to manage a business using different ways. Depending on the product or service you are trying to sell to your customers, you need to choose your business model. Having an understanding of the popular business models can help you choose the right business model for your business.

1. Business to Consumer

In the business-to-consumer (B2C) model, ecommerce companies will directly sell a product to the end-users without any need for intermediaries. In this model, the consumer will get the goods and will use them. B2C is the most common business model in ecommerce businesses as the entrepreneur will be able to see most of the profits. Remember that digital services can also be directly sent to the consumer using the B2C model.

2. Business to Business

In the business-to-business (B2B) model, while the business creates goods or services, they, however, create them to sell to other businesses instead of making them for the consumers. B2B businesses are usually much larger in production and have larger profits. If the businesses are using this strategy for the manufacturing process, then there will be recurring transactions, making this a profitable business model.

3. Consumer to Consumer

In the consumer-to-consumer (C2C) model, consumers will communicate with other consumers to order products or services. All popular modern ecommerce platforms manage their business using this way. For example, Amazon is an ecommerce company that uses this model. All sellers on Amazon are consumers who use Amazon Logistics to ship and fulfill orders to other consumers. eBay is also a similar ecommerce company where consumers negotiate with each other to decide the price and then ship the orders. Most of the freelancing websites where consumers buy the services of writers or artists will also fall under this category.

4. Direct to Consumer

In the direct-to-consumer (D2C) model, the business will be directly selling products to the consumers and hence, will not have to deal with any intermediaries or wholesalers who will be taking out some of the profits usually. While D2C is hard to establish, it, however, gives the most profits of all the business models. Streaming giants such as Netflix which creates content and directly sells it to consumers via a subscription model can be a good example of the D2C model.

5. Consumer to Business

In the consumer-to-business (C2B) model, consumers will try to sell their products for businesses to make use of. C2B is a different one of the lot because it is unconventional. iStock is a good example of this business model. On this website, photographers can upload the photos they have taken and businesses will buy them to use on their websites or blog posts.

6. Business to Administration

In the business-to-administration (B2A) model, businesses will make products and services for administrative entities such as governments. Most of the time, businesses need to bid with their proposal so that governments can choose the best one for them and allow them to provide goods and services. A government-wide acquisition contract is usually set up between the business and administration to ensure that everything works effectively. Governments around the world are also venturing into ecommerce businesses to handle some of their mandatory requirements.

7. Consumer to Administration

In the consumer-to-administration (C2A) model, consumers will directly try to sell their goods and services to administrations and agencies. For example, a lecturer in physics can use online consulting to teach physics because of an administrational requirement. Online tax filing will also fall under this category.

✚ PROS OF ECOMMERCE

It makes sense for a beginner to learn about the pros and cons of ecommerce business to gain a better understanding of the business model. The pros will be discussed first, followed by some cons.

1. Convenience

Ecommerce can be done 24-7 even during public holidays. Websites will always stay online around the clock and hence, it will become possible to earn revenue from sales even when you are sleeping.

2. Increased Inventory

With ecommerce, it becomes possible to provide more inventory than brick-and-mortar industries can hold. When you get an order, all you have to do is ship the product from a warehouse. Increasing your inventory options ensures you additional profits.

3. Lower Startup Costs

With an ecommerce business, it is possible to reduce the total costs involved in a business. As there is no need to have a physical storefront, all the money can be invested in logistics and the research and development (R&D) of the products you are trying to sell. Costs can be minimized on rent, insurance, and property taxes.

4. International Sales

When you are selling on the internet, your products are accessible to people around the world and hence, international sales are a common scenario. If you can arrange international shipping for your customers, then your business will not be limited by geography.

5. Retargeting

Retargeting is often impossible with the traditional business model. Ecommerce businesses, on the other hand, can use the details provided by customers with consent to send their new offers to the customers without any hassle. Ecommerce entrepreneurs can use social media and search engine marketing to direct marketing campaigns to their loyal customers.

▬ CONS WITH ECOMMERCE

1. Limited Customer Service

Customer support experience is one of the major cons of the ecommerce business. In traditional stores, there are usually employees who will be helping customers to understand details about different products. While chatbots can be created, they, however, are not efficient in communication most of the time.

2. No Instant Gratification

When people visit a store and buy an item, they can immediately take the product with them to their homes. Ecommerce businesses, on the other hand, will let the consumer wait for their delivery as they need to ship the product with their providers. Even though ecommerce companies such as Amazon are providing a one-day delivery option for their customers, the traditional way is still satisfactory currently.

3. Customers Can't Try Before Buying

All products have different feelings associated with them. Several customers decide whether or not to buy a product depending on how it feels in their hands or how it looks from a distance. Online purchasing doesn't provide this convenience for the customers. Most of the time, customers need to depend on images and videos, making it a hard decision for them. However, online businesses will be changing this soon with the utilization of AR and virtual reality (VR) technologies.

4. Business Is Highly Dependent on Technology

An ecommerce business is usually highly dependent on the ecommerce platform and the technicalities associated with it. If there is a vulnerability on your ecommerce platform, then you may lose all your money because of a cyberattack. Online theft and phishing are also some of the problems that ecommerce businesses are facing frequently.

5. There Is a Lot of Competition

As it is easy to set up an ecommerce business, when compared to a traditional business, there will be more people that are competing with you and are targeting the same customer demographics as you. Keeping up with the fierce competition is necessary for you to break-even in business. You need to be aware of internet marketing strategies and SEO techniques to stay in the business even if you are making meaningful products for your audience.

WHAT ARE THE FACTORS INFLUENCING ECOMMERCE?

Ecommerce is an ever-expanding industry and is giving neck-to-neck competition for the traditional business structure. In the age of millennials and Generation Zs (Gen Zs), who are most likely to spend money online, accessing a website or the internet isn't as challenging as it used to be. With popular culture now mostly being influenced by the internet and social media platforms, influencers are also keen to promote online businesses instead of traditional ones.

With a pragmatic shift in consumer behavior due to the recent pandemic, ecommerce has become a more viable business option now. Having an understanding of some of the factors that influence ecommerce can help you gain a deeper familiarity with the industry.

1. The Exponential Growth of Markets Outside of the US

For many years, ecommerce has been only popular in developed countries such as the US and UK. As a result, ecommerce companies have been limited to catering to a small number of consumers, which has, in turn, limited the amount of money they can spend on their businesses. The global pandemic, however, has increased the net consumer optimism toward internet transactions, and hence, there is a lot of growth in ecommerce businesses in the past few years especially in developing economies.

Now that entrepreneurs have more potential consumers ready to try their products or services, they can try different businesses with confidence. Businesses that target both domestic and international customers should, however, focus on logistics and maintenance costs as this may differ based on different regions. Remote work can be a viable option to solve these problems and limit your expenditure.

2. The Power of Automation

Automation is making it easy for businesses to do a lot of things in a limited time. Digital labor jobs can be eliminated with automated tools. Ecommerce businesses are constantly adopting tools such as Zapier to automate their tasks that don't need much detailed attention.

Chatbots are making it easier for businesses to resolve tickets quickly without having to hire a lot of customer service representatives. Businesses are also highly dependent on machine learning to improve the conversion rate in their business. Around the world, these ever-growing technologies are ensuring success for ecommerce businesses.

3. The Advanced Features Provided by Voice Technology

Due to its ability to connect users with different applications and services instantly with voice commands, Amazon's Alexa has become a huge success. Google Assistant, Siri, and Cortana are some other voice technologies that are becoming hugely popular with both millennials and Gen Z users.

Advancement in voice technology has also brought hope to the development of ecommerce. Amazon is already successfully trying to market its services with this technology. With the growing number of users, it becomes easy for users to quickly place orders or services and hence, will increase the overall profitability of ecommerce businesses. Google is also improving its search engine capabilities to recognize frequent voice searches.

4. Improvement of Progressive Web Apps

Progressive web apps are improving the shopping experience of users and are making it easy for ecommerce businesses to thrive even with a lot of competition. These web apps are not only providing quick speed but are also sending push notifications to decrease the cart abandonment problem. Mobile apps are advanced versions of progressive web apps and are making it possible for online businesses to become successful.

5. Improvements in Data Collections

One of the major reasons why the cart abandonment rate is constantly decreasing is that ecommerce businesses now have the correct data to target customers who are going to buy their products. Depending on the user's past spending, machine learning algorithms are also capable of providing better prices for the products listed on a website or store.

6. The Increase in the Impact of Social Media Presence

Several businesses are constantly improving their sales numbers because they are maintaining a good social media presence. All ecommerce businesses are trying to create their own social media brand strategy as users are often getting attracted to these campaigns. Due to the rise in in-app purchases on social media platforms in the past few years, it is safe to conclude that social media platforms are responsible for the increase in internet users' purchasing power.

Apart from learning about the factors that can guarantee your success in the ecommerce industry, you also need to be aware of some of the challenges that you may face while handling your ecommerce business.

CHALLENGES AND BARRIERS

Any type of business has its downsides and risks. Starting a business comes with challenges and barriers, regardless of whether it's online or traditional. You need to prepare yourself to handle some of these common mistakes that entrepreneurs usually make.

1. Choosing the Wrong Ecommerce Platform

It is important to choose the ecommerce platform to target your potential customers regardless of whether you are new to the ecommerce business or an expert. For example, Shopify is an ecommerce platform that everyone is aware of but not every business can work with Shopify. You need to do your initial research using search engine tools such as Ahrefs to judge whether Shopify is a good platform for your potential customers. Choosing the wrong ecommerce platform will not only annoy your customers but also make it difficult for you to scale your business in the future.

What Are the Factors That You Need to Consider While Choosing an Ecommerce Platform?

- What products are you trying to sell and is the platform used by your target demographics?
- What are your plans for scaling the business?
- How much are you willing to spend?
- Are you okay with templated designs for your website or are you looking for customized ones?

It is also important to remember while choosing an ecommerce platform that all your existing business workflow will function with it without any problem. A platform that does not integrate with your current business is nothing less than a disaster and will cause unnecessary headaches.

2. Not Understanding the Target Audience

To reach the profit zone, you can't just create a website or product and wait for sales to increase. With ecommerce, this approach is not enough to become successful. To understand what your demographics want, you must first research the market data. Rather than creating new cravings, you should satisfy their existing ones.

How Do You Understand the Target Audience?

- Verify whether or not your target audience needs the product. Don't create a fad but create a solution for your business to be successful.
- Understand the language that your target audience will most likely be comfortable with.
- Focus on your target audience when creating a marketing strategy.
- Try to understand your audience.
- Try to know about the solutions they have used before to solve their problem and the experience related to it.
- Develop engaging content for them to help your business become popular while also helping them.

3. Website Design

Website design may seem an unimportant thing for many but it is the most important thing that resonates with your business success. Choosing an ecommerce platform itself is not enough as these platforms always provide themes and allow you to customize designs so that you can create uniqueness for your business.

Step 1 of the guide helped you understand the technical definition of ecommerce along with the types of ecommerce businesses that exist. In a dedicated section, you got to understand the pros and cons of ecommerce businesses to look at the big picture of the business model.

Also, with info about the challenges that exist in the ecommerce world, we are now all set to learn about how to research an ecommerce business in the next chapter.

STEP 2

RESEARCHING YOUR ECOMMERCE SPACE

We all know how big Amazon is in terms of net worth. It is constantly growing and building a dominant empire in the ecommerce industry. It is believed that Amazon, however, accounts for less than 50% of all ecommerce sales that happen (PYMNTS, 2022). There are several other players in the market and the potential growth for ecommerce is astounding.

Ecommerce is not restricted to just a few big multinational companies but can be utilized by anyone willing to help their customers as no one did before. Ecommerce provides a huge opportunity for entrepreneurs who are interested in trying out their luck in the ever-expanding online business. Anyone can dream of getting into an ecommerce business or starting one. But to be successful, you need to move out in the right direction which is possible only with the help of ecommerce market research.

WHAT IS ECOMMERCE MARKET RESEARCH?

Research has always helped businesses. There are traditional approaches that businesses usually take to start a business. However, when you are dealing with an online business, these market research tactics might have become outdated. While it is not complicated, many are still confused because of a lack of awareness and good resources.

Market research in simple words refers to discovering what your target customers need from you.

Several Factors Will Affect Your Research:

1. Depending on the industry you are in, your research will differ.
2. Depending on your consumer demographics, the way you approach your research will change.
3. Depending on how well-protective your competitors are regarding their business model, your research approach will change.

WHY IS CONDUCTING MARKET RESEARCH IMPORTANT?

Doing research before starting is important due to the below-mentioned reasons.

1. To Get a Deep Understanding of Your Target Audience

To become successful in any business, you need to be aware of the demographics of your target audience. The research will help you to create new product ideas, create a customized marketing strategy, and use relevant copy-writing skills for your target audience.

The research will help you to create personas that will help you to understand the needs of your customers and the solutions you need to provide. The research, however, is not enough for you to become a pioneer in the market. You need to still implement and market your business but research is usually always the first step.

Online research is improved significantly because of terms of service that provide different metrics for you to research. In the research, you not only should understand what your customers want but also should focus on what they think and what they value. This qualitative research is important to make the customer purchase your product.

2. To Learn Customer Behaviors

When you research customers, you will also be learning about the patterns they will be using while browsing websites and apps. Learning about their usability patterns can help you improve their customer experience by making your websites usable for them. Understanding these patterns can also help you decrease the cart abandonment issue that is common with an online business.

Doing research can help you understand strategies that you can use to improve the retention of your customers and hence, increase the conversion rate for your products.

3. Find New Business Opportunities

When you start researching, you will start to find several opportunities that are usually hidden away from you. Successful people who are already following these methods or keywords don't want you to say their secrets and hence, they will be hiding them from normal users. With research, however, you can unveil these opportunities and make the most out of your online business.

What Will You Be Finding?

- new ways to develop your products
- understanding cross-border sales to improve your product sales
- understanding how to earn with subscription offerings
- understanding different business models

TYPES OF MARKET RESEARCH

To master the research methodologies, you need to be aware of two research methods.

Primary Research

Primary research is a research strategy where data is collected using internal sources. While primary research is a slow process, it is still the preferred way to research as you will be the sole collector of the data and information, and hence, analyzing the data can be fully trusted. With primary research, you will be the sole controller of the data that is being used.

What Are Some Examples?

- surveys that usually happen via online forms
- questionnaires that you ask people on social media platforms
- interviews with pioneers in the market or industry
- researching from online forums and groups who are interested in your niche

Secondary Research

Secondary research is a research strategy where data and insights are collected from other sources. Most of the time, entrepreneurs depend on secondary research because data collection is usually tough and a time-consuming process. However, due to the internet, we now have reliable statistics providers such as Statista that entrepreneurs can use. Even though you need to pay a few bucks to access these services, it is highly recommended to go with this peer-reviewed data instead of depending on public data for your research purposes.

What Are Some Examples?

- Government statistics are the most reliable way to collect data about the most important industries in a country. For example, if you are in the stock market industry, then the New York Stock Exchange (NYSE) reports are the most reliable for your research. On the other hand, if you are in the real estate industry, then data provided by U.S. housing corporations is a valuable source of data.

- Statista is a great resource for getting information about different industries and how they are performing in a particular year.

- You can use resources such as HubSpot to get a good understanding of the current industry trends. You will be able to read reports using the perspectives of different industries.

The only con, however, with this strategy is that data can be manipulated for whatever reason by both governments and the industries, and hence, usually a 5–10% of deviation is applied while performing research with these reports.

FIVE CRITICAL AREAS TO RESEARCH BEFORE ENTERING THE ECOMMERCE INDUSTRY

Anyone entering a business needs to conduct extensive market research about the latest trends and behaviors of the market and its consumers. To ensure that your research is of industry standard, you need to first focus on the five main areas.

Country Overview

When you start an online business, you will be expanding your business to all countries in the world. However, remember that still, the majority of your users will fall under only a few countries where digital shopping is prevalent. The US is the most popular country that most businesses will focus on to improve their earnings as U.S. citizens are more likely to buy products online because of the high security provided by credit card companies.

What Data Do You Need to Research?

A country has a lot of statistics associated with it. While you need to look at the statistics for your niche without failure, you need to also use the following five metrics.

1. GDP Per Capita

This metric will help you see where the country's economy is heading. There is a difference between gross domestic product (GDP) and GDP per capita. While GDP refers to the value of the goods and services produced by a country, GDP per capita refers to the GDP value divided by its entire population. To reach out to a large audience, you will need to analyze GDP per capita to determine what price you should use for your product.

2. Average Monthly Income

Average monthly income is another important indicator that will help you to decide what your pricing strategy should be. When you analyze the average monthly income statistics you will be able to understand the average potential spending of your target demographics and hence will be able to come up with a better pricing strategy. You can refer to the official metrics released by the IRS to calculate the average monthly income for your target demographics. Using websites such as Statista is also recommended.

3. Inflation Rate

In economics, inflation is a general increase in the prices of goods and services in an economy. Inflation can directly affect your product sales because people will stop spending more when there is inflation going on. Even though there is an inflation effect on retail stores, online businesses are going strong as of now.

4. Population Size and Demographics

Both these metrics can help businesses understand to whom they are catering their products. You can also further analyze metrics such as people with internet access and no internet access.

5. Main Populated Regions

This is the metric that you need to concentrate on if you want to restrict yourself to one particular area even with an online business.

Ecommerce Trends

Ecommerce trends are one of the most important things as they will help you understand what you are getting into, how fierce the competition is, and how rewardable the profits will be.

1. Market Size

Market size will help you understand the opportunities your niche provides. You also need to compare the growth of market size to decide whether the market is moving forward or backward. You don't want to risk your business in a failing market. You can also look at the predicted growth reports to judge the future of your products.

2. Online Consumer Insights

These metrics will help you to understand how your consumers behave and what strategies you need to use to ensure that your conversion rate increases. Details such as shopping frequency, payment methods, and average purchase amount are good indicators for this research.

3. Digital Consumption Overview

These metrics will help you to understand how your customers will be accessing your digital store and hence, you can adjust your resources depending on it. For example, knowing what are the popular browsers used by your customers can help you to create a well-optimized website for that browser.

4. Most-Trusted Brands

When you do ecommerce trends research in your niche, it helps you to learn about the most trusted brands in your niche and why they are successful. When you know why they are successful, you will not make silly mistakes while creating products for your niche.

Competitor Analysis

Competition analysis will help you not only understand your competitors but also implement the successful business strategies that they are already using in your business. You will also analyze their sales and marketing tactics to get the most out of your research.

Here Are Some Metrics That You Need to Focus More On:

- different product categories in which they are running their business
- pricing strategies they are using to maximize their sale
- shipping costs and terms
- payment methods that they allow
- return policy
- promotional activities being used
- marketing tactics
- regional pricing difference
- loyalty program
- app functionality

Social Media Analysis

Social media analysis of your competitors will help you understand how to attract the masses in your niche.

- Analyze their social media channels by finding out their post's engagement rate, average likes, and frequency of posts.
- Analyze the type of content that is being posted. Also, it is important to observe whether images and videos are being posted.
- Analyze whether they are running contests or using celebrities to promote their products on social media.

Consumer Survey

You can also use the five-second testing methodology to gather customer impressions on your competitor's websites.

What Are Some Questions That Can Be Asked in the Survey?

- What products do you think this website sells?
- Do you like this website?
- Do you think that this website loads fast?
- What are the best things that you like on this website?
- What is one annoying thing that you noticed about this website?

HOW TO CONDUCT MARKET RESEARCH

Market research is usually complex and can become quickly complicated if you are not focusing on your objectives and your end goals. This section helps you to understand the important steps that you need to follow for conducting market research that can help you provide relevant insights about the niche or domain you are targeting.

Conduct Keyword Research

Keyword research exists to help entrepreneurs to judge whether or not there is demand for their business ideas and product lineup. While search volumes don't directly reflect whether or not your product is going to be a success, it can, however, help you understand whether or not there is interest among consumers in the problem you are trying to solve with your product.

Keyword research will also help you to increase your organic traffic with the help of a dedicated search engine optimization (SEO) strategy.

There are both free and premium keyword research tools for you to look into. Ubersuggest and Google's Keyword

Planner are the popular free tools whereas Ahrefs and Semrush are the popular pro tools for keyword research.

All keyword research tools follow the same process as mentioned below.

1. Brainstorm Keyword Ideas

In the keyword research tool, enter the generic keywords that customers may use while searching for your niche. If you are not sure about these keywords, you can also enter the niche in the search box for the keywords to be automatically generated for you.

For example, if "best hair dryer" is a keyword that you are targeting, then the keyword tool will generate similar keywords and phrases for you to target to improve your organic traffic.

2. Analyze Google's Top Results

Once the results are generated, you can look at the top results for these keywords. These are your competitors and you need to understand what they are doing and how they are providing content to drive traffic.

3. Reverse Engineer

Once you have analyzed these top websites, reverse engineer their articles and try to create content better than theirs to beat the traffic and increase your search engine rankings. When you create better content, ensure that you are sharing it on social media platforms to improve your backlink score. Backlinks are the primary criteria that Google uses to rank pages.

In the end, you need to consistently maintain your dominance for those particular keywords and hence, you need to be constantly providing unique content.

Scope Out the Competition

To judge your market better, you also need to thoroughly analyze your competition as previously mentioned. Use keyword research tools to find your relevant competitors and find out some of the below-mentioned information about your competitors.

1. Business Model

Analyze their business model and find out how they are sourcing their product. Find out whether they are using advanced logistics technology to track their products.

2. Sales Funnel

Find out how the competition is trying to take advantage of the potential customers to make them recurring customers. Sales funnel is a concept where businesses will keep selling their products to customers continuously. Analyze their whole sales funnel to understand the strategy they are using.

3. Website

Analyze their website and the content management system they are using. If possible, find out the themes and plugins they are using to make their website load fast and look beautiful.

When you know the information about competitors you will understand what to do and what not to do in your own business.

Research Current Trends

When you are researching, you also need to check out what is popular currently with the help of services such as Google Trends.

These services will help you understand two important characteristics of your niche or products.

- Is there a growing or decreasing trend for the niche with the consumers?
- Does niche product interest exist throughout the year or only during certain seasons?

Analyzing these trends will also let you know fads that may be short-lived. You need to focus on trends that are consistent and can have long-term potential for your business to thrive.

Utilize Social Media

Social media is an innovation that has changed how we interact with people around us. With the help of social media, you will have access to several consumer insights and behaviors. Your initial market research should also extend to deal with social media research in depth.

1. Follow Influencers

When you follow influencers for your niche in social media platforms. you will understand the important trends and have a better connection with the audience in your niche.

2. Monitor Relevant Hashtags

Check out the popular hashtags for your niche and monitor them regularly to improve your organic traffic in the future.

3. Analyze Competitor Segments

Take a look at what the sentiment is about your competitors on social media platforms. When you know what are the shortcomings of your competitors, you can try to grab a part of your competitor's user base by offering better products.

You can also use advanced text analytics and machine learning software to have a more accurate picture of the market.

Leverage Forums and Customer Feedback

The last step for your research will focus on learning more about what your customers are wishing to have.

- Look for online forums that belong to your niche and check them regularly.
- Integrate with the forum users and try to discuss in different conversations.

- Ask questions and engage with the users to know their mindset and what they are expecting from businesses in their niche.
- You can also use *subreddits* to expand your knowledge of your customers.

Alternatively, you can also directly get customer feedback from your customers themselves with the help of the following strategies.

- Use tools such as SurveyMonkey to ask questions from your audience. You will get anywhere between 10 responses for 100 emails you send (QuestionPro, 2020).
- Ask your customers directly via video conferencing or email. Network with them and try to know what type of products they are expecting.
- Send automated emails to ask for feedback. At least 5 people out of 100 will reply to these kinds of emails. Any feedback is great in the long run for you to judge your market better.

STORIES

You can get a business idea from anything and can change it to a successful one if you have the right attitude and target a customer base who needs a solution to a problem. Take a look at some of the stories that will inspire you to strive for better innovations.

1. Beardbrand is an ecommerce business started by Eric Bandholz from his passion for beards. It is now one of the top-grossing ecommerce businesses in the self-care industry through the creation of unique products for maintaining a bearded lifestyle (Sourcify, 2019).
2. Beer Cartel is an ecommerce business that got huge success in the beer craft industry. It used innovative marketing strategies to reach out to its target user base and improve its services.
3. Bushwick Kitchen is a usual honey product. However, by using minimalistic marketing and public relations techniques, it got huge sales. This ecommerce business has focused more on letting its target audience know what they can provide and get results.

Step 2 of the guide helped you understand the process of doing research for an ecommerce business. While learning about the research techniques, you also understood what actually matters for an ecommerce business to become successful.

With a good understanding of keyword research and techniques to deal with the competition, you are now all set to learn how to identify what you need to sell in your niche.

STEP 3

IDENTIFYING WHAT TO SELL

U sually, niche markets are segments of larger markets that have specific needs, preferences, or identities that make them distinct from the larger market. For a business to thrive, you can either focus on the larger markets at once or can focus on niche ones. For ecommerce businesses, either approach can work depending on how well you are marketing your products. This chapter will focus on helping you narrow down to a niche that is both profitable and exciting for you to start your business in.

BENEFITS OF SELLING PRODUCTS ONLINE

In today's economy, having an online presence is as important as having a retail business in many fields. All retail businesses within their strength are creating new web apps or collaborating with ecommerce websites such as Amazon to ensure that they are reaching out to their customer base. By selling their products, these businesses are also going global like they never would have done before.

Here are some of the benefits that make businesses sell products online.

1. Cheaper Startup Costs

Everyone who has tried their luck in running a physical store always knows how hard it is to break-even in this business. You need to take care of several operations such as renting space, paying utilities, and dealing with wages for your workers. But, if you decide to sell online, then all these activities are not necessary or can be minimized.

2. Freedom to Move

Usually, when you start a retail store, you will be restricted to a particular neighborhood or a small region unless your brand is very popular. You need to cater well to your location and can further start new branches to expand your business. By selling online, you can, however, sell to all people without worrying about staying in one location.

All you have is the internet and help customers reach out to you.

3. Reach More Customers

Online shopping eliminates the barriers that are associated with shopping and, hence, makes it a lot easier for people to spend their money. Small business owners can use it to their advantage and sell their products to a new set of customers. While the profit margins may decrease when you start to ship your products internationally, you should, however, understand that your overall sales will increase.

4. It's Easy to Scale

When you sell products online, you can easily cross-check your sales records and decide what is doing better and what is not doing well. You can immediately take those off of your inventory in real-time to ensure that you eliminate your risks in the business. You can also use this as an opportunity to scale your well-working products.

5. No More Store Hours

The internet works all the time and hence, you will not be restricted by store hours that are usually a norm for businesses. Even when you sleep, if your products are good, you will receive orders. As there is no downtime for your businesses, the probability of them being successful also increases exponentially.

6. Better Margins

As most of your costs decrease, you can provide your products for low costs to your customers, allowing them to buy more of your products. This makes it possible for you to get better margins over time.

7. Track Sales and Shipments

Several entrepreneurs who start online businesses usually worry about tracking their shipments. However, remember that because of the newly developed management and logistics tools, it is now possible to quickly track your shipment and inform the customer. Improving the efficiency of logistics further can make it easier to track every step of the delivery process and automate it further.

HOW TO FIND WHAT WILL SELL IN THE TARGET MARKET

Deciding to sell online is an easy choice but the biggest challenge that entrepreneurs will usually find is to know what sells well within their target market. Irrespective of whether it's a single product or a bunch of products that are lined together, you need to be aware of what to do and what to not do.

One of the hardest stages in finding a business is to come up with good product ideas. Most entrepreneurs get stuck for a long time searching for a product and constantly researching to know whether or not they can make a business out of it. One of the biggest problems you will probably face is that the product you want to sell is already being sold by other companies with usually good reviews. With a lot of competition, you will often feel that niches are pretty saturated already and are, hence, hard to penetrate.

Irrespective of the competition, it is important to remember that there is always a way to penetrate the market mostly because people are always looking for alternatives. As long as people are eager to try new solutions to their problems, new products are launched all the time, which is great news for entrepreneurs.

Let us look at some of the popular strategies that can help you easily find products for your target audience.

1. Solve a Customer Pain Point

Most of the popular products are designed to take away the pain that the target customers usually face. It is not only effective but is a logical way to create new products for your target customers. For example, let us suppose that you are trying to create products for cat owners.

Usually, when you look at cat-owner products, most of them would be about toys that the owners can buy for their cats and kittens. If you dig a bit further, you will understand that most of the owners are not satisfied with the toys because they are not durable. If you try to create a toy that is more durable for cats then the target customers will pay more attention to your product. You can then further expand your collection of toys by offering more sizes, colors, and designs; developing your brand name; and expanding your business.

You can read online public reviews on Amazon or similar websites to brainstorm ideas about the next profitable ideas that can clear your target customers' annoyances and frustrations.

Active Hound is an example pet toy product company that has now extended its business to hundreds of different products in the same niche.

2. Appeal to Enthusiastic Hobbyists

You can create products for niches where people are passionate about their hobbies and thus, don't worry about spending hundreds of dollars to improve them. Understand consumer psychology and where it is more important for businesses to thrive. You will not only be able to create a product but also expand it to a line of products to increase your profit potential. For example, people inclined to any sport will be willing to update their gear to ensure that they perform better.

If your products are of the highest quality, these loyal hobbyists will also be loyal to your brand. You need recurring customers for building your successful business empire irrespective of whether you are doing it as a retail or online business.

Solé Bicycles is a good example of a brand that has followed this strategy to create a loyal fanbase of bicyclists who are willing to buy their products because they can easily link them to their personality.

3. Go With Your Passion

As an entrepreneur, you need to be more inclined to choose a niche that interests and intrigues you. However, remember that proper research should, however, go on to decide whether it has the potential to work or not. You can't start to create a new product in a very niche genre just because you are passionate about it.

You need to understand the markets and decide which of them is more inclined toward your passion. Choosing something with passion can improve your chances of creating unique products. When you love what you are doing, you will be more motivated to overcome the hurdles that usually occur while you are selling products. An example of this is the Bear Brand story mentioned in Step 2.

4. Consider Your Professional Experience

When trying to create a business, you will benefit when you can create a product in a niche in which you already have professional experience. Going this way works well because you are usually more knowledgeable than the average person in that niche and have chances for creating better products for the target audience. Using your expertise to create an online business and trying to market products that you want to use is a smart idea to enter the market with confidence.

RetroSupply is a good example of a company that has used this strategy. Its founder, Dustin Lee is a freelance designer who has been in the industry for more than 20 years and has decided to create a website where design assets can be shared between freelancers with fewer commission rates by the mediator. Dustin Lee has tried to make use of his professional experience to create a business model and you can do it too with both digital and handmade products.

5. Capitalize on Trends Early

To be successful in the business world, you need to predict the future and judge what will be working out. You also need to understand the current trends to streamline your business potential. Recognizing a trend before it becomes big can help you become a powerful leader in that niche. It will also help you to rank better in terms of SEO when people are searching for it using search engines such as Google.

You should not be confused with a fad and a trend when using this strategy. A fad is a sudden gimmick that has surged the sales of a product. Fads can be great for quick sales as they mostly depend on how well you market. All fads, however, will reduce their impact after a few months. Trends, on the other hand, will stay longer as the demand will be constantly increasing for the products that use these trends. This is the main reason why trends are more popular in the financial arena.

Knox Labs is a great example of a company that has understood this strategy. Knox Labs' founder understood that VR technology is the next trend in the future and wanted to help people utilize VR technology without the need for high-tech VR devices by using their mobile phones. Knox Labs has created a cardboard-shaped device to hold the mobile phone and be used as a VR headset. The idea was a huge success and has made more than $3 million in revenue for the company (Shopify, n.d.).

DISCOVER THE NEWEST TRENDS

To understand what are the ongoing trends, you can research using the below-mentioned techniques.

1. Use Social Media

Social media can help you easily check the ongoing trends and hype for several topics at once. You can look at the popular hashtags for social listening and identify different trends that are popular over a while.

2. Google Trends

Google Trends is a great service for you to look at different popular trends that people have searched for. When there is a spike in popularity for a term, you can research the reasons for it.

3. Trend Hunter

Trend Hunter is a popular third-party service that collects information about different popular trends for various websites and sources with the help of artificial intelligence (AI) and provides insights for the users of the service.

4. Reddit

Reddit is usually called the front page of the internet as anonymous people meet and discuss various topics with their honest thoughts about it. Even though it is true that people are a little mean on Reddit you can, however, use it to judge the real impact of various trends.

5. Read Customer Reviews on Existing Products

Customer reviews are a gold mine for entrepreneurs who want to improve from the insights given by their customers or to research the problems that are being faced by customers using competitors' products.

If your product is already live then you can use these customer reviews to understand the notable problems with your device and can use this information to create a new product that eliminates these problems. Note down the shortcoming and complaints with seriousness.

If you are a beginner, then you can also look at customer reviews to understand the strengths of your competitors and the products they are making. You need to ensure that you are giving the same qualities to your consumers to ensure that they are satisfied.

6. Find Product Opportunities in Keywords

Keywords used in search engines are a great way to market your products. If people are searching for keywords more than that particular keywords have become popular. You need to strategically find out these queries that the users are using and need to either rank for these keywords or pay for Google Ads to display ads for these keywords.

You can use tools such as Ahrefs and Semrush to find popular keywords for a particular niche or topic. You can then look at your competitors and find out what keywords they are mostly using. With keywords, you can get organic traffic which is essential for a business to thrive without worrying much about marketing tactics that need to be used.

The only disadvantage of building your business based on keywords is that changes in google searching algorithms can affect the traffic that you get and hence, your profits can be diminished. Google is also said to sometimes penalize users for various undisclosed reasons.

7. Litmus Test Before You Launch

For any product launch, the initial days are important as this is the time when passionate consumers will try your product. If people leave bad reviews during the initial phase, then your product will be destined to be a failure as people will lose interest in trying out your products.

Due to this reason, you need to upfront your investment before launch and ensure that your marketing is on point. When you secure interest with your potential customers, you will start to see fruitful results if your product matches their expectations. You can also use paid advertisements to improve your initial impact on sales.

8. Look at What Is Trending on Online Marketplaces

There are no better resources than checking on other popular ecommerce websites to understand what is trending and what people are showing interest in buying with their hard-earned money. We recommend you first check popular ecommerce stores such as Amazon, Etsy, and eBay before starting to look at some of your niche marketplaces. Amazon is a goldmine for entrepreneurs to find products that are selling extremely well in their niche.

All websites provide top seller lists for you to easily look into. If you are interested, you can also look at third-party tools that do the hard work for you and provide you with information about popular products in different marketplaces.

Amazon also provides ranks for products in different niches. For example, search your niche keywords on the Amazon search engine, and a list of products will pop up. You can now open the first search product to look at the bestseller rank in your niche category. Just move to the bottom of the Amazon page to look at different categories that particular product is ranking on top. Jungle Scout is a popular tool that makes it easier for you to look at Amazon's popular products in your niche with a minimal monthly subscription.

9. Research Products That Have the Potential to Give High-Profit Margins

When trying to resource your products, you need to give high priority to profit margins. While some products sell well, they, however, are costlier to manufacture and ship, and hence, your profit margins will slip drastically. Before deciding to sell a product, ensure that you have calculated both manufacturing and shipping costs to judge whether the products can generate a high return on investment (ROI).

10. Start Your Search With Related Products

If you are looking to sell mid-tier products in your niche, then you can use Amazon as a good research resource. Mid-tier products are usually not unique products but they sell well because they are usually bought along with the unique products. For example, a PlayStation console is a unique product but the controller for this console is a mid-tier product.

To get ideas for mid-tier products in your niche, visit any popular product in your niche using Amazon. On the product page at the end before customer reviews, you will see a section called "products customers frequently buy together." This is where you can find several products for your niche that can be sold to a larger audience.

11. Always Keep Searching

The modern ecommerce economy is quick and requires you to be attentive to get the most out of your business. You should never stop searching for products even if you have found a product that is being well sold. Keep searching on other ecommerce websites and keep researching to create products that can not only help you expand your business but will also help you make a mark in your niche.

HOW TO FIND THE BEST PRODUCTS AVAILABLE FOR YOU TO SELL

Selling products online needs a lot of research. You need to first ensure that the customer's need is being fulfilled with your product.

Customers are usually disappointed due to the following reasons.

1. Not having products to solve their need in the niche.
2. They are disappointed with the existing products.

When your niche audience is stuck with this problem, there is a scope for you to easily grow irrespective of the competition. You can now do research and expand your understanding of the target audience with the help of competition analysis.

Using the strategies in this section will help you achieve your goals.

Market Research

Once you have narrowed down the category or niche that you are confident enough to dive into, you also need to search whether there is potential to do business. The research will help you understand the market size and what you need to do to occupy a huge chunk of the market.

You Need to Ask Some of These Questions While Doing Research:

- What is the overall market size of this niche?
- Which demographics will be your potential customers?
- Who are your competitors and how to dominate them?
- How hard is it to beat your competitors in SEO and market worth?
- How is your product different from your competitors'?

Understand Competitors

When trying to search for products, you need to focus on what competitors are selling and how they are selling.

You Need to Ask Some of These Questions While Doing Research:

- What are the popular products of your competitors in your niche?
- What is the pricing of these popular products?
- Why do customers enjoy these products?
- What problems are these products solving for the customer?
- Are there any improvements that can be done to these products?

Research Target Markets

You can also get inspiration for some of the products when you do further research on your niche. Look at forums and read journals about your niche to understand what is next in the domain and how you can use these to create new products that sell well. For example, Apple has introduced MagSafe on their phones from iPhone 13. MagSafe makes it possible for businesses to develop a lot of new products such as magnetic chargers and wallets for smartphones. If you had predicted this technology would come to the new generation of iPhones by analyzing trade reports and production statistics, then you would have been prepared to develop MagSafe accessories that can be sold for huge profits during the initial days of the launch. Researching target markets will help you to grab the market quickly especially when a new technology emerges.

TYPES OF PRODUCTS THAT CAN BE SOLD ONLINE

Almost any type of product can now be sold on the ecommerce markets due to advanced logistics and a large user base who are willing to utilize the ecommerce business.

1. Commodities

You can order different types of commodities such as gold, silver, and minerals now with the help of online marketplaces. While some commodities such as petroleum and natural gas are still hard to get on online marketplaces, it is believed that within the next few decades, almost everyone can buy everything using the ecommerce business model.

2. Niche Products

Products that are part of a bigger market but have the potential to have their market are known as niche products. For example, smartphones are a market whereas flip phones are a niche market. Niche products are usually highly popular with ecommerce businesses because they can be targeted using content marketing to improve sales and improve ROI.

3. Physical Products

Most of the ecommerce purchases will usually be physical products. Physical products are the products that need to be packaged and shipped to the customer when an order is received. If you are selling physical products then you also need to ensure that you have good logistic support for your business to be successful.

4. Digital Products

Digital products are those that the customer gets access to as soon as they pay a fee for you. Online courses and e-books are good examples of digital products. Digital products require high-level marketing to make good sales as there is usually a lot of competition when compared to physical products.

PRODUCT DEVELOPMENT PROCESS

Once you decide on a product that works best for your business, ensure that you are following the below-mentioned product development process for the best results.

1. Idea Stage

Once you start to do research, you will get a lot of ideas about what to create for your target audience. Not all ideas can be practical and can work at this stage. After an initial review, you will be able to select a few ideas that can be implemented and marketed.

2. Idea Validation

Once you have only a few ideas to choose from, you can now start to validate these ideas using budget constraints and how much audience exists for these ideas. After a retrospection, you need to initially choose one product that you can develop immediately. If there are advanced ideas, note them down in your journal because you can always come to them back in the future while expanding your product lineup.

3. Product Development

Once an idea is confirmed, you need to now start approaching suppliers or manufacturers to make this product for you with your desired results. Develop a blueprint so that you can easily explain what needs to be done by the manufacturer. If it is a digital product, then you need to create your workflow to ensure that all the contents in the digital product are well developed.

4. Testing the Product

Once the product has been developed, you need to test it thoroughly before actually selling them to your customers. As initial reviews are important, you can also send review units for influencers and bloggers to get some good traction for your initial product launch. You can use beta testers to check what is good and what is bad with your product before launch.

5. Launching

Once the testing is completed and you have found no flaws, then it is time to launch your product to your consumers. In this process, ensure that you are utilizing your marketing potential to improve your sales.

The third step in the guide focused on helping you narrow down your niche and find the products that actually matter to the people. It also helped you get a psychological understanding of your audience and made you realize how to jump into the product development process.

With enough information about your target market, you are now all set to learn about ensuring that you have a good supply system for your ecommerce business to start.

STEP 4

ENSURING A SOLID SUPPLY SYSTEM

QUALITIES OF A GOOD SUPPLIER

For an online business to thrive, choosing the right supplier is essential. The process of finding the right supplier for your business can become complicated quickly, especially if you are not able to judge who a good supplier is and who is not. Choosing a supplier will result in how the quality of your product will be and can help you to limit any defects or flaws that are associated with your products.

If you choose the wrong supplier, then you have to deal with a lot of delays in shipping, quality, and returns. Choosing the right supplier will make the process a lot smoother and the percentage of satisfied customers will also increase.

To help you judge better about suppliers, we provide some of the important qualities that a good supplier possesses.

1. Quality Products

There is nothing more important than having a supplier who makes quality products. Selling mediocre or faulty products to your customers can damage your reputation in your niche. You need to find a supplier who is accountable for the quality of the products they make. If a supplier is not ready to accept their quality problems and is not willing to improve then it is a big red flag.

Most of the time, entrepreneurs need to verify the quality of the products by themselves. If you are not able to verify in person, then you can also hire a third-party inspection company to do the hard work for you.

The quality of the supplier is also usually directly proportional to the production capabilities. Whenever you start to create a relationship with a supplier, you need to find a way to measure their production capabilities. Either visit in person to verify their production capabilities or talk to a supplier representative to report for you. A supplier should provide you products with high quality consistently.

You will be knowing about the standard of the products a supplier provides by verifying some of the areas as discussed below:

- the raw materials being used for the product inventory
- the quality of control and how the shipment is being handled
- the capabilities of R&D of the supplier
- what certificates or licensing they are capable of
- how well they are handling the maintenance of machines and equipment

You can also ask for sample products if you are unable to estimate the quality they can provide.

2. Timely Delivery

To have a good relationship with suppliers, they also need to deliver the products you have ordered promptly to your inventory or to the nearest warehouse that you have booked out. Even if the products are of high quality, if the suppliers couldn't keep up with the demand from your customers, then you will be receiving negative reviews from the customers which will further weaken your sales.

Ask them about the maximum number of units they can manufacture in a business day for your product requirements and based on their answer, you can decide whether or not the supplier suits your demands. Some desperate suppliers can make false promises to get the contract from you. You need to do sufficient research and ask them for their previous client's details to verify the supplier by yourself.

3. Reliability

A supplier needs to be highly reliable and should be consistent in producing the products that they have promised to do for you. Unfortunately, in online business, you will be partnering with a lot of unreliable suppliers who will either decrease the quality of the products or decrease the production, claiming different reasons. Some reasons, such as global pandemics or worker strikes can be understood but most of the time, you will have to negotiate with them. With good research and communication, you can, however, try to make your suppliers reliable. Getting better suppliers can also be achieved by offering a higher price per unit.

4. Easy Accessibility

A good supplier should always be accessible for you to reach out to even if you are from different time zones. A quality supplier usually has a customer representative that will be able to answer your queries almost immediately. Having an English-speaking staff is very important, especially when trying to solve any problems.

Apart from the language, professional and open communication is also important to create an everlasting business with your supplier.

5. Competency

A good supplier should be competent enough to create products that are not only efficient but also game-changing. Suppliers need to be aware of the latest technologies that can improve the product's quality. If you find a supplier who is willing to provide you with the best variations of your products and are trying to improve the product quality for every shipment, then it is a golden deal for your business.

6. Stability

The suppliers also need to be stable with the quality of products even during the rush period when the production limits need to be pushed a little higher. Suppliers must keep up-to-date with the latest technologies used in the field to be stable in the business.

7. Variety of Options

A quality supplier when you provide a blueprint should be able to provide a lot of variations for a product design. If a supplier is capable of manufacturing different variations, then they have good quality production standards making them a good option for your business.

8. Discounts and Privileges

A good supplier also provides their consistent customers with discounts and additional privileges. You need to question the privileges the supplier provides before agreeing with them to ensure that the whole process is as seamless as possible.

9. Fair Pricing

Even if the supplier has modern technology and makes high-quality products, they should still be within your budget. You can't just agree with a supplier thinking that you can raise the prices further in the future. Negotiate with them and partner with the supplier only if you have a good ROI potential for your business.

DECIDING ON A BUSINESS MODEL

Identifying which business model you want to adopt will help decide on the best supplier option for you. Ecommerce is fabulous because it provides a lot of different opportunities and business ideas that entrepreneurs can implement with their capital. Even if the capital is limited, there are a lot of ways to make your business stand out from the competition. The idea of ecommerce mostly aligns with freedom because it provides entrepreneurs with a path that makes them more excited and yearning to do more in their niche.

While there are hundreds of options available for you to make use of the modern ecommerce economy, we will discuss some of the important ones that can help you make a better decision.

1. Dropshipping

Usually, when entrepreneurs start an ecommerce business, they need to get the idea, manufacture it with the help of suppliers, and market and ship it to the customer when an order comes.

It is a lot of hard work and requires a lot of patience. Now, what if this process can be made simple? This is where dropshipping comes to your rescue. With drop shipping, all you have to do is market your product and the rest will be taken care of by the supplier itself.

For example, if you are selling a pregnancy pillow for women, then you need to create a website and build an audience. Once you have enough audience members who are in the pregnant demographic, then you can contact a supplier and provide them with the blueprint so that they can send you your mentioned units. You can then divert these shipped units to a warehouse where they will stay until you receive orders from your audience.

Dropshipping can be a profitable option as long as you are setting prices more than what you are paying for your supplier

2. Handmade Craft Seller

Custom-made crafts by hand are very popular in the ecommerce industry. There are several popular websites such as Etsy and ArtFire that serve more than a million orders every year for customers around the world.

If you are not good at handicrafts, then you can outsource artists who can do the hard work for you. All you have to get is a good idea that can be marketed using ecommerce platforms such as Etsy. If you have a unique craft, then you need to develop a brand for yourself in the market to get huge profits. Once people start to see your talent, you will increase your reputation and can earn a good amount of money by doing what you love.

Startup costs for this path are extremely low especially if you are the supplier. Your only task should be to market yourself on social media platforms.

3. Niche Market Ecommerce Retailer

Not all niches have a lot of sales. Some niches such as fitness and electronics are more popular with consumers. However, remember that you can build a business from any niche as long as you are providing solutions for people.

It becomes easier to target if you are targeting a specific set of users on the internet. Building a niche market can also help you easily differentiate between various ecommerce companies.

All you need is a web-hosting service along with good content to drive visitors to your website. Once they are on your website, you need to hook them by trying to sell them your retail products or services. Focus on fewer products to manage your inventory and scale your business effectively. Having a few successful products is always better than having hundreds of products to sell.

4. Wholesaling

Wholesaling is most probably the toughest and most complex way to do an ecommerce business. While the risk is high, the returns are also huge with wholesaling. It requires a lot of capital as it needs the business to maintain a lot of inventory in its warehouses.

Wholesalers sell their products to retailers from around the world for less than consumer prices but at a margin that they can make profits. To be successful in the wholesale business, you need to have a lot of contacts and also personally have easy access to suppliers.

You can start doing well in this business with a few months of good research.

5. White Labeling

White labeling is a unique approach to start selling products quickly in the online ecommerce business. In this business model, when a customer places an order, the ecommerce company will get an existing product that has a license to be reused, repackage it with their branding, and ship the product to the customer.

Do you remember the fidget spinners which became hugely popular in 2017? Several entrepreneurs who are selling fidget spinners used the white labeling method to earn hundreds of thousands of dollars within a short time.

For the white labeling method to work, you need to first search the internet for popular niches and start to target the audience with CPA ads.

6. Private Labeling

While the white labeling method is a recent phenomenon, private labeling has been popular for decades in different industries. In a private labeling method, the entrepreneur will usually contact the supplier and will ask about what products they make the best for their other clients.

Once they list out the products, the entrepreneur needs to choose a product, ask them to do small changes and include your label, and sell it as a whole new product. Several luxury goods companies are believed to use private labeling methods.

For the private labeling method to work, you need to create brand value for your product. Use custom logos or a different cloth for your product to stand out from different brands that do the same.

7. Subscription

A subscription model is the latest popular business model on the internet. Even Google is trying to shift its services such as YouTube to the subscription model. In a subscription service, the business or service usually needs to provide valuable content so that the customers can purchase and access it.

You can't just create a subscription service and expect people to give away money for you. For people to believe that your service is valuable, you need to first create valuable content or solve a problem for them consistently. Almost all mobile and web applications are now using this model to have everlasting business irrespective of the domain.

NARROWING DOWN TO THE RIGHT SUPPLIER

Finding the right supplier is important for your business to constantly expand and scale itself with time. This section will help you understand how to choose suppliers from a lot of options available to you.

Types of Suppliers

When you start to search for suppliers, you will understand that there are different ones available for your
business.

1. Manufacturers & Wholesalers

Manufacturers and suppliers are the most preferable way
to find a supplier. Manufacturers manufacture the
product and hence, make it easy for you to customize the
products as per your liking. Wholesalers, on the other
hand, usually have contacts with manufacturers and can
help you get the products you want for a flat commission
rate.

2. Cash & Carry Suppliers

Cash & carry suppliers are usually large shops where you can just walk in and take your desired products after paying cash. If you are in a hurry and want products immediately, then this is a recommended approach.

3. Brokers of Specialty Products

Not all products can be directly obtained for your businesses. For some specialty products such as vending machines and highly technical products, you need to first contact a broker to obtain these products. Brokers of specialty products usually demand higher commission rates.

4. Membership Clubs

When you join specific membership clubs for a business, you will be able to meet suppliers who will be helping kickstart your business with products. Remember that these suppliers will usually only make business with the members of these clubs. It is, however, quite tough to get an invitation from one of these membership clubs if you don't have any contacts.

5. C2C Platforms

If you only need a few units then C2C platforms are a great way to make a deal. eBay and Craigslist are some good examples.

6. B2B Marketplaces

B2B marketplaces such as Alibaba are a great way to meet businesses from foreign countries such as China who are willing to supply to other businesses with minimal costs. You need to, however, remember that your country allows shipping imports from China.

Where to Search for Suppliers

While there are thousands of suppliers online trying to make a business with you, it still takes a lot of searching to filter the options you get and choose the best supplier from the lot.

1. Search Online

Use search engines such as Google and Bing to find both local and international suppliers for your niche. So many suppliers use websites to reach out to their customers and get their clients.

2. Join Professional Networks

You can also use professional networks such as LinkedIn to research popular suppliers in your niche. Most suppliers will have a dedicated page about their services to improve their reputation. You can search for their contact details on this page and contact them directly.

3. Subscribe to Trade Publications

Trade publications usually publish details about popular trends and talk about suppliers in the industry for every niche. When you read trade journals you will also get the latest technology that is being used in your niche. Knowing advanced information about the manufacturing process can help you choose better suppliers for your products.

4. Attend a Trade Show

You can also attend trade shows if you want to meet any suppliers who are trying to promote their business. Trade shows are usually arranged in cities such as New York and San Francisco. Please refer to your local Facebook groups to find out details about any new trade shows happening in your area.

5. Get Connected With Groups on Social Media

Social media is a powerful way to meet suppliers. You can particularly use Facebook groups to meet like-minded people in your niche. Just ping them, using the message option, whether they are interested in making your product.

6. Use Directories and Local Libraries

If you want to use the traditional way, then using whole-sale and dropshipping directories and public libraries is also recommended, such as SaleHoo and Worldwide Brands. However, remember that the information from directories and public libraries can be quite outdated for some niches. Just reconfirm the information you found using the internet before approaching them for negotiation.

7. Request for Local Referrals

If you have any good local suppliers nearby, then you can also message or meet them directly to agree with your business. With local suppliers, it becomes easier to negotiate, but remember that not all local suppliers can be trustworthy. Ensure that you have verified their manufacturing capabilities before agreeing with local suppliers.

Choosing the Best Supplier

When you start to send invites to suppliers after your initial research, you will start getting replies from most of them. With overwhelming options available, you may need to use the strategies mentioned below to choose the best among them.

1. Set Your Criteria

As an entrepreneur, you need to have some distinct expectations about the supplier you are going to make a deal with. Please try not to adjust or change your criteria just because you liked a supplier's reputation or communication capability. Irrespective of all the additional factors, in the end, all that matters for you is the quality of the products that you are selling to your customers and hence, you need to strictly follow your criteria before choosing a supplier.

2. Browse Your Options

Once you have invites to do business, you need to thoroughly research each of the suppliers. Do a quick Google search or read customer reviews to understand how well-functional they are. Start to narrow down your options depending on your requirements and choose at least 5–10 for the final negotiations.

3. Call for Bids

Send a message to all your chosen suppliers asking them to send their bids for a fixed number of products. Wait for all or most of them to reply to your queries.

4. Evaluate Bid Submissions

Once you get all bids from the suppliers, start to evaluate these bids and look at the best offers you got. Don't just go with the lowest bid because you also need to ensure that the quality is not missing.

5. Monitor Supplier Performance

Before making the decision, monitor the performance reviews that are given to the suppliers using websites such as Alibaba.com. If you don't find them on Alibaba, rely on Google reviews to monitor their quality performance.

ENTERING INTO SUPPLIER CONTRACTS

Once you decide on your supplier, you need to sign a contract with them to ensure that they will be providing you with quality products at the agreed-upon price. Doing business without contracts is not recommended especially in the ecommerce business.

This section focuses on some of the important questions you need to ask them before making a contract.

1. What Are the Payment Terms?

Asking about how they want payments to be processed is an important aspect. You can ask the payment providers they use and ask them how many days the invoices should be cleared. Usually, all the invoices are expected to be cleared within 30 days but if you explicitly mention in the agreement that the payment can be made within 60–90 days of the invoice being sent, then it will be a good negotiation for you in the long term.

2. What Will the Costs Be?

You can further ask them to mention all costs such as logistics, shipping, manufacturing, and insurance fees for you in detail so that you can understand the costs that are involved. After knowing the complete costs, you need to try to negotiate with them about some costs where a discount can be provided for you.

3. Do You Have a Liability Insurance Certificate?

Ask for written proof of liability insurance for all your products in case there are any damages to the products you order. Ensure that the insurance certificate is not expired.

4. Are You Going to Sell Directly?

Some suppliers do a bad job of selling similar products with a little bit of variation for a cheaper price in ecommerce stores after they supply you with your products. You need to ensure that your supplier doesn't have any malicious intentions as said above to compete with your product and grab your sales.

5. Is It a Guaranteed Sell-Through Policy?

Not all products can be sold. Sometimes, products fail and the stock remains. You need to be cautious about these situations and hence, need to usually agree about what to do with the remaining stock and how you can resell them to your suppliers. Of course, you need to compensate the supplier accordingly for their work.

6. What If Materials Don't Arrive?

Sometimes, products can be shipped late or can take a long time to be shipped. If you can't meet your deadlines or if so many of your customers start to cancel their orders because of this delay, you may have to make the supplier accountable for these cancellations. Ask them how they will compensate for the losses.

7. What Will Be My Expected Gross Margin?

Suppliers are usually aware of how many products they need to sell to reach their gross profit margin. Ask them for this information to confirm whether your gross profit margin estimates are realistic or not.

8. During Which Circumstances Will the Prices Be Changed?

Not everything goes as planned sometimes. Black swan events such as the global pandemic that devastated businesses just a year back can make the agreements be changed. Ask them about some of the exceptional conditions that can result in making some changes to the contract.

9. What About Volume Rebates?

If you require more products then ask how much discount will the suppliers provide if there is an order for more volume. All suppliers usually will be willing to take these additional orders even with a discount offer.

10. What Is Your Transfer of Possession Policy?

You also need to inquire about how the transfer of ownership process will happen. Sometimes, suppliers will ask you for the patent rights for the product for a reduction in manufacturing cost per unit. While it may seem like a good deal at first, you may end up regretting it when they start to create their product lineup based on your idea. We highly suggest you retain all the patent rights for your products.

NEGOTIATING WITH SUPPLIERS

As an entrepreneur, you often need to negotiate with suppliers to increase the profit potential of your business. In addition to increasing profits, you can also improve the quality of your products by communicating with suppliers in a way that they perceive as being important.

Take a look at some of the important negotiating tips from the below section.

1. Communication Is the Key

Your negotiations can have better results when you maintain constant communication with your suppliers. By being attentive to what the suppliers are saying and by responding to any doubts they have about your product blueprint, you will be able to leverage your chances in future negotiations. Communication will help you build rapport with the supplier, giving you better prices.

2. Research the Costs

Before starting to negotiate with the supplier or asking them to reduce the cost per unit, you need to be thorough about the actual costs the manufacturing process usually takes. When suppliers understand that you know these costs, your negotiation can work better.

3. Know the Lingo

When you are negotiating with the supplier you need to use the technical lingo that is popular in your domain. Talking without any of this technical lingo makes you look like an inexperienced businessman. Sounds like you know what you are doing and this behavior can earn you respect from the suppliers.

4. Discover Areas of Mutual Gain

When you pitch to them, say that there will be a mutual gain for everyone involved. Make them understand the profits that they can see when they start the business with you. Let them know that you are here to make a long professional relationship with the supplier.

5. Quote Multiple Suppliers

When you are trying to negotiate with a supplier, it is always recommended to share the prices quoted by the three suppliers of the competitors. When you show them the quotes, they can understand that you are looking for the best option in your budget and hence, they may try to provide you with a better deal.

6. Give Them a Reason to Make Business With You

You need to let the supplier know about your brand value and the audience to whom you are catering your products. If you have a good social media following then you can also share the links with them so that they can understand that you can be a good profitable relationship for them from a business perspective.

7. Have Your Deposit Available

When your negotiations are working well, don't forget to give them at least a 50–70% deposit to let them know that you are serious about what you are doing and want to get started immediately. Paying upfront also gives them confidence that you will be paying them on time.

8. Ensure That You Will Do Your Best to Reduce Any Risks

Suppliers are usually not so confident to start working with entrepreneurs especially if they are just starting as most of the time, the risk associated with the overall process is difficult for them. Ensure them the potential risks your business may face and what you are doing to not fall under those tough circumstances. Give them confidence that you will do your best to reduce both financial and supplier-focused risks.

With the fourth step of the guide, we provided you with information about how to find and negotiate with suppliers so that you can make a long-lasting relationship with your suppliers. Narrowing down suppliers using several criteria provided can help you while scaling your business further. A section about supplier contracts looked at helping you to be responsible for your ecommerce supplier relations.

With information to streamline your supply, you are now all set to learn about brand awareness and the complexities of business structures.

CREATING YOUR BUSINESS IDENTITY

NAMING YOUR BUSINESS

The business name is through which your potential customers or clients will know about you for the first time. We can go much further and claim that sometimes, a business name will be the sole representative for your business. Irrespective of how well or poorly your business does, your reputation will be carried with the help of the business name.

Several psychological experiments have proved how important a name should be for consumers to care about the brand. Your brand name should not only represent what your business is but also should be something that people can know what to expect when they hear the name.

As an entrepreneur, you need to understand what a good business name is and what is not. Your main goal is to design a name by looking at which of your customers can recognize what business you are doing.

Why Is It Important?

1. Creates Identity

For any niche and sub-niche, there are now competitors everywhere and new businesses are often blossoming. To stay in the business and to be profitable all the time, you need to create an identity for yourselves. For a business to be successful, it needs to have a separate identity. Not all the names will have the same tone associated with them because we have businesses in different categories and sectors. Your identity and demographics will change according to the line of business you are in. You need to let the consumers know what separates you from other competitors with the help of a good business name.

It is a well-known fact that consumers connect the products with their company name and judge how the products are going to be. For example, Apple is a household brand name and people vibe to it quickly because it is catchy and they can understand what to expect from an Apple product. Creating a unique product itself is not enough. You need to create a connection between these products and the name so that it creates an identity for your business.

2. Memorability

There are hundreds of thousands of businesses and brands in the market right now. People are bombarded with hundreds of options for any product they want to buy. With this amount of competition, you need to ensure that your business name is easier to remember. Having a complex name makes it difficult for customers to remember your brand and hence, you may lose some sales even when you make the best products or provide great services.

For example, companies such as Amazon and AMD have catchy names that make them easy for consumers to remember. We all know how successful Nintendo's game consoles are. But did you know that Wii-U, which is a handheld designed by Nintendo, had poor sales and ended as a failure? When the executives of Nintendo started to search for the answers to the handheld's failure they understood that the naming for Wii-U was quite similar to Wii and hence, many people thought it was just an extension of the previous console. Having confusing and similar names made it hard for people to remember the brand. It's not the sole reason but is one of the reasons for the handheld's failure.

3. Motivating Factor

Having a business name that you can relate to with your business can actually be a good motivating factor for an entrepreneur. The name usually comes from your work and the passion you put into your beloved business. Seeing it every day on your website or when people review your products can create a long-lasting impact on you. Your business name becomes a part of you and hence, you can't have a business name that you don't love or can connect to. You, however, need to understand that just because you like a complex name you can't name your business with it. You need to create a business name that you can connect to and, at the same time, your consumers can easily connect to. That's the only way to move forward while creating your business name.

4. Brand Recall

Brand recall is important for a business to have a good rapport with its consumers. When people remember your business name easily, it is definitely a good scenario. Whenever they have a problem that is related to your business, they will directly search for your brand in search engines. People are always busy and hence, may not remember all the things that you want them to remember.

For a brand recall to become easier, you should make sure that your name is as catchy as possible. Look at the popular brands and know how minimalistic they are.

5. Word of Mouth

For any business to thrive for a long time, consumers need to recommend your products or services to other potential consumers. People are usually happy to share a product when they love it. Word of mouth is very powerful for businesses and results in the growth of the company.

Having a good business name will make it easy for people to spread their views about your products.

6. Easy to Search

As most consumers today use search engines and social media networks to find out about their favorite products or to make a purchase, your business name should be easy to search for. You need to ensure that it takes less effort to search for your business name for your business to have an everlasting impact.

STEPS FOR NAMING THE ECOMMERCE BUSINESS

Choosing a name requires a lot of skill and this process expects you to have a piece of good knowledge about both your demographics and the market you are targeting. Naming a business is a mix-up of both art and science. Here are some guidelines to help you come up with a name that will help your business thrive.

1. Make a List

You need to first make a list of all the possible names that your business can be suitable for. Brainstorm different names and write all of them in a paper or list them out in an online mind map editor for you to easily take a look at all of them at once. Remember that all these words should be relevant to the business you are doing while being simple and creative.

You can use a thesaurus or online generators to use as inspiration while looking out for ideas. One example is Namelix which uses AI to create impactful and memorable names.

2. Narrow It Down

When you first generate a list, it is common to have words that don't resonate with your business idea. There will also be many names that are not catchy. During the narrow-down process, eliminate all the words or phrases that you feel will be difficult for an average customer to remember or search. Remember that you also need to look out for domain availability while creating an online business name, as having a different domain name can become hard for you to market your product. It will also become hard for consumers to come to your online store due to the difference between domain and business names.

3. Get Creative

When you start to create your business name, you can also use some creativity to rhyme the words or start different words with the same letter. Modifying or tweaking a word a little bit can also change the perspective of your brand. However, remember not to be too out of bounds while creating your names just for the sake of creativity. While references and smartness in your business name are a good idea, not everyone can, however, get what you are trying to say. Most of the time, literal words work better than over-creative brand names.

4. Compare and Test

Once you have narrowed down your names, individually compare them with each other and find out the few that are attractive to your business. Look at your competitors' names and compare with them to understand whether or not the name is good and can hold well in the long term. You also need to separate from your identity and hence, the name shouldn't be very similar to your competitors'. Names should reflect your business and be easy to pronounce and write.

5. Verify the Availability of the Name for Professional Use

Apart from checking the domain name for your new business name, you also need to make sure that the username is available for social media usage. Social media is right now the most popular way to connect with your customers and you shouldn't have a username that is different from your business name. To ensure that the business name is not already protected by copyright or trademark, you should also check the U.S. patent and trademark office. If you are not from the US, then check the official patent manager in your country.

6. Register Your Business

Once you have chosen your business name, it is important to register your business to ensure that no one steals it or uses it for their own businesses. Registering your business also makes it a legal company and hence, it will be possible to create trustworthy relationships with both customers and suppliers.

Once you have chosen a business name and are ready to register it, you also need to select the business structure you are going to use. The next section will describe in detail the different business structure models that entrepreneurs need to be aware of.

STRUCTURING YOUR BUSINESS

Several entrepreneurs usually don't understand the importance of the right legal structure and how you can easily solve several problems regarding taxation by registering your business with one. Whether you are a new entrepreneur or someone who has been in the business world for a long time, it is important to be aware of the below-mentioned details.

What Is a Business Structure?

A business structure is a legal way to determine certain aspects of your business. A business structure from a federal perspective also helps you know how much taxes you need to pay irrespective of your liability in the business.

A business legal structure is important because it can save you a lot of money and also help you avoid some unnecessary headaches while handling a business.

1. Taxes

One of the major reasons to have a business structure is to handle taxes effectively. As different tax rates are given for different business structures, you need to choose the correct one without burdening with high taxes in the future.

2. Liability

A proper business structure, such as a limited liability company (LLC), can protect your personal assets in the event of a lawsuit.

3. Paperwork

Different business structures have different documentation forms that need to be filled out. For example, if you choose a corporation as your default business structure, then your paperwork increases.

4. Registration

If you want to provide an Employer Identification Number (EIN) for your employees, then you may have to register your business with a business structure. If not, then the federal government will ignore your request to provide an EIN for your business.

5. Fundraising

Without a business structure, it becomes difficult to raise funds for your business via crowdfunding. Most crowdfunding websites expect businesses to provide their business structure to ensure that no fraud is taking place in the crowdfunding campaign.

Even though you can change your business structure anytime you want to, choosing the wrong structure can result in unnecessary tax consequences.

WHAT ARE THE DIFFERENT TYPES OF BUSINESS STRUCTURES?

Knowing about all important types of business structures can help you to decide what to choose for your business.

Sole Proprietorship

In a sole proprietorship, a business is operated by only one person. When you use the sole proprietorship you will be responsible for all the company's profits and debts. If you are a person who wants to be their own boss and have complete control over your business then this is the better business structure for you.

What Are Some of the Advantages?

1. Easy Setup

It requires very less paperwork for your business to be registered as a sole proprietorship.

2. Low Cost

As there are no separate licenses that need to be acquired to run your business, the costs are usually low.

3. Tax Deduction

A sole proprietorship usually has certain advantages when compared to other business structures while filing tax returns. For example, you can claim returns for health insurance with a sole proprietorship.

4. Easy Exit

With a sole proprietorship, it becomes easier to end your business whenever you want to. You will not usually be accountable to anyone and hence, the paperwork required is also very less. If something doesn't work, you can just dissolve the business and start a new one when you are ready again.

Many famous companies such as eBay and Walmart first started as sole proprietorship companies and later became the corporations that we know today.

The one con, however, is that with the sole proprietorship your personal and business assets are not separated and hence, can be an issue during legal disputes.

Partnership

When you want to manage your business with two or more partners, then choosing this business structure is a better idea. There are two types of partnership models in the business structure. A general partnership is the first one where the business is shared equally between the partners. A limited partnership, on the other hand, will provide more power to you while the other partners will be limited just to contributing capital and receiving profits.

This is a good business model if you want to enter into the ecommerce business with a family member or friend. It is, however, important to remember that you will be receiving profits for all the decisions made by your partner, and also you will be liable for all the mistakes they make.

Google is a good example of a company that started as a partnership-based company.

What Are Some of the Advantages?

1. Easy Formation

A partnership business structure is also easier to form. If you want to do business other than in the name of your partners then you need to apply for a doing-business-as (DBA) agreement. You also need to draft a partnership agreement to list out all the powers you and your partner have.

2. Growth Potential

When you have a partner, it becomes easier to meet suppliers and make agreements with them. Banks also prefer to give loans to businesses if there is a partner in the business. As credit scores are usually important to get loans, this approach is a better way if you don't have stellar credit scores.

3. Special Taxation

Partnership business structures usually have special taxation rules and hence, you usually need to use form 1065 to file your taxes and returns. Both you and your partner need to file income taxes regularly like in sole proprietorship as individual income but with different forms.

The major con with this business structure is that you will be liable for any mistakes that your partner makes. It is for this reason people who usually start a business with a partnership model will usually start with the people they trust.

LLC

An LLC is the most popular business structure that is used by ecommerce companies especially when they are just starting out. LLC is a hybrid structure where owners, partners, and shareholders will usually have limited personal liability with the business but will have flexible benefits such as a reduction in tax rates.

The LLC model is majorly used by businesses because it provides liability protection. With liability protection, your personal assets will not be liquidated because of others' decisions or because of the business not doing well. When your business starts to grow, it is important to migrate from a sole proprietorship or partnership to an LLC business structure.

Sony, Nike, and IBM are some of the companies that started with this business structure and have succeeded in the market.

The only con with this business structure is that it is quite costly to set up and as an LLC, you also need to maintain a lot of paperwork, hence, you need to hire a chartered accountant, which is an additional cost.

Corporation

A corporation's business structure is the highest form of business structure that exists. In this structure, the owners will usually be completely independent of their legal rights. If someone sues then it will be directed to the corporation instead of the owners of the business. Corporation fees vary based on state and country but there are significant tax benefits associated with this business structure.

There are also several variations of the corporation's business structure based on how big and regulated the business is.

1. C Corporations

C Corporations are big companies that have billions of dollars of turnover in revenue every year. Apple, Amazon, and Bank of America are some corporations that fall under this category.

2. S Corporations

If you are just starting out then this is where you fall as this is designed specifically for small businesses. With S corporations, you will benefit as double taxation can be avoided.

3. Non-Profit Corporations

Non-profit corporations help others in some way and hence, they are usually exempt from tax. If you are doing business not for profit but for service, then this is the business structure that you need to register with.

What Are Some of the Advantages?

1. Limited Liability

As a business owner, you will have minimal liability for your business and hence, this is a good choice if you have a lot of personal investments.

2. Continuity

Irrespective of the exchange of owners or even your death, your corporation will survive because one person doesn't hold the ultimate power over the business.

3. Raising Capital

When you get registered as a corporation, it becomes not so challenging to raise capital from investors.

WHAT ARE SOME FACTORS TO CONSIDER BEFORE CHOOSING A BUSINESS STRUCTURE?

Choosing a business structure can be quite overwhelming because a lot of choices get thrown at you when your business starts to gather attention from your potential customers. You need to be able to make a decision that can save you money and energy by considering some of the factors mentioned below.

1. Day-To-Day Operations

Depending on how your business's day-to-day operations are, you need to choose your business structure. For example, if your business requires a lot of wholesale transactions every day, then choosing either corporation or an LLC is a better choice.

2. Tax Liability

While choosing a business structure you need to make a consideration based on the fact that a business structure will reduce the tax payment for your business. Both LLC and corporation business structures are designed to help businesses reduce some taxes. You can also choose a non-profit corporation option as your business structure if your business is not working for profits.

3. Quantum of Paperwork

If you are not interested in checking and filling a lot of paperwork or are not in a position to hire a chartered accountant for the time being, then it is recommended to go with either sole proprietorship or partnership as it involves minimal paperwork.

4. Risk of Personal Liability

If you have personal assets and prefer not to lose them when something happens to your business, then we suggest you not go with either proprietorship or partnership business structure as you will be directly liable, and hence, your personal assets can be liquidated too.

5. Complexities Involved in Raising Funds

If you are running a business that is focused on improving its market by scaling, it means that you need a budget that can be possible only with venture investors. To pitch to these investors, you need to definitely go with the corporation as your default business structure.

STORIES

Business names have always helped companies reach an increased audience. Take a look at some of the success stories where a business name played a significant role to boost its popularity.

- Apple is a popular technological brand that has reached out to millions of customers not only because of its innovation but also because it's a household name and has an appealing icon.
- Skullcandy is a headphone brand that became popular because it reminds one of colorful earbuds along with producing aesthetically beautiful headphones.
- Etsy is an ecommerce business that makes no sense according to its creator. He wanted to use a name that is artistic but silly. Etsy stood out for him as it is both catchy and mysterious.

- Wish is a popular brand that helps businesses sell their products. As it resembles a "wish list," it became easy to market itself. A single word can also change the fate of businesses in the ecommerce world.

With the fifth step in the guide, you got to understand the importance of a business name and learned a process to create a unique name for your business. We also discussed the complexities of different business structures and what can be the best choice for you.

With all the foundational steps set up, you are now ready to venture into the real business world. In the next chapter, you will learn about the required licenses and permits that make sure that your business can continue without any legal hurdles.

STEP 6

OBTAINING LICENSES AND PERMITS

WHAT IS A BUSINESS LICENSE?

In every country, governments prefer to track and monitor businesses, and to make this happen, business permits and licenses are a logical way. When you have a business license, it means that you are officially recognized by the government as a business. Alternatively, with a business license, you will have some advantages such as tax exemption making it a better option for business too.

Is a Business License Needed to Sell Online?

All the licenses associated with a business usually change depending on the country you reside in. Different countries have different laws and hence, personal research about licenses is important to sell a product online. If you don't acquire the licenses, you may be fined. If you are trying to sell products in industries such as animal products and alcoholic beverages, then you will be fined huge amounts as these industries are usually heavily regulated.

Ecommerce businesses have recently become popular and most state governments have started to issue licenses for ecommerce businesses to organize their records better. You need to also get permission from the city and counties just to be safe in the future.

Most ecommerce business owners obtain a general business license from their local city or county and renew it every year or two.

When and How to Apply for a Business License

To obtain a business license, you need to follow the below-mentioned instructions.

- First of all, estimate the cost of obtaining a business license. Depending on the location you are staying the business license will usually cost between $100 and $500. Every time you renew your license, you need to pay the same amount.
- If you make constant pickups and deliveries of your products, the business license may take some time to be registered as your business will fall under home-based businesses. You need to first make an appointment with your city or county's zoning department to confirm that you are not violating any local zoning restrictions.
- Once the zoning verification is completed, you need to visit the local federal office in your city or county and download the forms that are required to be filled out for the business license.

- You need to provide details such as your business structure, your sales tax information, and the description of your business in detail.
- Once the information is entered and verified, pay the business license fee and wait for your license to be approved. Once your license is verified and approved, you will be able to manage your business without any legal problems. This process can take anywhere between one to two weeks.

When to Get the License?

You can start to get your business license even after opening your store and after you get a few sales. However, just to be safe and to ensure you get the deserved tax exemptions, you need to register for a business license even before opening your digital front store.

What Are the Types of Business Licenses and How Do You Obtain Them?

Every business needs to provide licenses for both the IRS and bank to ensure that your ecommerce business sails as soon as possible and is available for customers to make orders from you. You need to obtain several ecommerce business licenses to ensure that you are legally permitted to operate a business. Operating any kind of business with these licenses is illegal and can land you either in jail or you will end up paying a hefty fine.

While we have said the hard fact already, we want to relieve you by saying that all the licenses that you nccd to start your business are easy to obtain. All you have to do is make a quick research about your state laws and find out how to obtain the licenses mentioned below according to your state or country's regulations. Remember that different states and countries follow different tax regulations. Hence, you need to usually do your research to ensure that you are doing everything right. If you are not comfortable with handling your finances, then you can hire a chartered accountant to do the hard work for you.

1. Business Operation License

To operate a business legally, you need to apply for a business operation license. A business operation license allows you to open and run a business in your country, city, or state. All ecommerce businesses need to obtain a business operation license. You need to pay a small processing fee for your license to be obtained. You also need to confirm for how many months or years your license will be applicable. Before your license expires, you can, however, renew it to operate the business without any problems. Remember that operating your business with no license or an expired one can result in hefty fines and is also a legal crime.

2. EIN

An EIN is usually provided by the Internal Revenue Service (IRS) to ensure that you are a supported tax entity. If you have a working business structure such as an LLC or if you are planning to hire employees, then having an EIN is recommended. It becomes very difficult for you to file taxes if you don't have an EIN. You can visit the IRS website to apply for a new EIN.

3. DBA License

When you operate a business, it is not mandatory to do business with your legal name. You can use different business names to make sure that your personal assets and business assets are separated. DBA can help you easily get business bank accounts.

4. Seller's Permit

Governments usually place restrictions on people selling items. Not everyone can trade or sell the items they want to. You need to get a seller's permit legally to sell products online. Every state has its requirements to get a seller's permit. We suggest you check with the revenue department of your state to get the correct permits. Many ecommerce sellers get confused that a seller's permit is not required for digital products. However, it is not true. You need to obtain a seller's permit for a digital product or an intangible service.

5. Sales Tax License

Any business that sells taxable products using ecommerce needs to pay a part of the product price as sales tax. To pay sales tax in your state, you need to have a sales tax license. Sales tax also will usually differ from state to state and hence, we suggest you check out the rules before applying for a sales tax license.

6. Home Occupation Permit

As most ecommerce entrepreneurs operate their businesses from their homes, it is necessary to take a home occupation permit. If you have a separate business office with a permit, then you don't need to worry about this license.

7. Occupational License

Depending on the industry you are in, you also need to get an occupational license for your ecommerce business. For example, if you are selling merchandise on the internet, then there is no need for an occupational license. On the other hand, if you are providing special training for students, then you may have to acquire an occupational license.

Apart from these licenses, you also need to apply for basic license permits such as environmental permits and health permits for your business to be run without any problems from a legal perspective.

What Is a Seller's Permit?

A seller's permit is a special license that is asked for businesses that pay sales tax. A seller's permit makes it easy for federal officers to easily confirm your tax payments. The seller's permit completely depends on the state you are in. Not all states, however, will ask you to have a seller's permit.

A lot of people get confused between a business license and a seller's permit. While a business license provides you the permission to run an online or offline business in a certain location, the seller's permit will just identify that you are paying the sales tax for the concerned authorities.

Some states also provide temporary seller's permits for up to 90 days if you are not an established business yet.

OPENING A BUSINESS BANK ACCOUNT

When your business starts to grow, you need to separate your personal finances from your business finances. A lot of entrepreneurs ignore this and will end up paying a lot of taxes than they have to. Having a business bank account will not only save you money but will also not make you directly responsible for any copyright claims or intellectual property notices that can be given by businesses.

Business bank accounts will help you professionally solve this problem. Let us look at some of the important benefits a business bank account possesses.

Benefits of a Business Bank Account

1. Limited Liability Protection

When you create a business bank account, you will be limiting your liability for any suing or losses that the company may have to face. When you use an LLC along with a business bank account, any individual or business cannot ask you to repay funds that are not of business but yours.

2. Purchase Protection for Customers

When you have a business bank account, several banks and credit card companies will accept you as a merchant, and hence, your customers will have a stress-free transaction as these banks and credit card companies usually provide purchase protection.

3. Professionalism

When you bill your customers, having a personal name can be quite demotivating for them. A business name, on the other hand, looks professional and assuring for the customers.

4. Credit Options

Most banks and credit card companies provide way fewer credit options for individuals. They, however, provide larger credit options for businesses.

What Should You Consider Before Choosing a Business Bank Account?

Different banks are trying to do something different for their customers. Out of the overwhelming options available it can become tough for you to choose a good one. You can take a look at some of the options provided to evaluate the banks that you are more inclined to.

1. Fees

Every bank has different fee structures that they make available for their customers. You need to verify and compare the fees that you will be paying for different types of banks. Typically, personal accounts will have fewer features when compared to business accounts.

2. Sign-up Bonuses

Whenever you create a new business account with a bank, you will receive a sign-up bonus. Not all banks have the same rules, however, when choosing a bank, it is better to choose one that gives better sign-up bonuses. However, you shouldn't make your decision completely based on the sign-up bonus as some new banks can lure customers with this strategy.

3. Account Maintenance Requirements

One of the important factors to be aware of are the account maintenance requirements that are asked by the banks. If your desired bank is charging a high fine for not maintaining a minimum balance, then it is not a good idea to go with it.

4. Features

The bank account you will be choosing should also depend on the features the bank provides. For example, a mobile app can be a great feature that may usually be overlooked by customers. You need to list the different features provided by different banks and choose the one that includes features that you feel are more important.

How to Open a Business Bank Account?

Creating an online business account is often a complex process and often requires you to submit a lot of documents. This section focuses on helping you understand the process of opening a business bank account.

What Documentation Will You Need?

1. Articles of Incorporation

Articles of incorporation are documentation that assures the bank about how your business is structured. The business structure should usually comply with state rules. Irrespective of whether you are an LLC, limited partnership, or corporation, you need to provide articles of incorporation for a business bank account to be created.

2. Business Licenses

Banks will also ask for the necessary license files that can verify that you are legally permitted to do business in your area. By providing the business licenses, you will become accountable to the bank and give them confidence that you are a legit entrepreneur.

3. DBA Certificate

Most businesses use a different name while advertising, accepting money, or marketing. As an example, Coca-Cola is a great catchy name for a product, but the company can use a different name when interacting with suppliers and paying salaries to employees. It has always been a norm to separate business transactions with a different name and hence, banks usually want to know the fictitious name that you are using to handle your business transactions.

4. EIN

EINs are usually used by banks to avoid the identity theft that is usually common while taking business loans. You need to provide the EIN and social security number (SSN) if you are a sole proprietor. If it is an LLC or a partnership, then you can open accounts without an EIN. However, we still suggest you create an EIN for better managing taxes for your employees.

You can get EIN for your business by filing with the IRS.

5. Identification Documentation

In the end, you also need to provide mandatory identification documents such as a driver's license, voter's license, or passport for the bank authorities to confirm that you are a real business owner.

WHEN SHOULD YOU OPEN YOUR BUSINESS ACCOUNT?

It is recommended to open a business account before you will start accepting your first payment from customers around the world. You also ensure first that all your business licenses are acquired before attempting to create a business account.

Before the pandemic, most business accounts were created only when you visited the bank in person. Now, however, banks have created solutions to create business bank accounts right from your home with just a click of your mouse.

The sixth step in the guide has focused on providing detailed information about the licenses and permits that are required to run an online business. We also have extensively discussed opening a business bank account to make the process smoother for running an ecommerce business.

With enough information about opening an online business account, you are now fully equipped to create an online store. The next step in the guide will help you focus more on bringing your business to life.

STEP 7

CREATING YOUR ONLINE STORE

REGISTERING YOUR DOMAIN NAME

For an ecommerce business, a domain name is as essential as the business itself. With a bad domain name, you will lose a lot of sales. Due to the many services available right now on the internet, it just takes a few steps to get your desired domain name if available. You can switch domain names whenever you want to. However, we suggest you not do this as you may lose recurring customers who remember your business solely by your domain name.

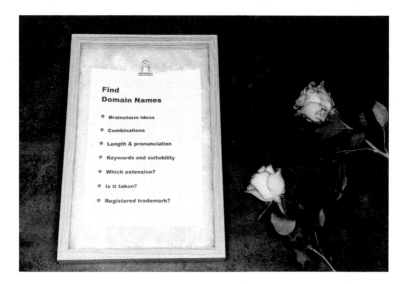

Follow the below-mentioned instructions to create a brand-new domain name for your business.

1. Choose a Domain Name

First of all, remember that your domain name needs to mostly coincide with your business name. Brainstorm and come up with a few catchy domain names that can be used for your business. There needs to be a connection between your business and domain name to make it memorable.

2. Check for Domain Availability

Not all domain names will be available for you to register. Use websites such as godaddy.com to check whether or not your domain is available. A domain name service (DNS) is decentralized and is universally recognized; hence, you need to make some compromises if your desired name is not available.

As domain names are universal, if a domain name is not available from godaddy.com, then it will be unavailable with any other available service.

Fortunately for businesses, there are usually domain resellers who wish to sell their domains for a profit. If you are fixated on a particular domain that is held by a reseller, then you can bid for it with the reseller.

3. Choose a Domain Name Registrar

A domain name registrar is a service that will usually issue your domain name to a DNS server all on its own without making you involved in the technical process. GoDaddy, Namecheap, and HostGator are some of the popular domain name registrars in the industry.

These providers will usually charge domain prices for a year. You can register the domain for as many years as you want to.

How to Choose a Domain Name Registrar

- Ensure that there is good customer service.
- Make sure that there is high-level domain privacy protection where your details will be masked.
- Confirm whether they provide hosting and SSL certificates for your website for better encryption.

Several ecommerce stores such as Shopify have their own domain and hosting services for their customers to quickly set up their ecommerce store.

CREATING YOUR ECOMMERCE WEBSITE

For an ecommerce business to go live on the internet, you have two approaches to use. One is by creating a website and the other one is by creating an app. App development is usually hard and requires both huge capital and resources. This is the reason why a lot of entrepreneurs, in the beginning, will start a website and when the business expands, they will scale their website to work with the help of a mobile app.

Why Do You Need to Create an Ecommerce Website?

- It is easy to set up.
- There are millions of customers you can target.

- Websites work on smartphones too with the help of browsers such as Google Chrome and Safari.

BUILDING AN ECOMMERCE WEBSITE STEP-BY-STEP

Building an ecommerce site is quite straightforward right now as there are so many sources and services available. With enough research, you will be able to create an ecommerce website that will last longer and can serve even millions of customers.

1. Select Your Ecommerce Platform

The first thing you need to do is choose an ecommerce platform to launch your digital store. There are several options to choose from depending on your preferences and will to customize your website.

The most obvious option for many businesses is to use WordPress as the default content management system to run their websites. With WordPress, it is possible to add thousands of themes and plugins to customize your website.

The other popular option is to use services such as Shopify that are fundamentally designed to work with ecommerce websites. These websites, however, charge a monthly fee to host your website. WordPress, on the other hand, can be installed for free on your hosting network.

2. Purchase a Domain Name

Once you have chosen the ecommerce platform, link the domain name that you have already purchased. Just link the DNS server of your website with the hosting service.

3. Find a Developer

Creating an ecommerce website needs a certain skill set. While it is possible to use basic themes and plugins to start running your website, it is, however, not a feasible solution especially when you have a good number of customers landing on your page to buy products. A dedicated web developer can help you develop your website with high encryption standards and with faster loading times. You can use websites such as Upwork to hire freelancers or Indeed to hire remote employees for your ecommerce business.

4. Pick Your Ecommerce Theme

The theme represents your website to customers who visit it. Ensure that your theme is bright and visible to everyone. There are thousands of themes for you to choose from websites such as www.themeforest.net. You can also customize your themes according to your liking. We suggest using minimal themes with fast loading times that can work in both mobile and desktop browsers for an increase in conversion rates.

5. Customize Your Ecommerce Template

Once the theme is set, you can also further customize your website with the help of templates and plugins. Plugins such as WooCommerce can help you to integrate various payment providers with a click. All plugins, however, come with a cost, and hence, you need to decide on plugins that will only make your website function better and that you feel are necessary.

6. Add Your Products

Once your website is set up you need to start adding your products. If you are focusing on only one particular product lineup then we suggest you use a dedicated landing page for each of these products. If you are selling a lot of products then using a carousel view is recommended.

7. Set Your Payment Options

Ensure that plugins such as WeCommerce are used to provide payment options for your ecommerce website. Using a Secure Sockets Layer (SSL) is mandatory, especially when your customer is making a transaction. We suggest using PayPal, credit/debit cards, Apple Pay, and Stripe as default payment options. While some businesses are using cryptocurrencies as payment, it is still not recommended as the crypto market is currently volatile.

8. Set Shipping Options

You also need to link the logistics tracking tool you are using to ship your products so that the customers can track their orders.

9. Preview, Test, and Publish

Once all these parameters are set, preview the website, test it and publish it online. Once the website is live, you can use Google Analytics to monitor the performance of your website and make any changes that are needed.

WEBSITE BUILDERS

If you are not interested in hiring a web developer due to a minimal budget you can also use free website builders that will do a decent job to create a website that works out of the box on both web and mobile browsers. While all the below-mentioned website builders are free to use, you can also premium versions to have more functionalities.

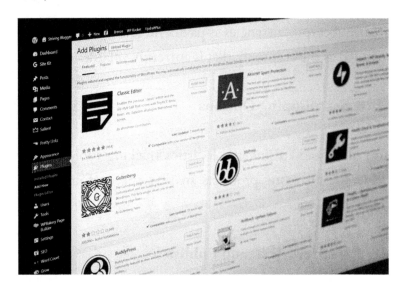

1. Wix

Wix is the most popular drag-and-drop website editor right now in the market. It has a large collection of apps that can be integrated into your website.

2. Elementor

Elementor is a unique website-building tool that uses aesthetic web elements to make your website as beautiful as possible. Elementor comes with a lot of third-party and plugin integrations.

3. Yola

Yola is a website builder tool that is optimized to work well with smartphones. It also supports multilingual websites making it an attractive option if you are targeting your products to sell in different countries with the same interface.

4. Shopify

Shopify is a store creator tool along with a website development editor that can be used by ecommerce businesses to host their websites and products. Shopify provides customized themes and plugins for businesses to make high-quality dynamic websites and ecommerce stores.

The seventh step in the guide has focused on giving your information about registering with a domain name and identifying the options available for you in an ecommerce business. We also focused on providing information about tools that can help you to create the front-end interface for your ecommerce business.

With your ecommerce website setup, it is now time to find ways to market your website to your target audience.

STEP 8

MARKETING YOUR ONLINE STORE

Irrespective of the scale of your business, you need to ensure that the details about your products are reaching your customers. For a business to succeed, understanding the customer's problems and providing solutions is not enough. You need to make sure that you are letting them know that a solution exists for their problem. How can you accomplish that?: Through marketing.

For a business to succeed and survive the competition, a marketing plan is mandatory.

WHAT IS MARKETING?

Marketing is a term that covers a lot of activities that businesses use to make people aware of the products created by companies. Marketing will not only help businesses to inform about their products but should also focus on persuading the customers to buy the products. Marketing will involve product and consumer research along with product design.

It is, however, important to remember that sales do not fall under marketing. While marketing motivates people to buy products, sales are the result of marketing. This section will help you understand different types of marketing and how to approach your business.

Why Is Marketing Important for Businesses?

Marketing helps businesses to achieve the six below-mentioned characteristics to make a mark in their niche or industry.

1. Effective Consumer Engagement

For your products to be sold, you need to first engage customers. Engagement is the main reason why businesses usually spend millions of dollars on advertisements. Ecommerce businesses use marketing as a powerful tool to reach out to their potential customers. To engage customers, you need to provide info about your products that they don't know yet but they would love to know. You need to create a hook with your customers and that will become possible only with the help of marketing.

2. Building and Maintaining the Reputation

Running a business is a long-term job for entrepreneurs. You can't just sell a product and move on with your life. The reputation of a business depends on long-term commitment and constant improvement of the product lineups. To intrigue people for a long time with your products, you need to improve your brand etiquette and ensure that the customers are aware of all the new improvements that you are making to your brands and services.

To let them know what your new features are, you need to build and maintain a reputation, which is possible only with the help of intelligent marketing.

3. Building Relationships Between Customers and Business

Businesses usually need to create bonds with customers and their experiences to create products they will love. Marketing will usually help businesses to maintain these bonds with their customers. As marketing will also help you learn more about consumer behaviors and psychographics, you will understand what the customer wants.

4. Boosting Sales

Good marketing will have a direct impact on your sales. When the effectiveness of your marketing improves, the sales will automatically improve as people will be keen to try your product. However, remember to not do any false marketing as it can give a negative impact especially if your product is nowhere near in reality to the marketing you have done for your product.

5. Staying Relevant

Marketing helps you to stay relevant in your niche. Because of marketing, even if you don't have any immediate products to unveil, you will still make money from your old products.

TYPES OF MARKETING

As an entrepreneur, you need to be aware of different types of marketing strategies that you can apply to your business.

1. B2B Marketing

B2B marketing is a marketing strategy where you will be selling products and services to other companies and hence, you need to market specifically for these clients after thorough research. The demographic groups you will be targeting are fewer but as you know, the exact companies you want to impress with your marketing strategy will be much more focused.

2. B2C Marketing

B2C is a marketing strategy where a business will be selling to consumers. As you will be targeting thousands of people at once, most of the marketing is done through advertisements.

3. C2B Marketing

In a C2B marketing strategy, the customer will do their best to sell their products and services to a business. Freelancers are a good example of C2B marketing.

4. C2C Marketing

In C2C marketing, a consumer makes mutual business with another consumer. A c2C business model is usually monitored by a centralized authority. However, the consumer will market their unique abilities to ensure that the other consumer will book them for their services. Gig economy workers who use websites such as Fiverr use this marketing strategy.

PERSONALIZED MARKETING

Personalized marketing is where the business should focus on marketing to every individual in a unique way. Creating personalized marketing plans for customers can improve the conversion rate. The only problem with personalized marketing is you need data to market to specific customers in a unique way. As customers are now becoming more aware of privacy concerns, the road to personalized marketing will become tough in the future.

What Are Some Examples?

- Use targeted emails to increase the reading rate of emails.
- Create customized shopping filters so that you can get small sets of customers with different opinions.
- Provide free trial offers for customers who have abandoned products in their cart.
- Offer free shipping for customers with abandoned carts to increase the conversion rate.
- Create customized coupons and provide them for recurring customers.
- Use custom video messages.

- Use retargeting with the help of cookies. Facebook is a good way to retarget your customers.
- Create dynamic content for customers.
- Create personalized reports.

CONTENT MARKETING 101

Content marketing is a popular way to market your products and services in the industry. All businesses in one way or another use content marketing to share knowledge about their services and products. Content marketing will also help you rank better in Google search page rankings and hence, will automatically increase sales.

What Is Content Marketing?

Content marketing is a marketing strategy where textual or media content will be used to promote the brand or build awareness about the service they are offering. Hooking customers with content can help your brand grow its popularity with your target customers.

How Can It Help Your Business Grow?

There are several advantages of content marketing that can help your business grow.

1. It Will Help You Reach Different Demographics

As content can be easily targeted and translated, you can reach different demographics. Personalized content can also be created to improve the conversion rate for your products that are linked using this content.

2. Help You Create a Web of Content

Content can be easily linked together, and hence, your marketing will extend like the web. For example, if a new version of a product is released, you can still promote the old product using your content.

3. Content Marketing Is Passive

Content is always shared, so even if you uploaded the content years ago, you will still get clicks and sales.

What Are the Types of Content Marketing Strategies?

There are several variations of content marketing that can be used by entrepreneurs to improve the performance of their businesses and increase brand value.

1. Blog posts that provide a personal experience and are designed in a way that the person is talking to the customer.
2. Articles that provide in-depth information about a particular subject or a solution for the problem the users may be facing.
3. Emails that hook the customers with important information instead of the cliched ones.
4. Ebooks that provide an in-depth guide about your product or what it can do.
5. Videos that provide education and entertainment at the same time.
6. Infographics that provide important information or a summary of a complicated topic so that it can be understood easily.
7. Courses that will let the customer understand how to use your service from scratch.

HOW TO GENERATE SALES AND LEADS WITHOUT SPENDING

The below-mentioned ecommerce strategies can help you generate sales without having to spend a fortune. Right ecommerce strategies can not only boost your sales but also can help you retain customers in the long run and beat your competitors.

Before trying to apply these strategies, you need to consider the three below-mentioned marketing mantras.

1. Understand your ideal buyers and find out what their pain points are in your niche.
2. Build your business based on solving customer needs. This is also a great way to have recurring customers.
3. Understand the interaction points between your business and customers to provide a better customer experience.

Ecommerce Strategies

1. Include Advanced Product Filtering

Advanced product filtering will help customers to find products based on different specifications. Ecommerce companies such as Amazon and Shopify have more than 250 product filtering options for customers to quickly look through their inventory.

Filtering products based on design, color, size, and price is popular with the customer as it will scour their needs.

2. Highlight New Products

When you run a digital store, you will usually have recurring customers who like your brand and want to buy the new products that you offer. It is for this reason you need to provide a special section on your digital front store to highlight the new products that you have now in your store.

To Increase Your Sales for New Products, Use the Below Strategies:

- Give urgency to your offers. Say to your customers that the offer is available only for a limited time.
- Bundle these new products with your most successful and popular products.

3. Offer More Payment Options

When you are doing an ecommerce business, it is important to cater to customers from all around the world. Most ecommerce businesses use only credit/debit cards and PayPal as default payment methods for customers. Not all customers, however, are comfortable with these options.

Contact different payment providers such as Stripe, Payoneer, and Wise to make them integrated into your payment system. If you want to be more professional, you can also start to use CMS platforms such as BigCommerce for your website, which allows more than 65 payment gateways into your digital store.

When you are adding new payment options, however, ensure that they are highly secure.

4. Give Discounts

All customers love discounts. Irrespective of how popular your product is in your niche, discounts can always drive more sales, especially with new customers. Discounts make your customers feel rewarded for buying a product for less money.

To motivate them to buy your products, mention your best discounts in different sections of your digital stores. With the strategic placement of these discounts, your conversion rate will increase exponentially.

You can also use services to create custom coupons for your customers. These coupons will only work for some time and hence, the buyer's dilemma about whether or not to purchase your product will be cleared away.

5. Leverage Social Proof

Ensure that the reviews for your products made by customers are available for other users to look at. When you show proof of customer reviews, people will be more motivated to try your product, and hence, your conversion ratio will increase. With this strategy, you, however, will also be losing sales if there are more negative customer reviews.

When you have more negative reviews, you should focus first more on increasing the product quality instead of just turning off the reviews section. Be accountable for your actions and you will create a good brand for your business.

6. Run Loyalty Programs

A successful businessman will always try to get new customers all the while keeping their existing customers. Most businesses make profits just because of the recurring customers.

Ensure that you are motivating recurring customers to make sales with the help of loyalty programs. Provide them with exclusive coupons, discounts, and rewards for their purchases. Making your customers feel important and valued is a successful step to scaling your business.

Ensure that these customers are redeeming their rewards as soon as possible by placing an expiration date for them.

7. Provide Discounted or Free Shipping

Ecommerce businesses usually charge a separate shipping fee, and sometimes these fees can be so high that your customers may not want to purchase your products. Research from VWO has stated that more than 44% of customers abandon their shopping carts because of the excessive shipping costs charged by ecommerce companies (Drip, n.d.).

You as an entrepreneur should use this as an advantage to get quick sales.

Here Are Some Times Where You Can Provide Shipping Offers:

- For a limited time during the peak periods, run campaigns where all your products will be shipped for free.
- Create a subscription fee for customers who make more orders with your business to reduce their shipping costs and ensure that you get confirmed orders for your business. Amazon Prime is a good example of this shipping strategy.

- You can provide complimentary shipping if the customers have purchased more than a fixed limit.

The eighth step in the guide focused on providing detailed information about different marketing tactics that can be used to make your ecommerce business popular. Information about content marketing can be used to create a marketing strategy for your website. Using this guide, we also tried to make you realize that brand awareness is more important than sales.

After setting up your website and marketing it extensively, you should now be able to start getting sales. Once your sales start to improve, you will need to depend on automation to manage your business better.

STEP 9

ELEVATING YOUR GAME

AUTOMATING YOUR BUSINESS

When you are managing a business, it becomes tough to track all the workflows and all the important details that are essential for your business to function as you expected it to. For a business to thrive, all the processes associated should be performed consistently even after repeated executions.

To ensure that your business is on track, it is important to be aware of business process automation.

Automating usually refers to the usage of programmatical techniques and software applications to automate all the processes and workflows that are associated with your business. Automation doesn't require human intervention and can occur without any manual operations.

The automation process can be customized according to business requirements, making it a viable option for entrepreneurs who don't have any experience with bookkeeping.

Business automation can work well with the following functions of a business.

1. Logistics

Logistics will be most improved with the help of automation in an ecommerce business. Automated shipment routing, tracking the shipment, and labeling the shipment are some of the automated tasks that can be performed.

2. Marketing and Sales

Marketing can also utilize automated technology. Sending marketing emails to customers, retargeting customers on social media platforms, and sales tracking are some of the use cases.

3. IT and Technical Services

It is possible to create automated reports and solve some of the simpler status reports and ticketing resolutions with the help of automation.

4. Administrative Duties

With automation, several HR-related functions such as employee benefit enrolment, performance monitoring, and tax withholding can be managed.

SEVERAL ADVANTAGES AUTOMATING YOUR BUSINESS PROVIDES

1. Will Increase Operational Efficiency

With the help of automation, it becomes possible to reduce the manual work that is involved between processes. You can minimize costs all the while handling your operations with the help of automation.

2. Productivity

Automation helps you and your employees to be as productive as possible. Instead of focusing on tasks that require repetition, you can use your resources to do important research and innovation.

3. Morale

Doing tasks repeatedly can decrease the morale of your employees and can make them feel that they are doing nothing important in their life. By automation, you can give them work that matters and they can be more passionate about it. An increase in the morale of your employees will automatically improve your company's performance.

4. Governance and Controls

Automation of your business as designed by your workflow practically eliminates the possibility of deviating from the regulatory guidelines and is hence, a more safe approach for businesses.

5. Cost Reduction

When you automate your business, you will be automatically avoiding a workforce that is not necessary and hence, can reduce costs for your business which can instead be used for further innovation.

6. Reduction of Errors

With automation, you will largely reduce the errors that are usually caused by humans.

7. Better Collaboration

With automation, it becomes easier to collaborate with different projects that are happening in your business. When collaborations become easier, any disappointments or frustrations that your employees may have while performing their duties can be reduced.

8. Better Analytics

With automation, everything will be recorded and hence, you will have better access to analytics associated with your business. Using analytics, you can research further to improve your shortcomings.

STRATEGIES TO IMPLEMENT AUTOMATION

When your business is small, you will be able to manage and monitor all the important workflows to minimize costs and maximize efficiency. However, when you start to scale your business there is no better way than automation to keep up your game in the industry. While hiring more employees is an alternative option, you will, however, be cutting down your profits if you chose this path.

For ecommerce, business automation is the only recommended option to maximize the potential of your business. We will take a look at some of the popular strategies to automate critical processes in your business.

1. Identify Functional Areas of Operation

With automation, a lot of entrepreneurs have a misunderstanding that all the areas of a business can be automated. However, it is not true. There is still a need for employees to intervene in your business process. As an owner of the business, it can be tempting to think about replacing everything with AI.

While it may be possible in the future, at present, AI is not so efficient to replace humans. So, your main strategy should be to separate different areas of your business and judge where AI automation can be rightly used. For example, customer service is an area where you can automate with the help of chatbots for basic queries. For advanced queries, you, however, still need to hire customer representatives.

What to Do

- List out all different areas in your business and subdivide them into hierarchical processes.
- Mark down the areas where you can automate and reduce costs.
- In these areas, you cannot automate; try to hire efficient employees.
- Ensure that the balance is not disturbed to have better results with your automation approach.

2. Create Standard Operating Procedures

Standard operating procedures (SOPs) are a default name for any business to manage everything effectively. Using an SOP will usually document the exact steps that are needed to operate. SOPs can be used by both employees and for automation.

While SOPs are a great way to manage your business, several multinational companies are still struggling to implement them in their workforce. You need to take it as a priority and ensure that SOPs are written for almost every stage of your business.

3. Identify Repetitive Tasks

When you find out the functional areas and have researched the SOPs, you will be able to identify the areas where the tasks are usually repetitive. You can now contact your business or operations manager, if relevant, to understand how repetitive and boring the tasks can be in this area.

Be compassionate about your employees and try to find solutions with automation for them or these areas. You, however, need to also list out risks and inefficiencies that may occur when you migrate from a manual workforce to an automation process.

You should also focus further to find ways to minimize these inefficiencies for a complete transformation of your business.

4. Prioritize Areas to Automate

While it is true that several areas need automation for business to thrive, you, however, also need to understand the initial costs that may be needed. For this reason, as an entrepreneur, you need to prioritize different areas from others.

Judge the priority based on how it affects your customers and how it can improve your operations. Create a score-card to ensure that you are choosing the right areas.

5. Digital Transformation

For implementing an automation process for your business you need not create complex software that works with your workflow. You need not start from scratch because there are already several companies focusing on creating automation software for businesses.

Companies such as Appian and Signavio can help you deliver better process management for your business without costing a fortune. Just ping their customer representatives with your proposal and you will get a quote from them. These companies will also ensure that the process is well-secured digitally so that no problems such as hacking can disrupt your organizational procedure and business workflow.

IDENTIFYING AUTOMATION AREAS

A few years back, automation was completely restricted to advanced manufacturing robotics. However, with awareness, businesses have understood that automation can be achieved for several robotic tasks that employees perform. Automation also can improve the workflow.

For ecommerce businesses, business automation will mostly depend on finding a way to change how your brand operates. This section focuses on providing you with information about some of the best business automation tools that you can use to take your business to the next level.

1. Zapier

Zapier is a tool that is created to automate several actions that employees usually make on their system. For example, automatically adding attachments to your mail account or automatically sending mail to a business cloud drive when an invoice has been generated are some of the tasks that can be automated with this tool.

Zapier can also be used to handle your business' social media accounts such as Twitter, Facebook, and Instagram. Zapier allows you to set thousands of automated tasks for your business with very minimal pricing. You can message their customer representatives with your employee number and the number of actions you are trying to perform and they will send you a quote.

2. IFTTT

IFTTT is a cheaper alternative to Zapier for businesses. It works exactly similarly to Zapier and can be used to automate actions. IFTTT has a free version and hence, if you want to try automation without any charges, this is a better version of Zapier. The IFTTT free version, however, is not suitable for teams. It can only be used by one person. With the premium version, you can, however, use it for teams efficiently.

The downside when compared to Zapier is that IFTTT doesn't provide multiple triggers for a particular action. If you want to automate your business workflow with conditionalized actions then Zapier is still a better choice.

3. ActiveCampaign

ActiveCampaign is software that is developed to automate your marketing campaigns. It can be integrated with advanced email marketing features and can be easily optimized for any size of business. ActiveCampaign is also affordable for startups and can be integrated with digital storefronts such as Shopify easily.

4. Hootsuite and Buffer

Hootsuite is a dedicated social media management software. You can control all your social media accounts from one user interface without worrying about posting them from multiple platforms. Buffer is a good alternative to Hootsuite if you are interested in working with teams for managing your social media accounts. Scheduling options are provided by both platforms.

5. Grammarly

Grammarly is a writing checker that will help you to verify simple mistakes that you may make. In one way or another, all ecommerce businesses write content to drive sales. Grammarly is a foolproof way to ensure that all the content you or your employees create is of a high professional standard.

6. Calendly

Calendly is an automation tool that can be used by businesses to schedule their meetings and tasks. Your employees can manage meetings, conferences, and deadlines effectively with this scheduling and reminder tool.

7. Xero

As your business starts to grow, you need to ensure that your accounting is of a high standard. Xero can automatically create invoices, schedule payments, and generate tax reports so that the financial management of your business becomes simple. Xero eliminates the need for a dedicated chartered accountant especially if you are a small business. When the business starts growing, you can, however, hire a chartered accountant to bookkeep and audit your business transactions.

This ninth and final step in the guide focused on providing information about automating your business. The guide helped you focus on finding areas to automate and scale your business better as it starts to grow.

By combining all the nine steps provided, you will be able to start and maintain an ecommerce business that will have the potential to dominate your niche. For any business model, a well-working blueprint is essential and we hope that *The 9-Step Ecommerce Business Guide* provided you with enough details about the vastly unexplored path of ecommerce business.

CONCLUSION

This book has included a 9-step guide for you to master the craft of an ecommerce business with information that helps you start a business and expand it over time to create a mark in the niche or industry you are targeting.

Here is a quick summary of the nine steps that you have learned from this guide.

Step 1: The Beginnings

The first step helped you understand the ecosystem of ecommerce business and different ecommerce business models. Understanding some of the notable barriers also made it easy for you to understand the complexities associated with ecommerce.

Step 2: The Research Phase

The second step made you aware of the research procedures that are important for an ecommerce business to thrive. Research is very important and will decide the fate of your business irrespective of the niche. Entering into business without significant research can have negative results.

Step 3: Finding the Correct Products

Once the research is completed, you need to find the products or services that you want to provide for your customers. Finding profitable products is a hard process and you learned about all the different ways that you can use to find the gold mine for your business.

Step 4: Everything About the Suppliers

The fourth step focused on providing you with information about how to meet suppliers, negotiate with them, and make an agreement with them. Suppliers are the backbone of your business and we learned how to get the most out of your supplier.

Step 5: Creating an Identity

Finding a niche and suitable products doesn't necessarily mean that you should start selling your products immediately. The fifth step helped you create an identity for yourself. We talked about business names and business structures.

Step 6: Everything About Licensing

The sixth step focused on helping you learn about how to acquire licenses and a business bank account for your business. Licenses are important for you to not have any legal disputes in the future.

Step 7: Creating the Store

The seventh step started to introduce you to the practical steps you need to perform for creating the store. From searching for a domain name to helping you create an ecommerce website, everything was explained.

Step 8: Everything About Marketing

The eighth step helped you to understand different marketing strategies to sell your products. Marketing is an important prerequisite for you to be a pioneer in your niche.

Step 9: Automating

The final, ninth step helped you to learn about the automation techniques that can be used to streamline your business workflow. Once you start to scale your business, it is important to not get overwhelmed and messy.

For a smooth transformation, you need to utilize some of the techniques mentioned.

The 9-Step Ecommerce Business Guide focused on providing well-researched and practical information about starting an ecommerce business. Do you now feel inspired to solve a problem like Melanie Perkins or start a passion project like Eric Bandholz? Well, I hope so.

You now know what it takes to build your online business from scratch. So, get out there and start building your way up in business!

If you liked our guide, please leave us a review at rebrand. ly/9StepEBG so that it can reach more people.

GLOSSARY

Abandoned cart: In ecommerce, it refers to an online shopping cart that is abandoned before the customer completes their purchase.

Analytics: This is the use of digital analysis tools such as Google Analytics or other paid platforms to track various metrics of interactions between an ecommerce business and its customers.

Automation: It is the use of technology to carry out tasks or operations without the direct involvement of people.

Business account: A business bank account is a type of banking account specifically designed to manage the financial transactions of a business.

Business license: A license granted by a government body to a business to allow it to legally operate.

Business model: A plan for the successful operation of a business, identifying sources of revenue, the intended customer base, products, and details of financing.

Business structure: The legal form of an organization under which a business operates and is recognized by law.

Competitor analysis: It is the process of researching, analyzing, and comparing the products and services of a business' competitors in order to gain a better understanding of the market and to identify opportunities for the business to exploit.

Content marketing: A form of marketing focused on creating, publishing, and distributing content for a targeted audience online.

Corporation: A type of business entity in which the owners have limited liability for the debts and obligations of the business, and the business is treated as a separate legal entity from its owners.

Demographics: The study of a population based on factors such as age, race, gender, education level, income, occupation, and location.

Digital technology: Any technology that is related to or enabled by digital computing, usually used to refer to the use of computer hardware, software, and networks.

Disruptive technology: This is an innovation that significantly alters the way that businesses or consumers operate. It has the potential to create new markets and value networks, and can disrupt existing ones, displacing established market-leading firms, products, and alliances.

Domain name: This is a unique string of characters that identifies a website or other online resource. It is used to locate and identify a website or other online resources on the Internet.

Ecommerce: Short for electronic commerce, it is the buying and selling of products or services over the internet—online. It can include activities such as online shopping, online banking, and online auctions.

Engagement: It refers to how customers choose to interact with a brand; it is the emotional connection between a customer and a brand. It is measured as a rate. The more engaged they are, the more they buy or promote a product or brand.

Entrepreneur: An individual who organizes and operates a business or businesses, taking on greater than normal financial risks in order to do so.

GDP per capita: This is a measure of an economy's output per person, calculated by dividing the gross domestic product (GDP) of a country by its total population.

Keyword research: This is the process of finding out what the popular words are that people enter into search engines like Google or Bing, then including them on your platform as part of your SEO strategy.

Inflation: The sustained increase in the general level of prices for goods and services.

Inventory: It is a business term used to describe the total amount of goods and materials held in stock by a company, organization, or individual.

LLC: This is a limited liability company—a type of business entity that is similar to a corporation, but in which the owners have limited personal liability for business debts.

Marketing: The process of creating, communicating, delivering, and exchanging offerings that have value for customers, clients, partners, and society at large.

Market research: This is the process of gathering and analyzing data about a market, in order to better understand the needs, wants and preferences of consumers.

Negotiating: Negotiating is a process of discussion between two or more parties aimed at reaching an agreement and resolving a conflict or dispute.

Partnership: A type of business entity in which two or more people share ownership and management of the business.

Product development: The process of creating a new product or improving an existing one for the purpose of marketing and selling it.

Retargeting: It is a type of online advertising that uses tracking technology to "retarget" users who have previously visited a website or viewed an ad.

Sales funnel: A visual representation of the customer journey from initial contact with a brand to purchase. It is typically divided into distinct stages such as awareness, consideration, and purchase, and is used to track the progress of prospects or customers through the sales process.

Segment: A segment is a subset of a larger population that shares common characteristics. It is used in market segmentation, which is the process of dividing a population into smaller groups based on demographic, geographic, psychographic, and other characteristics.

Seller's permit: This is a state-issued license that allows a business to collect and remit sales tax on taxable items it sells.

SEO: Standing for search engine optimization, it is the process of optimizing a website or webpage for search engines such as Google or Bing.

Strategy: These are the plans and tactics that an ecommerce business uses to increase brand visibility and increase sales.

Sole proprietorship: A type of business entity that is owned and run by one individual and in which there is no legal distinction between the owner and the business.

Supplier: A person or organization that provides goods or services to another organization or individual.

Target audience: The group of people most likely to be interested in a product, service, or message. It is important to identify and understand the target audience before developing a marketing plan, creating content, or launching a campaign.

Trends: Refers to the direction or pattern of change of a particular indicator or set of indicators over time. Trends can refer to a wide variety of topics such as fashion, politics, economics, and social movements.

Web apps: These are applications that are accessed over the internet through a web browser such as Google Chrome, Microsoft Edge, Mozilla Firefox, and so on.

REFERENCES

Alter, C. (2021, March 19). *How Whitney Wolfe Herd turned a vision of a better internet into a billion-dollar brand.* Time. https://time.com/5947727/whitney-wolfe-herd-bumble/

Dinarys. (n.d.). *Why is Amazon so successful? Amazon success story.* https://dinarys.com/blog/amazon-success-story

Drip. (n.d.). *15 cart abandonment statistics you must know in 2022.* https://www.drip.com/blog/cart-abandonment-statistics

Economic Innovation Group. (2022, January 19). *New startups break record in 2021: Unpacking the numbers.* https://eig.org/new-startups-break-record-in-2021-unpacking-the-numbers

FDR Library. (2016). *Great depression facts.* https://www.fdrlibrary.org/great-depression-facts

IRI. (2o22). *Recession report 2022.* https://www.iriworldwide.com/en-us/insights/publications/recession-report-2022

McKinsey. (n.d.). *2020 perspectives on the business impact of COVID-19.* https://www.mckinsey.com/capabilities/risk-and-resilience/our-insights/covid-19-implications-for-business-2020

Merriam-Webster. (n.d.). *Merriam-Webster dictionary.* https://www.merriam-webster.com/

Miva. (2011, October 26). *The history of ecommerce: How did it all begin?* https://blog.miva.com/the-history-of-ecommerce-how-did-it-all-begin

Olson, P. (n.d.). *Facebook closes $19 billion WhatsApp deal.* Forbes. https://www.forbes.com/sites/parmyolson/2014/10/06/facebook-closes-19-billion-whatsapp-deal/

Our World in Data. (2018). *The internet's history has just begun.* https://ourworldindata.org/internet-history-just-begun

PYMNTS. (2022, March 14). *Amazon's all-time high US ecommerce share: 56.7%.* https://www.pymnts.com/news/retail/2022/

amazons-share-of-us-ecommerce-sales-hits-all-time-high-of-56-7-in-2021/

QuestionPro. (2020, January 27). *QuestionPro vs SurveyMonkey: The best free survey software.* https://www.questionpro.com/blog/questionpro-vs-surveymonkey/

Seal, T. (2022, October 3). *Amazon boasts of 25% increase in British marketplace sellers in 2021.* Business Standard. https://www.business-standard.com/article/international/amazon-boasts-of-25-increase-in-british-marketplace-sellers-in-2021-122100300067_1.html

Shephard, J. (n.d.). *21 essential ecommerce statistics you need to know in 2022.* The Social Shepherd. https://thesocialshepherd.com/blog/ecommerce-statistics

Shopify. n.d.). *How Knox Labs validated their market with a splash page and made $2.9 million in 2015.* https://www.shopify.com/blog/116245573-how-knox-labs-validated-their-market-with-a-splash-page-and-made-2-9-million-in-2015

Sourcify. (2019, June 18). *How Beardbrand took a simple business idea and turned it into $100,000 MRR.* https://www.sourcify.com/how-beardbrand-took-a-simple-business-idea-and-turned-it-into-100000-mrr/

Statista. (n.d.). *Infographic: The most popular dating apps in the U.S.* https://www.statista.com/chart/24404/most-popular-dating-apps-us/

TechCrunch. (n.d.). *Canva raises $60 million on a $6 billion valuation.* https://techcrunch.com/2020/06/22/canva-raises-60-million-on-a-6-billion-valuation/

TycheSoftwares (2020). *Ecommerce terms glossary.* https://www.tychesoftwares.com/ecommerce-terms-glossary/

weDevs. (2022, May 17). *Amazon success story: 11 learnings for startups in 2022.* https://wedevs.com/blog/413420/amazon-success-story/

IMAGE REFERENCES

Alzayat, R. (2016). *Silver Android smartphone* [Image]. Unsplash. https://unsplash.com/photos/w33-zg-dNL4

Campaign Creators. (2018). *White printing paper with marketing strategy print* [Image]. Unsplash. https://unsplash.com/photos/yktK2qaiVHI

Cytonn Photography. (2018). *Person writing on white paper [Signing contract]* [Image]. Unsplash. https://unsplash.com/photos/GJao3ZTX9gU

Deziel, M. (2020). *Person writing on white paper [Audience and arrows]* [Image]. Unsplash. https://unsplash.com/photos/U33fHryBYBU

Eletu, A. (2015). *Person wearing suit reading business newspaper* [Image]. Unsplash. https://unsplash.com/photos/E7RLgUjjazc

Gios, J. (2021). *Free UK Image [Google UK]* [Image]. Unsplash. https://unsplash.com/photos/PDg180uwHvQ

Heyerdahl, C. (2016). *Silver iMac with keyboard and trackpad inside room* [Image]. Unsplash. https://unsplash.com/photos/KE0nC8-58MQ

Jessier, M. (2020). *Person using MacBook Pro on black table* [Image]. Unsplash. https://unsplash.com/photos/eveI7MOcSmw

Kaleidico. (2018). *Man wearing gray polo beside dry-erase board* [Image]. Unsplash. https://unsplash.com/photos/3V8xo5Gbusk

Kolde, B. (2017). *White and black laptop* [Image]. Unsplash. https://unsplash.com/photos/bs2Ba7t69mM

Konig, M. (2020). *[San Antonio ecommerce street sign]* [Image]. Unsplash. https://unsplash.com/photos/Tl8mDaue_II

Kwong, M. (2018). *Black Android smartphone near laptop computer* [Image]. Unsplash. https://unsplash.com/photos/rQRKEu9HnZo

Li, A. (2020). *Cargo ships docked at the pier during day* [Image]. Unsplash. https://unsplash.com/photos/CpsTAUPoScw

Morgan, J. (2021). *Black flat screen computer monitor* [Image]. Unsplash. https://unsplash.com/photos/ZjX-z2Q5zrk

NisonCo PR and SEO. (2021). *HD photo by NisonCo PR and SEO [SEO Scrabble]* [Image]. Unsplash. https://unsplash.com/photos/yIRdUr6hIvQ

Rumee, T. (2020). *Silver Android smartphone* [Image]. Unsplash. https://unsplash.com/photos/w33-zg-dNL4

Shatov, A. (2021). *Blue, red and green letters illustration* [Image]. Unsplash. https://unsplash.com/photos/mr4JG4SYOF8

Sikkema, K. (2019). *Stack of papers flat lay photography* [Image]. Unsplash. https://unsplash.com/photos/tQQ4BwN_UFs

Vi, L. (2021). *[Entrepreneur magazine Taraji P Henson cover]* [Image]. Unsplash. https://unsplash.com/photos/BMPuBdpjrr8

Winkler, M. (2020). *Brown wooden framed white printer paper* [Image]. Unsplash. https://unsplash.com/photos/mGrERgAbcBU

Printed in Great Britain
by Amazon